In 2019, Farren B. Ifield published *Paradigm Shift,* the first in this Blue Dreamer trilogy, and has now almost completed the third, *Awakening.*

Also to be published this year is his work of science fiction, *Systematical,* which is currently in the latter stages of production and due for release soon after *Twists, Turns, and Transformations.*

Concurrently, Farren is working on a medieval action/suspense while compiling ideas for a potential sequel to *Systematical.*

For Jennifer Ann Jones, with love

Farren B. Ifield

BLUE DREAMER: TWISTS, TURNS, AND TRANSFORMATIONS

AUSTIN MACAULEY PUBLISHERS™

LONDON • CAMBRIDGE • NEW YORK • SHARJAH

Ordering Information
Quantity sales: Special discounts are available on quantity purchases by corporations, associations, and others. For details, contact the publisher at the address below.

Publisher's Cataloging-in-Publication data
Ifield, Farren B.
Blue Dreamer: Twists, Turns, and Transformations

ISBN 9781645361695 (Paperback)
ISBN 9781645361701 (Hardback)
ISBN 9781645366010 (ePub e-book)

Library of Congress Control Number: 2020908963

www.austinmacauley.com/us

First Published (2020)
Austin Macauley Publishers LLC
40 Wall Street, 28th Floor
New York, NY 10005
USA

mail-usa@austinmacauley.com
+1 (646) 5125767

While writing these words, the world remains in lockdown, our future is uncertain, and it feels strange somehow to be publishing two more books this year. It seems, for many people, as it has been for me more often than I'd like to admit to myself, that finding the motivation and energy to continue with personal goals can be challenging in itself at this time. With this idea in mind, I would like to thank the readers of my first book for taking the time to review and share your feedback. After being isolated through injury for many years, external encouragement was scarce and so I'm fortunate now to have readers' words and their interest to remember whenever enthusiasm runs low. Thank you to you holding this book, intending to read it; you make it all worthwhile.

Lastly, I'm very grateful to Austin Macauley Publishers for your ongoing support in the publishing of my work, including this book, the second in my Blue Dreamer trilogy. With equal gratitude, for your work and confidence in my soon-to-be-released science fiction, *Systematical*, I thank you!

So long as we accept lies and deception, we will be enslaved.

Chapter One
Seeking the Invisible

For many a hoof-trodden mile, Sanura managed to avoid attracting attention from anyone inside or outside the slave wagon, while secretly trying to unclip and remove the shackles from her wrists.

"What are you doing?" Talia whispered, finally, with a great warning in her broken voice and without moving her generous lips very much at all.

Every other slave in their company appeared to be a strong male, obviously purchased for hard labor, so the two young women had quickly deduced the obvious and most horrid purpose for their acquisition. As a consequence, their minds had become as frayed as their tan dresses, which were not much better than light sacks, with holes cut into them for heads and arms. Side-by-side they stood huddled in the back corner. Together, hunger and tiredness added a bite of chill to the air and sought to transform a crisp, midspring afternoon into wintertime.

After passing a long line of new army barracks, the wagon turned northwest for a short distance toward a property on the east east-side of Black Sand Valley, just southeast of Vivian Piper's land in Riverside.

"I know where we are," Sanura said under her breath, spying one of seven men outside on horseback just a few paces away. "We're in the Midlands now. Black Sand Valley Township isn't far from here, to the north. My father used to take me hunting here a long time ago. Madeleine Fox lives here somewhere."

Sanura returned to her task then. She knew her kind of shackle well from years of harvesting crops; designed for children and for women with slender wrists, which defied the minimal limits of the most common adult-cuff designs. Countless times she had seen the pin-key used to open them, entering at the side to spring the cuff loose.

At her waistline, a rusty metal rod, a little longer than her fingers, jutted out from one of the timber slats in the side of the wagon. It was the right width to fit into the pinhole of the cuff and, although its very end had a short point like a nail instead of a blunt end like the correct key, Sanura believed, or hoped rather, that it would open the cuff all the same.

Twisting it while lifting with all her weight didn't work, so she tried then to twist it and hit it sharply at the same time, to somehow drive the pin in further and maybe blunt its rusty point. With the rod firmly in place, while wedging the right cuff between two steel bars for leverage, she waited for heavy bumps in the road before each new attempt, for the wagon to jolt, hoping to hide her sudden movement and the noise she made each time when striking it with the ball of her hand.

It proved a difficult, if not impossible, trick to accomplish, given that the short length of chain between the two cuffs prevented a long swing. Two attempts failed, but, other than Talia, she had only drawn the attention of one other slave so far, and he lost interest immediately anyhow. Along with all others, he was but the shell of a man; lifeless, overworked, hungry, bleeding somewhere, and aching all over.

It was only Talia who understood what her new friend was up to. "They will kill you!" she insisted, with a new flood of tears coming forth. She was almost always crying.

"It's not death I'm afraid of," Sanura replied bluntly, giving the cuff another thump at the same time. This time, the cuff sprang open, surprising both of them equally, and at the same time, the metal rod snapped off and stayed in the keyhole. Quickly, Sanura swung the cuff back around, hid the long rod in her fist, and covered the cuff with her other hand.

Talia knew what Sanura had insinuated, but her shattered mind couldn't stand to think of it. "You can't just run. You heard them, they're taking us to Del Hickory's farm. He's a monster. No slave escapes Hickory's. What are you going to do?" Skepticism drenched her every word.

"I don't know yet," Sanura admitted. "Just be ready for anything."

Talia held no hope at all. She shook her head. "How could you even find Madeleine Fox and what could she do for us anyway?"

They were both recently purchased at the same market and, although strangers prior to this day, they had both worked in the southern fields for the last eight years or so, not half a day's ride from one another. Del Hickory's men were at the markets buying more slaves to work his giant estate, when two of his men, Mitchell and Tanner, bought Sanura and Talia with their own money, when they happened upon the two of them, standing out together like flashing beacons in a market filled predominantly with men for hard labor.

In youth, their hair was clipped short, but had since grown past the shoulders again after being left alone in the fields for many years. Talia's dark-brown plaits were somewhat matted and Sanura's black spiraled locks were greatly in need of attention, but this slight disarray did nothing to detract from the natural beauty they both possessed, and Talia's unusual obsidian-blue eyes easily drew the attention of men.

"Don't give up, Talia," Sanura urged. "Be brave. Be strong."

The wagon rattled on down the driveway along the southern boundary, past Del Hickory's looming two-story mansion with rendered red walls, tall white pillars and creamy, marble steps, then came to a halt outside two main barns and a large shed on the west side, closest to the river. Housing numerous chains, a tall pole situated in the middle ground stood at attention, awaiting the next flogging order, and even in the shadows of the afternoon, blood stains of various tones were clearly visible across the timber and metal. Unseen howling dogs added yet another level of dread to the haunting scene; their new home.

Talia's lips quivered, wet with tears, when the wagon door opened and the male slaves were quickly shuffled off into one of the barns before the wagon door closed again, leaving just the two of them alone inside.

Hickory's men had been chugging on whiskey for most of the journey home, so intoxication was coming on rapidly throughout the pack. Some of them went to the house, others went to the other barn and it didn't take long for voices to get louder and for the ominous sounds of smashing bottles to find the young women's ears. One man was left to watch them, so they stood in desperate silence until Talia turned to Sanura, her eyes filled with horror to quietly ask, "Sanura, why are we still in here?"

Sanura only shook her head.

"Quiet!" their guard demanded.

A raised voice came to them then, turning both their heads. It was Tanner from inside the barn, and his aggressive tone suddenly grew louder when the door swung open with a "bang," as it bounced off a pile of empty barrels.

"I think you're forgetting your place!" he threatened. "Mitchell and I bought them ourselves fair and square. If you didn't gamble all your money away, you coulda done the same, so if any of you dogs even think about touchin' 'em, I'll kill you myself, yer hear!"

No one responded, but they could now see the man Tanner had threatened standing in the doorway with his chubby red face in the light of a lantern exposing a hateful sneer and great discontent. He took a grumpy swig from his whiskey bottle when Tanner and Mitchell turned to exit the barn, then helped the door slam behind them with a well-aimed boot. Quieter grumbles continued inside the barn then, as Tanner and Mitchell approached the wagon, bottle in hand, crunching gravel under their boots.

Talia gasped heavily.

"Be strong," Sanura whispered.

"Idiot!" Tanner spat from nearby.

Mitchell swallowed some liquor and coughed. "I thought you were gonna hit 'im."

"I was thinking about it," Tanner stated, and it wouldn't have been the first time he beat a man for talking back. At the wagon, he eyed the captives, running a hand through his thick beard and mustache in lewd contemplation. "You can go now, Donny."

The women's guard left them, as Mitchell swung the door open. Talia flinched and recoiled. Sanura remained still.

"While the boss's away, the boys will play," Mitchell laughed, earning a chuckle from his associate.

"Out!" Tanner demanded.

After pausing for a few moments, they both realized they had little choice but to do as asked and stepped slowly to the doorway, down the steps. The men seized both of them before they reached the ground and Tanner first grabbed Sanura by the hair to bring her face closer to his.

"Move when I tell you to!" he yelled, through clenched teeth, stinging Sanura's nostrils with the breath of single-malted fumes. When he grabbed hold of the chain between Sanura's shackles, he almost pulled the loose one right off her wrist in the process, and she only just managed to keep her secret hidden.

Mitchell took Talia by the chain as well and led her away. She screamed out briefly, so he jerked her shackles heavily and she cried out in pain once more, but only whimpered thereafter.

"Shut up!" he yelled, threatening with his bottle in the air as she cowered.

Tanner led Sanura to the shed. She didn't fight at first, but her mind worked overtime while her eyes examined everything in sight, from the buildings to the visible crops and the long tree line which undoubtedly revealed the location of the river. She heard Talia cry out again, as her own breathing began to accelerate rapidly. Tanner kicked the shed door open and closed it again after pushing Sanura inside, then slipped a knife out of its sheath at his belt.

"Lie down over there," he demanded, referring to a bed of strewn hay on the shed floor. After taking another swallow of apathy, he placed the bottle clumsily on the window sill next to the door. "This knife is for you if you don't behave yourself."

He twisted the finely-honed blade in the air, most satisfied with the power in his hand, and a wicked grin mirrored his intentions. The closed door sealed out most of the twilight and so he lit a lamplight on the wall which served well to highlight the hatred in his glazed eyes.

Sanura complied not to his command, only stood still while adding an extra sting of contempt to her furious stare. In assuming she would have only one chance to attack, her idea was to make him force her to do what he asked, so then she could feign falling down, only to quickly make a weapon out of the pin in her hand and strike unexpectedly. It was certain she needed to be fast and accurate for, after one attempt to injure him, Tanner would certainly make sure she wasn't capable of another.

Unfortunately, her wish came true. A quick backhand sent her backward and after stumbling, she was sure to fall facedown over a thin layer of straw. The slap didn't hurt too much, but Sanura moaned and writhed on the floor somewhat, pretending it had stunned her well, while beneath her chest, she was slipping her hand free of the cuff and gripping the rusty metal rod within her clenched fist, leaving it to stick out a good distance from between two fingers.

Tanner began to chuckle then, most proud of himself, then sank to his knees and gripped Sanura's shoulder to turn her over. In that moment, Sanura spun around rapidly, located his face and punched at it with all her might. She pulled back immediately then, ready to strike again, only to discover that she had stabbed Tanner directly in the eye and pulled his eyeball out with the rusty end of the rod. A trail of bloody chords now stretched from his eye socket to her hand.

In disgust, she flicked the rod away and cringed watching his pierced eyeball swing and bounce around. It took a few moments for the initial shock to pass and for Tanner to truly acknowledge what had happened. He dropped the knife unwittingly then and jumped to his feet, screaming.

Sanura grabbed the knife and also got to her feet, just as he bounced off a tool cabinet and returned with his arms flailing all around. She didn't back away, but slashed at him with the blade, cutting his forearms and his hands until he stopped advancing, then drove him back away from the door with a few more slashes about the air in front of him, the last of which severed the chords attached to his eyeball.

Before this occurrence, the injury was already too shocking for Tanner to act methodically and in any case, given how well his good eye now watered, he could barely make out his lost eyeball bouncing along the dusty floor, let alone take any worthwhile action. It was altogether too much to bear and by the time he regained any balance and composure at all, Sanura had snatched a key ring off the wall, burst through the door and was already running, knife and keys in hand.

***

14

Sometime after the people learnt the name Montgomery Swift, the man who had fallen to his death all the way from the hole in the ceiling to The Ledge, an adage began to grow in popularity, especially amongst daring climbers and workers who regularly braved dangerous heights within the enormous cavern of Blue Falls. Madeleine first heard the saying after a somewhat awkward discussion between the Guardians, as Annabel wandered off on her own, unhappily, stating, "I'm going to try the Plummet now. All the children are waiting."

Akachi called after her, "Annie, please don't do a Swifty!"

Annabel's new rail-ride, nicknamed The Plummet, was not at all like the leisurely Swing Rail which descended slowly to The Lake, with a handheld brake at the ready. The Plummet track began on a ledge above that rail and dropped steeply for a good distance, making for rapid acceleration and high speed. This initial plunge delivered enough momentum to rise up and pass through a wide hole at the top of a rock wall high above The Nook. From that point, the track descended again even more rapidly, all the way down to The Lake, swerving this way and that along the way, through open spaces, narrow passages, and gaps in rocky outcrops.

The harness for the Plummet wasn't a swing such as those used on the other rail, but a vest made of five wide straps which looped over the shoulders, between the legs, and around the waist, clipping all together in the center of the chest, into a quick-release clasp. The wheels were attached to the harness in the center of the back, so throughout the journey, the passenger travelled parallel, facedown, and locked into a forward position so that the body couldn't spin in any direction.

Although future models were thought to have some kind of braking mechanism, Annabel's prototype contained no brake and was designed purely for high speed. With much help from dressmakers, she even went to the trouble of making a light but tight swimming costume to wear, and also pulled her hair into a tail for added aerodynamic value. Up until the rail was ready, she ached every day to try it, and pondered so many times on the idea of coming home from a skirmish or from the slave markets to blast down the Plummet and into the water just moments later.

Victor made her promise to be sure he wasn't around when she planned to try it for the first time. When the engineers first strapped a weighted feedbag into the harness and sent it down the track, he was at the south side of the Hotpot as it whipped passed high above at frightening speed, but he couldn't see the rest of its journey from that location, for which he was thankful. Even though the designers had tested both the track and the harness countless times, with far greater weights than Annabel and through all kinds of stresses and strains, Victor still didn't like the idea of his daughter flying at such deadly heights and speeds. High points and drops in the track were designed precisely to build enough speed for the climbs. The very end of the track looped up just over the south side of the Lake following an overhanging ledge, and the height at the top of the loop provided just enough inertia for the harness and passenger to glide back down before coming to rest at a dip in the track on a safe shelf above the entrance to Crimson Cove. Yet, it was never Annabel's intention to return with the harness.

To make the task all the more daunting for engineers, Annabel asked for the quick-release mechanism to be designed so that she could snap the harness open at the rise over the lake and drop into the water. After hearing her design and location ideas, the engineers who built the first rail all stood open-mouthed at the prospect of such craziness, but it wasn't long before their imaginations went to town and they started designing and investigating Annabel's proposed ledges and outcrops for the path of the track.

Both the track and the harness had been ready for weeks. Yet, after seeing the speeds that their test dummies reached, all the engineers were both excited for the success of their design and very frightened that Annabel, and a Guardian of all people, would be the one strapping her mortal self into that harness, and so they demanded more testing be done, followed by another great inspection of the entire track, before her first run. Annabel was done waiting, yet she agreed, begrudgingly, letting the designers have their way and after they had gone above-and-beyond the call of duty, in terms of safety testing, it was decided this day would be the day.

When the children heard as much, they gathered at The Lake to watch her final plummet into the water. The Guardians were all together after their meeting at The Books and chose to remain, since most of the track could be seen from there, including the southeast side of The Lake where she would inevitably drop from the rail.

Madeleine shook her head after Akachi's comment, trying not to smile. Oni saw the irony in it, but didn't find it so amusing.

"Where did you hear that?" Misae asked. Like her sisters and Madeleine, she was both disgusted and amused. "Don't do a Swifty," she repeated with a scoff.

"I've heard some children say it," Sayen answered in her place. "But I think the chimney workers started it." She and Naira were not as talkative as Misae throughout the meeting, and looked now for any opportunity to add to general conversations.

Aside from Misae meeting with Annabel often, the three sisters hadn't yet spent much time with the Warrior Guardians, mostly due to some of the

Warriors' obligations and increased training sessions, and the atmosphere remained a little uneasy. Believing the cause to be mostly their non-Warrior status, the Princesses put extra effort into integrating themselves, without knowing that the tension they detected was actually within the Warrior Guardian circle itself. Nonetheless, to further their cause, they were also hoping to encourage Kachina to spend more time with them in her alternate role as Keeper, as they felt her input would be invaluable and, since she also spent most of her time with the four Warriors, she would certainly help to bond them all more expediently. It was upon this request that the meeting of the Guardians took a turn and exposed underlying animosity, many months in the brewing.

Annabel supported the Keepers' suggestion, with her hidden hope that it might help to calm Kachina some, by being in a supportive role, which may also find harmony with her Warrior training and bring about more inner peace. While Annabel's support was genuine and honorable, Kachina's growing suspicion floated to the surface and, although calmly spoken and making a half-joke of it, her insinuation was clear: First you keep secrets and now you want me to go and be a Keeper.

She referred to the discovery of Madeleine's father in her Book of The Doomed, and how Annabel didn't share the knowledge with her in the moment of realization. In the end, Madeleine decided to tell Kachina herself. The Guardians who knew about it agreed this would be the best idea and, although Oni also confessed to knowing this truth, Kachina saw it as a kind of betrayal from Annabel, since they were close and had experienced so much together, and for weeks, she fueled her cynicism. Feeling hurt herself, she didn't realize how deeply her distrust had disappointed Annabel, that she doubted Annabel would only ever have her best interests in mind.

Oni saw this reaction from Kachina not as distrust in Annabel, but as a general lack of trust in human nature and in herself. Although it was clear by Annabel's following silence and lack of anger that she may have believed this also, it did nothing to bring Annabel back from a kind of sudden despair, and at a depth that no one could completely understand.

Together with sending Annabel away, Kachina's words triggered a long, uncomfortable break in conversation and, as most were expecting Annabel to have responded with something at least, they were all surprised when she simply stood with sorrow building in her downturned eyes and said only that she was going to try The Plummet.

After some time, Kachina's saddened gaze turned to the hands in her lap picking at nails, contemplating the origin of angst, while feeling eyes upon her: yet, none of those eyes held judgment. Two, thin plaits swinging gently about her cheek bones somehow exacerbated the melancholy in her disposition. Even when braided, her hair was quite long again, and with wounds all thoroughly healed, she was very near the image of Kachina that everyone remembered.

Oni braved the precarious air with an earnest smile, which covered her gentle lips. "Kachina, I don't believe Annabel was trying to push you away at all or—"

"I know… I…" Kachina shook her head with remorse. Annabel's reaction made her think more deeply, to question her feelings. It would have been easier if she had become angry instead, thus providing Kachina with an avenue on which to vent anxiety. With a sudden wave of longing, she faced Misae then, hoping not to have turned another hand of friendship away. "I'm sorry, Misae. You asked me for help and…my mother's right, I've been neglecting my duties as a Keeper. It's just that sometimes when I stop moving or I'm trying to have a normal conversation, I just get muddled in the head and anger and…I say all the wrong things—" She was starting to choke up then, unable to continue, so she stood and began to walk away.

Akachi called after her, "Kachina, please don't leave. We need you here." She tapped the sandy granite next to her crossed legs, impelling Kachina to sit in the circle again, and in time, Kachina relented; her request made easier by the fact that the general population stayed clear of The Books whenever the Guardians chose to meet there and, being a quiet, non-invasive space, they were free to express themselves openly and even cry in peace if they wanted to, in good company.

"There's growing unrest throughout Blue Falls and Crimson Cove," Sayen said with great concern, though all present knew it. "We've been trying to mediate between the new arrivals and long-term residents, but at the moment, we're afraid it might get out of hand."

"Our mother's also going to Crimson Cove today," Misae added, "to spend time with all those asking for war to see if she can calm things down over there."

"With the sudden increase in population, people are beginning to miss spending time with a Greeter," Naira explained. "And sometimes, they start doing things to annoy others or go against our general unwritten rules."

Misae nodded, remembering all the complaints she had received already. "It was harder than we predicted bringing so many people all at once, and some people are calling for us not to bring any more, even after the reconstruction is finished."

"What does the Queen think about that?" Kachina asked.

"The same as all of us," Misae shrugged. "How can we stop saving people when there's more than enough space and food and water? As you know, we've stopped bringing people in for the time being, while we're rebuilding the entrances and the openings to Blue Falls and Crimson Cove and until we complete the work over at Riverside, but I don't think most of us would want to stop saving people after that."

Misae was right to assume at least that all the Guardians felt the same, and she received many nods for confirmation, yet no one could imagine an immediate solution for the disturbances.

"How big is Jalen's army now?" Madeleine inquired, remembering her last visit many weeks ago to the Panther's Den in Crimson Cove, where Jalen continued to collect warriors he dubbed the Panthers and the Shadow Warriors, the latter being an elite selection of the former.

"They're scary," Naira answered. "He said about two-thousand."

"And there're about 400 Shadow Warriors now," Sayen added.

"Gosh." Madeleine was amazed. "Considering the Shadows have to pass Ky Mani's tests, 400 is a lethal army in itself." She turned to Kachina then, "Have you seen Jalen fight lately?"

Kachina shook her head. She was still upset, and thoughts of Jalen were anything but comforting. "I haven't seen him in a while."

"He's got another ton of muscle," Akachi sniggered. "I think he could break right through a stone wall now."

"And with Ky Mani's training, can you imagine facing him?" Madeleine proposed, with raised eyebrows.

"You could beat him, Maddy," Akachi laughed, yet she was mostly serious.

"With a staff or sword, you could," Kachina agreed.

"Mm…" Madeleine uttered, reluctant to agree; aspiring to remain without arrogance for knowing how quickly a bout can turn around, only to result in stunning defeat for the one who seemed to be dominating the battle all along. "Anyhow, you wouldn't want to ever get close to him."

"See," Oni said, in support of Akachi's claim. "You already know how."

Madeleine shook her head and smiled. "Well, I don't ever want to find out."

This comment received a few giggles and seemed to ease the tension a little. They all believed the rift in the Guardians' circle was beginning to permeate out into the population, fueling unrest in many places. Lesedi and her daughters were all greatly challenged, mediating and bringing tensions to rest, while the Warrior Guardians' frustrations grew for the impeding effect this discord brought to their advanced training aspirations. Madeleine's concern for the future of the Guardians began to grow and Isi's recent words, being always the collective belief of the Blue Ones, kept repeating in her mind: The

Guardians will need to pass a series of tests of alignment before the gate can be opened. Madeleine could only ask, What test? What gate? Yet, Isi had leapt off The Ledge into the water immediately after that comment and so she couldn't question him further. She only said, "Come back you little brat!" while knowing he couldn't hear.

In silent question, Madeleine looked to Oni, believing her to be the most intuitive of all the Blue Ones, but also the most elusive in manner and speech.

Somehow Oni was already looking her way, yet with unobtrusive eyes and the usual soft smile across her mouth which, of course, never gave her thoughts away. She merely turned her gaze to Kachina then, while clearly speaking to all present. "Annabel is the keeper of a mystery," she stated. There was silence for a time while the Guardians looked to one another, seeking confirmation.

Only Akachi and Misae seemed to know something of Oni's suggestion.

"What mystery?" Madeleine was the first to ask. "And how do you know of it?"

"We don't know it," Akachi confessed. "Not Oni or me. We just know she has one. Only the Blue Ones know what it is, maybe."

Madeleine, like the others, sat both curious and baffled. "But you're both Blue Ones and you've known her your whole life, Akachi."

"So have I," Oni stated. "But Akachi and I, we're Guardians like you, and so it's hidden from us. Isi knows more, but he cannot tell."

"And you're okay with that?" Madeleine asked with surprise.

"Trust me," Oni answered. "If Isi doesn't want to tell you something, then you don't want to know it. Also, I trust Annabel, with all my heart."

"And the other Blue Ones have sworn themselves to secrecy," Akachi added.

"Now I'm more confused," Madeleine confessed. "Annabel isn't a Blue One, and she's a Guardian, so how does she know?"

"That's the mystery, but it's an important one, this is for sure," Misae said adamantly, surprising the others greatly, including her own sisters, and all heads turned her way. "I don't know it either, but I've been spending a lot of time with Annabel lately, planning for Riverside and I've been dreaming more clearly." She gestured toward her sisters then. "As you know, Ky Mani and Annabel have been helping us with meditation and teaching us all self-defense. I saw Annabel in one of my dreams, she was blocking a doorway and she was fierce, like she is in battle and frightening, very frightening, but still, my trust in her is the same. I believe like Oni."

Oni's smile broadened and she spoke with contrition, "She believes in you the same, Misae, but I don't think she was blocking a doorway, I think she's guarding it."

"Somehow, she blocks all the Guardians from seeing this secret," Akachi elaborated. "She passes through the door, but we can't follow her. I just fall down when I try and wake from the dream suddenly."

Oni nodded. "It's the same for all the Guardians, it's too powerful, but I don't believe it's Annabel who's blocking us."

"Have you asked her about it?" Madeleine queried, while fearing her question may have been a little too obvious.

"I have. She always says the same thing," Akachi answered, without offering any more.

"Well, what did she say about it?" Madeleine laughed. "What's with the mystery?"

"She only ever says, 'Do you trust me?' I know it's very important, but that's all she'll say about it, and since she was eight." Akachi revealed.

"Eight?" Madeleine blurted, greatly surprised.

"Ah uh," Akachi confirmed. "Or she just says, 'I believe in the Guardians.' The only other thing she's ever said about it was long ago to me and Jojo. She said her mother came to her on her eighth birthday. Since then, she meditates at Crystal Nest in the morning every birthday."

Madeleine didn't know what to do with this information. "She meditates there almost every day. Why do you question it? Maybe it's just something to do with her mother."

"It is to do with her mother," Oni agreed. "But also to do with us. The Elders have always believed the Prophecy is incomplete and the Blue Ones know there is more to be discovered, and we also feel it's something that could destroy the Guardians somehow or bring an awful fate to Blue Falls, which is why it's hidden from us. It's Annabel's calling. She's protecting something or someone."

"Maybe us. I think it's to do with the Guardians," Akachi proposed, "because she's been really down since tension began between you and Kachina…sorry," she cringed. "But I'm just being honest. I know you've all noticed how detached she's been since this happened and she's been pushing so hard to finish the work at Riverside."

The Guardians could only agree. They all sensed it; as if seeing any of them, long-term friend or not, made Annabel sad. Of late, she had actually spent more time outside of training with Misae than with anyone else.

Madeleine had been too preoccupied to notice this for weeks, due to matters related to Vivian's massive estate, working at the house next door, accepting slave wagons into The Drop, and with her written work including correspondence between herself and Julian. This barely gave her enough space to train with the Guardians, let alone spend time with everyone consistently.

After these latest remarks, her concern had risen to another level. She looked to the four Princesses, all of whom shrugged but for Misae, who seemed to believe in the importance of these events. Finally, she turned to Oni. "What do you think's going on, Oni?"

Although she believed in her words wholeheartedly, Oni didn't want to speak them. "I think we're all being tested; this is also Isi's belief."

"What?" The question was on everyone's lips, but it was Madeleine who voiced it first. "I remember, he said this to me too."

"I think Annabel expected something to happen by now, but it hasn't," Oni added, knowing Akachi had already disagreed with this idea, "and she's like this because she can't talk about it."

Akachi thought more on it and something began to ring true. "I don't know why she'd keep anything from me, but if she has, she must have a good reason. She's like my sister, I trust she's doing what's right, but maybe you're right, Oni," she confessed.

"Is Oni ever wrong?" Madeleine sniggered. She noticed a bare smile from Kachina and this made her think of Annabel's recent remark: Maybe I should've told Kachina straight away. I don't always know what I'm supposed to do, but you have to make it right with her, Maddy, because it could ruin everything. Until this moment, Madeleine believed Annabel simply referred to peace within the Guardian circle, but now she saw the connection to Oni's beliefs. What did Annabel mean by that? She began dissecting Annabel's words, I don't always know what I'm supposed to do, when suddenly, she felt an urge to lay her thoughts out for all the Guardians to dismember. "I don't know why, but I think Oni's right." She turned to Kachina then, after finding the courage to speak the words, "Kachina, I don't know what to do about my father being in your Book of The Doomed, about what he's done to you—" She stalled then, as Kachina looked down again, away from attention, struggling with memories and emotions. This brought Madeleine to the verge of tears immediately and she realized all at once the stress this had brought upon her, upon them both, and certainly upon all the Guardians. "I wish it could just go away and we could go back to the way it was. I don't even want to think about it, it's too upsetting and when I don't know how to fix it—"

"I don't see how either of you could fix it, since neither of you are to blame," Oni stated. "Perhaps it's not for you to fix, but to overcome. Ky Mani also believes we will be tested in many ways. And it wouldn't be much of a test if it was easy for us, would it?"

"Have you asked Ky Mani about Annabel's mystery?" Madeleine questioned, knowing it was Ky Mani and Nanook who initially shared the prophecy with all the people.

"Yes," Akachi replied, and then adopted Ky Mani's calm, prophetic voice while quoting him: "It's not my path to fill my thoughts with such things."

"That sounds like something Ky Mani would say," Madeleine giggled, amused by yet another failed voice imitation from Akachi. "An answer without an answer."

"It's good when Jojo's not around, I can do voices without getting a punch in the ribs," Akachi shared gleefully. "Hey, I'm getting better at your Vivian's voice, listen, Maddy, Well I do declare, I'm madder than a wet hen." She had improved somewhat, but the accent was still way overdone, although it never failed to amuse. After all the giggling ended, she asked, genuinely, "What did you think?"

"I think you're lucky Jojo's not here," Kachina replied, finding laughter in all present, and shocking herself for being of a mind to think of something humorous to say. Akachi scowled, but also failed to completely hide her own amusement.

Kachina flashed a glance Madeleine's way, filled with hope, and she was pleased to find the same hope in Madeleine's eyes. She turned to her fellow Princesses then, offering, "I'll come with you after this and make some plans okay?"

Naira nodded happily. "Thank you."

"Even just a day here and there," Sayen proposed, "and you won't be alone. One of us can stay with you until you're happy doing some things on your own. It's up to you."

Misae, most relieved, took a deep breath and pulled a long lock of spiraled fringe out of the corner of her mouth to speak, "Thank you, Kachina. The Riverside wall is finished now, so I'll be there with Annabel until the rest of the work is finished."

"I still can't believe you volunteered for that," Naira declared, and it sounded as if she were impressed, yet, in truth, she feared for her sister's safety.

Misae detected this and although apprehensive herself, facing the first time outside Blue Falls since her arrival, the mission brought on an excitement that she hadn't felt in a while, if ever. "I have protection the whole time, Naira. You don't have to worry."

"I know," Naira replied, pretending. She wasn't as strong as her sisters, and Misae's brave words did little to curb the fear. Her nerves were still somewhat shattered, even with all her months in Blue Falls and, after believing she had already lost Misae one time already, it seemed it would take a long time to expel the fearfulness.

"And she's been training with Ky Mani and Annabel for ages now," Madeleine added, hoping to help rid the sisters of their fear. "You're pretty dangerous now, Misae, yes?"

Misae smiled with modesty. "I'm getting better. I like the sword, but I'm better with the knife at the moment."

"Well, I don't know anyone better to be with when you're outside, than with Annabel," Akachi stated, for extra reassurance. "She's always there to protect you when you can't protect yourself. One time, she knocked a man out just for running into me in the street on purpose."

Madeleine smiled. "That's sounds like Annabel."

"You're joking?" Naira was astounded. "Did anyone see?"

Akachi shook her head. "Nup. We took a shortcut down the alley between the markets and the stables, and this man was just, I don't know, full of hate, I guess. He bashed into my shoulder as he walked past. I went down pretty hard."

"What did Annabel say?" Sayen's eyes were wide open also, eating up the story, and when it came to Annabel, although such stories seemed never-ending, they were never too much.

"She didn't say anything," Akachi answered. "When he knocked me down, he turned around and started to say, 'Why don't you watch where you're going?' but Annabel hit him before he finished. Right here, with the knife of her hand on the side of his skull, and the second hit under the chin with an elbow. 'Bam!' He was a big man, but her first strike stunned him, made his whole body go limp and it looked like he was gonna fall over, but her second hit made plenty sure of it. She hit him so hard, I couldn't believe it." Remembering what followed, Akachi tried not to laugh out loud. "I don't know if I should tell you what we did after that."

"What? You have to now," Misae demanded.

Too much objection followed, so she yielded. "Okay, we dragged him next to one of those manure trailers and…took all his clothes off—"

"What! No, you did not," Madeleine contended.

It was difficult for Akachi not to laugh now, and she struggled to finish. "Yes, we did. We hid his clothes, tied his feet together and his hands behind his back, and then tipped the trailer of manure over him."

A wave of laughter passed through the circle then, but Naira and Sayen were too shocked to manage more than hesitant sniggers for a long while.

Akachi, although in hysterics with her own story, managed to add, "We just left the trailer upside-down on top of him and ran off."

"Oh my gosh!" Madeleine exclaimed. "Why haven't you told me that story before? I wish I could've been there when he woke up."

All present were, more-or-less, picturing a naked, filthy man trying to wriggle his way out from beneath a trailer of stinking dung like a dirty worm, but, in fact, the owner of the trailer returned before the man regained consciousness. After assuming and cursing the work of hooligans, he pushed the trailer back over to go to work, refilling it, but his second swing of the shovel hit the bound man's thigh and his head shot up out of the pile as he cried out in pain, spitting chunks of manure all the while.

"So anyhow," Akachi concluded, "I know Annie, she'd die protecting you."

They all pondered silently on the story for a while and on the previous discussion regarding Annabel. Madeleine wondered how Annabel felt at this time. "I'll try to have a long talk to Annabel tonight, okay," she advised. "I'm not sure yet what I can do, but—"

"You can't tonight," Misae cut in. "It's already late and we're going to Riverside straight after she tries the Plummet. I think you know; the slaves arrive this afternoon."

"Yes, I knew that much," Madeleine admitted. "When will you be back?"

Misae shook her head and shrugged, realizing then that only she and her sisters knew of their plans. "We don't know for how long. We just have to see."

"That's alright." Madeleine was somewhat shaken, but hid her feelings well. She looked to all the others and noticed Kachina's eyes were locked onto the ground again. "It will be okay. We'll talk soon enough. I'm meeting with Julian later so I don't know when, but maybe I could go to Riverside and talk to her while she's there. What do you think, Oni?"

"Sometimes, you can worsen the hole in the dam by trying to patch it up from the outside," Oni answered.

It didn't help appease her worried thoughts at all, but Madeleine understood Oni's warning.

Kachina was beginning to understand Oni's ways and intuited her insinuation before turning to Madeleine. "Maddy, I know you're not a Keeper and you've been so busy, but the Drop will be closed soon, so maybe sometime you could come with me to work with the Princesses. What do you think? It might also help the Keepers if another Warrior knows about their plans."

The idea was a little daunting under the circumstances and she longed for a swim, a nap or some alone time before meeting with Julian, but Madeleine wasn't about to deny Kachina's hand of friendship. "That's a great idea," she accepted, with a deep breath of fortitude. "I can come with you now for a while if you like."

Oni smiled, yet even she only knew a part of the magic she had just helped to weave.

***

Albeit harmless, many children teased Elan for his seeming attempt to rival Annabel's shadow, and he didn't mind so much. Annabel was the one who rescued him, killed his monsters, and held him in her arms all the way to a paradise he could never have imagined. He loved Artetha very well, who frequently looked after him, yet Annabel had become his whole world and, as he, like so many other children, didn't have any idea where his parents might be, she would always stand tall as the one who succeeded where they failed; the one who snatched him from the grip of devastation and abuse, then brought him to a place filled with protection, love, and wonderment.

Hundreds of children awaited Annabel's arrival at the very edge of the Lake on the north side, being the best vantage point to witness her journey along the Plummet all the way from The Nook to the water, yet Elan easily found his way to the shoreline. A place had been kept for him and before he arrived, the children had been competing, though in a friendly manner, to be closest to Elan outside the space they saved for him.

Although younger than the majority, and relatively newer to Blue Falls, he was well-loved by all the children and revered by many, as they also knew that he often trained with Annabel one-on-one, and this, they saw as a very rare privilege. The fact that he also trained with Isi – a Blue One devoted to being a voice for all children; orphaned, blue or otherwise – just attracted more adoration. He was believed to be the greatest young warrior of Blue Falls, and his rapidly-increasing abilities astounded all his peers. Yet, they didn't fear Elan, for he was always gentle. However, they did fear facing him in warrior training, even those years his senior, as their defeat was most certainly assured.

Despite his natural talents and magnetic spirit, Elan was humble and giving, and yet, mostly oblivious to the attention he gained. His mind explored all things at all times, and he strived only to be like Annabel and Isi; the young voices and carers for the children, the Warriors who would never fail them.

Yet, in this moment, his mind only imagined Annabel's long-awaited flight down the Plummet, and his eyes remained fixed on the point of the track where he knew she would first appear. This initial sighting would only be a glimpse until she appeared again, sailing through the opening high above The Nook.

"There she is!" Elan shouted, pointing with great excitement.

The children who managed to catch her whizzing past The Books, with arms flat at her sides like the wings of a plummeting bird, gasped with

26

amazement at the neck-breaking speed at which she already travelled. They all wanted to say something, but their mouths just opened in silence, anticipating her reappearance. Before she came into view again, they first heard her scream with delight which, from their distance, sounded like a hawk crying out. Then, with arms out again, she passed through the stone opening so gently that they could never have imagined the frightening speed she reached just before the rise over this wall nor the masses of adrenaline pouring into her blood, and all with a heart pounding so heavily, she felt like it might snap in two.

Despite having thought about it too many times to count, Annabel wasn't completely prepared for the rapid acceleration which the first descent produced. To make it even more exhilarating, she knew the second part of the track was not only faster and longer, but twisted and turned rapidly in many places. Without realizing, she held her next breath for a good distance after that first scream of delight.

The children couldn't believe how quickly she weaved her way down along the southern wall, and for Annabel, the ride was so incredibly breathtaking, she'd almost forgotten to prepare for disengagement and was at the rise above the Lake before she knew it. Even so, she hit the clasp at her chest at the exact moment she had anticipated, which was just before her speed began to decrease rapidly, believing this would allow her to continue rising upward for a short distance once free of the harness, and this is exactly what happened.

Once releasing the clasp, she opened her arms again and flew into the air. The harness slipped away behind her and for a moment, she was neither falling nor rising; purely weightless. All the children screamed out in that instant and some shouted her name as she brought her arms together while her body turned in preparation for the long dive. It was a great drop from there, so correct positioning was imperative, and she had practiced the technique many times by diving from high ledges into the lake. Practice, of course, was to avoid a bellyflop, and the training proved worthwhile for hardly a splash was made upon entering the Lake.

Absolute silence ensued, until Annabel's head and shoulders breached the surface, then the children all cried out again, jumping up and down excitedly, and when she finally walked out of the water, she met with an embrace of congratulations from Elan.

"My turn!" he exclaimed.

Annabel shook her head and smiled, still reeling from her experience. "Not yet, Elan," she said flatly. "No way. I'm hiding all these harnesses."

Elan raised his eyebrows. "There's more than one?"

***

When the sound of at least 100 cheerful, screaming children drifted up from the Lake to find Queen Lesedi, a great and unexpected smile came over her face, and long before it truly registered in her mind that Annabel must have just tried the Plummet for the first time.

The fact that only joyful voices danced around her on the wind denoted Annabel's survival through an endeavor, Lesedi herself felt dangerous and without adequate purpose. She could certainly understand being attracted to the potential exhilaration of the ride, but couldn't imagine finding the courage herself, nor the want nor need, to attempt such a potentially fatal stunt.

More pertinently, Lesedi reserved a special place in her heart for both Annabel and Madeleine, and couldn't imagine losing either one of them. After rescuing her, they also found her three daughters and brought them all together for a new beginning in a safe haven. Such a debt, she felt, could never be repaid, and so Annabel's reckless adventures triggered another recent fear; that Misae would be on the outside soon and out of her sight for some time. Although completely supportive when Misae first volunteered, she felt her heart skip a beat at the same time and, after losing all three daughters once already, knew there was a great chance for her to become overprotective thereafter.

Lesedi understood this mechanism well, and never failed to analyze her own motivations and actions, hoping to avoid selfishness and to offer her daughters and her people guidance without subjugation. Where her daughters were concerned, this proved to be the most difficult undertaking for a traumatized parent, yet Lesedi found a way to exact her purpose, albeit painful and exhausting. She gave Misae her blessing and went about assisting her in the planning for her new mission.

On the flip-side of emotion, the more positive side, she felt it a miracle that her daughter, one of them at least, had recovered so well from horrible experiences that she could venture out from the cocoon which was Blue Falls and into the outside world again. For this reason, she couldn't deny Misae the opportunity to consolidate her newfound courage.

Elated, positively excited children in the present moment revealed another obvious blessing to Lesedi. She contended with a great many challenges at this time yet, as her reputation portrayed, she managed to recognize the positives amidst the conundrums and to acknowledge the wonder of Blue Falls; that it could provide such a magical place for the children in these violent times. Their high-pitched roar was well-timed, bringing with it much needed energy, hope, and determination.

She had just come back through the tunnel into the Entrance after a meeting with Jalen and his warriors in Crimson Cove, only to see all the names of the lost on the way through, and her heart sank yet again under the sheer weight of the growing numbers.

After Annabel's whole Book of Dreams system became completely overrun with new arrivals, and her third book was filled in no time, it was decided that her dream-book idea needed to be expanded upon, before recording and remembering lost ones became Annabel's only function in life, or before her brain exploded with information, whichever came first. So when the long tunnel between The Drop and Blue Fall's entrance was complete, Taneli and Jabari adorned some of the columns of the main archways along its length with sculptures of the Guardians. The tunnel was then dubbed the Hall of Dreams upon the idea of people filling-in a loose page of what would become a page in a new Book of Dreams and posting it along the wall in its alphabetical place. This way, new arrivals could look for themselves along the walls when they entered, and seekers like Annabel and Madeleine could peruse them anytime. Nanook adored the idea of making each new Book of Dreams thereafter, knowing they would only ever hold the pages of the found.

Nonetheless, while Lesedi adored walking through to see her magnificent daughters immortalized in stone, it was forever hollowing to see all the pages of the yet unfound, and the bracelets and necklaces that some of the children had made and left for the unlikely but most anticipated arrival of parents. Equally heartbreaking was to read messages left for lost lovers, knowing they were written months ago, and having to halt the rescue of the enslaved while reconstruction took place added another level of urgency and dread to Lesedi's aspirations as Queen to her people.

No matter how many new arrivals they brought in nor how many of her people were reunited with loved ones, it never felt like enough, not anywhere near enough. So many people inside Blue Falls were still living a kind of nightmare, being safe-and-sound while a loved one was undoubtedly being punished somewhere in the outside world, and the percentage of the saved slaves barely measured at all against the percentage of the unsaved. As ever, the task remained daunting like an avalanche.

Lesedi discovered long ago that one of her greatest challenges as a leader would be to find continual hope and perseverance in the midst of such unstable times and to propagate these traits within her people, knowing that so many could barely endure their own raging hearts.

With great surprise, she discovered in her meeting with Jalen that it wasn't Jalen after all, inciting the idea of war, but the Panthers themselves, and in fact, their leader was actually trying to bring about peace by way of giving them a purpose in creating the Panthers, which, at times, satisfied anger more than lazing around in paradise. During his weeks cutting the tunnel from Crimson

Cove to Blue Falls – some people believe single-handedly – Jalen exhausted the greater part of his fury and frustration. Upon realizing the value of putting his body to work in order to hush his mind, he redirected his energy into becoming a better warrior and into making warriors of broken men; to be stronger of mind and to be prepared.

The Panthers were made mostly of men, and most of those had seen their children slaughtered or their loved ones dragged away, seemingly forever. Most commenced training with anger dominating their purpose, and of course, almost every bout was lost for them before it even began. Their patience seemed non-existent and any initial composure was doomed to be quaked by visions of past horrors while they listened vaguely to instruction and exhausted themselves in seconds with overzealous and thoughtless movement.

Jalen's purpose for creating the Shadow Warriors was to separate dedicated, highly trained warriors from blood-thirsty maniacs, which also provided a training path, such as a set of disciplines leading to inner balance and, of course, greater skill. He asked Ky Mani, Annabel, and Oni for their help in guiding the men, not only to bring about more order to a rapidly growing rabble, but for his own lack of training. The subsequent shortage of confidence, this brought about only threatened to undermine his endeavors and, not wishing to create an army of uncontrollable killers, he forgave his desire to create his vision on his own and sought the help of a trusted few.

Yet, rumors were easily fueled by people in need of drama and when word began to spread that Jalen planned to lead his army of Panthers outside to wreak havoc on the world, Lesedi thought she should venture into the Den to investigate matters for herself.

While searching for Jalen, it didn't occur to her until it was over that she might have been subject to a demonstration, one made far more impressive by the unwitting part she played. One of the Panthers said she would find Jalen in the Den, training with some of his Shadow Warriors, and so it came as a surprise to find the large cavern vacant when she entered. It was lit well-enough, with a line of lanterns along every wall, but it was only Lesedi's second time in the Den, and so she walked out into the center of the sandy floor, expecting to find another unknown section, yet discovered nothing more. The extent of every niche and wall seemed to be lit, but only training apparatus, crates and equipment could be seen in any direction, so she turned to leave, most puzzled. In the next moment, she was greatly startled, so much so that she let out a great gasp and froze on the spot.

All the shadows within the cavern began to move around and transform, becoming the shapes of men, permeating the stone walls, and dropping from the ceiling with hardly a sound. Before she could draw another breath to gasp again, she was surrounded by at least 50 Shadow Warriors who suddenly began flailing about in mock battle, using all kinds of weapons with great mastery.

Once realizing there was no danger present, Lesedi found herself being very impressed by the illusion of so many all at once together with the silence they managed to keep throughout the ambush.

Jalen walked through the circle in that moment, as all the warriors halted and bowed to their Queen. "Forgive me, my Queen," he had said, bowing his head also, "I hope we didn't frighten you too much, but I wanted to show you how great they are."

After she'd caught her breath and looked around in wonder at where they might have all been hiding, Lesedi replied with one raised eyebrow and conscientious nodding, since words had momentarily forsaken her for the return of a steady heartbeat. She did, however, find enough voice to tell them once again, that bowing wasn't necessary.

Sometime during the meeting, Lesedi realized that Jalen had actually done a great service for Blue Falls and Crimson Cove in forming the Panthers and Shadow Warriors; providing the men with a more profound outlet than the relatively small training sessions with Ky Mani in The Dojo, which couldn't possibly cater for thousands anyhow. Perhaps, she pondered, if not for Jalen's initiative, Blue Falls might have already been roaming with wild avengers fueling war and bringing about a great disturbance.

"Jalen, I'm sorry," she confessed upon her new understanding. "I was led to believe you were inciting a pointless war."

Somehow, Jalen wasn't insulted. "I understand why you might think that," he offered, most accepting, while hoping to appease the guilt in his Queen. "Given my past, this is my undoing. As much as I want to squash all who enslave, I would never lead men knowingly into a slaughter and I would never go against the wishes of my Queen or my Princesses."

Lesedi faltered somewhat in the wake of these unexpected words. Somehow, they seemed dizzyingly gracious coming from such a colossal man, and his underestimated devotion almost won him a few tears. No one Lesedi knew well had seen Jalen for quite some time, and she began to wonder if anyone was even aware of the obvious change she had detected in both his demeanor and his motivation.

In great detail, Jalen explained to Lesedi the path of the Panther, which led to being acknowledged as one of the elite Shadow Warriors. They practiced in all manner of ways, mimicking all kinds of conditions, and trained amidst the Dark Forest, in the caverns, in the water, and throughout the hinterland outside at night. Teachings included rock climbing and swimming, the making of weaponry, silence and camouflage, survival and healing techniques, strategy in the field when unarmed, and facing weapons of all kinds and, of course, primarily, Ky Mani's martial and weapons training.

During the Shadow Warrior's test, the hopeful one must first defend themselves easily using a number of weapons and also hand-to-hand against a series of specific attacks from Ky Mani based on the skills they had learned during their training with the Panthers. Most hopefuls passed this phase, because it became blatantly obvious very early on in training how incredibly difficult it was to achieve that level of skill that no one but the worthy usually attempted the test. By the time one reached anywhere near this level of skill, arrogance had been well and truly demoralized into nothingness, and so the only ones who tried were the ones most capable of making an informed and impartial decision regarding their own skill level.

However, the test against Ky Mani was but the penultimate. For the final test, the hopeful must face a Warrior Guardian and defend themselves successfully during a series of bouts with and without weaponry. Yet, the true purpose of this test was never divulged to the aspirant, for it was only those accepted, the ones who finally passed this test, who understood its true and essential purpose. So, all the Shadow Warriors, once accepted, kept this purpose a secret, knowing well that to speak of it could destroy the unity within the Shadow Warrior force by way of unnecessary and dangerous hotheadedness during training and certainly in the event they ever embarked on an actual mission.

New hopefuls always assumed that the final test of facing a Guardian was just another, yet more difficult test of their martial skills, but Jalen asked for the participating Guardian to help him create this illusion, for the real purpose was to test mental and emotional aptitude.

Jalen knew, through Ky Mani's advice, that there held no place in a team of elite warriors, whose lives depended on one another during a skirmish or the like, for someone driven by anger and revenge. From his own experiences also, Jalen knew that someone in this state-of-mind only thought of themselves and could easily sabotage even the best-laid plans. His final test incorporating a Guardian was created purely to expose these emotions and motivations in order to drive them out and away before the warrior next attempted the test.

Jalen chose Annabel and Oni specifically to take part in this test for how easily they frustrated and aggravated their opponents; Annabel, due to her impossible, lightening-like skills, her fierce but steadfast demeanor, and how quickly she could defeat her opponent, and Oni for the delicate smile which never seemed to leave her placid face, as she so gently and effortlessly brought her opponents to their knees.

Many times, hopefuls were defeated just through sheer exhaustion alone derived from spending ever-increasing amounts of energy trying to make some sort of an impact, while the Guardian themselves had hardly moved at all the whole time. Oni's smile was born of her untouchable and never-ending love of life, yet her opponents, in the heat of battle at least, saw it as a mocking grin from someone so easily and gently exposing all the flaws in their offense and defense. It was demoralizing for the most experienced warriors, let alone those still motivated and controlled by self-sabotaging emotions.

Those hopefuls most in denial about the rage in their hearts were the ones who usually exploded the greatest, after just minutes of exponential failure. This test never failed to bring their rage to the surface in its ugly completeness. Some, after many failed attacks, dropped their weapons and ran at Annabel or Oni like wounded psychopaths, only to be brought down even quicker, yet this only added salt to the wound of uselessness and fueled more frustration. Many dropped to their knees after this, to let out a long and almighty scream, born off complete and utter frustration, which more often than not, ended in gut-wrenching sobbing and convulsive heaving, seemingly strong enough to break the lungs.

While expecting perhaps to be ridiculed, and feeling ashamed for having targeted a young woman with their inner anger, instead, they were met with complete understanding from all present, and a hand of friendship from whichever Guardian lifted them to their feet to offer further guidance. Only the Shadow Warriors, Ky Mani, and a select few were permitted to attend the final tests, and the failed hopefuls were assured that almost all of their fellow warriors had been through exactly the same transformation at some point in their life and were hardly going to judge them.

After this experience, the warrior's urgency seemed to abate in most cases, and that once wasted energy could then be redirected into focusing on the perfecting of skills and in helping others within Blue Falls. When a warrior passed the first test but failed the second, they only had to face the second test again, and it was clear to all very quickly if they had transmuted the old ways or not. It didn't matter if they prepared for future attempts, knowing the measure of the test, because that kind of rage would always reveal itself. It could not be controlled, and this was the whole point of the test.

Lesedi left the Panther's Den with great surprise and adoration for what Jalen had achieved already in Crimson Cove. His suggestion, that it might help to bring the Panthers more peace and less frustration if their Queen were to make a point of visiting just the Panthers sometime, was well-received. Being aware that most of the Panthers, especially the most dedicated, rarely ventured out of Crimson Cove, she agreed that a personal visit from her might help them to feel more a part of the whole, more supported, more understood. Together, they set a day for the next visit and agreed that Jalen should tell them immediately to give them time to think of any questions they may want answered. Lesedi planned to bring Sayen and Naira also, hoping to make it an even more significant event for them.

Following her feared yet undeniably successful venture to see Jalen, Lesedi enjoyed her walk back to the top of Crimson Cove, noting how quickly the once-vacuous space had developed into its own self-supporting city, much like Blue Falls. All manner of workshops were steadily multiplying throughout, and it now had its own version of Blue Falls' HotPot, called the Red HotPot, where kitchens of many kinds grew in number and variety.

For long-term Blue Falls residents, spending a day in Crimson Cove was almost like an adventure to another country, and vice versa, with alternative food to be tried, new places to explore, and events exclusive to Crimson Cove or Blue Falls to be experienced. One of which being the Panther's Tournaments, where archery together with knife, axe, and spear throwing were the main spectacles which never failed to bring about enjoyment for all, and greater unity between the two caverns.

The next stop on Lesedi's unwritten agenda was The Nursery, a smaller cavern on the floor-level of the mid-northern wall of Blue Falls, where every single Blue One was born and where she was told she could find Isi meeting with the Blue Ones, as they often did, in their unofficial home. It became customary, somehow, for all expecting mothers to give birth inside The Nursery, and the space held everything needed in relation to childbirth. Artetha or Awinita, usually both, attended every birth, and mothers made the choice between giving birth in or out of a small pond inside, which was constantly refreshed by a small stream of river water from above, and the perfect size and depth for both mother and carer to reside during the birth, without the fear of drifting off with a strong water current.

Over the years, the Blue Ones and their mothers had filled every possible space inside The Nursery with something green and growing. It now seemed much like a jungle inside, beginning with two grape vines completely surrounding the entrance, which, over time, had narrowed the passage to the extent where no more than two people could enter side-by-side, when it was wide enough for at least eight in the beginning.

On her way in, Lesedi picked a bunch of red grapes to appease slight hunger – admitting to herself that the impulse held more want than need – and took a deep breath to honor the healing energy which the Nursery always seemed to offer upon entering.

After walking through and around the never-ending mesh of plants and vines to more or less the center of the cavern, taking in an abundance of delightful fragrances all the way, she suddenly realized that the space was unusually deserted. Normally, she would have seen at least a few Blue Ones by now, sitting in small groups or sleeping amidst the green gardens somewhere, but, so far, she hadn't seen a single soul. However, she was yet to reach their meeting place at the far side of the cavern, and since she could hear faint singing now, she figured that's where she would find them.

Yet, it was a single voice, soft and most accurate in tone, drifting through the leafy paths, and she soon recognized it to be Isi's. When the way opened again to another small pond surrounded in moss and ferns, Lesedi saw him, sitting alone and cross-legged, facing her way but singing with his eyes closed, in a voice almost worthy of a whisper.

"Sampa...Thípi...where are you...? The world is crying...where are you...? And when the sky begins to fall... Will all the Guardians hear the call...?"

Lesedi paused at a distance to enjoy the sight and Isi's beautiful yet sorrowful melody until he finished and opened his eyes. She knew the song well. Being based on an ancient legend regarding a hidden paradise called Sampa-Thípi, where the people once found freedom, it was the subject of many songs and stories and also popular throughout Blue Falls for its likeness to the Blue Falls' legends.

Isi's eyes opened with expectation and a smile quickly found his lips upon seeing the queen. He had grown considerably since Lesedi first met him, sporting longer hair, and the sapphire beads within his lochs almost rivaled Ky Mani's bead-for-bead now. It seemed to be a growing trend, inspired by Ky Mani, who originally replaced his wooden beads with sapphire beads, and the Guardians fueled the idea by regularly adorning their own hair, headdresses and clothes worn in ceremonies with the same. Many people saw the beads now as a piece of the Guardians' amulets, a piece, in essence, of the much loved Guardians themselves, so Nanook made them automatically from sapphire and ruby offcuts while he worked, knowing they would be used in no time.

Lesedi quickly realized that Isi was not only expecting her impromptu visit, but had somehow cleared the Nursery of all Blue Ones for the occasion. If she didn't know him better, she might have been spooked, but she merely returned his smile and went to kneel in front of him as he bowed there on his knees.

"Isi?"

Cheekiness stole his smile. "Yes, my Queen?"

Lesedi failed to keep a completely straight face. "How many times have I asked you not to bow to me?"

"Why does the Queen dislike this so much?" Isi answered, without answering. "Your people love you. They would fan you and drop grapes into your mouth every day if you wished it."

Somehow, this amused Lesedi greatly, especially with the taste of grapes still in her mouth, and the relief she felt after meeting Jalen made way for a good, long belly laugh.

"Oh, Isi, you always make me laugh," she confessed, after recovering somewhat. "Can you imagine me lying over a long settee being fanned and fed grapes?" Her elaboration found for herself another burst of laughter. Finally, she settled and asked, "Do you remember when I first arrived in Blue Falls?"

"I don't think anyone will forget that day, my Queen," he noted with surety.

"No, I mean, just you," she reinstated. "You were my Greeter and you saw my heart like no other has ever seen it, with all its scars and weaknesses."

"I saw no weaknesses, my Queen," Isi argued. "I saw a mother desperate to find her children and to free her people. This is far from any weakness, and I remember, you were very strong."

Isi's words removed Lesedi's amusement and replaced it with awe. She sighed, almost longingly, and confessed, "I wish I could see what you and the Blue Ones see, Isi."

Although Isi didn't answer in words, his expression hinted at the possibility that Lesedi may not wish for such things if she knew more of them.

"Is it a burden?" she asked, and saw a reaction in him that she hadn't seen before, leaving her to wonder if anyone had ever asked him that question. His eyes turned downward for a moment – something rare for Isi, to avert his gaze – and he was, of course, the unsung leader of the Blue Ones, yet, however inherently wise and perceptive, still a young man with human needs.

"My existence is no more a burden to me than yours might be to you, my Queen," he answered carefully.

Lesedi let him get away with dancing around her question, but to ask another, more relevant to her current cause: "How did you know I was coming to see you today?"

"I dreamt it, as you dream," he said, simply. "But I'm dreaming all the time."

"Heavens, Isi, you actually answered that question directly," she noted in disbelief.

Isi giggled a little, something which always seemed to surprise Lesedi no matter how many times she saw his dimples expose themselves to that extent.

"It's because you asked in full honesty, admitting your suspicion and proving your lack of fear for the answer," he explained. "If you asked instead, 'Did you know I was coming to see you?' my answer might have been different."

For some time, Lesedi pondered on this idea and the more she thought of it, the more expansive it became. "I'll have to think more on that later," she admitted then, after a long pause, then dared to suppose, "If you knew I was coming, then you probably know why I'm here, yes?"

"You fear for Misae?" Isi intuited. "And you want to know what the Blue Ones see of her future. It doesn't take a Blue One to work that out, my Queen."

After taking a deep breath, Lesedi exhaled heavily and her eyes alluded to the fear in her heart. "No one wants to talk about the Guardians, Isi," she said with a good pinch of frustration. "Not the Guardians themselves, including my daughters, not Ky Mani, not Nanook. The Elders refuse to talk about them too, but they don't mind saying to the people that they think the prophecy is wrong. How can I learn more about the prophecy and the Guardians, three of which are my daughters, if no one will speak of it?"

"The prophecy isn't wrong," Isi said succinctly. "It's just a part of a greater prophecy and missing some information."

"Then why haven't you tried to inform the people?" she asked, then abruptly raised a hand in realization. "Wait, let me guess, to protect the prophecy?"

***

The train from Port Harroway to Black Sand Valley took a good day-and-a-half, depending on the number of stops and, of course, on how long the driver chatted to each familiar station master along the way. Julian was grateful to have a sleeper, even with the narrow bunk his economy ticket offered, as his sleep had been disturbed for many days.

Despite lethargy, derived from his journey to the station before sunrise, he never slept well in the daytime, and after tossing and turning for a long while, he thought it better to try to turn his body clock around by staying awake until nightfall. Meeting Madeleine in such an exhausted state was something he hoped to avoid, but it didn't seem as if he had a choice in the matter, so, with journal in hand, he headed for the dining carriage.

Shyness led him to a more private table at the back corner where he settled to browse a menu, hoping to consume his mild anxiety. A waiter approached immediately, swinging a towel over his forearm.

"Good day, sir," he greeted politely. "Will you be dining?"

Julian hadn't thought of it. "Ah…yes, thank you. I'll take a look and I'll have an earl grey tea to start, please."

"Very good, sir."

The waiter went about placing cutlery and condiments over the starchy-white table cloth. Julian looked around the carriage and noticed a table of four looking his way, aristocracy for certain; always obvious in manner and style. Both men and one of the women regarded him with dissent, but one woman seemed to enjoy casting her eyes upon him. Her look denoted familiarity and great interest.

Julian quickly turned his gaze to the waiter's work while subconsciously adjusting his dark corduroy jacket and forcing strands of his wavy brown hair back behind both ears. "Thank you," he said graciously once the table was set.

"Very good, sir."

Since he never knew if his moderate level of fame would attract good wishes or abuse, Julian avoided attention wherever possible. Passion for his work and beliefs also found him dropping the reins on his extreme views and, more often than not, his controversial ideas were ill-received. So, he did his best to ignore the eyes upon him and opened his journal to the page he had prepared for Madeleine.

Fearing he may have annoyed her to some extent when they last met, for insisting that she may have been incorrect regarding certain aspects of the prophecy, the Guardians and Blue Falls, he went to great lengths collecting the crux of his research together in the hope to explain his findings more thoroughly. It was extremely important to get the facts right and not just for the integrity of his work – being based almost entirely on the Guardians and the prophecy – but to end the disagreement with Madeleine. The very last thing he wanted to do at this time was to upset or repel her in any way. She was very clear in telling him that it wasn't a suitable time for her to think of beginning anything on a romantic level, yet he hoped the future had other ideas.

Until now, Julian's romantic interests had been fleeting and without substance. No one had truly taken his heart like Madeleine, and so he reminded himself regularly to respect her wishes, hoping not to ruin what they already found through overzealousness, regardless of what the future may hold. This frame-of-mind was difficult for Julian to adopt. The more he tried not to think of Madeleine in this way, the more he found himself lost in his dream of what might be, and had consequently written and torn up more letters of adoration than he would like to count. Delving deeper into his research didn't help greatly as a distraction, since the more he checked his facts, the more conclusive his findings and this inevitably maintained the lack of resolution for he and Madeleine.

After much written correspondence, containing Madeleine's warning that – given all the recent killings – his life may be in danger if he were to speak with Black Sand Valley slave owners against slavery, he decided instead to travel about earlier than planned to continue researching for his book in the hope to ascertain further knowledge of the intricacies of the prophecy at the same time. There was no point pushing to see Madeleine immediately when he felt eagerness might only serve to work against his aspirations, and in the meantime, he hoped his patience might prove the depth of his devotion.

Meticulously, he had checked and rechecked translations to the Guardian Prophecy from three separate sources, one being scriptures in the oldest known recorded language of Aramaic, and noted that they differed slightly – in storytelling and in certain minor details – but they all agreed on the numbers of people and places. Not only did they agree, but two were very specific regarding origin and gender of the Guardians.

Julian was lost for not knowing what to do in such a predicament. His intention this day was to go over the notes again, but at a quick glance, he realized that no aspect of his research was yet to be reexamined at least 50 times. Much to his disappointment, believing Madeleine to be more knowledgeable on the subject than he, the new information only validated his original beliefs and left him facing her again with an even stronger opinion.

"Your tea, sir." The waiter placed a wooden tray down with a small porcelain teapot steaming at the spout. "Have you chosen?"

Although Julian had looked at the menu many times, he didn't read much of anything written there. It merely served as a calligraphic backdrop to his thoughts. "Um. I'll have the vegetable soup please."

The waiter nodded and left him alone again. Although he chose abruptly, the air quickly cooled as the train chugged alongside a high ridge in the hinterland east of the Midlands and the idea of a bowl of hot soup already had a warming effect, leaving him thankful for rash decisions.

After pouring some tea, he added a sugar cube and subconsciously tapped the top of it until it crumbled. One spin of the spoon broke it open then and sent the pieces spiraling, while his mind rested in no man's land. His dreams of late had been most unsettling, seeming to portend catastrophic events and, although he tried not to think of them, he was reminded often and yet again while watching clouds of sweet granules disintegrate.

Before waking suddenly and preparing to meet with the train, he was dreaming of flying with Madeleine, and although she appeared as a black bird, he knew it to be her somehow…leading him somewhere. He tried to catch up, but her speed kept increasing and he could only travel behind. Their destination, a rocky mountainside where a path had been made, spiraling all the way to the base with a wider part of it housing a number of mortars, made enormous by the tall ancient beings who worked them. Stone pestles with silver-tipped handles slowly circled inside them, powered by a type of pendulum activating a series of cogs. One such cog, lying horizontal above the pestle handle, seemed to move the pestle without a solid part connecting them, as if they were locked together, yet kept slightly apart by some unseen matter or force. Somehow, he knew the work was done silently, meticulously, and with a mindfulness one would not dare to interrupt. As they flew past, he noticed large barrels of olives, lemons, and apricots; the kernels of which were being removed and poured into mortars with other ingredients. A line of sickly humans not too far down the path, with darkened eyes and lumps beneath the skin, meditated with small vessels in hand, seemingly awaiting the completion of the ancients' work.

Madeleine slowed down as they soared around the mountain and hovered above a wide tor where she dropped and turned into her human form as she touched down on stone. Julian did the same and was about to turn to speak with her when he noticed a man standing at a distance in full battle garb, holding a large sword. Without a word, the man started running at him at full speed, with the obvious intention of attacking, yet Julian stood weaponless and at the very edge of a great precipice.

He turned to say something to Madeleine, only to find she had disappeared and the man was already upon him anyhow, leaping into the air from a few paces away before directing a boot into his chest. The impact sent him backward, and as he met with the open air, he recognized the man; it was himself, gloating, with a pleased and victorious smile.

Julian attributed his inability to sleep thereafter to this inordinate dream leaving him to ponder on all the possible reasons why he would dream of Madeleine leading him to his self-administered demise. It was most unsettling and contradicted his every idea of Madeleine's integrity. Together with his inability to prove Madeleine correct regarding the prophecy, he felt a great dread come upon him and it didn't help that two burly men in bowler hats at the other end of the dining carriage were clearly eyeing him with intimidating, hateful glares.

The waiter returned with a bowl of soup and a side plate with a bread bun and a ramekin of butter.

"Your soup, sir." He cleared his throat then. "Sir, one of the lady passengers said you might be Julian Winters, the author. Is it true?"

The answer stalled on Julian's tongue. "Yes, that's right."

"Well." The waiter, pretending or not, seemed delighted. He placed a napkin over Julian's lap. "It's not often we have someone of renown in our modest country diner carriage. I can't say I've read your books, but I will have to now. Enjoy your lunch, sir."

"Thank you." Julian never knew exactly what to say when people spoke of his work, especially when comments were neither here nor there. "I hope you enjoy…whatever you happen to read," he stuttered.

The soup was surprisingly delicious, yet perhaps only made remarkable by Julian's neglected appetite, due to a world slowly-but-surely filling with strangeness. He could almost feel pieces of hot potato drop to the bottom of his hollow stomach but, after only a few gulps, his appetite faded yet again; stolen by the dilemma of how he might tell Madeleine that she was wrong about the prophecy in so many ways.

***

Isi read the queen's frustration clearly, but could only answer in truth. "Yes, it's true we protect the prophecy, but also because we are not permitted to see everything, and since there are many possible futures, it's not always obvious right away which of those futures will triumph. Some visions we know will be unbelievable and misunderstood anyway, and so we don't share them."

"Like what?" Lesedi asked, most curious to understand.

Isi thought on it for a few moments before an example came to mind. "Between the day you arrived and the day all four princesses were found, I had a vision that your daughters were separated and sold to the darkest of monsters. I saw Kachina being beaten, I saw Naira's eyes frightened beyond sanity while a horrid man led her around by the neck and I saw the wounds of all your daughters. In the same vision, I saw Annabel covered in blood, holding a sword also dripping with blood, and then I saw her weeping with a little boy in her arms. All these visions were real and they happened, but the princesses were all found and rescued, and both Annabel and the boy, who was Elan, were actually safe in that time of the vision. Do you think it would have helped you if I told you any of that while the princesses were still lost?"

Lesedi didn't have to think about it for long. "No, not at all. It would have made things so much worse."

Isi shrugged in agreement. "It's difficult to explain why, because the emotional energy of the visions is more revealing than the visions themselves, but for me and some of the other Blue Ones, these visions told us that all the princesses would be returned to you safely and that they would all heal, but, of course, we never have proof. You wanted to hear this more than anything, and I knew it was the truth so I said it, in a way, that day," he explained. "If you remember."

41

"I remember, you were positive," Lesedi acknowledged. "Back then, I thought you were just a naive and hopeful child. All right, well, now I want to hear more than anything that Misae is going to be safe." She swallowed then, almost regretting having asked the question, as she voiced it indirectly.

"Will you be seeing Misae before she leaves for Riverside?" Isi asked and, because he didn't immediately ensure Misae's safety, his question rattled the queen's composure somewhat.

Her breathing had almost halted completely by the time she answered. "No, I think they would have left by now, why?"

Acknowledging her fear, Isi smiled gently. "Do you trust me, my Queen?"

His question should have brought more worry, but it wasn't the first time he posed it, and she started breathing again, acknowledging that Isi had never failed to speak only truth to his queen, nor failed to come through with his promises.

"You've asked me this before," she stated. "The answer is still yes."

"The Guardians are tested in many ways, you know this," he reminded her, yet Lesedi only nodded slightly, warily. "Today is one of many important days to come for the Guardians, for all people."

"Today? Why?" It was the first time Lesedi had heard this idea. "The day's nearly over."

"It may be more important than any other day before it," he emphasized. "It will also answer many of our questions about the Guardians. Something very important is coming, a revelation. It must be great because the Blue Ones have been blocked somehow from seeing beyond a certain point. Many of the Guardians will be tested before the end of today in preparation for this coming event."

A wave of confusion came over Lesedi. "But they're all here now except for Annabel and Misae."

Isi didn't respond, but Lesedi was beginning to understand his silences, that they revealed more than his words sometimes. "You make me feel like I'm playing with fire."

"It's very important that no one interferes with the Guardians' natural choices at this time," Isi explained. "Especially if the reason is fear, for what the future might bring. This is not for us to control."

Since this was Lesedi's own philosophy, not to attempt to control outcomes, she could hardly disagree, and hearing it spoken by another dragged her own fear into the light. She looked into Isi's eyes then, not knowing how to feel about the current set of circumstances, only recognizing all at once that the unusual feeling she'd endured all day was surely related to the topic at hand, to Isi's speculations.

Isi sat in silent contemplation then for a long while, simply gazing into Lesedi's worried eyes. She didn't know what to make of it, but to her, it seemed as if he were deciding whether to speak or not.

Finally, he voiced his thoughts. "Your trust in me is an honor, my Queen," he said first, unexpectedly. "And since my trust in you is the same, I would like to tell you something about this day, but before I do, I want you to know what I'm trusting you with so you can decide for yourself if you want me to share it with you."

"Go on," Lesedi prompted, feeling her stomach hollow-out a little more.

"I'll tell you first that it won't take away your fears about Misae," he forewarned. "But it will help you to understand the importance of the day and the importance of your resolve."

"My resolve?" Lesedi asked, stunned. "Why me?"

"What I will tell you, if you wish that is," he answered, "will give you the power to ruin the future for the Guardians and for all your people. Tonight marks a turning, a great step in the prophecy, and the part Misae will play is as crucial as each part of all those involved. If any one of them were to fail, then the future will hold only doom for them and for Blue Falls. So, if you interfere with Misae's natural choices in any way, it will most likely lead to great misfortune."

"Great misfortune," Lesedi repeated the words with concern. "Isi, what are you saying? What's going to happen?"

"We don't see events unfolding continuously like that," he explained. "We see enough of each part played to understand how they all piece together. We don't see success or failure; we just see the choices that will have to be made."

"I'm not sure if I understand that, Isi," Lesedi admitted.

Isi pondered for a moment, seeking a more useful explanation. "Oni and Akachi won't be tested because they're Blue Ones and they will never fail to act on their greater wisdom, but all the others will be tested today and in more ways than you or I could ever imagine, on selfishness and loyalty. I'll tell you about Kachina. The first of her tests is over for tonight. If she has succeeded, there will be a future test to confirm she and Madeleine are on the good road. We dreamt today Kachina will also be given the choice to assist the Guardians somehow and to make amends in some way, or to turn away and go deeper into herself, into the darkness. She will be right on the edge of this choice, for she has many scars and she will have to initiate this step herself in some way or the chance will be lost forever."

"Did she succeed?" Lesedi asked, remembering Isi had said her test for tonight was over.

"I don't know," Isi admitted. "Overall, it's not one of the most important tests to come, but for Kachina, it's one of the most important tests of her life. Naira and Sayen will be tested on their ability to overcome fear of worthlessness and inferiority to the Warrior Guardians, and they too will have to initiate some form of greater connection to further align themselves with the Guardians. This is what today promises, to open the opportunity for all the Guardians to unite in the future, to prepare for greater tests and obligations to come."

"The Guardians were all united when my daughters and Kachina arrived," Lesedi argued.

"No, this marked the time when the queen and princesses were reunited and rejoined their people, and when eight Guardians came together, but not the time when all the Guardians will be united," Isi explained, most certainly.

"What is Misae's test?" Lesedi asked hesitantly then.

"Misae will have to find her true self," he said simply and he could have predicted the queen's next question.

"Will she be in danger?"

He didn't hesitate in responding, "Yes."

Lesedi let a small gasp escape and eventually asked, "Have you seen what might happen if I interfere?"

With a nod denoting horrid things, he answered, "The death of at least three Guardians will be assured and the fate of Blue Falls will be to crumble in disunity."

Lesedi's mouth gaped open for a long while before she spoke again, "And yet, you tell me she will surely be in danger, and I could send someone to fetch her within the hour and—"

"Destroy everything we know," Isi concluded, in her stead. "Do you see the greater responsibility of the Blue Ones now and of the Guardians and of the queen?"

"Yes," she acknowledged. "But how does it help you to know these things? How does it help the people?"

"Because we see the importance of the interconnectivity of mindfulness and we are alerted to important coming events, not just to assist the Guardians, but for all, and when in situations like the Guardians' meeting today, you can be sure that the Blue Ones, Oni and Akachi, would have assisted in the transformation and harmony of relationships to help enable the strengthening of future unity. This was the most important aspect of their meeting today." Isi paused for a few moments before continuing, to be sure that Lesedi had compiled this information in her mind for later access. "And with my insights, when my queen comes to me for council, I can tell her with confidence that she should be more afraid of her own fear than anything else at this time because fear could lead to disaster, but faith in her daughter's ability to adapt and survive will help her to fulfill the calling."

Lesedi took a very deep breath then and let it all out at once, seeming to expel the anxiety which had gripped her all this time. She thought for a long while on all Isi had revealed before responding.

"You didn't have to see me at all today," she discerned. "You could have easily avoided me until tomorrow and avoided this conversation altogether and so avoided giving me information that could ruin everything."

Isi shook his head. "I never want to be someone who avoids their queen," he determined. "Or anyone, for that matter. If we are honest with ourselves and others and go without fear, there is no need to avoid confrontations. In any case, it is the opposite that I seek. It was a surprise for me to be your Greeter when you first arrived, but it was not a random coincidence. The future is calling, and it called us together."

From the moment Lesedi first met Isi, she felt a certain destined element, but could never quite determine its significance. Only now she was beginning to understand. "Why?" she asked, while believing his words to be true.

"You, the Guardians, and the Blue Ones have a greater purpose outside the one you are aware of, my Queen," he revealed. "And if we honor each other's trust, this day has the ability to create an unbreakable bond between all of us to carry into the future. In the new world, the unity of the Guardians, the queen and princesses, the Elders and the Blue Ones is of absolute importance. Without it, we have nothing, we have no future. So, I feel it is my calling to offer myself as your personal council today and for always. It is my plan to tell you now something of the greater prophecy that I know of, and after today, if the Guardians succeed, you will know the worth of my council and we will both know the value of each other's trust."

"Are you going to tell me the outcome of tonight?" she asked, with a mind swelling with intimidating possibilities.

"We're permitted to see the various levels of both outcomes, of failure and success," he admitted. "But we're not permitted to know exactly which one will be. So, the Blue Ones will continue to act as if we have no doubt that the Guardians will succeed because our support, our belief, and encouragement has a positive effect on all of them, on the energy that comes to them. If our energy is fearful and doubtful, this will have the opposite effect and they will be burdened by it."

"As it would be with my energy and belief," Lesedi realized.

Isi smiled warmly. "You are very powerful, my Queen, and highly intuitive. When giving Misae your blessing for her mission, it was empowering, and in doing so, without fighting her on it, it has increased the faith she has in herself."

"How did you know I didn't fight her on it?" she queried.

"Because she went to Riverside," he answered plainly, with a touch of a smile. "She would have obeyed you as always, and stayed if you asked, or if you made it seem like it would be a great burden for you if she went. You see now, the true power you have?"

"I might have already destroyed everything," Lesedi supposed, and after reflecting on this and many other ideas, she continued with much less urgency. "You trusted me, Isi, and I understand now why it is so difficult to share what you see. I won't betray this trust, and I also understand that you're not able to see the outcome of tonight, but what does your intuition tell you?"

His eyes awash with sincerity and hope, Isi lifted his chin and with pride, answered, "I believe in the Guardians."

***

When Jimmy gave the word that the last of the slave trader's wagons had trotted away, Annabel removed her Penelope wig and went to fetch Misae from the house.

"It's all yours now," Victor declared, boarding his carriage, ready to leave Riverside himself after his last delivery of supplies for the day. "See you tomorrow. Good luck and keep safe."

With a high timber fence now surrounding the inner grounds and mansion of what was Chester Flinch's estate, and an equally tall, reinforced hardwood gate at the entrance, anyone could walk around the property freely without the fear of being seen by outsiders. While the fence was being built by a team of Caucasian workers, Vivian spread the rumor that it would serve to minimize the use of slave handlers, but what they were actually developing at Riverside was a decoy to eventually draw any possible attention away from the west side of the Midlands, away from Blue Falls.

Uninvited, unwanted visitors of all kinds – authorities, the generally curious and treasure hunters alike – were forever increasing and, when rumors began to spread about the possibility of a secret hideaway on the west side of Black Sand Valley harboring hundreds of runaway slaves, it was decided that the Riverside property situated on the east side should become a decoy somehow. At the same time, major changes should occur to the physical makeup of The Drop, the entrance to Blue Falls, and also to the process of delivering new slaves, in order to guarantee continued secrecy.

It was agreed to by all that The Drop to Crimson Cove would soon be sealed permanently and that the hole in the ceiling of Blue Falls would no longer be hidden inside the chimney walls but beneath a huge pile of large granite rocks carefully arranged over an open steel framework. This would still allow for rainfall to pass through in streams and, instead of one wide beam of light, hundreds of smaller beams would shine through the network of gaps in the design, which were made to align with the path of the sun. Since the height of the chimney walls themselves stole a good portion of light, and the new creation also contained a layer of large, quartz, crystal rocks below the granite layer in order capture more sunlight, it was assumed that the difference in overall light emanation would not be so noticeable. The opening at Dead Man's Fall provided enough light for most of the day anyhow on its own, and they also kept in mind the contingency plan of placing reflective materials over the walls around Crystal Nest, to bounce more light inside, but for the time being, this seemed unnecessary.

In addition to these reconstructions, the greater part of the opening at the Entrance would be sealed with granite boulders, then covered with dirt and foliage, including thorny bush as a deterrent, and the barn which once concealed this doorway would be moved further away. The only way to enter Blue Falls thereafter would be through a smaller doorway hidden behind a large swinging stone within a maze of boulders, underbrush, and trees.

If the predicted war eventually found its way to the higher western farms of Black Sand Valley, Blue Falls and Crimson Cove could easily be exposed by the complete destruction of either Vivian or Victor's barns which concealed the Drop and the Entrance, or by demolishing the chimneys hiding the opening in the ceiling of Blue Falls. The latter of these scenarios would almost certainly result in major injury or death for anyone on the Ledge or around the ponds at the time of the collapse. Changes certainly needed to be made and safety plans created to protect themselves as best they could, such as utilizing Vivian's Riverside land on the east side.

When discussing how difficult it might be for only white people to manage the arrival of slaves to Riverside, and to convince them that they had come upon a safe place, Misae volunteered for the task she described as, "Worthy of a princess."

For Misae, the marble-lined foyer of the Riverside mansion felt like enemy territory. She stood alone there at this time, adorning her blue Guardian dress with a half-smile of hope and determination, with her amulet on brilliant display and, although extremely nervous, she looked very much like a princess. Sayen and Naira had loosely braided her hair, entwining each braid with a string of sapphire beads and brought them all together into a single, high-sitting ponytail.

She jumped when the door opened, but it was, of course, Annabel who appeared, as expected.

"I'm sorry I left you alone for so long," Annabel apologized. "But everything's locked up now. It's just you and me, and Jimmy for extra security. There's no rush. Whenever you're ready." She smiled heartily then, for the anticipation of meeting the new arrivals with Misae, but also for the pride she felt for her fellow Guardian. "You look amazing and you've been so strong. A true warrior."

Misae laughed briefly and welcomed the release, yet a moment later, she was on the verge of tears. "Thank you for helping me do this." Her words might have been the most genuine Annabel had ever heard, and they were followed up with a strong hug.

Annabel's expression turned serious then. "Remember, this is your land, your people, and this is your time." She readjusted braids in Misae's hair then, having disturbed them during their embrace.

Smiling with great warmth, Misae decided, "I'm ready. How many are there?"

Annabel answered with a half-smile, half-grimace, "43 men and 18 women."

Misae's face went stark for a moment. "What? That's—"

"61," Annabel smirked, enjoying Misae's partly stunned reaction. "C'mon, let's get their chains off."

The barn Chester Flinch had built to store harvests and to house his slaves was enormous and, after restoration for the many fence workers and for the new arrivals, including the addition of two fireplaces, cooking stoves, comfortable bedding, and all manner of food supplies, it was a modest but homely space indeed. Yet, for its current occupants, all still chained and recovering from a long uncomfortable journey, it was just another lock-up, another farm where they would be worked, then worked some more.

They all stood abruptly as the huge doors creaked open and when Annabel, the young white woman who had somehow transformed from black-haired to blonde since they last saw her, walked into the barn side-by-side with their princess, Misae, complete stillness fell upon them. Shock dominated every face and, as suddenly as they stood, they all knelt and bowed.

Misae stepped forward and shared a nervous smile with Annabel before speaking, "Hello my beautiful people, I'm Princess Misae, and it warms my heart that you recognize me, but please don't bow to me, ever, I demand it." All the people rose again, though confusion still reigned. "This is Annabel.

She's a Guardian like me, a Warrior. I will not speak of this again and I will ask you to do the same please. At Riverside, when outsiders are around, she will pretend to be someone else, which is what you all saw today, but you have no reason at all to fear her. She's going to help you with your chains now, so please help each other and remove them all."

Annabel began removing chains from wrists in the front row. No one moved at first, but one-by-one, they slowly followed her lead.

"First," Misae continued, with inner delight for how quickly her fear had dissipated. "If anyone has any serious injuries, please come to the front." A long pause ensued during which no one moved. "Don't be afraid, Annabel is an experienced healer and I'm good myself, so we'll treat you now if you think it needs immediate attention."

Her last words brought two women and one man to the front. Annabel ushered them to sit on chairs by a large wicker basket which opened at the front to reveal multiple shelves and pockets containing all manner of healing solutions and cleansing materials.

As Annabel inspected wounds, Misae continued, feeling stronger in every new moment. "This piece of land is surrounded by a high wall so no one can see you here." Misae paused then, as her attention was repeatedly drawn to Tamaya, a woman with roughly-cut lochs of thick black hair standing toward the front, twisting her hands together while chewing on her lips. Misae presumed the woman too afraid or shy to speak. "Are you injured?" she asked, merely guessing.

Tamaya shook her head rapidly for a moment before speaking nervously. "No, I am a healer, my Princess. I can help…Annabel…i-if you want."

Misae smiled and gestured for her to do as she suggested. "Please, yes."

Annabel waved her over and pointed to the basket. "Thank you. Everything you need is in here."

Misae became distracted again for a short time, watching Annabel show Tamaya where to find things, being one of those moments she knew would be remembered forever, very distinctly. "When I'm finished, these doors will remain open like they are now and you are free to go anywhere at any time, including this barn, the house, and all this property. You will be notified if outsiders are coming here and what to do. All these crates and baskets here are for you. They're filled with food, clothes, and things for cooking. We had to keep the clothes plain-and-simple for when outsiders come here, but there's more than enough for everyone." Misae knew this would all take a while to sink in and to be believed, so she didn't bother elaborating on these ideas for now. The next item required carefully chosen words, so she took her time with each idea. "We have a project to complete here and it's for the protection of our people, but you are not expected to help us. Everyone is free to walk out the gate anytime and no one will try to stop you. If you decide you don't want to stay and help with this project, we can also take you to another place where you will be safe and free. I feel this would be better for you than trying to make it on your own out there, but as I said, you are free and we can easily bring more people until we have enough to do the work, so the choice is yours alone."

Annabel looked up from her work to share a proud smile with Misae.

Tamaya had unwittingly paused with her hand in the air, holding a piece of bloodied gauze. As with all present, she was greatly shocked by circumstance, and when she looked across to Annabel, she was met with a piercing blue stare. Somehow Tamaya denied the urge to avert her own gaze as she wanted to know what she would find in Annabel's face. A slight smile on Annabel's lips remained and her eyes, as daunting as they were at first to look into, eventually revealed friendship and trust. It was all somehow believable and Tamaya continued, with tears of relief attempting to blind her from her healing work.

"That's enough for today," Misae added. "For the rest of today and tonight, just eat and rest. Cook whatever you like. Our people have prepared so much food for you, you won't believe it until you see it. There are showers in here and another three in the house, so you will all be fresh with clean clothes and full bellies in no time. Some crates are filled with bedrolls and blankets, just sleep anywhere you want to, in here, outside, or in the house, it doesn't matter. Remember, you don't need permission to do anything here, and you can sleep for as long as you want to. No one's going to wake you." This idea gave Misae a great smile, upon remembering her first night in Blue Falls with this realization; that her sleep would not be disturbed and she would also, most certainly, wake to gentleness and peace. "Tomorrow morning, I'm going to walk around the property with Annabel to go through the plans again and get things started. We'll all meet here again at around midday tomorrow to go through the plans. Please decide before then what you would like to do so we can get whatever replacements we need and organize to relocate those who want to go to our other place."

Misae crossed to Annabel then to help with healing. The people were slow to move, but once a number had started taking up towels, clothes, and heading for the showers, other hungrier souls went about pulling food baskets out and arranging platters over tables for all to share.

Annabel glanced up to Misae while busy cleaning a gash in a woman's leg, which threatened to harbor a nasty infection. "Misae, you are beautiful, and you speak so beautifully. Why were you ever worried?"

Although reluctant to speak, all present in the healing circle agreed with nods.

Misae was touched. "Thank you, Annie." As humbly as ever, she asked, "Do you think I missed anything?"

"No," Annabel replied. "And it doesn't matter anyway. There's always tomorrow."

Once people had begun to spread out, a number of other wounded bodies approached the healing circle hesitantly, being too shy to announce themselves earlier. Annabel and Misae looked up when enough had gathered to draw their attention.

"Only if you have time," one woman said. She moved clumps of hair thick with dried blood out of the way to reveal a weeping graze around her neck.

"We have all the time in the world," Misae replied. "Come and sit with us."

***

During his last visit to Black Sand Valley, Julian saw a patch of grass along the river in the parkland surrounded by huge fig trees and thought it would be a great place to take Madeleine for a surprise picnic. It was off the main road but an easy walk, and, at first, Madeleine was somewhat reluctant, since they didn't have much time this day and also for being stressed about the turmoil in Blue Falls. Yet, after a few deep breaths, a stroll down the hill and having Primrose graze nearby, she sat on a rug with Julian and began to relax.

It was rare also for Madeleine to be near Primrose without riding her. The sound of her soft hoof-beats on the earth and the tearing and munching of grass nearby always had an unexpected but calming effect on her, and she was thankful for Julian's surprise, yet she stood abruptly not long after sitting down, stating, "Just a moment, sorry."

A nearby clump of thistle revealed itself to be the source of her distraction, and when she began breaking stems off at the base, collecting a number together, Julian's curiosity got the better of him.

"What are you doing?" he asked, smiling confusedly. She had just asked him what he found on his trip only to jump up and run away a moment later. Although he toned his excitement down a great deal, he was overjoyed for being on a picnic with Madeleine. It didn't matter to him what they discussed and he also didn't mind procrastinating as long as possible before discussing something with the potential to bring about tension.

"It's Prim's favorite," Madeleine informed him, laughing at herself. "I just saw it and I didn't want to forget." She took the bunch of thistle to Primrose, held it out, and an instant later, it was being devoured.

"I can see. She really likes that," Julian acknowledged.

Madeleine smiled joyfully. "It's like dessert for her." After brushing soiled hands off on her jodhpurs, being thankful they were black, she returned to sit again with Julian who still grinned with adoration.

"What?" Madeleine sniggered, mistaking his amusement for judgment. "I'm not very ladylike, am I? I'm getting worse, you know."

"I wasn't smiling at that." Julian wanted to say that, every time she did such things, she stole a little more of his heart. "It's just good to see you after so long," he said instead, yet earnestly all the same. "And I really don't want to spoil things, but I don't think you'll like how I'm going to answer your question."

Madeleine pursed her lips and glared a little, though a hint of a smile was still there. "Hmmm," she uttered.

Julian took a deep breath, pulled his journal out of the wicker basket, opened it to a specific page, and handed it to Madeleine. The page contained a table of sorts, outlining the origin of each collection of information and the conclusions to each finding. Each column ended with virtually the same information but for minor details.

"This is where each legend or piece of the prophecy came from," he explained. "And these are the translations. Only some were the complete prophecy as you can see, but even the minor parts all agree."

Madeleine was surprised at the amount of work he had done correlating all the information. "Gosh, Julian, you've gone through so much trouble." She focused now on the numbers he had put together. "These numbers, this is what you were saying last time." There was a question in her flat statement, but she knew what he would say.

"Yes." He didn't want to be too emphatic, not yet. "I can't tell you how many times I've gone over it all. You see, it's always eight and three, nine and two, or ten and one."

Madeleine wished she could just say why she believed him to be incorrect. "I'm sorry, Julian, but from my understanding, the numbers are wrong. This one is correct." She pointed to one of the less-complicated interpretations. "It says there are eight Guardians and that's true, but these other…" She shrugged dismissively.

"But that one is incomplete," Julian stated gently. "Well, it's not incomplete, it's just the part of the prophecy you've come to learn, but I feel it's not the whole truth. It's the prophecy up to a point which marks a special event."

"You're saying there're eight females, which is true," Madeleine agreed. "But there are no males."

"According to these findings, there is, one," Julian argued, and added gingerly, "It's saying that the Guardians of this era are ten females, not eight, and one male. It's written that the last 11 Guardians were made up of eight males and three females, if my research is valid, but you seem so sure about it all. I don't know what to say about it."

Madeleine was careful in choosing her words. "From what I've come to learn, this is incorrect."

"I don't know what to do about that," Julian confessed. "And I don't know where to go with my book now."

Madeleine saw Julian's genuine concern and that he wasn't interested in having an argument at all and took time to look through his notes more thoroughly. Again, she wondered at the possibility of showing him Blue Falls and trusting him to meet all the Guardians, including herself in a manner. Then he could see for himself the personified evidence of her version of the prophecy and go about writing his book with a clear conscience. She wasn't sure if the Guardians, the queen, and Victor would agree to it, and also feared the whole process might jeopardize the secrecy of Blue Falls, but it seemed for the sake of this argument that another solution may not present itself.

She tapped three columns on the page. "These all speak of one male."

Julian nodded, pleased she was at least considering his ideas. "You see, two white, nine indigenous, ten females, one male, two Warriors, nine Keepers. Ten-one, nine-two, eight three, all the way…11. It's always 11. I don't know what it means and the translations vary, but three sources of the prophecy even speak of nine Guardians being born on the outside, and two on the inside, whatever that means. One scripture calls two of them Blue Guardians, if I've translated it correctly."

"Blue Guardians?" Madeleine repeated, shaking her head in denial. That much she knew to be true; both Oni and Akachi were Blue Ones. "But also, there are four Warriors, not two, and one of them is both Warrior and Keeper."

She was almost arguing with herself. Julian sensed this and responded gently.

"This may be for Blue Falls, but descriptions of the vessel speak of 11 Guardians, two being Warriors, eight Keepers, and one who is both Warrior and Keeper, this one is the link between both types." While he held her attention, Julian pointed to one of the oval-shaped lines within a symbol he had sketched and added, "Also, they all speak of two secret caverns above this."

"What is it?" Madeleine regarded the whole symbol and noted its similarity to the one on the ancient coins found in Blue Falls, but for the position and nature of certain lines. One of the three elongated ovals was larger than the other two, which almost sprouted out from that one, and a single vertical line was drawn coming down from these three.

"An exact translation is difficult, but it's like the utopia, the paradise," Julian explained. "But it's also like a vessel of liberation in some texts. I've come to realize, or believe rather, that we're confused about it because we're actually dealing with two prophecies, not just one, and one relates to this other realm. The other relates to the legend of Blue Falls."

"But these three represent the cascading waterfalls and this line is the river," Madeleine stated.

"This one is the river, yes, but according to the scriptures, these three are the three hidden places of sanctuary. It speaks of one of them being a world unto itself, the one they call the vessel or the realm." Although tentative, Julian was relieved to be sharing this information with Madeleine finally. "And in one text, they call that single line, the river, and in others, they call it the waterfall."

"Same thing," Madeleine muttered aloud, while very deep in thought.

"Same?" Julian's ears pricked up. "What do you mean?"

"Well…waterfalls are on the river," Madeleine explained, hoping to cover her slip-up.

Julian wasn't convinced. His eyes narrowed for a moment, suspecting a greater truth, and he leant back against the trunk of a fig tree with folded arms. "Madeleine," he said after time, yet she still hadn't looked up, only pretended to clean her thistle-stained fingers some more. "I do understand that you might be protecting people, but I also get the feeling you know far more than you tell me."

Madeleine bit her bottom lip and after a long delay, said only, "Perhaps."

Julian smirked, resigned to his ignorance, and shrugged. "All right, I won't ask more. I trust your reasoning."

Madeleine was delighted to hear this and it only added to her conviction that he could be trusted with the whole truth. Yet, she felt it a sense of duty to ask first for permission from the others before deciding if he would be invited into Blue Falls, and she was about to hint at this idea when she saw two people walking toward them. "Those men are coming this way," she noted, with suspicion. "Do you know them?"

Julian looked back over his shoulder. "They look like two men from my train."

"Were they friendly?" flatly, she asked.

Julian shook his head. "No, not at all."

Madeleine took a deep breath. "Maybe it's time we got going, it's getting late anyhow."

They began to pack as the men approached.

"Howdy," Julian greeted as they arrived, while continuing to pack.

"Leaving so soon?" one of them asked, with a malevolent grin and much intimidation. "I thought we could join your little picnic here."

Madeleine walked straight to Primrose without a word, removed her sheathed sword from its long leather saddlebag at the horse's flank, and returned to continue packing. "We're just leaving," she said with a threatening glare for both men. Julian became very worried and there wasn't a single soul in any direction to call for assistance.

"We wanna know why your man here wants to cause trouble for businessmen in the slave trade," the same man added.

His associate had been eyeing Madeleine's stick, and finally asked, "So what's that for ay?"

"What's what for?" Madeleine replied, knowing.

"You went and got that walking stick when we came over," he insisted. "What do you think you're gonna do with that ay?"

This kind of intimidating behavior found Madeleine's complete intolerance. She had well-and-truly seen enough of it and quickly intuited the intention of these men.

"Why is that your business?" Madeleine said without turning. They had finished packing. "Good day, gentlemen," she said, heading for Primrose.

"I just made it my business," the man sneered, gripping Madeleine's arm as she passed, while his friend watched Julian's reaction very closely.

She dropped the picnic blanket then, but her stick was still in her right hand and her eyes darkened. "I suggest you let go of me immediately."

Julian then moved in order to go toward Madeleine. "Look, boys, your fight is with m—"

His words were cut off as the other man pulled out a cudgel, ready to attack him, but an instant later, Madeleine's stick found the side of his head and his hat went tumbling. A hefty "crack" rang out and long before he folded to the ground, her second blow struck the inside elbow of the man holding her and the sharp impact forced him to let go. While grimacing and gripping his arm, he looked to his friend in disbelief and then to Julian, noting that Julian seemed just as surprised.

"Well, you wanted to know what it was for," Madeleine said then. Her stick was in both hands now and in the air, as she turned sideways to the man, waiting. "Now you know."

The man's anger rose quickly. "I'm going to kill you both," he said through gritted teeth, while pulling out and releasing a switchblade.

"Actually, no," Madeleine retorted, now with a gaze most deadly. "I'm going to kill both of you."

Julian hadn't the chance to be shocked by Madeleine's statement, before the man lunged at her, thinking to surprise, but she spun away from his arms easily and brought the stick around to meet with his left kneecap in full force. The sound of the blow was most sickening to Julian, more so for the man of course, and his pain so great, that he hit the ground heavily on his side without attempting to brace himself at all. After gripping his knee and grunting like a wild pig for a while, he tried pointlessly to rise, but Madeleine knocked him out with a snap-kick to the head before he even came close to standing again.

Primrose watched on, prancing nervously on the spot, feeling the aggression and brutality from afar.

"Click." Madeleine drew her sword from its hiding place.

Julian suddenly found the breath to speak. "Madeleine? What are you doing?"

"What do you think they were going to do to you, Julian? To me?" Her sword was in one hand, stretched out, awaiting orders. "Dead or hospitalized for months, that's where we'd be. If we leave them like this, it's just a matter of time before they come after us, and with more men to be sure. This is the war, Julian. This is the dark side of the war you joined long ago. It wasn't a fluke. They came for you because to them, you are the enemy, and so is anyone in your company."

"How did you...?" Julian still battled with speechlessness. They didn't have time, but he wanted to ask how she could do all those things. It all happened too fast. "What are you going to do?"

The time for timidness had long since passed and Madeleine's resolve was just strengthened by her own words, so she looked over the terrain once more to be sure no one had seen the event so far.

"No one comes down here at this time," she portended, with a stillness chilling Julian to the bone, and as she looked into his eyes, the fire in her own almost turned him away. "If you don't want to watch, you can take Primrose and meet me at the hilltop."

Julian didn't move for many moments and Madeleine expected him to object somehow, but finally, he took a breath of seeming newfound resolution. The fury in her presence, which first shocked him beyond reason, suddenly drew him infinitely closer to her. "Let me search them first. Maybe we can find out who they are." He started going through one of the man's pockets. "And

I'm staying for whatever happens. I don't know how, but it was me who brought this on us."

Madeleine wanted to smile for Julian's trust and support, but she was about to kill two people and it didn't feel right, so she smiled inwardly instead.

***

With a fragmented mind sparking with impatience and fury, Madeleine returned to Blue Falls, and it seemed her aggression had abated not at all on the ride home. She longed for Crystal Nest and meditation.

Although some had detected her unusual level of ferocity, Madeleine didn't speak to anyone much, especially not about the details of her conversation with Julian on the Guardians and the prophecy, but only to tell them about the attack on Julian and herself.

Sleep deprivation became more evident when she stepped out of the Lake and headed for Crystal Nest, with dizziness morphing the rocks and grass around her. She would have gone somewhere to sleep instead, but knew it would throw her whole sleep pattern out, so a swim followed by meditation seemed like the next best thing. Besides, something indescribable seemed to be urging her to do so and, since learning that to follow these intuitions usually led to a greater understanding of some kind, she decided not to fight against it.

On her way past the north orchards, she picked an apricot, a plum, and a peach to eat along the way, hoping the energy they delivered would support the journey which, although not a great distance to walk, and an easy one at that, seemed too much in her delicate state.

As usual, the light increased again as she stepped out of the Dark Forest and headed up toward the opening where the crystals showered her with warmth and energy, even so late in the day. She closed her eyes for a few paces, breathing deeply, and opened them again before stepping between tall crystal shards into one of her favorite places to meditate on the south side of the nest, amidst crystals of all shapes and sizes. A small patch of moss-covered granite in the center was just wide enough for Madeleine to sit cross-legged or to sit with her legs stretched out while leaning back against one of the crystal walls. The opening which led to this spot became narrow and inside almost felt like a crystal cocoon, somehow making it very easy for one to slip into a meditative state and many times Madeleine had also fallen asleep there. On each occasion, her dreams were intensely ominous, yet not frightening.

In an attempt to free her mind from the residue of tension derived from killing and from disagreements with Julian, she focused instead on the sound of Dead Man's Fall, which wasn't loud at all in this place, yet its distant, consistent hum lulled her into a more relaxed state-of-mind. It wasn't long before she imagined flight again, as she did so often during meditations, copying her regular lucid dreams of flight just above the water and the land.

This time, she found herself gliding above gentle waves, following a shoreline, feeling the sunlight caress the surface of her wings. The taller waves made for more fun as she flitted into the pipelines and darted out just as the funnel closed behind her, splashing blue droplets over her blue-black feathers. Her breathing was long and deep, and she was lost in the wisps of wind taking her away, making effortless her flight above the blue.

The sea turned rough then.

Am I dreaming now?

She had no time to think on it. A wave approached rapidly, an enormous wave, heavier than a thousand elephants, and she flew too low to rise above it in time before it passed. There was no choice but to enter its emerald pipeline which had suddenly curled up and over her, and to fly fast and straight toward its opening. Suddenly, a rush of wind came like a blessing to push her faster through the funnel, and, at last, she was blasted out of the end, left flapping this way and that, struggling to regain equilibrium.

After finally managing to hover calmly again, she found herself in the direct path of a sailing ship, and had to beat her wings rapidly to move out of its way. As it passed, rising high above, she barely escaped a brush with the railing before it lunged down again between the waves, sending curtains of water into the air, to the starboard, port, and ahead of the bow. The hull creaked away its stresses and strains as the stern came alongside, and Madeleine looked down to see Nathaniel, her father, working the rigging on the deck with his eyes fixed on the horizon.

Suddenly, that scene vanished, and Madeleine was walking down a crystal path to a doorway with blue light emanating from all its edges. She heard a woman's voice in her mind then, "Enter truth."

Madeleine's eyes flashed open and she sat still for a long while, waiting and hoping to draw that line somewhere between dreaming and wakefulness while trying also to blink away her father's image. Still dazed and with her mind elsewhere, her eyes fixed themselves on one large crystal and on the smaller crystals around it. The light reflecting and refracting in that space added sharp lines of light to the surfaces and edges of crystals, making it difficult to find actual physical edges with the eye.

This illusion added more dreaminess to Madeleine's condition, so she stood, abruptly hoping to awaken muscles as well as her mind. After that experience, she didn't want to meditate anymore and was about to leave when curiosity finally gave way to the intangible edges of the crystal she was staring at just moments ago. There were hints of other colors within its clear haze also. Madeleine noted a blue tinge and moved her head around the side of the crystal to see a strong flash of blue and remembered the hallway which appeared in her meditation. When her eyes finally adjusted to the surface of this crystal, she peered behind it, hoping to see more color present itself and noticed instead a narrow passage there, one she hadn't seen in all her times meditating in that space. It was an odd complication of formations, creating the illusion of a dead-end in a pocket of crystals, yet, when looking with a certain focal depth, a space wide enough to walk through revealed itself, so Madeleine slipped through the gap.

On the other side, a corridor between quartz and granite led the way down a path with uneven steps seeming to curve back around to the north. Madeleine followed it and the way was soon filled with thunder from the waterfall, too loud to be anything but very near. As the hallway turned north, it leveled out and widened behind the curtain of water which was Dead Man's Fall. At first, the sight and sound was astounding to Madeleine; with a stone wall on one side, immense torrents on the other, and every surface saturated and dripping. A fine mist also filled the air and thickened as Madeleine moved quickly past the waterfall and into a small cavern which curved away from the water slightly, becoming a niche harboring slightly less bedlam.

While pausing there to contemplate the discovery so far, she took a few deep breaths and looked about. At first, nothing of consequence presented itself, even though more than enough light penetrated the fall to see all surfaces within the empty space, so Madeleine went back to look throughout the passage more carefully. Again, she found nothing significant, so returned again to the cavern to inspect the walls closely, looking for writing or the like. At one point, she saw a blue flash of light appear in one of the walls and stepped back to look over that section again. There was no blue to be seen thereafter, and a frown crept over her bewildered face, deeming the sight to be merely imagination running rife and wild.

Am I still dreaming? Of this, Madeleine was yet to be certain. She didn't know what to think of the space she had discovered. It seemed and felt significant, yet offered nothing of merit. Confusion took hold. She turned on the spot a couple of times, preparing to drop the idea of finding anything of importance and went over the visions in her meditation once more. The doorway from her meditation came to mind again and she stepped toward the wall once more to inspect the surface.

A great gasp escaped her then, loud enough for her to hear it herself over the roar of the fall. The closer she came to the wall, the stronger the blue lines became, and when she came very close, the lines brightened and spread out to form the outline of a doorway, embellished with fine, vine-like patterns surrounding a curved line of three diamonds, one of which was a brighter blue than the other two. The doorway was majestic to the eye, magnetic energetically and somehow familiar to Madeleine. She reached out and placed her palm on the brighter diamond. In the same instant, everything within the blue lines vanished and the entire doorway turned into a sparkling blue hue, causing her to snatch her hand away quickly and jump back. To her surprise, the doorway faded away again into plain granite.

Madeleine couldn't believe it and her urge was to open it again and walk through, but didn't know what might be on the other side or if she could return thereafter. Yet, that something which led her to the doorway now compelled her to enter, so, before allowing herself a change of mind, she stepped forward until the door showed itself again, placed her palm over the diamond, and walked into the blue haze.

***

Chapter Two
Trickster

Sanura had covered a good distance before the men got wind of what happened to Tanner and began their pursuit. When she first bolted out of the shed, they were all singing in the barn, and it took a while for them to hear Tanner's chilling screams for help. Mitchell heard the calls sooner, but he had to tether Talia first before coming to Tanner's aid, and so he took even longer to arrive than the others.

In flight, Sanura's thigh collected the handle of a wheelbarrow behind the shed as she rounded the corner and the impact deadened her leg for a long while. Enduring crippling waves of pain, she grunted heavily and limped for many paces, but someone yelling, "There she is!" was enough to push her forward through the agony.

Upon reaching the northern fence line, another of Talia's screams drifted down on the breeze and the volume was such that she could only be outside again, which gave Sanura a little more faith in her idea, since she didn't know where Talia had been taken earlier. Her chancy plan was filled with unknown quantities, she knew, but it was the only plan she could come up with, the only plan which gave any hope to rescuing Talia.

Most of the men would come after her for certain, maybe all of them if she wasn't found quickly, and this would hopefully leave Talia unguarded long enough for her to double-back and set her free. It would be darker by then too, which would certainly help the cause. Yet, she needed, somehow, for the men to believe she continued to run away, and the solution to this part of the plan didn't come to her until she reached the top of a high bank at the river's edge and spotted a pile of large rocks nearby.

Torch flames and the silhouettes of men blinked in and out of view, flashing past clumps of trees not too far downstream and they were closing-in on her fast. There was barely enough time to act, let alone think through this part of the plan, so she dropped the knife to remove her cuffs completely; finding strange annoyance in how easily they opened with the correct key.

After hastily fumbling through the larger rocks, she found one she could lift and also throw a good distance, then stood waiting for the right moment.

The men were nearby in no time and they slowed down knowing the river was close, but since barely enough light existed – for their untrained eyes anyhow – to negotiate through the bushes and trees safely, they were unlikely to find her in the underbrush if she remained completely silent. However, Sanura hoped for another scenario to unfold.

Knowing they would be listening carefully, she let out a short scream of fright, as if she had fallen, before throwing the rock far out over the bank. As the splash sounded, she snatched up the knife and the keys, then stepped back and slipped to her knees beneath the brush again.

"She's gone in the river!" someone yelled. "Over here!"

Altogether, the men moved quickly again, running to an open space just a few paces from Sanura's face. As hoped, one of them found her cuffs at the edge of the bank and showed them to the others. Her heart pounded and her lungs heaved in and out heavily while they stood there with torches, trying to peer past the brush along the edge of the river.

In frustration, one of them finally exclaimed, "I can't see anything down there!"

"I told you we'd see better without the lights," said another.

"Shut up," came a third voice. "Go back and get the dogs. We'll meet you down there."

They all ran off then and Sanura didn't waste a moment. She too was up and running again, back to Del Hickory's farm.

***

The hull of Nemesis bounced heavily off the side of the jetty. Creaking and groaning with discontent, it lunged back and forth against the timber posts with each new incoming wave, and Captain McGregor, at the prow, might have lost his footing in the collision, but his sea legs had endured many a new helmsman and their struggle to bring the ship to port in such unforgiving waters.

"I said a starboard!" he bellowed. "Now bring to! What's wrong with you men!"

The waves were never great at Port Harroway, given its safe position inside Emerald Bay, but the wind was high this particular morning, and his exhausted 12-man crew battled lazily with the rigging.

"Sorry, Captain!" called the disappointed sailor behind the wheel. "I'll do better next time."

"There won't be a next time if you sink my boat!" the captain retorted. "Let's get it tied off. All hands on deck!"

In all his trips to Port Monte in the north, the captain had never experienced a worse time off of it. The crew he put together for this shipment was inarguably the most incompetent yet, and he was very thankful to be at port again, to be rid of them.

Two out of seven were sick for almost the entire week-long journey, and one of them spent most of his time wallowing in self-misery below deck or leaning over the rails, offering the contents of his stomach to the sea.

In exchange for free passage, food, water, and a small wage, the captain expected the crew to help load and unload the cargo he imported and also man the sails throughout the voyage.

"Let's go, men! The sooner you get this cargo unloaded, the sooner you get paid!" he hollered, then under his breath, added, "And the sooner you're out of my sight."

Much to his regret, he never found enough work to keep experienced sailors employed permanently, so he could only do his best to put crews together each time as best as he could from the mixed rabble who offered their services, being men who had little or no money but wanted to get to one port or the other.

This latest crew failed in almost all possible ways, and to make the trip a complete disaster, the captain's cargo of slaves somehow escaped and slipped into the water just north of Port Harroway in the middle of the night, swimming to freedom in the hinterland, northeast of the Midlands and Black Sand Valley. There remained only the dry goods and equipment, which he also hauled, with which to redeem his costs, and this disappointing result left him wondering if a change of employment for himself might be in order.

After the men unloaded his cargo into awaiting wagons, the captain received his payment and subtracted the cost of the slaves from the whole share before the crew lined up for their reduced rewards. None of them disputed the shortfall, knowing fully well they had failed miserably, except for Williams, the captain's most unfavorite selection, who came last in line.

After half the promised wage fell into his calloused palm, Williams pulled nervously at his long mustache and beard, remarking, "Only five pieces?"

The captain was unforgiving in his own defense. "Williams, you're the worst sailor I've ever come across," he stated. "You were hardly on deck and you were green the whole bloody time. You did half the work so there's half the pay. Be thankful you're gettin' that, now be gone with ya, and get some flamin' sea legs before offering your services as a sailor again."

The captain turned without another word and headed for his cabin for a stiff brandy or three.

Williams wandered off with his pittance and headed for the railway station. It was enough to purchase a train ticket to Black Sand Valley and a couple of meals perhaps, if he kept it simple. Knowing the journey to be a day and a half, he was very thankful since he had nowhere else to sleep. The train at least offered a sleeper, warmth, and no massive undulations to bring up his latest meal.

Walking on solid ground felt like a blessing, after battling illness for so long, and he denied the urge to kiss the hardened dirt beneath his feet all the way to the ticket office. At the window, he rehearsed his alias, Terry Williams, as he did so often, in the fear that he might utter his actual name in a moment of absent mindedness, before realizing a name wouldn't be needed to buy a ticket anyhow and that he merely overcompensated for his need to remain incognito.

The Ticketmaster asked, "Destination, sir?"

"Black Sand Valley, thank you, I take it there's still an afternoon train?"

"Yes, sir, that's it on the platform. It's leavin' in approximately 45 minutes. Will that be first class or economy?"

"Does economy still come with a sleeper?"

"Of course, and there's the dining carriage, but the amenities are not the same for economy."

"That's fine, I'll take economy."

Ticket in hand, he made straight for the train and his cabin with a sleeper, which he imagined calling his name, as he floated down the long, narrow aisle.

They can wake me if they want to see my ticket.

Sleep is all he wanted; uninterrupted, unwavering, warm, comfortable sleep. He didn't take the time to wash in the small basin provided, and the thought of eating still made his stomach turn, so he fell onto the bunk, slipped his shoes off with his feet, and let his head sink deep into the pillow.

Sleeping off illness was the only course to take, and he thought for certain that he would be counting pixies in no time, but instead, after feeling the softness of the pillowcase on his face and smelling lavender in the fabric, he was abruptly reminded of home, his old bed and the warmth of his wife, Helen, by his side.

They were estranged, somehow, for many years, before his own daughter sent him away with no promise of redemption. Yet, after many transformative experiences in between, he not only failed to comprehend how he came to let that life slip away, but could no longer recognize the man he was in that life; neither his thoughts nor his motivations. Since then, he had starved for weeks at a time, slept in all manner of dangerous places, taken a beating from drunks for simply asking them for a handout, and received more abuse and demoralization from failed job applications than he wanted to remember.

Somewhere along the way, the idea of a warm, safe place to sleep became more important than what the neighbors thought of his social position or impressing the boys at the club. He realized that the all-too-illusive hand of friendship was something to be desired far more than silverware or expensive suits.

Broken were his misguided aspirations and quickly replaced with unrecognizable dreams; dreams which had already manifested but couldn't be seen for the misconception of his existence, for the darkened endeavors which had taken his mind and soul.

My daughter will never forgive me.

After all his trials and desperate times, the hand of friendship he longed for came from the most unexpected of places, a place which proved only to fuel self-loathing and his feeling of unworthiness.

After days of sickness with drenching fevers at night, the captain and crew had left him in the sick bay below, next to where the slaves were chained, fearing that whatever made him so ill might be contagious. His second night down there proved to be the worst, with a soaring fever and a head seeming ready to explode, while delirium set in for a good long while.

In the midst of his torment, a hand reached over to place a cool, wet cloth over his forehead. When he became alert enough to look, he realized the hand belonged to a slave, a middle-aged woman, who recoiled when he spun his head around in surprise, expecting abuse, and only went back to helping him once he had calmly laid his head back down again. She replaced the cloth regularly all night long, fed him water on occasion, readjusted blankets when his bones rattled, and his fever turned on the third day.

As he began to make a recovery and feeling obligated to work, he tried to stand, only to realize that it was way too soon to move at all at that time, so he stayed for almost another two days during which he spoke to the slaves more and more. He learned where they all came from, what had happened to them and their families, and a mix of information regarding cultural practices and healing methods.

It was also the first time he had ever shared a smile with a slave, with someone who wasn't white and, after these days, the idea of these people leaving the ship in chains and being whipped and beaten was suddenly unconscionable, yet, he had witnessed this everywhere, his whole life, without blinking an eye.

What was wrong with me?

It was he who set the slaves free, and not by accident. He slipped them the key and a sheathed fishing knife on the last night, after telling them exactly where they were, what they had to do to make it safely to shore and to the hinterland, situated in the north of Port Harroway. They were to wait for his signal in the middle of the morning and he didn't disappoint them.

"Thank you, Terry," Layla, his temporary healer, had said to him. "How can we ever repay you?"

In that moment, all the wrongs he'd ever committed came rushing to the stand to deny him any pardon, any reciprocation. "You owe me nothing," is all he could think to say.

The woman took his hand in hers and he felt a warmth he hadn't felt in many years. "I am Layla," she said. "We will never forget what you've done for us, and we will pray you find your happiness again."

Is that even possible now?

True happiness; the last time he felt it, felt real joy, was the day his daughter entered the world and his wife was still the love he thought would never expire.

What happened to me? What happened to my mind?

Surely, enough time had passed for his daughter to forgive and for his wife to remember what he was for her at one time, and to spare him from a life which was now more of an existence than a journey. Life had somehow become hollow and meaningless, while discovering that his happiness just before this time was only an illusion, a masquerade, based on the accumulation of unimportant things and attempting to impress people who cared as little about him as he did for them. He felt he was yet to live, to truly live a single day, and now that he knew how he might obtain such a blessing, it felt as if he might have already destroyed any chance of finding this for himself and all due to his actions while not in his right mind. It didn't seem fair, yet he had no one to blame but himself.

The only course of action was to try and at least give himself the chance to be forgiven, to make amends somehow, even if this quest consumed the rest of his days. The fact that it was happening would be enough for him now, more than enough; for that miracle to manifest itself.

How can I expect them to forgive me, when I can't forgive myself?

***

Misae had enjoyed many stories already regarding Annabel's innate gift for bringing people together and how she seemed to attract this phenomenon. Having never the reason to be outside of Blue Falls before the Riverside project, and of course, for not being a part of the outings to slave markets, Misae didn't think she would ever have the opportunity to witness a magical moment like the ones which had become legend, including her own rescue. It was Annabel who had recognized her that day, somehow, in a field of horror and torment. Soon after, she was reunited with her sisters and then her mother, in a paradise like no other.

From within, being the perspective of the lost and separated, it's a story of great fear, even greater relief and a miracle, however dominated by urgency. From without, it's legend, an impossible yet undeniable story which only the blessed get to see firsthand, and it was this perspective Misae hoped to experience one day, just to witness the beauty of it without experiencing the terror and the pain. While ever hopeful, she never imagined it would happen at all, let alone on her first day out of Blue Falls.

She, Annabel, and Tamaya had been healing wounds unendingly, for the line of injured continued to grow unexpectedly, moving from more serious conditions to those still severe enough to have been included in the first wave of patients, and would have, if fear and shyness hadn't kept them away. In the meantime, people had brought soup for the healers and a spicy rice mixture wrapped in grape leaves and strips of pickled bamboo shoots.

It was Misae's turn to eat, and so she sat, watching the others treat the last two patients while gorging heartily. "I didn't realize I was so hungry," she confessed.

Annabel looked up, eyeing the tray of rice rolls again. "Same for me, until I started eating. That soup was so good. Can I have another one of those…?"

Misae held out the tray. "I'll never get used to how much you can eat." She watched Annabel squeeze the entire roll into her mouth, then struggle to chew it while continuing to work. Tamaya joined her with a giggle and they in turn amused Annabel so much, she almost choked trying to swallow the last of it.

"I'm sorry," Annabel pleaded at last. "You can see the silver table setting is wasted on me."

During the treatments, Misae and Annabel had discussed some of their plans, and Tamaya detected a few secret elements. Curiosity reigned, but she kept her most important question to herself for a long while, hoping not to incite a mass interrogation, but still desperate to ask all the same and hoped for a private opportunity to arise. Once the final patients left to explore their new home and the healers began cleaning the area, her wish manifested.

"Thank you, Tamaya," Misae said, placing her hands together and bowing her head with gratefulness. "We weren't expecting so many."

"Yes," Annabel agreed. "It's a blessing to have such a great healer here with the people. That is, if you don't mind helping if—"

"I don't mind at all," Tamaya interrupted. "It's what I love to do."

Misae shared a smile with Annabel in knowing each other's joy for having successfully completed the first task of their project and with an air of unity.

"We might be bringing more people later," Misae informed her. "And sadly, there's always injuries among them, so you'll probably have more healing than you want."

"That's okay, I don't mind." Tamaya meant every word. She gained healing skills from her grandmother and mother, and enjoyed practicing them more than any other skill. "Will the men here be asked to go to war?" she asked tentatively. "You mentioned we're building a kind of battlefield." It was a question; she really didn't understand.

"No," Misae answered. "We wouldn't ask anyone here to go to war. All of you will be leaving here once the task is completed and long before anything like that could happen. The first of these tasks is to create an emergency escape route for the people working here just in case. We'll bring trained warriors here when the need arises."

"We believe war is coming, and so does the rest of the continent. Armies are starting to gather around the Midlands now," Annabel added, and knew she had to be careful with her wording thereafter. "When the war comes, it won't stop until they regain total control of all the regions and the people. The killing, the questioning, and the torture won't stop until they find everyone working against them and anyone hiding."

Misae nodded and elaborated, "We're hoping to trick them into thinking they found what they're looking for and demolished it."

"So they stop looking," Tamaya intuited. "That's a big project for something that might not even happen. There must be something very valuable to protect." She saw the glance Annabel and Misae shared in response to her speculation, but, after learning more of the plan, it was clear, too much was at stake for them to be flippant with information, even mildly, and so her next words were chosen like ripe fruits amongst the turned. "I understand there are things we can't talk about and I respect this, but I need to ask..." Suddenly, her voice broke up, thinking of her next question, and tears were quickly forming. "In the other place you spoke about, are there any children?"

Annabel and Misae looked to one another; Misae, a little frightfully. Annabel had been in this situation many times and knew how to dance around the truth.

"Have you lost someone?" Annabel asked.

Tamaya started crying and nodding all at once. Her face met with her open palms and she couldn't speak for a long while. Misae sat her in a chair and dried her eyes with the blue sleeve of her dress.

Annabel, although sympathetic at heart, adopted a more serious tone. She looked about to note that most people had congregated outside to where a bonfire grew steadily and there was nobody close enough to hear their conversation. "Tamaya. It's all right, we can talk," she insisted. "We just can't be specific about anything, it's extremely important."

Tamaya nodded; she understood. "I don't care about anything else, just my boy."

"There are many children," Misae confirmed.

This news found a surge in Tamaya's hopeful tears. "Orphans?"

Misae nodded, "Many," then looked to Annabel, somehow knowing that Annabel experienced the same realization at the same time; that it was probable more people at Riverside would be missing children and other loved ones who could be in Blue Falls.

"Misae..." Annabel began, only to silence herself with dread for a moment. "Why didn't we think of this?"

Lost for an immediate solution, Misae could only hope. "It's okay, we'll work something out."

Annabel found a slight smile, one of thanks for believing in Misae's potential to be a clear-minded leader like her mother, staring each challenge in the face and working through it methodically.

However reluctant to be hopeful, excitement twisted on Tamaya's tongue. She didn't know what to say about her child first.

"Describe him," Annabel posed, placing a gentle hand on her shoulder. "Take your time, there's no one else here."

After swallowing fear and gathering herself together somewhat, Tamaya wiped the sting out of her crying eyes to embrace the opportunity to speak of her son. "He'd be, let's see, about seven now. He's got, well, he did have, black hair down to his shoulders like his father, slightly curly, and he's got brown eyes and...well, I don't know what else I can tell you about him."

"His name maybe?" Annabel prompted with amusement.

"Oh, that would help," Tamaya replied, mocking herself, while denying another wave of tears. "His name is Elan."

***

All was silent but for her own delicate footsteps, as Madeleine walked slowly from the doorway through to the end of a narrow corridor. She only looked back once to note that the door she came through had vanished again, before continuing to the end where she paused upon discovering that the next space seemed to be filled with light, as if it were under the sun.

An archway, which appeared to be made of pure sapphire, separated the corridor from whatever lay beyond, and Madeleine eyed the symbols carved into it, 11 in all, running right around its surface. Although familiar, she didn't understand the script, and so she didn't think on it for long before peeking around through the opening.

A type of vestibule lay beyond, surrounded with a low ornate wall made of small, white, decorative pillars and a railing sculpted from light-blue obsidian. After stepping through, she edged her way slowly to the railing to look out over the edge, where she let out a great gasp.

While pointlessly covered her mouth after the outcry, she quickly stepped back a few paces and dropped to her knees in order to touch the ground with both hands, hoping to rid the sudden and great dizziness.

It took a while to stand again, but eventually, she managed to do so and went back to the wall. Somehow, she stood on a small plateau on a mountain top. Green hills cascaded down and out as far as she could see, with rivers and waterfalls dividing land with silvery lines and splashes of blue in every place. Mist filled some of the valleys, and in one place, sheets of rain fell over a forest of pines.

An eagle soared nearby. Its screech struck Madeleine like an electric shock, as she turned suddenly to find someone standing on the other side of the passage. She gasped again and brought her hands to her chest as the figure floated over, pulling back the hood of its long, emerald cloak.

A blonde woman, with startling blue eyes, smiled with great warmth when she lifted her head and met with Madeleine's stunned face.

"Hello, Madeleine," she greeted.

Madeleine recognized her. "You're Freya, Annabel's mother."

"Yes, I was Annabel's mother," she answered.

"Was? Are you not alive?" Madeleine's head was a quagmire of questions already and she was still in shock. "What is this place? How is it possible?"

Freya walked to the edge of the vestibule to look out over the land. "Call it what you will. This part is the realm of the Guardians known as Attunga, which Annabel used to call Annabellia when she was younger."

Madeleine went to stand beside her. "Annabellia, I've seen that name, it's in her first Book of Dreams," she recalled. "She's known of this place all along?"

"Since she was eight," Freya smiled, then her voice became solemn. "It has been a great challenge in her life, carrying the burden of this secret all alone for so long and also keeping it from her father, but now she has a friend to share it with. This brings me great joy."

Madeleine remained stunned. "Why hasn't...why couldn't—?"

"It is forbidden." Freya turned abruptly and her eyes held a warning. "Three Guardians must be led to this place themselves when it is decided, as you were, or the gateway will not open for the people, and all will turn to turmoil."

"Turmoil?" Madeleine repeated, trying to understand. "What gate?"

"I can only tell you certain things," she explained. "Sharing the wrong information could ruin everything. Annabel can answer many of your questions. The door you came through can only be entered by a Guardian, and once this door is unlocked by three Guardians, you can open the gateway for the people and they will be saved."

"Saved? Where is the gateway?" Madeleine asked. She was starting to feel a sense of urgency; feeling very far behind. "And who is the third Guardian?"

A frown came over Freya. "I am sorry, but I cannot answer this question because I do not know and also, I couldn't tell you if I did. Annabel can tell you where the gateway is, but she has never known for certain which of the Guardians will be drawn to the door, and it is not guaranteed that three of you will be awoken to its existence anyway. However, I can tell you that dark times are coming."

"You mean, if we don't open the gate?" Madeleine assumed.

"No," Freya answered, with certainty. "It is sure, these times are coming. The darkness wants to enslave all of mankind, but in the future, the people will not be in chains and shackles and yokes as they are now. It will be all the people this time and it will be done with mind-control. The people will even defend and fight for the ones who enslave them."

This made no sense to Madeleine. "Why?"

"Because they will not know what they are doing? Their minds will not be their own." This idea saddened Freya immensely. She rested both her hands on the railing as if to counter a great burden. "The enslaved will even shun and ostracize the ones who try to awaken them to the truth." She paused in mourning for a long while then before turning to look into Madeleine's eyes again. "They will poison everything. Lives will be shortened very quickly, and sickness will be prevalent. First, they will do their best to twist the truth about the world, as you see they are already starting to silence the ancients and the indigenous. They will burn books, enforce their lies, and once this is done, they will intoxicate the earth with giant fires that will touch the sky and melt anything in their path. They will lift the sky and when it drops, the earth will shake and crumble. They will experiment on the people with all kinds of chemicals and mind-control weapons for many generations, until the people are oblivious to being enslaved and they will change the very essence of the human spirit."

Madeleine found no response at first and was hesitant to ask anything now, after seeing the sureness in Freya's disposition and was, altogether, perplexed by an influx of new thoughts and ideas. "Why? How can we stop it?"

Freya shook her head. She saw the fright growing rapidly in Madeleine's face and didn't want to answer, yet knew she must. "I'm sorry, Madeleine, there is nothing anyone can do to stop it. The very end is uncertain, but the beginning is sure, it has happened. The face of the Earth and its balance has already been altered so much. All the people of Earth would have to stand up all at once against this plan, but when so few know the truth, and the majority supports the system, enlightening all the people all at once becomes an impossible task. Some will try to stop it, but they will be silenced quickly, and the shadows will have assistance from other worlds."

"Other worlds?" Madeleine repeated; it was barely a whisper.

"They will learn secrets and have advanced technology and weaponry," Freya elaborated. "Those of the light will also have help from other worlds, but of a different kind, non-destructive of course, and there will be a secret war, masked by other wars and by more lies. Lie and truth will become one, completely convoluted. In the end, very few will know the difference, and most won't even care."

Madeleine went to lean against the railing, needing a moment to absorb this awful information, and tears began to blur her vision. "Freya, I don't understand. What's the point in doing what we're doing here if what you say is going to happen anyway?"

"Saving the people we do save will preserve ancient knowledge which would otherwise be lost to the people in the new world order. We cannot save all the people," she stated with great sorrow, "And besides, it is what they want."

Madeleine stood straight again abruptly, shaking her head in disagreement. "That's not true, Freya. We don't want this. Why would we want this?"

"It's not what you want, Madeleine, nor the Queen, nor Annabel, nor my beautiful Victor," she agreed. "But all of you, together with all the people you've rescued, still only equate to one in millions. Existence will become about the self and not about the whole, and so, people will be disunited. They will be divided and completely vulnerable to enslavement. When the majority is apathetic and also opposed to the minority, this leaves you with nothing, as both your allies and your enemies will be working against you. We can only save a number of people from this now and hope in the distant future the human spirit will turn again and awaken in unity against the shadows."

"But, Freya, you're right, there are just thousands here, it's nothing," Madeleine argued. "There are millions across the Earth."

"There will be billions, and they will all be enslaved, but the greater percentage will not be in shackles." Her eyes turned to the ground momentarily then, and she sighed deeply. "If three Guardians are enlightened to the doorway, together they can open the gates for the people. When the first of many wars begins, the lives of millions of white people will also be devastated, and a number of them will be guided to seek the same refuge with you. They will have the same chance to enter this realm if the gate is opened. Only the Guardians can open and close this gate, remember."

There was already an overload of information to process all at once, but Madeleine contained too many additional questions to stop voicing them and knew the greater understanding would have to wait for later. "Why has the Guardians' doorway opened for me? Why now?"

"It is difficult to answer in completeness, but partly because, as with Annabel, you found your true path, despite your challenges in doing so," Freya answered proudly. "This proved your worthiness to be one of the three Gatekeepers of the Guardians of this realm, and proof that mankind in Earth is still somewhere on the path to the light."

Madeleine hesitated before her next question, being unsure if she truly wanted to know the answer. "What happens if the third Guardian doesn't awaken and we fail to open the gate for the people?"

Freya turned back to look into the distance as a flock of green and red lorikeets swept passed them. Her voice took on a somber tone, "Then this realm will remain sealed and all you know will meet whatever fate awaits the rest of the blinded population who will go willingly to their subjugation whilst idolizing their enslavers."

"We can still fight them," Madeleine argued with reserved defiance.

"You could not defeat them with an entire continent of armies and all the weapons you can find, not even with millions. There are too many blinded and willing to support them and all they create," Freya's voice held much conviction. "And those who try to stop them will be nothing more than a convenience for weapons testing." She turned to Madeleine again then. "I'm sorry, Madeleine. I would hug you if I could, but I am not the human form of Freya. I know this is all difficult to believe and understand."

Madeleine slowly and unwittingly shook her head from side-to-side with stark-eyed realization. Finally, she uttered, "Why me?"

Freya smiled, though her heart filled with sadness. "This was Annabel's question exactly, as it was mine."

"This is why Annabel was so supportive of the Riverside project, creating the decoy," Madeleine realized, feeling more dread. "She doesn't believe the other two Guardians will find the doorway."

"It's not that she disbelieves it," Freya argued. "But what do you see in the Guardians' circle now? Imbalance. Rage. Unrest. Revenge. Distance. Division. The Riverside decoy was the joint idea of the queen, the Keepers and Victor, none of whom know anything about this realm yet, but it's also Annabel's idea of an alternate plan, hoping to keep the people as safe as she can where they are now, in case the gate is not opened. You know Annabel, like you, she would do anything to protect the innocent."

Suddenly, Madeleine's conversation with Julian crossed her mind and she asked abruptly, "Freya, are there more than eight Guardians?"

Freya's sorrowful expression hadn't changed, but she clearly withdrew from the question. "I cannot speak of this, and I must go now, but first—"

"Wait, please, Freya," she pleaded. It was too soon and Madeleine hadn't even begun to exhaust her questions.

"Have patience, Madeleine, you will know all in good time," she consoled. "Make sure you don't stay very long at all this time, for there is danger outside the Guardians' realm, and you must first understand the implications of time. If you were to go far enough, you would come upon the blue gates which lead to the outside of this realm, but do not pass through these gates without Annabel this time."

"All right," Madeleine agreed. "I won't, but—"

Without another word, Freya floated to the edge of the plateau only to vanish into thin air. Madeleine went quickly to the railing to look out and all around, but found no sign of her at all. Then, her mind and eyes adjusted to the view again, and she drew the deepest of breaths, being unable to imagine a more glorious and majestic sight than the one before her now.

For a long while, she cast her eyes over the realm, fighting a flood of tears born of fear, apprehension, and wonderment.

Annabellia, she remembered again, and it somehow brought about a smile. Just how much time have you spent in here, Annabel?

***

Tanner's endless, murderous screams from the ground floor of the mansion turned Talia's shaking into systematic and violent trembling. Beside herself, she was, yet, sitting alone on blood-encrusted dirt, chained to the whipping pole outside in the courtyard. Her vivid imagination of what horrific fate awaited Sanura and herself was easily detailed with Tanner's explicit, torturous ideas shared at the top of his voice.

The smell of dried blood, combined with intense fear, made her reach a number of times while she struggled to breathe through convulsions of high anxiety. By the shadows in the window light, she could tell that a number of men were darting around inside, trying to appease Tanner and help him with his injuries. He was so completely wild, wilder than anything Talia had ever witnessed before, and he kept howling for them not to touch Sanura, but to bring her to him. "Bring her to me! Bring her to me!" he yelled over and over amidst his agony and horror. Dogs in the kennel howled in unison.

Talia could only imagine, What did you do, Sanura?

She saw a torch light then, returning from the fields. Ignoring her completely, a man flashed past and returned soon after with two dogs on leashes. The small hounds practically strangled themselves in their enthusiasm to bolt away, adding greater challenge to the man's well-intoxicated mission, and he struggled just to stay on his feet.

To her great surprise, the moment the dogs were out of sight, Sanura appeared at high speed, running low from behind the shed, and she was there, removing shackles, before Talia had time to acknowledge her presence. She almost shouted with joy, but quickly silenced herself. "You came back," she whispered, with a shivering wave of relief choking each word, while her freshly split and swollen bottom lip made for painful speaking.

"Of course I did," Sanura answered flatly, checking the surroundings every second moment. "Are you all right? Did he…?"

Talia shook her head, looking at the tear in her dress. "No, he heard the man yelling and…"

Sanura didn't need to hear the rest. The shackles were off. She took Talia by the hand and lifted her to her feet. "Follow me, this way. I bought us a bit of time, but we have to move fast."

Just as Sanura spoke these words, she halted Talia again and turned her attention to the first barn. The men had left the door wide open and there was no one in sight. The only people seemed to be in the mansion where Tanner still bellowed-out agonizing, deadly threats.

"Wait. Hold this," she said, leaving Talia with the knife, gasping with fright and surprise, as she ducked low and ran to the barn.

"Sanura?" Talia whispered after her, like a muffled scream. "Where are you going?"

After peering inside, Sanura rushed in, grabbed one of the oil lanterns off the wall and unscrewed the oil cap quickly. She tipped oil over a couple of dry hay bales and a table, then removed the glass tube to let the open flame bite into the fuel. As soon as it took, she dropped it, snatched another lantern off the wall, and bolted outside.

Sprinting low again, she went to the slave barn, unbolted the door and slid it open. After poking her head inside, she entered and stayed for longer than Talia could bear, before leaving them with the lantern and returning quickly.

She took the knife back. "Let's go."

"What did you say to them?" Talia asked, as they made for the shed. "How many are there?"

On their way past the shed, Sanura ran inside, grabbed the lantern off the wall and smashed it over the hay-ridden floor before they started running for the river.

"I don't know, about 20 or more," Sanura answered, finally, picking up her pace a little. "I told them most of the men were at the river with the dogs, so they'll get caught in no time if they go that way. I told them to go north, it's hinterland over there and they've got a good chance of finding a hideaway if they go quickly and go now. I also told them to set fire to their barn before they go."

Shocked, Talia asked, "So why are we heading for the river?" She was yet to pick up her pace and Sanura had to slow down.

"Because we'll all get caught if we do the same thing," she insisted, coming to a complete halt. "Please trust me, I have a plan, but let's get to the river first."

Talia suddenly launched herself at Sanura and hugged her tightly. "Thank you," she stuttered. "Thank you for coming back for me. I trust you; I'm just scared."

"I'm scared too," Sanura admitted. "But we're together again, and we're free."

***

Annabel flashed Misae a knowing but apprehensive glance, as Misae had already drawn breath to express her excitement while realizing it would be more prudent being completely sure before giving a mother false hope. Yet, after further analysis of Tamaya's face, especially her eyes, both she and Annabel were almost sure.

Elan couldn't remember his mother's first name, only remembered calling her momma, and they assumed this to be memory loss due to trauma or that he was simply too young upon separation to have known her name well-enough.

Tamaya wondered what else she could describe about her son to help them. "Elan's a common name, isn't it?" she propounded.

"It's a beautiful name, that's why," Annabel replied, with sincerity.

While Tamaya searched for something else to add, Misae stole Annabel's attention and secretly pointed to her left eye. Annabel nodded with a hopeful smile, knowing Misae shared her thoughts, and gestured for Misae to speak.

"Tamaya, does your Elan have a kind of freckle…" Misae pointed to her left eye again. "Just—"

"Yes!" Tamaya blurted out. "It's a birthmark, on the edge of his eyelid!" It only took nods and smiles from both Annabel and Misae for her eyes to start glazing over again. She cupped both hands over her mouth to prevent a scream from escaping and only took it away when she trusted herself to speak quietly. "Y-you know him?" It was more of a statement than a question. She could see it in their faces, the Guardians' surety.

Misae giggled, "Everyone knows Elan. I can't believe this. We better not be wrong."

"I think we're going to lose our only healer at Riverside," Annabel stated, yet happily.

Misae's eyes filled with tears also, thinking of little Elan with all he had endured reuniting with his mother again.

Tamaya started shaking, writhing her hands together, and she swallowed heavily. "Is he…where…who's looking…c-can I…" She didn't know what to ask first.

Misae took her hands and held them, hoping to calm her down. "He's healthy and safe. Right now, he's with our friend, Artetha, or thereabouts, he gets around a bit, but Artetha looks out for him when Annabel's not around. She's also the greatest healer we've ever known."

Tamaya, still greatly shocked, looked to Annabel and back to Misae, wondering how her boy came to be in the care of a young white woman and a princess, and two Guardians.

"He's in very safe hands," Annabel reassured. "And his will is very strong. You definitely have a warrior there."

Tamaya seemed familiar with this idea. "His father is a warrior. I don't know where he is, but…" She looked to the ground then and while her mind drifted thinking of Elan, an idea came to mind. "I don't have to leave; he could come here. Could he? Then I can stay and help you."

Annabel and Misae shared a curious gaze; they hadn't thought of this.

"Actually, I think Elan would love that," Misae supposed. "And it would only be until the work is finished I guess."

After much thought, Annabel found no reason to contend Tamaya's suggestion, yet knew it wouldn't be fair to deny all people but for Elan's mother the potential to reunite with loved ones before moving them to Blue Falls.

"Misae, we have to make a new plan," Annabel decided, taking a very deep breath. "Maybe we should have just brought people over."

"We could have done that," Misae explained to Tamaya. "But it made sense to save more people at the same time."

Although Tamaya knew not what was at stake nor what the two Guardians were protecting, she envisaged enough of the picture to understand the dilemma they faced.

Misae had an idea. "What about this? We ask everyone here to write down their names and the names of people they've been separated from. You can look through the list yourself, Annie, and we can also take it home and the others can look through it. If there's a connection, then we bring those people together in either place and get more in for Riverside if we need to."

"Misae, you're brilliant," Annabel stated with relief. "Because I can't keep up any more. I used to know everyone and I think I still know all the children, but there're too many new arrivals now." She turned to Tamaya, "Sorry, Tamaya, you don't know what I'm talking about, but you will soon."

"We could post the list in the Hall of Dreams somewhere for everyone to go through," Misae added. "Then everyone here will know right away and there won't be any urgent reason to go and search."

Annabel smiled and joined Misae in a sigh of relief, after fearing they might have reached an unsolvable conundrum on their journey.

"I'll do it," Tamaya volunteered. "I'll collect all the names tonight and tomorrow when you're doing whatever work you have to do."

They were very pleased for this offer. "Thank you," Misae replied. "Now, what about Elan?"

"Easy," Annabel said. "They're making three trips tomorrow, so we can ask them to bring Elan back with them on the second."

"And they can take the list back with them on the first trip," Misae added. "So the people will know the list is already there before Elan arrives."

Tamaya brought her hands together as if in prayer and started weeping again; great tears of joy. "My boy. I'm going to see my boy," she uttered. It was almost a whisper; still half-question, half-statement, and something yet to be completely believed.

"I'm sorry we can't do it tonight," Misae said in earnest.

Jimmy walked in then and paused at a distance, upon noticing the tears. "Annie, is everything all right?" he enquired nervously, feeling somewhat intrusive.

Annabel smiled and waved him over. "Jimmy, this is Tamaya, Elan's mother."

Jimmy removed his cowboy hat and scratched his head. "Well, I'll be," he said with amazement, and with smile lines revealing themselves as he looked for Elan in Tamaya's eyes.

"You know him too?" Tamaya asked.

Jimmy chuckled. "Who doesn't know Elan? He's a wild one." He looked to Annabel then and shook his head. "Annie, how do you do it?"

Annabel shrugged. "It's not me."

"Yeah, that's what you always say." Jimmy didn't believe her. "Tamaya, is it?" he confirmed. "This girl rescued your boy with her own hands and killed the monsters who had him roped off like a wild horse."

"Jimmy!" Misae objected.

Annabel shook her head with love and disgust.

"Well, it's true," Jimmy stated, raising his hands in defense. "Tamaya, Elan is so good now, don't worry, he's strong and confident, and all the children follow him around like, well, like he's Annabel." He chortled for a moment and after the silence which his brash words brought about, asked, "So when are we going?"

All three women looked at him blankly, so he elaborated, "Are we gonna take Tamaya over now or should I go fetch Elan?"

Tamaya shot an excited glance to all present.

"Oops," Jimmy mumbled. "Was that not the plan?"

"You and Victor have been back and forth three times today," Misae empathized. "You must be exhausted."

"Well, at least I don't have to carry anything this time," Jimmy concluded happily. "Besides, I kinda have to now, since I mentioned it."

Annabel and Misae both smiled and nodded.

"I can take the smaller carriage," he realized. "It'll be quick. Which way do you want to do it?"

"I know it seems safe here, but I don't want to leave Misae alone yet," Annabel explained. "And we can't all go."

"We were planning to ask Victor to bring Elan on your second trip tomorrow," Misae added.

Tamaya began to shake again, trying to contain her excitement, and she didn't want to demand anything, but hoped, in silent desperation, that a solution could be found this night.

"Okay, I'll go back on my own and bring Elan with..." He pondered on it for a few moments, thinking aloud, "Sherman's at the black markets...Victor will be asleep already probably. I could ask him, I guess, but he's real tired. They'll have to be white just to be safe, so there's only Maddy."

Misae was unsure. "I don't know, she's been so busy too, managing The Drop for weeks."

"Well, there's no more new arrivals now 'til we finish rebuilding," Jimmy argued. "And Maddy told me she's coming into town again tomorrow anyway. I can drop her over there to make it easier, if she wants."

"Jimmy, you're so good," Misae said with thanks.

Annabel might have said the same, but she alone knew something of her uncle's crush on Madeleine, observing also that he never missed an opportunity to offer her a ride to wherever she wanted to go or to pick her up, even if it meant going well out of his way.

"What if she can't, or you can't find her?" Annabel posed.

"She's easy to find," Jimmy smiled. "Anyway, I'll find her eventually, it just means you'll be waiting longer, that's all."

"I don't mind," Tamaya blurted out, then surprised Jimmy with a strong embrace. "Thank you." Her words were stifled; choked by gratitude.

Jimmy didn't expect a hug nor did he think it was any great gesture, considering what would be the outcome of his efforts but he returned the embrace nonetheless. "It's okay, it's nothing."

"It's everything," Misae corrected. "We'll save you a spot by the fire."

"And we'll have another supper ready for you," Annabel added.

"Another supper?" Jimmy patted his belly-full of soup and spicy rice, feigning objection. "Well...all right then," he sniggered. "I'll be back soon."

As soon as Jimmy left, thinking of what was to come, Tamaya sat on a crate with a pounding heart and started picking at her hands.

Annabel nudged her with an elbow. "C'mon, let's go sit by the fire with everyone."

Tamaya agreed, thankful for the immediate distraction. "Do you have a book or something? I'll start getting the list together."

Although in awe at Tamaya's selflessness in the last moments before seeing her child again, they found her idea to be very sound, given that Elan would soon be arriving, and questions would surely come raining in from all directions.

***

Madeleine stayed for a good while, though within Freya's stipulations, juggling new information and a plethora of unanswered questions. She first walked down a pathway lined with emerald and sapphire statuettes on pillars made of lapis lazuli, which led to a lower plateau where she sat in long grass before an endless view of meadows, tree-lined estuaries, and lakes flourishing with wildlife.

When three animals approached her, she thought at first that they were dogs of some kind, but as they drew closer, she was startled to find they were, in fact, horses, miniature and very friendly. They trotted over and danced around her, rearing and playing. One of them rubbed its neck on her shoulder as it passed and the gentle whinnies they let out made Madeleine laugh aloud. After inspecting and sniffing her for a while, they settled into grazing quietly nearby.

If I'm dreaming, let me sleep, let me remain here, let me be.

A crow landed on the ground near the horses and Madeleine heard the wind on its wings as it swooped down for a soft landing. It didn't caw on arrival, but hopped onto one of the horse's backs and started picking at the hair in its coat, while it plodded along, swishing its hairy hooves through the lush grass.

For Madeleine, it was difficult to leave, as it seemed exploration could prove endless, yet her thoughts cycled repeatedly over Annabel, Blue Falls, and the Guardians. Regardless of time considerations, she wanted to speak with Annabel right away, to share her discovery, and as she made the choice to leave, the crow flew away, leaving a long caw lingering in its wake. At one time, a long time ago, its call would have unsettled Madeleine, but now, it brought her courage somehow, and a feeling of connectedness. It was time to leave, so she said goodbye to her new, equine friends with a ruffle of the forelocks and a stroke on the nose. "See you soon, beautiful creatures."

While strolling back up the path with a mind awash with complications, Madeleine thought she heard the crow caw again and wasn't too sure but, after realigning her thoughts, had the most welcome insight which started her running for the door. In all the time after speaking with Julian about the Guardians, she failed to remember that it was Nanook who had discovered the names of the Guardians in his visions before engraving them into each of the eight amulets: supposedly eight, and not 11, as Julian's research denoted, unless, of course, Nanook decided to keep that information to himself.

***

"Did Annabel really kill the men who had Elan?" Tamaya asked, after returning to sit next to Misae on one of the long makeshift benches which the creators of the bonfire put together using large pails and planks of hardwood. Three large, flaming logs were beginning to hollow-out now and burn with brighter yellows, oranges, and reds, and although she wasn't cold at all, Tamaya held her hands out before the blaze. It was a long time since she felt this sensation, as firewood was never wasted on slaves, and its heat teased like a prelude to the great warmth she anticipated feeling when holding Elan in her arms again.

Annabel stood well out of earshot, explaining to another group of people the purpose of the list being passed around. Tamaya worked on it for a long time until Annabel offered to take over for a while so she could enjoy one of the teas being brewed over the coals. Being so unused to such a blessing, let alone having choices, it took Tamaya a long while to decide between sassafras tea or one made with a host of ingredients including wintergreen, raspberry, spruce, snowberry leaves, and cherry twigs.

"Yes," Misae answered. "It will be one of the most well-known legends because on that day, there were so many witnesses. She slit two of their throats and put her sword right through the other one's heart."

Tamaya cringed, then her face flattened in disbelief.

"Madeleine told me she gave them a good beating first," Misae added with reserved humor. "She killed them because they threatened to seek revenge on them and the children, and maybe because she just wanted to. She's a bit of a cat like that."

"She saved my Elan," Tamaya acknowledged. "I hate to think what might've happened to him."

"Don't think about that," Misae recommended, shaking her head at the very idea.

"My Princess?" came a nearby voice. A man stepped through the many blankets covering the exhausted and sleeping to kneel before Misae and Tamaya; not in worship, but to avoid looking down on them. "If you remember, I am Shenandoah. Since you told us, we've all been discussing the choice you've given us."

"Yes, Shenandoah, you have all night and all morning to make your choices," Misae reinstated. "What did you want to ask me?"

"I having nothing to ask of, my Princess," he said proudly.

Misae noticed that he wore a tan shirt and brown drawstring pants which were brought across from Blue Falls, made by the dressmakers who long ago created a workshop in a cavern in the north-dubbed Needlewise, where clothes were made and mended for new arrivals and existing residents. They created the queen's and princesses' dresses, the Guardians' specialized clothing, and also items like the light, spring poncho Shenandoah also wore, of running horses, handwoven on a loom with auburn, black, and green thread. It provided the perfect cover for such nights; not nearly as warm as the longer, double-layered winter ponchos, yet more than enough to defuse the crisp night air.

Splashes of green in the material accentuated the color in his eyes, and in them, Misae saw much kindness and understanding.

"The people have asked me to speak for all," Shenandoah told her then. "I've been around to everyone and we've all decided we want to stay with you and work on your project as you've asked. We feel blessed that you have given us so much already."

"We have only given you what is rightfully yours," Misae deduced, while denying tears of gratitude, and would have let them flow but for her want to appear a stable leader. "You've decided so quickly, I am honored."

These words convinced Shenandoah that he was somehow face-to-face with a modest and beautiful soul, sitting with her people, demanding nothing, yet giving everything. "Some of us have worked in the mines, on the railroads, and in the fields. You have many skilled people here, my Princess. I myself have built mine tunnels and worked in smelting factories where they make machinery and weapons."

Annabel approached hearing Shenandoah's last words, as she sat again with Misae and Tamaya. Her eyes trapped his when he looked into them, and he failed to look away immediately. Though a deeper blue than usual under the stars, her gaze also seemed to capture the flames that warmed his back, and he saw a sleeping dragon within.

"Then you must be a gift," Annabel stated. "Would you like to oversee the construction?"

Shenandoah, a little stunned, looked to Misae, back to Annabel, then to Misae again.

"It was a plan made by the queen, a great warrior named Ky Mani, and my father," Annabel explained. "We were going to walk around with my father tomorrow and go through it all again, now that all the materials are here. You could come with us."

Misae looked to Annabel with a knowing smile and barely managed not to laugh. "I think Victor and my mother will be very happy to have you here managing it with us."

Annabel shared Misae's amusement, yet maintained her confidence. "We would have been fine, but with your experience, you're far more worthy."

"And we'd get it done so much faster with the three of us, with you overseeing it all," Misae added. "That is, if you want to, of course."

Words failed Shenandoah for a time, being gratified by their trust, but also due to his own fear of failure. "It would be my honor," he said finally. "I hope I have the skill."

"How much do you know about black powder?" Annabel asked then. "And blowing things to smithereens?"

***

Chapter Three
Hunted by the Prey

Whistling away happily, Nanook sat, cutting another facet into a ruby stone, which would soon add color to a new Book of Dreams, when he felt eyes upon him. Although not at all unfamiliar with this feeling, these eyes felt very powerful and brought his peddling to an abrupt end. The cutting stone ground to a halt as he turned to see Madeleine standing in the doorway, arms on hips, and with a stare which would frighten someone who didn't know of her lethal skills, let alone one who had watched her battle many times and every time in awe.

"Maddy!" he greeted excitedly, bouncing off his stool. When he noticed that she hadn't moved a muscle, but for her eyes narrowing a little more, he halted abruptly halfway across the cavern, causing his long dreadlocks to sway forward and back again, tinkling with ruby beads all the while. "Maddy?"

Madeleine took a long time to answer. "Show them to me."

She was calm, but Nanook had never seen her so determined; so very serious. It only took a second to realize she had discovered his secret somehow, and to act ignorant would be futile. He looked past her.

"It's only me," she assured. "I want to see them please."

Nanook went to a long chest of drawers, removed the bottom drawer completely and reached inside the cavity to retrieve a drawstring bag. Without a word, he dropped it into Madeleine's hands.

"How long have you known?" she asked flatly.

"From the beginning, Miss Maddy," he confessed.

Madeleine didn't open the bag right away. She waited for his eyes to meet hers again, and when they did, she struck them with a stare like spears of emeralds.

Nanook preempted her first question. "I couldn't, Maddy. The queen and princesses were reunited, eight of the Guardians were brought together, and the people were celebrating. What could I say?"

"It's only part of the prophecy, Nanook," she replied, without altering her gaze. "But I think you know that already."

Looking down at the drawstring back in her hands again, she found herself caught momentarily somewhere between wanting and not wanting to know the answer to her question.

"I see a lot of death in my visions, Maddy," he explained. "Hundreds of thousands. I see a horrible, terrible war. I don't want to be responsible for doing something against that which might prevent this war."

Madeleine drew the bag open. "Are you seeing what is or what might be?"

"Of that, I am not certain," Nanook's answer seemed most truthful to Madeleine. She found this assurance in his eyes, yet he filled them with worry. "I do know there is more at stake than I can imagine myself, but I'm not permitted to see it, something very powerful blocks me from seeing more than I see, and this is why I'm afraid to speak of it."

Madeleine now understood apprehension of this nature and became disheartened for the inability to share her new knowledge with Nanook. One day, she thought.

"Have faith that you will understand in time," she could only offer. "Does Annabel know? And what about Ky Mani?"

Nanook shrugged. "If Ky Mani knows, he's never mentioned it, and if he does know anything, he may feel as I do, that it's most unwise to talk about it." He paused then, not knowing what reaction his next words may bring. "And Annabel, yes, she knows. You see, we only knew who eight of you were. Annabel, Akachi, and Oni were already here. You were well-known and not too far away, and we knew the four princesses of course, but the other three were a mystery, and now, two are still a mystery."

"Only two, well, who's...?" Madeleine finally tipped the bag up and, as expected, three amulet cases slipped into her palm. Ironically, all three cases came out right-way-up, insisting that she turned them all over to discover the names engraved in the back. This gave her the opportunity to procrastinate a little longer. Two of the cases were embellished with diamond-shaped rubies and the third, a sapphire of the same shape, as were the designs of the other Guardians' amulet cases.

"One sapphire case," Madeleine observed aloud. "That means there's another ruby amulet inside, like mine, yes?" She looked up to Nanook in wonder.

"Indeed, one other with fire like your own," Nanook replied, with his frozen face predicting the Guardian's surprise.

Madeleine returned his smile, though hers dimmed quickly with a wave of foreboding. "Why do you think you were shown the Guardians' names, I mean, all of them, including Annabel's?"

"To be certain, they would all be acknowledged in Blue Falls as they manifested," he answered, without hesitation. "And to be sure no one could be mistaken for a Guardian, although I don't believe it would be possible to impersonate a Guardian. Your natural skills are undeniable. Anyway, I couldn't think of any other reason why the names would come to me. Perhaps, I just dream too much and this is the price you pay, to have knowledge you cannot share."

Madeleine took a deep breath and turned one of the ruby cases over to discover the name, Elan, inscribed in the back. She gasped aloud and left her mouth open in surprise for a long while thereafter. The second ruby case revealed, Talia, and the sapphire case, Sanura.

Madeleine voiced the names, "Sanura, Talia," then looked to Nanook in question.

"I don't know," he shrugged. "Are you angry with me, Miss Maddy?"

"No, of course not, Nanook. I'm not angry with you." She took another deep breath, returned the amulets to the bag, and gave it back to Nanook. "I've just had a lot of life-changing events in my life already, and I thought I had things more or less worked out, but it seems I've only just begun."

"As have we all, my dearest Maddy," Nanook's experience had decided, and his warm smile filled with adoration.

After hugging Nanook to be sure he felt no guilt, Madeleine left and stopped by The Books on her way to the entrance. She pulled the first Book of Dreams out and flipped between the inside and back covers, reading through Annabel's years of doodling. Between the two sections, certain words stood out from the rest; she saw Annabellia, Forgotten Ones, I will free you all and When will the war be over?

As she replaced the Book of Dreams, Jimmy's voice rang out from the north side of The Books.

"Maddy!" he called, approaching quickly. "I knew I'd find you here."

This amused Madeleine. "I only just got here."

"Well, lucky me," he smiled. "Hey, I wanted to ask for your help with something, I—"

"Okay," she interrupted. "But it can't be right now, I have to go to Riverside."

"Really?" This stunned him slightly. Madeleine turned again, leaving. "Wait, Maddy, I—"

"Jimmy, is someone dying?" she asked flatly; meaning to have a touch of humor, though she also endured a certain level of stress.

"Well…no," he answered. "But—"

"So talk to me when I get back, all right? I really have to go." Suddenly, she was on the move again.

"But, Maddy, I'm going to Riverside!" he called.

Madeleine halted and turned. "Oh."

"I'm taking Elan over, and I wanted to ask you to ride with him," he explained. "His mother came to Riverside today. I can take you into town from there in the morning if you want, or we can lead Primrose on the back of the carriage. Whatever you like."

Madeleine knew she had been brash and this news added a weird mix of wonder and excitement. "Elan's mother's at Riverside? Amazing. Jimmy, I'm sorry. My mind's on a thousand things. That's unbelievable."

Jimmy only smiled; after finally getting the message through.

"I need to change," she said abruptly, with a rush of impatience. "C'mon. I have to be Vivian at least until we're inside the Riverside gates. Where's Elan?"

Jimmy had to jog a few steps to catch up with her. "He's with Artetha in the healing bay. I told him he's going to stay with Annabel, but they asked me not to tell him about his mother yet."

"All right," Madeleine agreed. "Mum's the word."

Jimmy sniggered, "Good one."

***

"How did you get away from them?" Talia asked.

They slowed to a fast walk momentarily to catch their breath. After many minutes of freedom, Talia's distress had settled somewhat and she was no longer crying involuntarily.

"I made them think I jumped in the river, just over there." Sanura pointed to where she threw the rock into the water. "They'll be looking for me downstream, for a while anyway, and I'm hoping when the dogs don't get my scent down there on the banks, they'll think I kept swimming downstream with the current, and continue looking that way for a while." She listened with intent for a moment then, as they watched torch lights meander below where the river curved to the east, and they could still hear the dogs as well. "This time, we make new tracks and head downstream for—"

"What?" Talia halted. "That's where they are."

Sanura took Talia's hands into her own. Her fingers were sticks of ice, and she rubbed them while knowing her own would be the same. "You're freezing."

"I'm all right," she said, while shivering revealed a lie.

"This is what we're doing," Sanura spoke quickly. They didn't have time to stop and talk for long, but she knew it would give Talia confidence to know the plan. "We climb down the bank here, cross the river, and sprint along the edge downstream on that side 'til we get to the bend in the river. We make it look like we went into the water there, but we don't, we sprint back again the same way, go into the water here, and walk as far as we can upstream through this shallow part before we leave the water again. The dogs will get turned around and hopefully it'll take them a long time to find our tracks again because they'll have come all way upstream to find them. You see? We've got time to do this. You can see where they are."

Talia thought about it for a moment and soon understood. She nodded, "I'm sorry. I understand. If we just run from here, they'll catch up eventually," she elaborated, assuming Sanura's train of thought.

"That's it," Sanura confirmed. "We have to trick them again and keep tricking them. Dogs are too fast. They'll pick up on this new trail and it will lead them back downstream for a while anyway, I hope, because they will have to go all the way upstream to pick up our real tracks and they won't know what side of the river to search on. Yes?"

"Yes," Talia nodded again and, although the gesture looked more like shaking than anything else, she saw the greater purpose of what initially seemed like the craziest action to take.

"The water might be cold," Sanura confessed, as they made their way down the bank. "But running will warm us up." She met with Talia's eyes when they reached level ground to be sure she was listening, and looked into them with conviction and ferocity. "We have to run like the wind, Talia, like the wind on fire. Are you ready?"

With gritted teeth, Talia rubbed her hands together rapidly and took a few deeper breaths before ensuring, "I'm ready."

***

For most of the ride thus far, Elan sat with his head sticking out the window of the carriage under a waxing crescent moon, taking in the nighttime version of a world he hadn't set foot on in many months. He often sat with Annabel on the edge of the cliff next to Dead Man's Fall, looking down upon the land, questioning his Guardian friend on every aspect from the waterways to the hills and valleys. From this vantage point, he learned the landscape well from high above, and in his dreams, he flew over it many times, though being amongst it brought on a new level of excitement.

As they descended along Valley Road toward West Bridge, which led to both Black Sand Valley center, if one were to turn north from there, or to Riverside heading east, Madeleine watched Elan from the opposite bench and since he was so silently and deeply occupied, she let her mind wander over all her new revelations.

Jimmy was an expert driver. He kept a good pace, not too fast nor too slow, and although she felt bad for him having to ride upfront alone, she was thankful for having the time to sit quietly without conversation. She decided to lead Primrose along on the back of the carriage for returning to Blue Falls later tomorrow, but accepted Jimmy's offer to take her into town in the morning anyway, so she didn't feel so bad about this night, knowing she could sit upfront with him then.

The motion of the carriage, together with the rhythmical hoof beats of the thoroughbred upfront, teased and taunted Madeleine's sleep deprivation. Before too long, she closed her eyes and let her head rest against the padded corner of the bench, not thinking for one second that she could fall asleep with such a busy mind, but just a few moments later, there she was, dreaming again... And flying at head height through a forest of pines, trying to catch a glimpse of a boy running for his life at high speed. It was Elan, and with three wolves on his tail, closing-in on him fast; massive wolves, dwarfing his nimble frame.

Suddenly, Elan halted and turned with his fists in the air.

"No!" Madeleine yelled at the top of her voice, yet only the caw of a crow was heard.

She knew the impact alone would kill him, and there he stood, with eyes of steel fixed on his predators, waiting.

Madeleine was too far away to save him. She could only cry, "Elan!" and close her eyes to the scene...

Elan's excited voice drifted deep into Madeleine's dream and lured her back to wakefulness. "Maddy!"

She didn't know it, but it was the fourth time he had called her name.

"Maddy, I saw a slave girl!" he said again, before returning his gaze to the shadows along the tree line. "I can help her."

"What?" Madeleine was at first wondering how she fell asleep, but Elan's impatient voice bore in like a siren alarm and his surprising claim worked like smelling salts. She opened her door and stood on the sideboard to look around and talk to Jimmy.

"Jimmy!" she called. "Elan saw someone. Have you seen anything?"

Jimmy shook his head and halted the horses. They weren't too far from the bridge now. "Nothing, Maddy, not here." He looked around then. "I can see torchlights down along the river and on the bridge. See 'em?"

Madeleine saw the flames, four maybe five, remembered Elan's claim and knew at once that a slave was being hunted; a girl, if Elan was to be believed. "Elan said he saw a slave girl."

"They must be hunting her," Jimmy supposed. "I can hear dogs further downstream. You hear 'em?"

"Yep." Madeleine heard them too, but it didn't register in her mind until Jimmy mentioned it. She ducked back into the carriage then to ask Elan again what he had seen, only to jump back up, urgently searching for Jimmy's face in the moonlight.

With widened eyes of disbelief, she called, "Jimmy, Elan's gone!"

***

Every moment seemed like an eternity for Tamaya, while waiting to see her son, and so, she went again to assist the people in recording their details to keep herself busy, at least for a while. Annabel and Misae sat in their own space, enjoying the quiet and the tranquil atmosphere by the fire, while only the largest logs prevailed, crackling and spitting in contention, sending sparks spiraling into the air. Almost all the timber had been reduced to a giant pile of bright yellow and orange coals by this time, yet the fire produced more heat now than when the logs were all aflame.

Misae watched one cinder rise high on a warm current until it faded to nothingness under the stars. "I've been having some very strange dreams," she confessed in that moment, "About my purpose. At least, I think that's what they're about."

Annabel spoke carefully on the subject, "You're very important in this world, Misae, Sayen and Naira also, but you are gifted in ways you haven't imagined yet. Dreams and visions will help you on your path."

"We are the Keepers, I know," Misae agreed, modestly. "Why are you so protective of me? Of us? You could've gone with Jimmy."

Annabel shook her head. "The queen made me promise not to leave your side unless someone's life depended on it, and maybe not even then."

"Hmmm," Misae grumbled. "Sounds like my mother. Even after all my training with you."

"I told her you were already lethal and she looked at me like I was out of my mind," Annabel chuckled. "She said, 'Annabel, my Misae is a gentle

90

Keeper, don't go turning her into some bloodthirsty warrior.' So I said, 'But you haven't seen her dodge a spear yet.'"

Misae laughed aloud. "No, you didn't!"

"Yes, I did, but she finally realized I was joking." Annabel laughed some more, remembering Lesedi's face in that moment.

Misae frowned. "Good one, no wonder she's so protective."

"Actually, she relaxed a bit after that," Annabel remembered.

"Well, it's taken months for her to accept that I want to practice," Misae sighed. "Even now, I don't tell her when I'm meeting you at the Dojo. I just don't want to see that concerned sideways look anymore. You know the one?"

Annabel smiled knowingly. "With just a touch of disapproval?"

"That's the one," Misae groaned.

Tamaya came back to the fire to sit with them again, and Misae turned to her after choosing some words carefully. "Tamaya, I was thinking earlier about Elan arriving and about how long he's been with us and well, you already know he's close to Annabel, so—"

"It's all right," Tamaya interrupted, intuiting Misae's purpose and thought to save her from the pain of it. "I know what you're going to say. Elan will probably run to Annabel and look at me like a stranger."

"No one can replace a mother," Annabel demanded.

Misae breathed a sigh of relief, knowing Tamaya had already prepared herself.

"I don't mind," Tamaya said in all honesty. "It might take time, and I won't be jealous, Annabel. We owe you everything. You saved my boy."

Annabel placed her arm around Tamaya's shoulder. "Why don't we sit together when he arrives and we'll work with whatever comes?"

Tamaya smiled and an overwhelming wave of happiness brought her to tears again.

The sound of distant hoof beats turned their heads then, growing rapidly in volume, and the high-speed rattle of the carriage shot Annabel to her feet. She could tell immediately that Jimmy was flying down the driveway and something had to be wrong.

She took up her sword, bolted to the gate, followed slowly by Misae, Tamaya, and Shenandoah, and opened it just as Jimmy and the carriage came to a frazzled halt outside. Primrose snorted her annoyance, prancing and stamping at the ground. The thoroughbred at the harness maintained a little more composure, but appeared jumpy all the same. They hadn't run far, maybe minutes at the most, and surely spent next-to-nothing of their great energy and stamina, but the sprint was at a sudden and unrelenting speed, inspiring nothing but sheer flightiness in both horses.

Jimmy told them quickly what had happened and that Madeleine had taken her sword after deciding to go after Elan on foot.

Tamaya sank to her knees.

"It's all right, I know what Elan will do," Annabel intuited. "He knows the land very well. If he finds them, he'll lead them home, and if he doesn't find them, he'll eventually go home the same way anyway." She turned to Jimmy. "If I ride straight northwest from here through the properties, then turn southwest at the boundary, maybe I can get to the falls before they do."

"Hey, the girth is loose," Jimmy warned, as she ran to Primrose. "We just threw the saddle on to bring it over."

"Thanks," Annabel answered gratefully, thinking of the one and only time she rode off with a loose girth and found the ground with her head in seconds. This mistake, a rider only makes once, but she may not have thought of it under such urgent circumstances. After adjusting the saddle blanket quickly and tightening the girth, she gave the skittish Arabian a few words of encouragement and a pat on the neck in the hope to settle her down enough to mount. "C'mon, Prim," she urged, finally finding the stirrup, and swung into the saddle. "We have to fly."

Primrose started spinning on the spot again instantly. When it came to high speed, she needed no encouragement at all, in fact, Madeleine spent most of every ride trying to discourage it.

During one of Primrose's spins, Annabel looked to Tamaya and met with her eyes. "When they're safe, I'll come back for you," she promised, with a surety which Tamaya could only believe, then turned to both Jimmy and Shenandoah with the same certainty. "Look after Misae. If anything happens to her, and both of you are still alive, I'll kill you myself."

A moment later, Annabel and Primrose had disappeared into the night and only galloping hooves could be heard; thundering beats, so rapid that the sound frightened all who heard them leave.

Misae lifted Tamaya to her feet. None of them knew immediately what to say to her whilst it was clear, by her duly frozen state, that she imagined all kinds of horrible scenarios.

***

When Elan slipped under the bushes next to Sanura and Talia at the river bank, they both almost screamed aloud. After tricking the dogs and the men a number of times, they had suddenly found themselves surrounded and were desperately searching for a way to escape again. It seemed a number of men got wise to Sanura's tricks, for when the other men followed the dogs downstream for the third time, three of them continued upstream anyhow and one of them found his way ahead of them. The other was not far downstream and the third was somewhere in-between and too close for them to enter the water to continue heading upstream.

Once realizing who had just invaded their temporary hideout, Talia and Sanura looked to one another, astounded, and couldn't think of what to say to him at first. Talia was bordering on hysteria again, shuddering all over from the cold, and a nasty gash on her shin brought continuous throbbing pain with it, threatening to slow her down.

"It's okay," Elan whispered. "I can help you, but we need to get upstream to the falls."

"Why the falls?" Sanura asked, her voice so low, it was hardly audible at all. She was cold also and very tired, but she hadn't lost focus.

"My people are there, trust me, it's the only way," Elan quietly assured.

Sanura pointed in each direction of the three torchlights, shook her head, and muttered, "We're stuck, you see? And the dogs will be here soon."

Elan thought for a moment, then whispered again, "If we can get around this bend, there's a wall on the other side of the river. It's not high, but above it there's a track, it goes along the high bank for a long way, I've seen it." He looked about quickly then to note the position of the men again, before continuing, "Annabel says, when you're being hunted and outnumbered by the enemy, try to injure one of them and when the others come to help them, that's when you make your escape. I'll go, I'm small and I can sneak under the bushes and get away fast."

Sanura regarded Elan in disbelief; a strange young boy with blue-beaded braids in his hair, speaking of war strategy.

"Give me the knife," Elan said then, yet his eyes were fixed on the enemy's lights. "Stay right here. When I get back, we run, cross the river, climb up to that track, and keep running. Yes?"

Sanura hadn't blinked yet. She held the knife in the air. "You want me to give you this and let you go after them? Are you crazy, little boy?"

Elan snatched the knife from Sanura's loose grip quicker than her reflexes could stop him, then flipped it back and forth deftly in one hand. Lastly, he tossed the blade from his left hand to his right without watching the knife, but, instead, looked to Sanura with confidence and determination.

"Who is Annabel?" Sanura's face went blank and Talia had stopped crying at that point.

"If they catch me, get to the top of Dead Man's Fall and go to the only farmhouse you can see from there." Elan readied himself for flight then.

"Wait—"

"There's no time. Get ready to run." Elan didn't wait. He turned, dropped his head, and disappeared into the shadows a moment later.

Sanura turned to Talia wide-eyed to watch her friend's frightful face fill with awe. They could only wait now, but Sanura studied the landscape nearby to ensure they were prepared if Elan should succeed.

In no time, Elan was downstream, crawling through the underbrush until he came into the path of the man closest to them. He awaited his moment, then rose slowly to his feet before lunging forward and stabbing the man in the back of the thigh with as much strength as he could muster. He felt the tip of the blade pop through the skin and slice through muscle like butter, before he pulled it out again. The man yelped, gripping his leg, and flashed his torch wildly all around, searching for the source of his wound.

Yet, Elan was already gone. Beneath the brush he went, being careful not to give his position away by crashing heavily through the foliage, but he need not have worried. The man's screeching calls for help easily drowned out his little footsteps, even at a sprint.

Both Sanura and Talia heard the man cry out and the dogs howl in response, revealing they were much closer now. Another three torchlights could be seen further downstream, not too far away, closing in on the scene, with the dogs evidently in tow.

Heeding the desperate call for help, the man to their north ran downstream again and the man to the south headed upstream at full flight. Their three torches were rapidly coming together at one point.

Elan's plan had worked. As the man flashed past them, Sanura helped Talia to her feet and rubbed her shoulders and arms, hoping to generate warmth, but her hands were so cold themselves that the effort proved pointless.

"One more run, okay?" Sanura whispered with encouragement. "You can do it."

Talia responded silently but with a wistful stare into Sanura's eyes, just as Elan reappeared, panting heavily but from the thrill of his attack more than energy exertion.

He gave the blood-tipped knife back to Sanura and started moving. Sanura ushered Talia to go next and she followed them, glancing back every second step to ensure no one followed.

They rounded the bend at a sprint and found, as Elan had said, a low wall on the other side of the river, yet the track he spoke of could not be seen from that level due to a large willow on that bank blocking most of the view.

"It's up there," Elan whispered, pointing to where he knew the track to be, and slipped into the water without a sound.

After a quick analysis of the immediate landscape, Sanura was happily astonished. If she had known the terrain herself, Elan's suggestion would have undoubtedly been her own. Once across the water and on top of the wall, they would be out of sight and running again on the other side of the river in no time. She imagined that, after the men sorted out their injured friend, they would have to find their tracks with the dogs again and find where they entered the river. Yet, it wouldn't be obvious which way they went after that or where they came out again, because the opposite bank seemed mostly inaccessible. They also couldn't cross with the dogs in that place, so they would have to search for another way around and then hope to happen upon their scent once again somewhere on the other side, while this could also be any distance in either direction.

It was a better plan than Sanura could have imagined. She slipped in straight after Elan and reached up to help Talia silently do the same. They were across and climbing in seconds, and it wasn't too difficult an ascent, but Sanura stayed close to Talia throughout, just to be sure. The last thing they needed was for one of them to fall and not only risk an injury, but to make a giant splash in the process.

In any case, they reached the top of the wall without a hiccup, and none of them stopped to look back. The ground was soft and sandy on this high track, and clear of foliage, so they were immediately and rapidly covering ground; Talia, with newfound energy, derived from knowing they were already so far away from the men in only a minute or two. She looked ahead to Elan and noticed that he kept looking back to make sure he hadn't left them behind.

His presence was somehow comforting for Talia, while his courage brought about a feeling of weakness within, upon reflecting on the afternoon. Her blanket of fear began to dissolve somewhat and she realized, all at once, the great weight her utter despair must have brought upon Sanura during their escape. A little shame came her way and while in the depth of these thoughts, her pace slowed a little.

"Do you need to rest, Talia?" Sanura called. "We can probably stop and rest for a bit now if you want."

"Thanks, but no," she called back, with a strength in her voice Sanura hadn't heard yet. "I don't want to stop." After picking up her pace, she was quickly on Elan's heals, who was only running half his full speed anyhow. "Go," she impelled him. "I can run. Go."

Elan stretched his legs out. Sanura smiled inwardly for her friend's own revival, as she suddenly had to quicken her pace in order to keep up with them.

***

Thinking she didn't have any chance of tracking Elan at night or spotting him from the ground level, Madeleine stayed high on the rise of land west of the river instead, and sprinted as fast as she could until she passed the first group of torchlights. She was hoping to get ahead of Elan and wait for him upstream where she could only imagine he would go. All the while, she berated herself for losing him and wondered if she could ever face his mother, or Annabel for that matter, if he were to meet with some terrible fate this night.

The only way to get to the top of Dead Man's Fall from Madeleine's current location, she knew, was to go around it and up along the ridge to the Brighten Farm and Blue Falls. She hoped to find Elan before anyone of course, whether he'd found the escapees or not, and to place herself between him and the men, but, since Elan wasn't carrying a torch, she couldn't be sure how far upstream he might have travelled by this time.

Suddenly, she halted, thinking she heard a voice and it was soon confirmed with subsequent outcries; a man's voice, not a boy or a woman, Madeleine was relieved to discover.

On the move again, she watched three lights come together and saw another three approaching those from further downstream. The dogs howled and the men started shouting to one another. Madeleine imagined that one of them had fallen and seriously injured themselves, judging by the level of pain in his urgent voice.

The grumbling of Dead Man's Fall quickly grew louder as she reached the base of the cliffs beside the falls and peered down along the water. The river shone like a winding strip of moonlight and while making her way down to level ground, she saw three silhouettes downstream slip into the water one after the other. They were far too distant to note any distinctive features, but Madeleine imagined that only escaped slaves would be entering the river so unobtrusively.

This gave her confidence that she was ahead of them and that their hunters were not dangerously close behind, so after crossing the shallow plateau onto the other side of the river, she found a large cedar tree, slipped behind it into the shadows, and waited.

***

Almost everyone at Riverside was oblivious to what had transpired and had long since wandered off to sleep anyhow. Those few who remained, including Shenandoah, were still hovering around the fire, while Misae and Jimmy took Tamaya for a short walk, hoping to calm her down. Not too long after Annabel left, they had wandered close to the main gate, as two of Del

96

Hickory's men, Dale and Shearer, bolted up the driveway on horseback, jumped to the ground and called out as they beat on the timber. Their horses could be heard snorting loudly on the other side, stamping heavily at the ground.

Jimmy and Misae looked to one another with surprise and a touch of fright.

"I'll get rid of them," Jimmy whispered. He ushered Misae and Tamaya back against the fence next to the gate, out of sight, and opened it just enough to show his face. "Evening, boys, what is it?" he asked flatly.

The two men were much larger than himself, and looked like they'd ridden through an inferno. The drenched neck of one of the horses came into view momentarily behind them.

"We're looking for two escaped slaves," Shearer said, spitting tobacco to the dirt. "Looks like they came up by your land, thought they might have jumped your wall."

"Ain't seen nobody, and the gate's been locked since sundown," Jimmy stated. "There's no getting over this fence, and escaped slaves aren't about to trap themselves inside an unknown place anyhow, are they?"

"Mind if we take a look, just to be sure?" Shearer insisted, noting how nervous Jimmy seemed together with his urgency to get rid of them. "They told me to check all the places on this part of the river."

Jimmy didn't get time to respond before Dale pushed forward and invited himself inside.

"We won't be lo—" Dale began to say as he entered, but Misae's presence quickly silenced him and he rubbed his eyes in disbelief.

"Well, what do we have 'ere?" Shearer said with equal surprise, tipping his hat up and scratching his hairy jawline. "Look who's all dressed up like a princess. Havin' a party, are we?"

The two men chuckled under their breath for a moment.

"Something like that," Jimmy replied flatly.

"What you got in your hair there, little princess?" Shearer asked, in ridicule of Misae.

Tamaya recoiled further and further. She couldn't get far enough away, soon enough.

"None of your business," Misae replied coldly. She had seen too many men like these; invasive, bullying, and all without reason.

Shearer scoffed and looked to Jimmy. "Are you just gonna let her talk to me like that?"

"These are not your slaves, and this is not your property," Jimmy replied, hoping to divert the discussion. He nodded toward the gate. "It's late and I didn't invite you in, so I'll thank you to leave now. I told you, we haven't seen your runaways."

Back at the fire, Shenandoah had been watching with blood-boiling anticipation, ready to enter the scene if things turned bad, and he would have approached already but for the fear of causing a problem when there might not have been a problem to begin with. He couldn't hear the conversation clearly, but intuited that it wasn't very friendly, and so his heels were dug in, ready to run.

Shearer wasn't distracted by Jimmy's suggestion, and his eyes of hatred hadn't left Misae at all. It was clear that she had already offended him and he wasn't going to let it go easily. He reached out to grab one of the locks in her fringe to inspect the beads, but Misae pulled her head away. His eyes narrowed then and he tried again, but this time, Misae slapped his hand away.

"Don't touch me," she demanded with eyes of disgust. "Creepy monster."

The man's rage grew like wildfire and he lunged forward, trying to grab a handful of Misae's hair. "How dare you!"

Shenandoah started sprinting the moment he saw Misae slap the man's arm away. He knew this wouldn't go unpunished, regardless of slave ownership, and he wasn't about to wait around to see what might happen next.

Jimmy moved too, but was surprised to find that, instead of backing away, Misae moved forward while blocking Shearer's arm again, and struck him heavily in the throat with the knuckles of her bent fingers. Out of reflex, he pulled his knife out in that moment, only to drop it again immediately to clutch at his neck with both hands upon realizing that he couldn't draw breath at all.

Misae took up his knife and looked to Dale, who took a long while to react to the most unexpected turn of events and had only just pulled his own knife out.

"I'm gonna cut you up!" he threatened on approach.

Jimmy was about to move again, when almost the same thing happened.

Misae flashed forward in the instant Dale moved and dragged Shearer's knife along his neck as she slipped passed him. A stream of blood sprayed out all over her face and dress, yet she spun around, unmoved, ready to strike again.

Shearer was still attempting to breathe. He managed to stand upright and was getting ready to defend himself, but before anyone could move again, Misae had turned rapidly and sent the knife deep into his chest. When she jerked the knife out again, she flipped it around in her hand, slashed the side of his neck open, then turned back to Dale and shoved the knife into his heart, while he choked on his own blood.

Neither man stood for long thereafter. "Whump, whump" and the blood started pooling.

Shenandoah had screeched to a halt not too far away when Misae cut the first man's throat open. It was only a moment later that the second man went down and so he hadn't moved at all since then, only froze in wonder, with both hands on top of his head, looking down upon the warm corpses.

Both Tamaya's hands covered her open mouth and all present might have been expecting Misae to be frightened and quivery after that, yet she was decidedly calm. After shooting a quick glance to everyone present and still alive, she stated as a matter of fact, "That's two less monsters out there, hunting slaves and friends." Then, after a few moments of contemplation, she called, "Shenandoah?"

"Y-yes, my Princess?" he replied, yet stunned to the very core.

Misae looked up to him, neither grimacing nor smiling, but gently resolute, with blood still dripping off her face, hair, and hands. "Could you please help me bring their horses inside?" she asked, most gracefully, wiping drops of blood off the end of her nose.

***

It wasn't the first time Annabel had ridden Primrose, but it was certainly the first time riding at breakneck speed through relatively unknown territory at night. She knew well the general layout of the land in these parts, but not the ground itself, nor the usual hidden dangers like potholes, logs, stumps, and low-lying branches. There was no choice but to trust the highly-tuned instincts of her equine friend and give her enough rein and autonomy to ensure she could also make her own choices as to the safest paths to take.

In one place, as they came bolting over a small crest and met with a stream, they had only a split second within which to make a directional choice before plowing headlong into a small nest of trees. Their speed was too great to halt in time, so she quickly turned Primrose in toward a sandy path which ran alongside the stream and, although the Arabian eventually complied, she first leapt further to the side without being asked to do so, before turning in again. They met with the sandy path a little further ahead than Annabel intended, but, once there, she realized that her initial request would have taken them under a low branch, and Primrose had saved them from disaster. The mare herself would have made it through, yet Annabel would have been swept off at high speed by a massive cedar branch hiding its twisted form within the shadows, and she slowed Primrose down for just a moment after that just to stroke her neck lovingly.

"Thank you," she said, before they took off again.

Turning southwest at the border of the property, Annabel could see firelight flickering in and out of view in the direction of the river. She had already caught up to them, the hunters at least, and knew, for certain, she and Primrose were heading in the right direction.

A few minutes later, the distance roar of Dead Man's Fall could be heard, and so they eventually slowed when Primrose acknowledged that her sprint was over. Snorting in acceptance, she reducing her pace to a reluctant and sideways prancing trot. Speed was like an addictive drug to her, and walking calmly, the most challenging of comedowns.

Annabel listened carefully then, hoping for any sound to give away the position of the hunters and the prey. She knew it wasn't possible to go much further riding Primrose if she wanted to remain unnoticed, and so looked about for the best place to leave a horse in safety. A circle of trees near a narrow stream presented themselves well, and the grassy patch they encircled seemed like the perfect place to graze.

After walking Primrose inside, she jumped down, picked a bunch of grass and fed it to her, hoping to settle her down faster and also entice her to remain. At the end of such a ride, Primrose was like a ball of fire, but a few gentle strokes and a shh or two pacified her enough for one to believe she wouldn't bolt away at least. Just to be sure, Annabel placed another bunch of grass in her mouth and waited until she settled a little more.

"Stay, girl," she said with one last pat on the neck, then slipped her sword out of the saddlebag gently and stepped away slowly so as not to startle.

A path through the trees quickly led her in the fall. Once there, she stayed on the east side of the water, knowing one must pass by that way to get to the top of the falls, and found a cedar tree which looked good to climb for gaining a better view of the river. The position was also suitable, strategically, for she could see across the grounds all the way to the water from there, and also all of the plateau. So, she was sure to spot anyone passing through, even in stealth, and if she saw the men before seeing Elan, she would take them out of the picture and search for him then.

Following the shadows, she found her way to the tree when a voice called softly from nearby. "Annie, it's me," she heard, yet her sword was unsheathed instantly and she was ready to strike before realizing who had spoken.

Madeleine stepped out of the shadows. "I'm sorry, I didn't know how else to call you without giving you a start, or getting myself killed."

After replacing her sword, Annabel went to give Madeleine a hug. "Looks like we had the same idea. Have you seen him?"

Madeleine stepped back with even greater respect for her friend for not immediately impeaching her for losing Elan, leaving only self-deprecation to deal with. "I'm not sure, I saw three people cross the river downstream, not too far from here, and—"

"Three?" Annabel interrupted, to be sure.

Madeleine reconfirmed with a nod. "They were being sneaky. Who else could it be? Elan told me he saw one slave girl, but maybe there're more."

Annabel ushered Madeleine to walk with her, back the way Madeleine had come. "What side did they cross to?"

"The other side," Madeleine remembered.

"Okay, that means they have to come out over here on the left of the plateau," she pointed ahead. "Or go back into the water, one or the other, because, you know, it's only cliff on the other side next to the fall."

Madeleine knew it; she was just there.

"Let's hide near that spot," Annabel pointed. "We'll see them coming."

After crossing the plateau, they stepped behind a granite curtain jutting out from the base of the cliff which was just deep enough to conceal them both it its shadow.

"Thank you for coming," Madeleine said then, with great appreciation.

"What did you think I'd do?" Annabel jested. "Sit around the fire, roasting marshmallows, while you had all the fun?"

Somehow, this put a tiny smile on Madeleine's otherwise distraught face. She took a deep breath of hope before they stuck their heads out and locked eyes on the riverbank, both praying for Elan's appearance.

It wasn't long before their prayer was answered. Running low, and stepping light along the shadows, came Elan, followed closely behind by Talia, then Sanura. When they came close, Annabel and Madeleine stepped out and stood side-by-side in front of them.

Elan recognized them immediately, but his accomplices cowered in shock for the sudden and silent manifestation of two people standing like immovable monuments.

"Maddy! Annie!" Elan leapt into Annabel's awaiting hug and then Madeleine's. "I found them!" he exclaimed then.

"I can see that," Annabel replied, with a smile of excitement.

Madeleine's smile was a little more reserved. "Ah uh, so you did," she uttered, rivaling her beloved Neema's loaded responses. Her heart almost fell out of her chest when she saw him. It was a great relief and an even greater blessing to see the two young slave women at his side.

Sanura and Talia slowly rose to their feet once realizing they were in the presence of allies. It was difficult to accept at first, with them both being white and all, but their great love for Elan and vice versa stood as undeniable proof of their trustworthiness. Sanura dropped the knife.

When they became aware of the women's discomfort, both Annabel and Madeleine removed their coats at the same time and handed them over, while sharing a smile of appreciation for their unexpected harmony in offering.

Hesitantly but graciously, they both accepted, buttoned them up and pulled them in close, allowing themselves to finally acknowledge their frozen state, now that they had some relief from it.

"Are you cold, Elan?" Annabel asked.

"No," he answered bluntly, too elated to feel it even if he were cold. "This is Annabel, and this is Madeleine," he said, proudly introducing his friends. "They're both Guardians of Blue Falls." He covered his mouth then, but it was too late. "I'm not supposed to say that outside. Sorry, Annie, sorry, Maddy."

Under the circumstances, neither Guardian could care less; being too appreciative of Elan's presence and safety.

"Blue Falls?" Sanura repeated, then turned to Madeleine, who had left her Vivian wig in the carriage and now adorned the moonlight with her red, high-drawn ponytail. "Are you Madeleine Fox?"

"Well, look who's famous," Annabel chuckled.

Madeleine sent Annabel an amused glare before answering, "Yes, I am. How do you know my name?"

"Your work is well-known in the south," Sanura answered. "I don't believe it; I was going to try and find you somehow." She turned to Talia then, "Wasn't I, Talia?"

Talia nodded rapidly, still adjusting to the sudden turn of events. She was thinking with more strategy now, and less emotion, and her small taste of freedom had given her a giant appetite for it. "Do you think we should keep moving?" she prompted. Although still a long way off, the dogs could be heard intermittently over the falls.

Only Madeleine noticed Annabel's reaction to Talia's name being spoken, for she too, was breathless for a time. Annabel hid it well, swallowing the obvious exclamation she wanted to make, and pretended not to be moved. "Talia, is it?"

Knowing it would only complicate matters under the pressing set of circumstances, Madeleine suppressed her great urge to say, Your friend must be Sanura then. Plus, she wasn't completely sure, but it just seemed obvious somehow.

"Yes," Talia nodded. "And this is Sanura."

Knowing she would surely give away the surprise and excitement in her own eyes, Madeleine didn't dare look at Annabel in that moment, but noted

Annabel's cleverness in hiding her greater awareness. No one could have understood her tiny sigh of joy but for Madeleine.

"Well, Talia and Sanura," Annabel said, once she had regained her own composure. "Looks like you're in good hands." She turned to Madeleine then, hoping for confirmation that Madeleine might have assumed her next suggestion and received a smile of agreement. "Take 'em home, Elan. We'll take care of the men. We can't let them follow us any closer to home than this."

Elan's eyes widened with another wave of excitement. "Me? Just me?"

Sanura and Talia were also greatly surprised.

"So far, we haven't done a thing," she added. "It's been all you, Elan. Do you want to complete your mission on your own?"

Elan's smile beamed even brighter. "Yes!"

"It's not far from here," Annabel assured the two women. "It's uphill all the way, but only ten minutes, walking quickly, and there's no way you can get lost."

Talia sighed for the very idea of safety and freedom being so close, and her feelings were obvious to the Guardians. Although she also believed it, Sanura was still in awe at their discovery, and she had many questions, yet, knew this was not the time to voice them; not at all.

"No one can get to you now without going through us first," Madeleine added, giving them extra reassurance.

"And that's just not going to happen," Annabel insured, with a flame in her eyes instilling instant faith in both escapees. "We have to go to Riverside first, Elan, but tell them we're coming back there tonight after that, okay? And take them both to Artetha first."

"Okay, I will," Elan ensured.

Annabel unnecessarily adjusted both the women's borrowed coats as if attempting to make them warmer. "Artetha will heal all your wounds. Take your time on the way. You're safe now," she said. "The only people you might see between here and home are our own Panther Warriors who train outside at night sometimes, and if they see you, they will only help you home."

"They'd probably carry you," Madeleine jested.

Annabel retrieved Sanura's knife, noting its well-balanced design and finely-honed blade, and knew, at once, that it was specially crafted for fighting rather than survival. "Where on earth did you get this?"

"It belongs to one of Del Hickory's men," Sanura answered.

"Sanura took his eye out," Talia was pleased to tell them.

Annabel shared a knowing look with Madeleine. Del Hickory was their new target for investigation and potential eradication. After hearing already so many of his horrid exploits, they knew Del Hickory saw himself as the hopeful, new, self-appointed overlord of the Midlands; like the late Chester Flinch who they had successfully taken down.

Annabel raised the knife to inspect it more closely, finding blood stains. "You took his eye out with this?"

"No," Sanura answered. "But I cut him up a bit with it."

"And Elan used it to injure one of them," Talia added, not knowing how the Guardians would react to such information.

They all looked to Elan then, who quietly enjoyed the memory of his attack. "I stabbed him in the leg," he told them. "He's hurt real bad."

Somehow, the Guardians weren't greatly surprised, but they still shook their heads in wonder.

"So, these are all Hickory's men?" Madeleine asked, for confirmation, after a moment to accept the lack of compunction in Elan's words. Both escapees nodded. "Do you know exactly how many there are?"

"No, not exactly," Sanura admitted. "Sorry. There were three close to us, and maybe two or three with dogs further down the river. Earlier, we heard two of them shouting out to the others about going back to get horses, but we haven't seen them, and maybe more came, I don't know."

"There're two dogs," Talia added. "I saw them. Little hounds."

"That's good," Madeleine said with relief. "We can just scare them away if we have to. I don't want to kill any dogs."

"Me neither," Annabel agreed, then showed the knife to Sanura. "What do you want to do with this?"

Sanura shrugged, "Do you need it?" Both warriors shook their heads again. "Can I keep it?"

Annabel flipped the knife around and extended the handle to Sanura. "From this moment on," she said with credence. "You two don't need to ask permission for anything."

Sanura took the knife, albeit slowly and hesitantly, for Annabel's words rocked the very ground beneath her feet.

"Better get going now," Annabel suggested. "We'll see you in a couple of hours, all right?"

Elan nodded and started heading off, but had to turn back after a few paces to usher his two new friends along. "C'mon, this way."

However, they were both reluctant to leave, thinking of the Guardians facing enemies which they themselves created.

"They're the darkest kind of monsters," Talia said, without the restraint of disgust.

"We know this kind well, unfortunately," Madeleine replied, with equal disdain.

Annabel clicked the sheath of her sword open and drew the blade into the air in the blink of an eye. "And this," she said with the contrast of utter calmness, "has finished more of them than I can remember."

"You should be worried for the monsters," Elan stated then, turning all their heads. "Not the Guardians."

This somehow made them feel better about leaving with Elan. Sanura wanted to offer to stay and fight, but she knew exhaustion would probably make her more of a burden and less of a counterpart anyhow. They had been running, climbing, and swimming for hours and hours, and just knowing it was over, broke her body into pieces. She suddenly felt all the pains she'd been suppressing all along, and knew Talia would be feeling even worse with an open wound in her leg. "Thank you," she said to the Guardians, and Talia offered the same with equal gratefulness.

"Thank yourselves, and Elan," Annabel said plainly. "We haven't done anything yet. You would have been almost home by now if we didn't stop you, and the men haven't even tracked you this far yet."

Elan's shyness shone through, although he knew he'd done well, and to avoid more attention, he ushered them away again. This time, they followed, after leaving smiles of adoration for the Guardians, and before too long, Elan had led them part way up along the ridge and out of sight.

Annabel turned to Madeleine then, "Can you call Prim?"

"Prim?" Madeleine repeated, greatly surprised. "You rode here on Prim?"

"I flew here on Prim," Annabel admitted. "I tell you, I love that horse."

"Well, you can't have her," Madeleine stated. "No wonder you got here so fast. I was going to ask you how you did it."

As they walked back across the plateau, Madeleine placed two fingers together over her bent tongue and sent a high-pitched but melodic, three-toned whistle echoing throughout the canyon. A moment later, a whinny from Primrose echoed in reply. Madeleine smiled and whistled the same again. "You know this is just going to give us away, right?"

"Yep, and good," Annabel answered with scorn. "I'm tired. I don't want to go hunting monsters one by one and I want to put Tamaya's heart to rest as soon as we can."

"Elan's mother?" Madeleine supposed. "Me too." Given the guilt she felt for losing Elan, she wanted the same, and exhaustion also crept her way. Annabel's words reminded her that she was already yearning for sleep many hours ago.

It wasn't long before Primrose came trotting through the tree line and made her way over to Madeleine before halting in front of her, snorting and prancing on the spot. Unexpectedly then, she let out another long whinny.

"Oh!" Madeleine exclaimed. "Did you think Annie left you behind?" Both she and Annabel consoled her with gentle strokes across the neck and shoulders, which settled her down somewhat.

Annabel confessed, "I think she saved my life at one point, didn't you, girl? I nearly knocked myself off on a tree branch at flat gallop."

"She's very smart," Madeleine acknowledged, with great adoration, then turned to Annabel with a knowing grin. "So, who do you think the third will be, to find the doorway?"

Annabel's head turned so fast, it might have given her whiplash.

"I feel stronger since I was inside too," Madeleine added, knowing only Annabel could know what that meant. "Is this normal?"

"Yes," she answered quickly, both shocked and elated all at once. "Normal for a Guardian." After taking a few moments to fully accept Madeleine's insinuations, she asked with impatience, "You're telling me this now?"

Madeleine shrugged. "Sorry. It didn't feel right to tell you before I knew Elan was safe or in front of three Guardians, who don't even know they're Guardians yet."

"Oh my heavens, you know everything!" In her excitement, Annabel hugged Madeleine as if she were a lifeline of some kind and drew her close enough to squeeze some air from her lungs. Madeleine returned the hug with equal force, in recognizing this moment to be extremely significant for her friend; for both of them.

Madeleine nodded toward the approaching torchlights then.

"I used to think it would be Kachina, but after meeting Kachina, I think it might be Sanura," Annabel answered finally, seeing the lights also. "You?"

"Well, I was wondering why Oni hasn't found it already, or Akachi, because they're Blue Ones," Madeleine queried. "And Oni's meant to be the most gifted of them all."

"No, it doesn't make sense for a Blue One to find it," Annabel calculated. "Think of your life and how you've been tested. I figured you would be one of the three."

Madeleine didn't have so long to ponder this idea, as two of the men were at the edge of the tree line now and another two were closing in behind them. It was clear by the way their torches danced about that they were moving quickly. Yet, she did have a small revelation: "This is why you encouraged me so much to meditate at Crystal Nest."

Annabel merely smiled, then offered a half-grimace comprised of guilt. "But I didn't say where to meditate. And I encourage it anyhow."

After a mystified shake of her head, Madeleine returned her thoughts to the most pressing matter at hand. "So," she began, recapping. "If what Elan said was true, then one of them is down, which means at least one more is looking after him. That leaves four to six men or something, and two dogs, I guess, and maybe others on horseback?"

"I don't know about that." Annabel wasn't convinced. "I haven't seen or heard any horses, and if it's true, don't you think they would have set the dogs loose and followed them on horseback? It's so much faster."

This did make more sense, but Madeleine shrugged. "We'll see them on the way back anyway if they're around."

"Okay. Do you want to put them in the river when we're done?" Annabel proposed.

"I don't feel like dragging them over there," Madeleine confessed. "But, yes, that's perfect. Then no one will know exactly where they came from without a massive search."

Annabel thought for a moment. "Maybe we can lead them to the river somehow, before we kill them."

A plan came to Madeleine. "I've got an idea. I'll—"

"Uh," Annabel interrupted, raising a hand. "Just do it, I'll catch on. If I mess it up, I'll drag them over there myself, okay?"

Madeleine smirked for Annabel's laziness, then turned toward the torchlights and called, "Hey! Over here! Help us!" She lowered her voice then while waving her arms around. "Why do they have torches anyway? You can see better without them in this light."

"They're afraid of the darkness," Annabel deemed, waving also. "Even though darkness is what they are."

Two men were upon them in no time and another two joined them moments later.

"Oh, thank heavens you found us!" Madeleine blurted but in her most eloquent voice. "Did Daddy send you?"

"What?" one of them said, after sharing his surprise with the others.

The dogs were close now, howling in frustration.

Madeleine continued with desperation, "We've been lost for hours, and runaway slaves just attacked us."

"Slaves?" the same man asked.

Annabel caught on fast, "They stole my horse!" she exclaimed, looking frail and frightened. "And they took our coats too!"

Madeleine rubbed Annabel shoulders. "It's okay, we're rescued now. We're safe, okay?"

Another two men approached with the hounds then, and the Guardians both looked around, but couldn't see more torchlights anywhere.

"They had a big huntin' knife," Annabel added, dramatically. "Now what's a slave girl doing with a huntin' knife?"

"Was there two of 'em?" he asked then.

"Yep, two girls," Annabel answered. "Where's Daddy?"

"Look, I don't know who your daddy is," he snapped, impatiently. "We're looking for slaves who done escaped Del Hickory's farm. Sounds like the same ones who attacked y'all. Why'd they only take one horse?"

"They didn't," Madeleine explained. "My pony threw her off and the other one left her there and kept ridin'. She's over by the riverbank."

The men jerked their heads around all at once to fix their eyes on the river.

"What?" one of the new arrivals asked. "Is she alive? Is she injured?"

"Don't rightly know," Madeleine answered, between howls from the dogs. "We didn't wanna go over in case she attacked us or her neck was broke or something. I don't wanna see that."

"It'd serve her right," Annabel scoffed. "Scarin' and threatenin' good folk like that."

All the men ran to the water together with the dogs while the Guardians retrieved their swords and followed. At first, they walked slowly, then as soon as the men had collected together again at the riverside, they swept in at full speed. Before any of them had the chance to draw a weapon, they were spending their last breath looking into the beautiful and ferocious eyes of their most unexpected life-enders.

The Guardians didn't drag out the attack, as the men were never going to present any kind of challenge anyway. It was over in a heartbeat and, although the dogs voiced their disapproval, they backed away from the momentary frenzy. When all the men finally went still and silent, they stopped howling and sat nearby, looking over the men in quiet contemplation.

After rolling all the bodies into the river, they tossed their torches in after them, stamped out a couple of small but ambitious fires they left behind, then looked to the undernourished foxhounds, who hadn't moved at all the whole time.

Madeleine went to them, to test their friendliness, and they didn't seem to mind her presence at all. In fact, one them started wagging its tail as she approached, so she knelt down to pat them and removed their leads and collars at the same time. "You puppies want a new home?" she asked them, as if expecting an answer of some kind. "Looks like a boy and a girl." She looked up to Annabel. "They could be Riverside hounds?"

After Annabel answered with a grin of approval, they went to get Primrose and started making their way back to Riverside.

"C'mon!" Annabel slapped her thigh a couple of times, encouraging the dogs to follow. "If they actually stay with us, what should we call them?"

After a few moments of contemplation, Madeleine suggested with a laugh, "What about Foxy for the boy and Bell for the girl?"

"Foxy and Bell!" Annabel repeated. "I love it. Okay that's it then."

***

It was lucky for Mitchell that he volunteered to help the victim of Elan's knife attack back to the estate and left the others to continue the search without him, for although he could never have known it when making that choice, no one else would make it back alive that night.

Exhaustion set in, after limping only halfway home, for Mitchell had slowly but surely become a human crutch for Bill, once his wound prevented him from putting any weight on that leg at all. Mitchell progressively crumbled under the burden, while wondering why he was still fumbling through the bush after so many hours, and his energy for the hunt had all but depleted. After all, he wasn't the one missing an eye, so why should he destroy himself by going back out again? When he knew home wasn't too far away, he started to dream of a whiskey bottle and taking his boots off in front of an open fire.

Bill howled and cursed all the way home, adding additional annoyance to Mitchell's already exasperating night, and it wasn't until they'd turned northeast and over a crest, which gave view all the way to Del Hickory's property, that his complaining ended.

With great astonishment, they halted in their tracks, upon seeing three infernos where two barns and a shed used to be. They could hear distant voices, shouting orders with panic and great discontent. The startling vision distracted Bill from his agony temporarily, as they edged their way to the mansion which was now a silhouette in front of a giant red glow. Red against red, the mansion looked to be the orchestrator of wildfire itself, standing high and mighty before its violent creation.

The men continued to argue with one another: "There's nothing we can do! Well, we can't just stand here and watch it burn! What are we supposed to do, huh! What's your bright idea, Harry? You wanna take a whizz on it? Why don't you try that, huh…! Shut up, you two…! C'mon, whip it out, Harry, take a leak on it! I'll take a leak on you if you don't shut your trap!"

Cursing went on and on, yet neither Mitchell nor Bill heard a word they said. It was obvious to anyone that the buildings were long gone. Flames stretched into the night sky at least twice as high as the barns themselves, and their walls were already beginning to collapse.

Mitchell now understood why no more men had come to help them, which frustrated him even further, because he was planning to vent his anger and frustration out on them and no longer had an immediate outlet for it.

As they rounded the house, he could see Tanner through the window, pacing back and forth with a bandage around his eye socket and more bandages covering his arms. He was no longer screaming, but it was immediately clear to Mitchell that his fury hadn't lessened at all, not at all. Even more insulting for Tanner was the fact that he was covered in wounds made with a blade honed by his very own hands; a blade he kept proudly sharper than a razor. Tight bandages had stopped the bleeding, but agony still flourished, and a deep, sickly ache had set in, emanating in waves from within his eye socket.

Upon seeing Mitchell at the doorway, struggling to make it through, together with Bill into the foyer, Tanner held his tongue until Bill slumped into a chair and Mitchell dropped to his knees on the marble tiles.

"What happened to him?" he asked with a raised voice and dreaded expectation.

Mitchell panted heavily and his mouth was very dry, so he limited his use of words, "S…stabbed…in the…leg."

"What? Stabbed?" Tanner's diagonal head bandage also covered one of his ears and he wasn't sure if he'd heard stabbed in the leg or stumbled in the lake.

"Ah uh," Mitchell nodded. "I need water."

Tanner looked to Bill squirming in his chair and then to Mitchell again who seemed to have resigned himself to giving up. "Well, did you find them!?"

They both shook their heads.

"Where are the others? Are they still looking!?" he demanded, impatiently, but the men hadn't enough energy to care in the slightest.

This time, they both barely shrugged. Bill had lost a lot of blood, yet dizziness helped to mitigate his pain somewhat. "I need help," he uttered, trying to stop his head from lolling back into the chair.

Tanner was at the window then and he could feel the heat from the fires even from that distance, and with a wall in between. Flames from above the barn constantly flickered about in the periphery of his vision, catching his attention again and again, and it angered him further to have to turn his head to see the whole scene with one eye every time.

While watching the buildings disintegrate, in his mind, one idea rose high above all the night's misadventures and sat like an ominous gargoyle ready to pounce. Their boss, Del Hickory, was due back from his trip to the southern slave markets tomorrow, and, as Tanner knew all too well, the man was mean and unforgiving on his better days.

***

Chapter Four
The Sweetest Storm

Artetha had just asked Awinita if she noticed how many Blue Ones had collected at the Entrance, and if she knew why, when, most unexpectedly, the taps rang out, announcing two new arrivals who both needed medical attention. They were delighted that the code promised no critical injuries, but since no one planned to come to Blue Falls this night, let alone bring newly rescued slaves, they could only wonder, and then wonder some more, if the Blue Ones' presence was all but coincidence.

Yet, the taps were only ever used for one purpose. This was a golden rule, so healers were never called in without reason and thus, although surprised, the healers were in place and ready for the new arrivals in seconds. Since the people of Blue Falls hadn't heard the taps for so many days, curiosity soon rounded up a large crowd and brought them to the Entrance, hoping to see what surprise would enter Blue Falls so late on this night. Excepting, perhaps, the Blue Ones – who watched on quietly from a distance, sharing whispered words – all were astonished, and none more that Artetha, when Elan entered proudly with two young, bewildered slave women in toe.

With matted hair and skin streaked all over with dried river mud, they were certainly a sight to be remembered, and Elan was hardly recognizable beneath layers of muck. Yet, Artetha noticed him right away and looked to a stunned Awinita then to the Blue Ones, only to note that the queen was now standing next to Isi at the front of the crowd, seemingly as unsurprised by the spectacle as the Blue Ones themselves. Turning her attention back to Elan, she quickly checked him over for wounds and upon finding nothing but a few scratches and a continued smile, she joined Awinita in assisting the women to sit up on the beds. Although Elan had accidentally given away their destination, they were still so distracted and shocked for having found Blue Falls, that injuries were forgotten and exhaustion seemed to have vanished somehow, for the time being at least.

Elan stood by the beds. "This is Artetha," he said, half-pointing. "And this is Awinita. They are the greatest healers of all time."

Both healers smiled but with hesitance.

"Elan, what's happened?" Artetha asked, with much urgency. Both she and Awinita were already preparing to see to the wounded ones. "Is Annabel outside, and where did these women come from?"

"I'm Sanura, and this is Talia. Elan helped us to escape." Sanura's fat lip was now caked in dried blood, as with Talia's, and since she hadn't moved it much for a while, it stung greatly when she spoke and left her grimacing with every word.

"No, Annabel went back to Riverside," Elan replied. "But she'll be here in a couple of hours she said."

"All right," Artetha was pacified by that, yet more for the fact that Elan showed no signs of there being anything more to worry about. "We'll talk about it later. Let's get these two all cleaned up." She gently took the knife out of Sanura's hand. "I'm just going to put this on the trolley here, okay?"

Sanura nodded. She'd almost forgotten it was in her hand. "Please take care of Talia's leg first. I'm okay."

"We can look after you both at once, don't you worry," Artetha reassured her. "We'll clean up your wounds a bit, then we'll dress them properly after you've bathed." She looked up then to note that the queen was no longer standing next to Isi. However, Isi's eyes were upon her, still and unmoved. It was a little unsettling, as her instincts told her something of importance was taking place. Looking back to Sanura, she helped her out of her coat. "This looks like Annabel's."

"Yes, it is," Sanura confirmed, too overwhelmed to think of anything else to add.

Artetha looked to Elan again with a questioning eye, and the gaze he returned sent a chill down her spine; like those of a wolf or a fox, biding time.

***

"You know, I'm getting better at killing without getting blood on me," Madeleine declared.

Annabel sniggered a little. "Yeah, you learn some tricks after a while. Aren't you going to ride Prim back?"

"What? And have you walk next to me like my peasant slave?" she answered, joking. "No, from what you tell me, I think she's earned her rest, but thanks for reminding me." After halting Primrose, she unstrapped the girth and threw the ends of it over the saddle, then unstrapped the bit from the bridle to take it out of Primrose's mouth and dropped it into one of the small saddlebags.

They walked on. Primrose didn't need to be led, she just followed alongside Madeleine wherever she went and found a grassy patch to eat if Madeleine ever dawdled anywhere for too long, at a picnic or whenever she stopped to pick flowers.

"Annabellia is magical," Madeleine remembered, smiling with great warmth, thinking of the wonderment found in only the short time she spent there. "How on earth have you kept that to yourself all this time?"

"I didn't have a choice," she admitted, still in disbelief that this day had finally arrived.

Madeleine sensed her unsureness. "Are you all right? Freya said you were eight when you first saw it. It's a long time to bear such a secret. I'm not sure if I could've kept Annabellia to myself for so long."

"Yes, you would have." Annabel was sure. "It's weird when you call it that. I was a little girl when I named it, and before I went outside of it."

"What should I call it?" A thousand questions accumulated in Madeleine's mind.

Annabel shrugged. "The ancients call in Attunga, the high place, but we can call it whatever you want. Who knows how long it will be just you and me." She sensed Madeleine's confusion then. "I'm sorry. All right, tell me what you know already?"

"Not much," Madeleine confessed. "I went in, I was talking to Freya and she left suddenly, then I went to Nanook and saw the other amulets and—"

"You asked my mother something about the Guardians, didn't you?" Annabel was certain and Madeleine nodded curiously. "Don't ask her about the Guardians," she sighed, with the history of disappointment clear in her voice. "About the future anyway. My mother will vanish every time." She paused then, noting the urgency and inquisition in Madeleine's face. "Maddy, there's so much to tell you. I don't even know where to start."

"How about with Attunga?" she proposed. "What is it?"

"It exists inside the greater realm. Only a Guardian can enter Attunga," Annabel explained, taking on a more serious tone. "The animals have no predators there except for the very small ones. Birds, reptiles, and insects are the only carnivores. In its own way, it's in perfect balance, and has been for millennia. This is why the animals have no fear of humans, because they've only ever seen Guardians who leave them untouched. The Guardians have only ever eaten vegetation and fish."

"That's true," Madeleine acknowledged. "I never wanted to eat anything else, but I had no choice when I was younger."

Annabel nodded; it was no surprise. "Beyond Attunga is the greater realm. Some of the people call this world, Chanté Wičháȟpi, which means something like 'the heart of the stars,' but the ancients from the north call it Ista, which means the 'eye,' and in the east, it's Kmwh-yah, which is difficult to translate, but it's close to 'of the stars and from the light.' The people in the south, the land closest to the Guardians' realm of Attunga, call it Sampa-Thípi, which means 'beautiful home,' and the ancients in the west call it Allawah, which means something like 'make this your home' or 'remain here.'"

"People?" Madeleine was too distracted by this idea to hear the names distinctly. "I didn't see anyone."

Annabel smiled. "That's because you didn't leave the Guardians' realm which is in the south. If you walk north from there, down the mountain, you come to the gates and step into the greater part of the realm which the people inhabit. You would have seen it from a distance. It's another world. I use different names depending on which people I'm talking to, but mostly I call it Sampa, so we can call it that if you like, or Sampa-Thípi, whatever you want. There are hundreds of thousands of people."

"What?" Madeleine repeated the word unconsciously. "Hundreds of thou—?"

"Yes. There's an ocean, two large land masses close together, with lakes and many islands. When I first entered, I was eight, and almost all the realm was enslaved again by the Timuillain." A wave of sadness swept over her then.

"Wait." Madeleine raised her hand. "Who are they? The Tamu…"

"Timuillain. They're different, they're ambitious and greedy, not all of them, but mostly all of them." Annabel paused on that point, seeming to reflect on sad times. "They're taller and stronger, and they despise all other people. Some think they are not entirely human. They only want to dominate and enslave, and they did this completely when the realm went hundreds of years without a single Guardian. They destroyed all the human records they could find, burnt all the books, lied to the people about everything, distracted them with misleading information and horror, and exterminated anyone who tried to share the truth until the truth was almost impossible to find."

"That's starting to sound familiar," Madeleine said under her breath.

Annabel merely raised her eyebrows in agreement and continued, "You see, the problem we face is that we need Sampa to protect the people of Blue Falls from a worse fate coming to Earth, but if they were to enter now, we'd be walking them from the peaceful Blue Falls into a land still divided after long-term war. My mother freed many during her time, but when she disappeared, the people had no Guardian again for eight years, until I entered, and in the meantime, the Timuillain started to destroy my mother's work. I've spent many years freeing people and rebuilding their trust in the Guardians because they started to believe in us again during my mother's time, but then she failed to return one day like the Guardians of the past, and some believed she had abandoned Sampa. They didn't know she died in Earth giving birth to me."

Madeleine was suddenly having one of those moments she remembered from when she first walked into Blue Falls, when an inundation of information and questions threatened to shatter her mind. All of a sudden, she halted. "Wait, how could you help free the people when you were only eight years old? I don't understand."

"The Guardians' abilities are heightened in Sampa," she explained. "We're much stronger, and the people know it. They know every one of us and they were waiting for me like they're waiting for all of us, to lead them into freedom. They have powerful seers, like our Elders and our Blue Ones, who know the prophecy of Sampa and Blue Falls. Unfortunately, the Timuillain also know the prophecy well, and do everything to oppose it."

"The prophecy which includes 11 Guardians," Madeleine realized. She stared at the ground where she walked while Annabel's information did battle with her belief system, and, while her bewilderment flourished, Annabel's joy grew rapidly until she was practically bouncing on the spot.

"You're so excited," reservedly, Madeleine noted. "I'm sorry, I was excited to tell you, but now, I'm... I thought it was just another space, like Blue Falls and Crimson Cove. It's a lot to think about."

"And there's so much more to tell you, I haven't even started." She moved them on again, increasing their pace two-fold. "C'mon, we'll never get back. I'm excited about so many things, Maddy. It will take you a while to see the greatness of your discovery, but when the people see you, it will be the greatest and most celebrated event in all their history. You may or may not want to know it, but you're also one of the favorite Guardians of all the people."

For a long time, Annabel had been telling the people of Sampa about all of the Guardians and giving them updates, knowing how it brought them hope. They knew everything about all the Guardians, including those who people of Blue Falls were yet to discover, and long ago had built a coliseum for each Guardian where they go to pray and meditate on their arrival. As she thought of this, Annabel's joy waned and sorrow found her voice again. "I'll show you soon. There's something the people want from us, which can only be done by all the Guardians together, but you know one more Guardian has to awaken and find Attunga on their own first, like you and I did, before all of us can enter. It's like this, I think, to be sure all the Guardians are united, and with integrity, because if we rival in any way, if we go to war against each other in there, then devastation would come to Sampa without a doubt. I believe we are each tested for this reason. Sadly, people pray for their favorite Guardian without knowing if they will ever witness their arrival."

This idea struck Madeleine deeply and it suddenly placed everything into perspective. Unconsciously, she almost drew them to a halt again. "That's possibly the saddest thing I've ever heard."

Annabel sighed. "It's no one's fault, but try watching them walk to the coliseums to meditate and pray, while some of the Guardians, like you for a long time, hadn't even arrived at Blue Falls yet, let alone found the doorway. They're tired of war. The Timuillain just keep bringing it back no matter how long and how far we battle, and I'm only one Keeper. I bring peace to one place, while they're secretly attacking another or conspiring to attack. I can hold it off for a long time, but it always returns, eventually. I'm not the strongest of the Guardians, and I'm so tired of it too, Maddy."

Madeleine hadn't thought of war yet. "How have you survived through so much? And if you've been at war so much, how are you still alive? And why aren't you scarred all over?"

"You'll see soon enough," Annabel teased, unwittingly; it was just too much to explain all at once. "Things are a little different for us in there, for the Guardians, I mean. Something happens to us when we walk through the doorway and we're not so easy to kill in that realm." She huffed then and with sarcasm, added, "Of course, you find the doorway while I'm at Riverside."

"Bad timing, I'm sorry," Madeleine admitted. "Wait," she said abruptly then. "You confused me before, but I didn't want to interrupt. You said you weren't the strongest Guardian and you called yourself a Keeper by mistake, do you remember?"

"I remember," Annabel said with amusement. "But it was no accident."

"All the Guardians agree that none of us could come close to defeating you in a battle," Madeleine argued. "Not yet, anyway. There is no doubt. We prove that every time we practice."

"In Blue Falls, maybe," Annabel agreed. "And in Blue Falls, I'm a Warrior. In Sampa, the Warriors of Blue Falls who enter are not the same. In Sampa, there will be nine Keepers and two Warriors, instead of nine Warriors and two keepers like Blue Falls."

"Only two Warriors in Sampa?" Madeleine questioned. "You and me?"

Annabel shook her head. "No, again, not me. In Sampa, I am a Keeper."

"So, if Sanura, Talia, and Elan are Warriors, that means Blue Falls has eight Warriors and three Keepers, including Kachina, who is both," Madeleine argued.

116

"Sorry, wrong again," Annabel said assuredly. "Kachina is always both, in both places, but there are only two Keepers of Blue Falls, all other Guardians are Warriors. Misae is a Warrior, she just hasn't realized it yet. Sayen and Naira are the only Keepers of Blue Falls, and, of course, Kachina, if she chooses to be, so, again, in Sampa, there are just two Warriors, plus Kachina. Believe me, two is more than enough when you see what you can do, when you see what just a Keeper like me can do, but Kachina may be a Warrior there also if she's needed or if she wants to be."

"So if you're not a Warrior of Sampa, then who is the other Warrior?" Madeleine asked, though she had the answer already, and, knowing this, Annabel didn't respond, but waited for Madeleine to remember the Amulets.

"I can't remember whose Amulet was ruby," she admitted, after realizing. "But I think it has to be Sanura."

"Sanura," Annabel agreed. "Who, I also think, will find the doorway."

"Why?" Madeleine asked, being most unsure herself.

"It makes sense, don't you think?" Annabel was almost convinced. "I bet we'll find Sanura was responsible for their escape, and maybe this day, she was tested, along with all of us, and when you think about it, what would be the point in us being tested, going through all the things we've been through, if the third Guardian to open the door was already in Blue Falls?"

Eventually, Madeleine nodded in agreement. Although she believed Annabel completely in these matters, and also had Julian's research to draw on, it wasn't easy reformatting the structure of the prophecy in her mind. "I was about to ask why you haven't said anything all this time, but I already know why. There's too much at stake and you don't know what you could do to ruin things."

Annabel agreed with age-old discernment in her eyes. "You've got it. That's why Nanook almost swallows his tongue whenever you ask him about it."

Madeleine surprised herself with laughter, having seen Nanook in this state herself. After a while, a new awareness settled down upon her. "Now I understand why you are the way you are," she revealed. "It all makes sense now."

Annabel smiled broadly. "By the way, I'm sorry, but Elan beats you by far when it comes to popularity with the children of Sampa."

"I can't wait to see it all," Madeleine shared with excitement, while daunted by the tasks at hand. "How can we do it all? There's Blue Falls and Riverside, and now this...and this, Sampa, this is another life in itself. How have you done it all this time?"

"We are the chosen." Annabel shrugged. "Do you want to ignore your calling? You can't. If it was in you to abandon it, you wouldn't have made it to the doorway or even to Blue Falls for that matter. I feel we have much pain but equal beauty and joy, if you know where to look for it."

In the moonlight, Annabel's eyes took on a darker shade of blue again. Madeleine looked into them for a moment, trying to look past the young woman in her earthly vision to see the Guardian who, for so long, was surely desperate for support and long-term companionship. "Now I see the greater importance to protect Blue Falls," she determined. "Because if it's discovered and destroyed, then both Blue Falls and Sampa, and all the people in both places, will suffer." This was one of the pains Annabel mentioned, the pain of such an impossible burden, and she felt the weight of it building already. "Tell me what I need to do."

"You only need to be yourself," Annabel answered, simply. "The Timuillain leaders are afraid of me, but do you know what they fear the most at this time?"

"What's that?" Madeleine had no idea, but the wicked smile taking over Annabel's face shook the very ground beneath her feet.

"The day one of the two Warrior Guardians enters Sampa," Annabel replied, smile unmoved. "But mostly the day Madeleine Fox sees what they've done and responds accordingly."

***

When Annabel and Madeleine returned to Riverside, Misae was out of sight, busy in one of the bathrooms of the mansion. They first saw the stark faces of Jimmy, Tamaya, and Shenandoah, then two strange bodies lying dormant on the ground, and asked urgently, in two-part harmony, "Where's Misae?"

"She's fine," Jimmy ensured. "She in the house, cleaning up."

Annabel quickly inspected the dead, then looked over to see the men's horses, still saddled, but grazing placidly on the short grass nearby. "What happened?"

"Misae happened," Jimmy answered. "They came here looking for the runaways, then started making trouble."

Tamaya nodded cautiously in Jimmy's support, then asked with great fear, "Elan?" and let a giant sigh escape when the Guardians both nodded and smiled.

"He's safe again," Annabel confirmed.

"Well, now we know why the men on horses never showed up," Madeleine deduced.

Annabel ran for the house, leapt up the front steps three at a time, belted through the front door, and finally found Misae in the bathroom at the end of the hall. She had bathed, changed out of her dress, which was now sitting in a pail of cold water, and had chosen to wear a pair of tan pants and a light-blue shirt from the clothes brought over for the slaves.

After seeing Misae simply standing calmly at the mirror fixing her hair, Annabel took a deep breath and leaned against the doorway.

"Takes a long time to get blood out of your hair," Misae said flatly. She looked over to Annabel momentarily but continued to work on her braids all the same. "The only reason you would be back is because you found Elan," she intuited. "How is he?"

"Me and Maddy could've just stayed by the fire," Annabel supposed, and only partly in jest. "Warrior baby had it all under control."

Misae smiled. "Did you find the slave girl?"

"Ah uh, there were two," Annabel stated. "But we weren't completely useless, we found a few of the men who were hunting them."

"Found, huh?" Misae repeated with sarcasm. "Did you find them like I found two of them?"

"Yes." Annabel smiled but with some reserve, knowing it wasn't an easy thing at all to end a life, no matter to what extent that life had been taken by the darkness, especially for the first time. "How are you? Do you have any injuries?"

Misae shook her head. "I know why you didn't tell me. I never would have believed it." With puzzlement lingering, she turned to face Annabel. "I moved so fast, Annie, I frightened myself, and I didn't have time to think about what I was doing, it just happened. It wasn't the same as when we practice."

"Failure in practice doesn't end with your death or the death of one of your own people," Annabel suggested. She was impressed by Misae's composure, however, she decided to take a few more moments to confirm for herself that Misae had indeed dealt with her confrontation in a most balanced manner. "Your mother's going to kill me," she predicted with a nervous chuckle. "Anyhow, Jimmy volunteered to stay for the night, and we're going back with Tamaya now. Are you finished?"

"I'm finished," Misae answered, pulling her now bead-less braids back over her shoulders. "But I'm not coming with you. I'm not leaving my people now." She collected the sapphire beads and her amulet. "Keep these beads for me and give the amulet to my mother. She can wear it until I get back, if she wants to."

Seeing the resolution in her fellow Guardian, Annabel took the items and didn't think to contend the requests. "As you wish, but she's going to kill me twice now. It's on your head."

"My mother will have to find her own peace with it," Misae stated, gently but adamantly. "I'm exactly where I should be." She turned and embraced Annabel with great warmth then. "Thank you, my sister."

"I didn't do anything except disobey the queen," Annabel shrugged. "And I'm about to do it again."

Misae smiled. "Well, I don't see any greater emergency than reuniting a mother and child," she concluded. "Especially one who just had her heart ripped out another time thinking he was lost again. Remind the queen of when she lost her daughters if she gives you any trouble."

"All right, warrior princess," Annabel agreed, with adoration. "I'll see you in the morning. Look after Foxy and Bell for me."

"What? Who?" Misae screwed her face up.

Annabel sniggered. "You'll find out."

She left Misae then and went back to the others to find that the corpses had been removed.

"I told them to drop the bodies in the river," Madeleine informed her. "I'm going to leave Prim for the night so we can take the thoroughbred and the carriage, and take the men's horses with us. I thought we could set them loose on the other side of the bridge. What do you think?"

Annabel nodded in approval. "They'll probably find their own way home from there, if they bother trying." She smiled then as she looked over to the fire to see Foxy and Bell interacting with the people already, accepting food scraps with relish. She nudged Madeleine to look in their direction.

Pleasantly surprised, Madeleine noted, "I guess they're staying."

They both looked to Tamaya then, standing somehow patiently by the carriage and went over to her.

"Tamaya," Madeleine said with a serious tone. "Since you're Elan's mother, I feel it's necessary to say that no matter what you see on the way, you're not allowed to jump out of the carriage and go after it, all right? Not at least without telling me first."

***

Once again, Nanook's polishing stone ground to a halt. He didn't want to believe it, but, again, he felt eyes scratching down the back of his neck, and, this time, he turned to see the queen standing in the entrance.

He jumped to his feet and bowed, "My Queen," then looked up to see that the queen hadn't moved a muscle.

"Show them to me," she said flatly. "And don't bow."

Nanook did a doubletake and had to blink away his vision of Madeleine standing there, saying exactly the same thing not a few hours earlier, minus the part about bowing. Without delay, he went to his secret drawer again and took the bag of amulets to the queen.

Lesedi offered but a faint smile as she pulled the bag open and let the cases fall into her hand. Just two of the names exposed themselves: Sanura and Elan. She didn't need to flip the last case over but did anyhow, just to be sure, then looked up to Nanook, who stood waiting, meekly. Not knowing what reaction to expect, it came as a great surprise when she simply kissed him on the forehead before leaving again without a word.

On his way back to the grindstone, he wiped his brow and attempted to shake the tension out of his head.

"I'm too old for this," he muttered to the piles of gold and myriad gemstones sparkling in the firelight all around.

***

When the Guardians entered with Tamaya, Elan was standing just outside the healing bay, surrounded by children all listening to his version of the night's events with hungry ears and mouths agape. He heard their entrance and expected to turn and see Annabel and Madeleine alone, but when he noticed a third person between them, his story slowly faded into nothingness while his eyes slowly opened wider and wider. It wasn't until Tamaya came very near that he was absolutely sure he was looking at his mother. His gaze moved from Annabel to Madeleine, then back to Tamaya, as he took a few hesitant steps in her direction. A second later, he flew into her awaiting arms, shouting, "Momma!"

Tamaya wept frantically and practically crushed Elan in her arms. Until this moment, she hadn't allowed herself to completely believe she was going to see him again, and only now did her anguish begin to crumble.

Both Annabel and Madeleine were wiping tears away in seconds. In all the time they had to think about it, they still weren't prepared for seeing Elan's expression when he first saw Tamaya.

"And we were worried he wouldn't remember," Annabel said aside to Madeleine.

They left mother and son alone then, knowing the reunion would be unending, and went to the healing bay to see that the new arrivals had washed and were now sitting in light gowns, having wounds dressed and hair embellished.

Sanura saw them first and subsequently pulled a loch of her hair out of the dresser's hands, as she jerked her head around to look at them. They stayed a few paced away for a while to watch the silent goings-on, surprised by how the women's appearance had changed so significantly. Although they both shared swollen lips and Talia's cheek gleamed to some extent with hints of black and green, wounds did nothing to lessen their overall beauty. Talia was particularly striking in appearance, with bright blue, hawklike eyes which seemed to give her a perpetually sorrowful but stormy gaze.

Artetha saw the Guardians also, yet only shot a glance their way before refocusing on the wound at hand, a gash in Sanura's arm, made when she snagged on a stick beneath the water during one of their river crossings.

Annabel whispered to Madeleine, "I think I'm in trouble."

"Annabel?" came Artetha's motherly voice.

"Yep, here we go," she whispered again.

"What's a little boy doin' running around in the jungle in the middle of the night?" Insinuations were blatantly obvious.

Annabel grimaced. "It's not a jungle. More like a forest."

Both Sanura and Talia struggled to hide their amusement.

"Don't give me that, you know very well what I'm sayin'," Artetha insisted. "And don't you two laugh. You should stay away from these ones, they'll get you in all kinds of trouble."

"It's my fault," Madeleine confessed. "He ran off before I could stop him."

"We brought his momma over," Annabel offered in defense, albeit completely unrelated, and pointed across to where Tamaya still embraced her son.

"What?" Artetha stood abruptly and looked about until she found them. After watching on for a while with a hand over her heart, as if to still it, she went back to her work with tears threatening to blind the way. "Well, if that isn't one of the most beautiful things I've ever seen." After shaking the jitters out of her hands and regaining some composure, she went back to work. The sight had weakened her resolve somewhat and the next glance she shot over to Annabel and Madeleine was a little less mean and held just a pinch of adoration. "Hmmm," she muttered with a half-smile, then raised her eyebrows without looking up to ask, "Where's Misae?" and let the question sink in before adding, "I was just wondering, Annabel, since you were never supposed to leave her side."

Annabel flashed a worried glance to Madeleine, then one of apprehension to Artetha who merely shook her head and, after a tsk, added, "Well, look who's breaking all the rules tonight."

The two patients smiled again, receiving another shake of the head from Artetha, just as the queen entered the healing bay with Isi at her side, followed closely behind by Naira, Sayen, Oni, Akachi, and Kachina.

Annabel gulped and uttered, "It's been nice knowing you," to Madeleine, but was surprised to see Lesedi first approach the new arrivals, both of whom were stunned by the sudden presence of their queen. No detailed discussions had taken place yet, and so they had no idea what to expect regarding Blue Falls. They both made a move to stand.

"Don't you dare get up," Lesedi said. "Especially if it's to bow to me. I won't have it. I've just come to see, how you are? Artetha?"

"Nothing too serious," she was happy to answer, then nodded toward Talia. "This one's got a nasty gash on her leg, but it will heal perfectly before too long."

This pleased Lesedi greatly. She looked across the way to Tamaya kneeling in front of Elan while they spoke excitedly to one another. Elan was waving his arms about in that moment, elaborating on a story he shared, and it seemed that Tamaya constantly battled the urge to take him up and into her arms again. When they weren't wiping tears away, her hands writhed together as if impatiently collecting all his memories.

The queen looked about, appearing to confirm Misae's absence for herself and, when her eyes finally rested on Annabel, almost all eyes fell upon her also.

Annabel cringed somewhat under the weight, but she, together with all the Guardians and the healers, were shocked when the queen finally spoke the words on her mind.

She lifted her chin and a shy smile came over her lips before she asked of Annabel and Madeleine, "I'm assuming Misae has everything under control at Riverside?"

They were both stunned into silence for a long while, but they caught Isi, Oni, and Akachi's sneaky smiles nonetheless.

"She's a born leader, my Queen," Annabel answered in time, secretly doing backflips of joy in her mind for somehow evading impeachment for all the night's conundrums.

Lesedi's smile increased a little then, for the confirmation that Misae and all Guardians remained unharmed despite apparent misadventures. She didn't particularly want to know the details just yet. It was enough for now to know that no one was harmed. "All right, we'll talk tomorrow sometime, after these two have had the chance to settle-in."

Sanura spoke as Lesedi turned to leave, "My Queen, there's something I need to tell you about our escape, if you have time."

"Of course," Lesedi answered, turning back again. "I wanted you to rest, but if you think it's important…"

"Yes," Sanura said, while Talia also nodded. "We freed all of Del Hickory's slaves when we escaped, about 20, 25 maybe, I don't know for sure, but I told them how to get to the hinterland in the north."

"Del Hickory," Lesedi repeated, disgusted by the name. "You escaped Hickory's farm? My goodness."

The escapees both nodded again, as did Annabel and Madeleine.

"Yes," Sanura confirmed, then continued with hesitance. "We also…burned all his barns down too."

Grins started to appear amongst all the Guardians.

"Sanura took one of their eyes out," Talia added.

Annabel dared to say, "We killed six of his men tonight."

Smiles grew rapidly all round then, while Sanura and Talia looked to Annabel and Madeleine, shocked and pleased all at once.

"Elan stabbed one of them," Talia revealed, without thinking too much on it.

Artetha's head whipped around and her eyes widened greatly, yet she was struck speechless. Akachi laughed aloud, infecting others until they sniggered.

"We also adopted two of his dogs," Annabel said, cringing, fueling humor into laughter for many. Even Queen Lesedi couldn't keep all her amusement at bay, but she was, however, shaking her head at the amount of carnage the Guardians had left in their wake in a single night.

"But," Madeleine said with pride. "We did set two of his horses free."

"Is that meant to make it better?" Lesedi queried, satirically.

"Only because they were branded," Annabel stated, receiving another burst of laughter. "Otherwise they were pretty and I would've kept them."

Madeleine shrugged, "Oh, I think I might've killed two of his men yesterday too."

The chuckling took a long while to dissipate after Madeleine's last words, and the queen didn't quite know what to do with all the information for now.

"Let's meet early in the morning, Guardians," she said finally. "To talk about what we can do for the ones who were freed. It's a lot of people, and if they're hiding in the same place we hid, then we can't just go in there with wagons. I'll bring Jalen in on the meeting." She turned to Kachina then. "How do you feel about that, Kachina?"

The idea made Kachina's stomach drop, but she hid her reservations completely. "There is nothing more important than the Queen's and the Guardians' work."

After a smile of adoration for Kachina, Lesedi looked to all the Guardians with the same proud smile and left them with one last comment: "May all my daughters and all the Guardians be blessed for all time. Tonight, you have achieved something very great."

Madeleine and Annabel shared a mutual look of curiosity, both wondering how much the queen knew and, more appropriately, how she came to know it. They both looked up to her entourage then and voiced the same realization in harmony, "Isi."

"That little fox," Annabel added, affecting Isi's resolve not at all with the accusatory glare she sent his way.

***

After sitting silently for many minutes at the edge of the clearing, listening for any noise which may allude to human presence, Mosi decided it was safe for the people to cross the open space in order to reach the brink of hinterland northeast of Black Sand Valley and the river beyond. With intent, he had listened to Sanura's instruction, and, since they were yet to see any signs of being followed, and everything she told him had come true so far, he wasn't about to stray from her guidance in the slightest.

He, himself, had only arrived at Del Hickory's estate that day, along with Sanura and Talia, but many others in his company had been Hickory's slaves for many weeks. These were broken souls, in need of constant reassurance that they still had reason to hope and to stay strong. They had been running for many hours now, only stopping briefly every so often near waterways to replenish thirsts and to rest overworked legs, and so, energy levels were dangerously low, if not fully depleted.

Mosi drove them forward, knowing that the pain they were willing to put themselves through now may very well decide their freedom, and as he ran, for the first time in a long while, he allowed himself to think of his love and his child. Feeling his feet pound over the earth again, his chest burns and his heart race, reminded him of his warrior days and returning home exhausted after practice to hold his baby boy and to kiss his mother's beautiful smile.

Nothing could replace their presence in his life again, or even come close to rivaling that dream, and the open space within which he found himself reopened his imagination somehow, only to fill it with heartbreaking desires once again.

Run.

It began to rain then, and for them it was a blessing, knowing it would only serve to cover their tracks. When they had almost made it across the open field, Mosi saw a number of shadows moving along the tree line and raised his hand to halt everyone behind. For many breathless moments, they watched in silence until Mosi decided to investigate alone.

Crouching low and stepping silently, he came a little closer and paused again to look over the tree line. Soon after, he spied movement again and then clearly saw the silhouettes of two or three people treading carefully along the edge of the forest. By the moonlight, he could tell they were slaves and while still keeping low, he ran to them, calling softy, "Hey! It's all right, don't be frightened."

A few moments later, heads popped up all over the place, and one figure came to him, a woman, approaching hesitantly, bearing suspicious eyes.

"It's all right," Mosi insisted, then turned to the open field and signaled for his party to rise and join him.

The woman came close and Mosi deemed her to be roughly his age, perhaps a little older. Her chest heaved in and out, she limped heavily, and her shortly chopped hair was riddled with pieces of debris.

She panted, "Hello."

"Hello," Mosi replied, as all the people from both parties gathered around them. "I'm Mosi. I'm taking these people to the hinterland in the north. Where are you going?"

The woman wiped the combination of light rain and sweat out of her eyes. "Same as you. Where did you come from?"

"A farm in Riverside. A very bad farm," he answered. "You?"

"They're all bad," she stated. "We jumped a ship and swam ashore. We've been running since early morning."

"It's not far from here," Mosi said, hoping to ease her pain a little.

She nodded, "I know this area too. I used to come here hunting with my husband and my daughter. I'm Layla."

Mosi smiled, his first for the day, and looked down to Layla's feet to discover the bulge in her ankle which obviously caused her to limp and cringe.

"I can carry you the rest of the way," he offered, and before she had time to object, he lifted her off the ground and nodded for all to follow.

Layla didn't fight it. Only the want for survival had kept her going this long, and the pain had reached almost unbearable levels. Nonetheless, it wasn't long before they entered the dense forest at the edge of the hinterland and, after continuing a good distance deeper inside, they found a cavern near a stream large enough to shelter all from the rain. The river way promised food along its edges, together with fish within its waters, and, of course, drinking water, so it seemed the perfect place to nest, for now anyhow.

After sitting Layla down on a large stone inside, Mosi wiped away most of the water streaming down his face and looked about the cavern.

"Thank you, Mosi," Layla said with much gratefulness.

He just smiled and picked up the only stick inside, a long, thin, cracked pine branch still strong enough to take a good bending, and broke away one end of it to a point with his fingers. "I'll go now to get some firewood before the rain sets in, and I'll take this spear just in case."

"We have a knife," she announced with glee, and it was quickly shuffled along to him through the crowd.

Mosi pulled it from its sheath to inspect it, scaling edge and all, and shook his head happily. "Perfect."

Before too long, they would be hard-pressed trying to find timber outside dry enough to burn, so his plan was to search right away and then gather whatever food they could find. He knew Layla's people would be too exhausted for the moment to do more than fall unconscious on the floor, which is exactly what most of them did the very moment they stepped inside, so he quickly gathered a few of the others and set out to find what they could by way of firewood.

At the base of the cliffs beneath rock ledges was always a good place to look first, before the rain really set in, and the two, long rock walls extending out and up from either side of the cavern offered great promise. These places always produced something, and Mosi was pleased to find many a dry log and stick, sheets of dry tea tree bark, and pine needles; everything needed to build a fire.

They rushed their surprising find back to the cavern and it wasn't long before the thin strips of frayed bark pieces, which Mosi had placed over a split in the back of a sheet of bark, started smoking and flaming under the friction of the stick he rubbed back and forth along the crack. He blew on it then, ever so gently, as it was very easy to overdo it with eagerness; yet it became obvious to all hopeful onlookers that he had done it hundreds of times before. After placing a few tiny sticks over it, he waited until they caught alight, then added larger and larger sticks until the flames were sure to take hold.

Watching the fire grow brought a smile to everyone, even the most fatigued, and faces began to reveal themselves more and more as the glow expanded throughout the cavern.

Mosi placed a stick as thick as his wrist gently over the fire, then went about collecting stones with which to build a circle around it on the sandy floor. Others had returned with another great load of wood and so the reserve they had now brought great hope to everyone's heart, not only for the promise of long-term warmth, but for the feeling of homeliness it offered. It didn't matter that they were in the middle of nowhere, they were free spirits sharing the warmth of a fire after enduring a desperate and painful journey.

"I'm going to see what food I can find now," Mosi said then. "I'm very hungry, so all of you, from the ship, must be starving."

A crack of thunder rang out as he spoke and a massive surge in rainfall promised to saturate any remaining dry timber, in any place, but it didn't matter, for they had enough and they would certainly use it sparingly just in case.

"Don't you want to wait for the rain?" Layla suggested.

"I don't think this rain is going to stop for a long while," he predicted with a smile. "And I don't know about anyone else, but that makes me very, very happy."

Layla smiled, knowing exactly what this meant also; the promise of freedom, at least for a time. When he darted out again with a few helpers, she limped her way a little closer to the fire and knelt down gently, with her injured ankle out to one side, taking the warmth into her hands. She didn't mind her injury now. Aside from experiencing much worse in all her days, it was enough to be warming herself before a fire in the hinterland, free, and awaiting no command.

The heat on her cheeks and the crackle from the fire brought visions of her daughter to mind, running home after an adventure with her father, with reddened cheeks and a great smile, holding their fishy supper in the air with pride. For Layla, after so long withstanding their separation, sorrow had become a constant friend. There were no great ups and downs, no great waves of depression. A deeper kind of sadness just remained at all times, as if attached to her very soul; omnipresent and acutely felt whenever something triggered her to smile. Every day, she prayed for the time when all would be free and she could search for her family.

One day…

Despite the challenge under rainfall, cloud cover provided extra light, allowing Mosi and his party of gatherers to return with cattails, strawberries, milk thistle, comfrey for wounds, asparagus, dandelions, lots of wild onions from the riverbank, and mussels, all of which they delivered in makeshift baskets made from tattered shirts. Mosi and one other, between them, were lucky enough to spear five large, sleepy perches in a shallower part of the stream, making for plenty.

Suddenly, they had a miniature smorgasbord on their hands and felt it such a blessing that no one wanted to appear greedy. It was all laid out as best as they could, using rocks and clothes and lines of sticks, but no one jumped at it, as one might expect from the starving and tired, 39 in all.

Mosi began to crush comfrey leaves inside a curved piece of bark with the blunt end of a stick. Layla knew what he was doing and took it out of his hands.

"Thank you, I can do it," she said. "Go and eat something, sit for a while. I'll make enough for everyone."

Mosi didn't hesitate for too long. He took a deep breath and tried to relax a little, which proved to be a great challenge after fleeing in desperation for so long, even with the good cleansing he had just received from the storm.

One with the most fishing experience volunteered to chuck all the mussels and clean and prepare the perch, since they only possessed one knife, and as she cut the flesh into strips, helpers collected and skewered the pieces onto sticks ready for the fire. Onions were then lined around the outer edge, where coals quickly formed just inside the ring of stones, and asparagus laid over the warm rocks. Soon, delicious aromas began to drift up and around the cavern, flooding mouths over with anticipation.

"You remind me of my daughter's father, Montezuma," Layla reminisced, after watching Mosi hand out the comfrey poultices she had prepared. He still hadn't eaten anything, yet he was also waiting for some of the fish. "He's a hunter, not a warrior, but like you, he's always defending and providing and caring for people. All the best of human qualities."

Mosi responded only with a modest smile.

"Do you have a family?" she dared to ask; it was always a precarious question.

"Somewhere," he answered with great yearning.

Layla could only assume his tentative mind. "Sorry, if you don't want to talk about it."

Mosi shook his head, breathing in deeply, "I don't mind."

"Sometimes, it hurts more than others," she empathized. "But I like talking about my daughter because I feel close to her when I do, and it makes me feel…it makes me sure that I haven't given up on her, you know? After ten years, you have to find a way to accept as well as to hope."

He understood well. "I'm the same, it can bring joy to think about them and it can bring the worst kind of pain. I'd sooner take a whipping than to feel that pain as I have sometimes."

"It breaks the soul into pieces, doesn't it?" she asked, with no need of an answer. "How many children do you have?"

"Just one, Elan, he was four," Mosi said, trying to keep strong for Layla, yet speaking his son's name always brought on a wave of despair. "We were hiding in a place much like this and we survived for so long, but, you know, the slave hunters came, as they always do, dragged my son and his mother, Tamaya, away to…somewhere. I don't even know if they let my son live."

That was enough for Mosi; his own words. Sadness attacked in full force. It was a long time since he had mentioned them, spoken their names aloud, and it fueled that malevolent fire in his heart yet again.

Layla felt responsible for his pain. "Mosi, I'm sorry."

"It's all right," he reassured her. "I never want to forget them. When I am free, I will search forever."

A great crash of thunder sounded, causing everyone to cringe inside their warm nest, anticipating whips and pain, though smiles soon came upon them all again, as they celebrated another great surge in rainfall and thunder thereafter, without flinching at all.

***

Chapter Five
Repercussions

Tanner was all set to send men out again that night, when a storm swept in and a veritable ocean fell down from the skies. As if being mocked from above, the downpour only began once the barns and the shed were already reduced to smoking heaps of charcoal, and then continued relentlessly until the sun's approach could be seen on the horizon.

Pacing the halls all night, Tanner continued to smolder along with the buildings outside, but with latent rage bubbling and stewing in his soul. Six men were still out, searching, and he could only imagine them being forced to haul themselves up all night somewhere undercover, awaiting respite from the maelstrom.

Every so often, he thought of something to say, to voice some abusive and threatening aspiration, but since all others had turned in after leaving the fires in the hands of the cloud makers, he was left alone with his frustrations, swallowing contemptuous words one after the other. They filled his stomach, making him sick, and churned around in his head until he started smashing things involuntarily. First a few vases met with the wall, then a lamp found his boot at high speed, and later, after cutting himself trying to pick up pieces of the vase, he lost his mind for a while longer, until someone woke and stormed out with, "What in hell's name are you doin'! This is the boss's stuff, have you gone mad!?"

Yes, even if temporarily, his answer could only be yes.

The gutters dripped long after dawn. Rivers of water had washed ash and chunks of charcoal all over the grounds, stretching all the way to the steps of the house, leaving dirty scars across marble surfaces. Oddly enough, a few thin trails of smoke still emanated from beneath the ruins, like gentle remnants of the blistering force which destroyed them.

Mitchell only woke when Tanner kicked the bed, which he had fallen into for the rest of the night, after stating he was, "Going to rest for a few minutes."

Tanner shouted at him in blissful slumber, "Get up! How can you sleep!?"

Mitchell leapt to his feet, reeling, expecting immanent doom or something like it, only to find Tanner standing over him, sweating profusely, ever insane with rage.

After that, Tanner stormed out to wake all those still sleeping, only to be surprised to find that Bill didn't wake up, even after his second boot met with his shoulder. The man had wandered off in his delirium to fall unconscious over a bed, leaving his stab wound to bleed dry. In their preoccupation, no one had thought of him and, as a consequence, assisted Elan in exacting his first ever kill.

***

In the late morning, before going home, Del Hickory dropped into town for supplies and quickly found himself wondering why all the townsfolk stared, pointed, and whispered more than usual when he and his men pulled up at the roadside with two long slave wagons packed to the brim and wandered over to the Produce Store. His arrogance could only assume that the growing audience formed for his ever-increasing notoriety, and it wasn't until the store owner, Kevin O'Brien, said a word or two, that Del got wind of there being something more to discover.

Kevin loved nothing more than a good gossip. This event shone out like a bonanza in his hands, and he couldn't believe his luck for being the first to enlighten Del Hickory of his up and coming torment.

By early morning, the bodies of Hickory's men had collected themselves inside an inlet on the north side of town, giving the aristocratic passengers of a riverboat something interesting to talk about for the rest of the day. The sheriff had organized to have them extracted already, but he was still down there at this time, inspecting the bodies.

"I'm sorry to hear about your men, Mister Hickory," Kevin mentioned as he entered the store. "Do they know what happened yet?"

After regarding him curiously, Del looked around to note that all eyes were still aimed his way. "What are you talking about?" he uttered, feeling the hairs stand up on the back of his neck.

"Why, don't you know yet?" Kevin said with hesitance, yet lapping up the fear mounting in Del's eyes.

"I just got back," he stated, with impatience rapidly building. "Don't I know what?"

"Some of your men washed up in the river this morning and…" he hesitated again. "One of your barns was on fire last night. I don't rightly know what happened, but some folks told me they saw it all the way from the north side of town."

Del was still thinking about the dead men when the idea of his barn burning slapped him into action. He turned to direct the men at his side, "Doyle, Will, ride ahead on home, will you, and see what's goin' on."

They left quickly, as Del turned with a sneer, raising one side of his thin mustache, chilling Kevin to the bone. His frozen eyes seemed to grab hold of Kevin's throat and squeeze it, as he tipped-up the front of his wide-brimmed hat to wipe thinned-out grey hair back against his scalp. "I'll be back some other time. Have a pleasant day."

After pulling out again with the wagons, Del stopped at the river where the sheriff and many spectators had gathered, and walked down to the water to see six of his men lined up along the bank. No one stood too close, as all the bodies were bloated, covered in mud and river grass, and the smell drove them all back. Only the sheriff dared to venture up close, and that was with a scarf over his mouth and only a few moments at a time.

Sheriff Larry Downer wasn't at all like his well-respected and loved predecessor, Stanton, and he knew Del Hickory well. Both being ex-army, they found a natural affiliation and often shared stories over a few shots at the club.

"Howdy, Del," he greeted on Del's approach, most concerned.

"Sheriff," Del replied, still gawking in disbelief at the men. The smell hit his nostrils then and made him reach before backing away a few steps.

"I wouldn't get too close," Downer warned him, all too late. "You just gettin' back?"

Del pulled out a handkerchief to cover his nose and mouth. "Yeah. What happened to these boys, Sheriff?"

"Well, they were in the water for a lot of hours," he stated. "They've been stabbed and some had their throats cut. So far, we don't have any witnesses. While we're talking, we also found two men in the parkland upstream a little ways, but they've been dead a lot longer than these fellas. They didn't have any identification on 'em, but I know I've seen 'em talking to you up at the club sometime, so, not now, but I'll get you to take a look at the bodies when you get things sorted out." He looked to Del for a response, but his silence prevailed. "Anyway, there's nothing you can do here right now. I'll sort this out. We can discuss it later. I suggest you get down to your place, Del. I'm hearing all kinds of rumors."

Del nodded, with a mind clearly working overtime, as he headed back to the wagons.

"Oh, Del?" The sheriff called after him. "One last thing. Someone found two of your horses a bit further over yonder," he pointed. "They've got your brandin'. You should pick 'em up on your way home."

He only received another hesitant and worried nod from a most bewildered Del, who stumbled a little on the uneven ground under his feet when he turned to leave again.

***

After his picnic of death with Madeleine, Julian stole the dead men's wallets to discover that they were both in the possession of a check from none other than Del Hickory, and so he checked-into Black Sand Valley Hotel under the false name of Walter Mitten, feeling certain he had become a target.

Being so traumatized immediately after the event, when the hotelier, Barnaby Dixon, questioned him on the origin of his name, he had answered, "I don't know, I only just thought of it." Pleasantly surprised, he was to discover that his host had difficulty hearing and that he needed to raise his voice somewhat to be understood anyhow.

Upon first sight of Del Hickory's name on one of the checks, Julian had to read it again a few times before thwarting denial, for in one of his recent articles, he had singled-out and impeached a number of slave handlers and traders for being unnecessarily brutal, and Del Hickory was one of those he wrote about. Finally, he perceived this as no coincidence, and that it confirmed he was a target, for a good beating at the very least, and if not for Madeleine, both of them would either be floating in the river by now or on their way to the nearest hospital, very worse-for-wear, just as she had deduced.

Madeleine, who are you? What are you? Julian had never seen such skill and speed in the art of hand-to-hand combat; every movement precise and full of subtle intricacies, like the wings of a bird in stunning motion, and all without hesitation. It seemed likely that she didn't need the stick or the sword at all. Was it that she preferred to use it, or perhaps chose to use it in order to ensure a risk-free conquest? He didn't know, of course.

Julian wanted to write his thoughts out, as they resonated well with his current works. While they came with confidence, their deaths were sealed from the moment they decided to attack. Somehow, she saw it coming, long before a threat was even made, and although she gave the men one last chance to simply walk away, they heeded not and, for the dear price of wickedness, they paid.

While pondering these ideas, Julian was struck with an idea; that Madeleine may always be so cryptic and ambiguous regarding her knowledge of the Guardians because she not only knew them well, but also received combat training from them. The more he kneaded this notion, the more sense it made and he wondered, due to his own actions, if he had brought trouble upon Madeleine, which she may have otherwise avoided, and, by association, made her a target also. He could only hope that she wasn't seen with him.

Del Hickory's going to think I killed his men.

Although Madeleine saw the checks before she left, Julian had no idea how well she knew of Del Hickory's violent reputation, and it frustrated him that they weren't to see each other for a couple days. There was no way to warn her, when the plan was for her to leave a note for him at the hotel when she had time to see him, and he only knew that she wasn't staying with her mother, so this left him with nothing but himself to worry about. This, he did with ease.

Later in the morning, from somewhere within a frenzy of thought, came an idea to disguise himself, and it was fortunate that he decided to head uptown to find what he wanted because he might have bumped right into Del Hickory himself if he had headed downtown instead.

Being well-known for wearing a short top hat in the streets, Julian's first stop was the general store to pick up a tartan beret and, although he didn't smoke, while in the same street, he obliged the sudden urge to buy a pipe and subsequently held it awkwardly in his mouth wherever he went. As it slipped from side to side, he was forced to keep adjusting it with his hands, making it obvious to smokers and non-smokers alike that he was, for whatever reason, pretending to use a pipe; not to mention its pristine condition and that it never once bellowed any smoke. His presence would have surely been far less conspicuous without it. Nonetheless, he endured with the farce throughout his shopping trip and, after hearing no news about the death of Hickory's two men but everything about six new bodies found this morning, the butterflies in his stomach gave birth to thousands.

Given the circumstances, an important one being that Madeleine knew not the alias he used and would inevitably leave a message at reception for Julian Winters not Walter Mitten, all he could do was attempt to work on his book until Madeleine came to see him and hope that she didn't come across anyone with ill intentions.

Upon re-entering the hotel, Barnaby didn't immediately recognize him.

"Welcome to Black Sand Hotel," he said brightly. "Barnaby Dixon at your service."

Julian took the pipe out his mouth to speak and also removed his beret. "No, Mister Dixon, it's me, Julian, I mean, Walter. Walter Mitten. I checked-in last night if you remember."

"Oh, he-he, I didn't recognize you with your costume on," he said, delighted. "Good one."

"What do you mean costume?" Julian contended. "This is my hat and my old pipe."

Barnaby snatched the pipe out of his hand, surprisingly fast for his age and fragility, to inspect it more closely. "Mister, if this is your ol' pipe, then I'm a pickled radish."

"I like to keep it clean, is all," Julian mumbled in defense, snatching it back.

Barnaby didn't hear him. "You goin' to one of 'em masquerade parties?" he supposed.

"What?" Julian's mind was still on his questionable disguise, and overrun with emergencies, so it took some time to comprehend Barnaby's question.

"With your costume," Barnaby elaborated. "Like a costume party folks have on occasion."

Julian understood now but just shook his head, staring blankly.

Barnaby was both amused and a little befuddled. "Well, it ain't my business none-the-how. How do you like your room anyway?"

Julian hesitated, hoping to answer as politely as possible, since the hotel had lived up to its reputation well for having small rooms, for being dingy in general, and Julian could hardly deny the rumor after experiencing it for himself. "It's…adequate."

"Well, don't go all crazy with the commendations now," Barnaby responded, with his wayward eyebrows high in the air.

"No, it's fine," Julian backpedaled. "I was hoping for something larger, but it's fine."

Barnaby huffed a little but finally let it go, in the most part, or pretended well to do so.

"Has anyone left a message for me, by the way?" Julian asked then, thankful to have thought of a subject change. "Or for…anyone?"

***

While the remnants of his men stood in fear, awaiting verbal lashings, Del stepped down from the wagon and proceeded to spin around and around on the spot, with astonishment washing over him in giant, unending waves. His hat flew off in the process, but he kept spinning with his hands on his head, waiting to wake up from the nightmare.

Mitchell ran to pick up his hat, only to have it thrown back at him violently as Del met face-to-face with his anger. More frightening was the sudden quiet and deliberate tone he adopted.

"What happened here?" he asked calmly, yet utter rage building within became palpable very quickly, and none of the men wanted to answer.

Doyle answered for them, upon which they all realized they should have answered for themselves, for Doyle's summary lacked the begging and pleading in which they would have soaked each and every word.

"Apparently, Tanner and Mitchell bought two young slave women when they went to the market for you," he said bluntly. "One of them took Tanner's eye out, set all the slaves free, and burned your barns down."

"B-boss," Mitchell began. "It's not—"

Del cut him off, as his rage peaked and he let out an almighty roar which lasted as long as his breath would allow. "Shut up!"

He panted heavily then, allowing for the sudden lack of oxygen, while spinning around again, waving his hands at the destruction all about. "Are you trying to tell me that a couple of slave girls did all of this!" he screamed. "Where are they!?"

Again, none were quick to answer, but Tanner somehow found the courage. "We haven't found them yet."

"What!?" Del's face turned bright red then.

"B-but some of the boys are still out, looking," Mitchell added with a positive bent. "We haven't given up."

"You haven't given up!? Haven't given up!?" Del repeated, then laughed hysterically for a good long while before coughing and speaking again with much sarcasm. "So the men are still out searching, are they, Mitch? And where exactly are they searching, do you think?"

"Well...I don't know at this time," Mitchell confessed.

Del laughed briefly again. "Don't know at this time. Genius! And what have you been doing all this time while they were out, looking?"

"I had to fix my eye," Tanner said in defense, as if it would bring about immunity for him alone.

"I was out, looking," Mitchell answered. "But Bill got stabbed so I had to help him home, then...I rested...for a bit."

"Rested?" Del suddenly calmed again. All present knew this wasn't a sign of good tidings. "Did you have a nice little nap then, Mitch?"

Mitchell almost nodded in reply, but knew this was like putting his head inside a bear trap. He could only offer, "I'll go out looking again now, boss, and for the others. Don't worry, we'll find them all."

Del's rage heightened again. "You idiots couldn't find your own asses! How could you lose all the slaves?" He spun around then, pointing to the wagons. "I've got 50 more in those wagons and nowhere to put 'em! Nothin' to feed 'em! Nowhere to store the harvests! I don't give a damn about your two runaways! How's it going to help me to find them? Huh? How!? I know more than you and I wasn't even here! The men ain't out looking for your girlfriends! They're all lying dead in the river! You idiots! We're supposed to be setting up shop to fulfill a contract for the army! Now we can't do squat!"

He had much more to say but rage, in its completeness, somehow demanded silence for the time being, and he stormed into the mansion instead. Tanner and Mitchell were too shocked by the news of the dead men to find any words to say to each other. None of the men knew what to expect thereafter and, until they heard Del yelling again inside the mansion, they had forgotten about the condition of the house with filthy footprints, blood spatters, and smashed items littering tiles and carpet. They only remembered Bill, and looked to each other, startled, when they heard Del shouting, "Get up! I said get up, you idiot!"

The ranting and raving went on for a while longer then, until Del returned with a stock whip in hand, the weight of which he knew all too well. "Do any of you even know that Bill is dead!?"

No one said a thing. His men also knew Del's whip well, having witnessed many times their boss's keen use of it on the slaves and often celebrated his refined skills. At this point, all feet were glued to the ground.

"Boys," he said to Will and Doyle as he rolled the whip out to its full length and readied himself. "If these two move, cut both their throats open."

Either Doyle or Will would have done it without hesitation, Mitchell and Tanner knew it. They were both large men, experienced in all kinds of violent ways, and their expressions hardly changed from that of hatred because of it.

Del pointed the handle of his whip at Tanner and Mitchell. "Take your shirts off," he demanded.

"Boss…?" Mitchell uttered, as both he and Tanner hesitated. "What are— ?"

"All right, cut their throats," Del interrupted.

Doyle moved to comply, but paused when Mitchell raised his hands in compliance, stating, "Wait! All right!"

Tanner said nothing. He wasn't as hopeful at this point that any kind of reprieve was coming their way and took his shirt off when Mitchell finally did as he was told.

"It's your throats cut or a good whippin'," Del ensured. "And I'm not even gonna tie you up. You're just gonna turn around, stand still, and take it like good little idiots. Got it? And when I'm done, you're gonna start work and you're not stoppin' until I have me two new barns and one new shed. Got it!?"

Del wasn't one to make idle threats. Long before his heavy whip stopped coming down, both men wished they had opted for the throat-cutting instead. Each lash came emphasized with an abusive word or two and, by the time Del vented the better part of his rage, the men lay fetal in the ash-ridden dirt, taking additional lashings to their legs and arms.

After that, Del was extremely sweaty, and used the wetness to slick strands of his fine hair back over his head. The shredded men moaned unendingly, and they were only moving slightly by that time, like sluggish red and black worms squirming in the mud.

"Well," Del said, most pleased to have exhausted his temper. "That felt good. Right, now what are we gonna do with all these slaves?"

***

First thing in the morning, Misae gathered all the people together to instruct them on what to do in the case of outsiders coming to the property. Having been surprised once already by their unwanted visitors of yesternight, it was Misae's aim never to be surprised again, so she made everyone aware that when the brass bell at the house sounded, they were to take their predesignated positions and go about looking like real slaves at work.

Misae's brief but instructional, full-dress rehearsal was meant to be a serious one, yet it quickly turned humorous when Jimmy, with his lithe frame and harmless smile, did his best impersonation of an aggressive, demanding slavedriver while more successfully bringing repeated laughter upon every new take.

"What?" Jimmy asked at one time, genuinely disappointed in his performance. "Isn't that what they do?"

Misae was very amused by this time, especially upon seeing Jimmy's plaintive face. "No, Jimmy," she giggled. "It's not like that at all. If only that were the worst of it. But it doesn't matter, I think everyone knows what to do now, yes?"

After receiving amused affirmations from all, Misae turned to Jimmy. "Thank you, Jimmy, and don't worry it will work out fine."

Jimmy smiled, finally, upon hearing a carriage approach the gate and ran over to take a look. The signal for the coast being clear was a long whistle, so Jimmy let one fly before opening the gates for Sherman.

Although they hadn't slept much at all, Madeleine and Annabel decided to return to Riverside in the morning, after a short meeting with the queen and

Guardians, Ky Mani, and Jalen. Victor was inclined not to make any more deliveries to Riverside until things blew over, and so he came along with nothing but himself, and Madeleine and Annabel came disguised as Vivian and Penelope Piper to ensure the integrity of their masquerade; knowing also that these false identities could bring them close to the enemy without suspicion, whereas Madeleine and Annabel could not, in most circumstances anyhow. Victor's reason for being at Riverside could be to talk business with Vivian, plus he could also hide in the house and not be seen at all. Jimmy and Sherman were not well-known like Victor, but they were known, however, to help out a lot of people, so the purpose for their presence could easily be justified.

No one knew exactly what might eventuate after the Guardians' secret endeavors of the night, and so they felt it more prudent to be out and amongst it all with ears and eyes open rather than to hide away, as hiding in plain sight proved more effective anyhow.

Both Misae and Jimmy were surprised and delighted to see Tamaya and Elan exit the carriage first, followed closely behind by Victor, Madeleine, and Annabel.

"Finally found each other, I see," Jimmy stated happily. Tamaya's smile hadn't waned since she saw Elan for the first time, and she merely broadened it in reply.

Victor and Sherman were still compiling the whole story together in their heads, after being inundated with information on the way over, but they were quick to catch up after so many successful years of deception and cover-ups, and it was fortunate for all that they were so well-organized because it wasn't long before Del Hickory himself unexpectedly rolled up the driveway with two wagon-loads of slaves.

Being so cumbersome, the wagons' approach was slow, and so after the bell was rung, everyone had plenty of time to get into their places, ready for the first real take after only one morning of planning and rehearsal.

Despite their efforts, it was just Del himself who entered the gates. He left Doyle and Will back at the house, to ensure that the men went straight to work, and came to see Vivian with his drivers. Both Madeleine and Annabel were quick to adopt their respective characters.

Victor and Sherman took the dogs and stayed inside the house, and Misae, along with everyone else, went about working as a slave under Jimmy's supervision.

"Good day, Mrs. Piper," Del greeted them, with something like a smile, removing his hat respectfully. "Miss Piper."

"Good day, sir," they both replied with their best southern accents.

"Due to the negligence of my men," he continued. "I'm in a bit of a pickle, and I wondered if we could come to some arrangement whereby you might be able to assist me and I would, of course, compensate you for your trouble."

"I'm happy to help if I can, Mister Hickory," Madeleine offered. "Does this have something to do with a fire at your place? I heard a rumor this morning."

"I thought I smelt smoke last night," Annabel added.

"Yes, unfortunately," he nodded with remorse. "My barns burned down last night and I just got back today with the slaves I bought. I got nowhere to keep them now, so I thought, if you had the space, I could kind of agist, er, if you will, my slaves with you and pay you a fee, I don't know, per day or…" his words faded out, upon noting that she began to think deeply, potentially formulating a solution.

"Hmmm," Madeleine sounded, after a suspenseful pause. "Sounds like a lot of counting money and fluffing around. Tell you what, why don't we just make this easy for both of us? You're in a pickle, but you're in luck. I did some trading yesterday and I haven't been to the bank yet, so why don't I just buy your slaves outright, right now, then when you're ready, you can just buy more slaves. That way, we don't have to—"

"Why, Mrs. Piper," he interrupted, most surprised. "That's mighty generous of you. I don't know what to say, that just solves my whole problem in one fell swoop. I'd be most humbly in your debt." So relieved he was, for his next plan was to send his men to ask some farms on the west side, but he didn't believe they would find a solution there. After that, his only option was to return to the southern markets in the hope of selling the slaves again.

"Not at all, neighbor," Madeleine said modestly. "I can easily sell them on, and don't you worry, I know how to make a profit from those hillbillies out in the west." She raised a hand in the air then. "Now, I'm not planning to take advantage of you, neighbor. I know you get cheap prices in the south, so I can probably pay you piece for piece. I'll make my profit on the other end." Madeleine smiled with a little greed then. "How many are there and what did you pay?"

Del was still in awe. After the morning he'd endured, Vivian was a golden chariot, however he feared the numbers would be too high. "There's 50 of them," he cringed. "Men and women, but all in good health. I paid seven-and-a-half-thousand in all."

Madeleine pondered for a moment, "That's—"

"One-fifty on average," he said, solving the calculation in her mind.

"Not bad at all," she exclaimed, seeming most impressed. "In that case, you've got yourself a deal, neighbor. Are they shackled?"

Momentarily stunned, he could only nod.

"So bring them on in," Madeleine said, pointing to an area just inside the gates. "Put them over there. My boys will transport them out of here later. I'll be back in a minute with your money."

By the time Madeleine returned, the last few slaves were joining the rest inside the gates. She handed the payment over to Del, who didn't count the contents of the bag, but smiled with admiration as best as he could, hindered by nasty frown-lines.

"Count it if you like," Madeleine offered. "I counted it twice."

He shook his head upon leaving. "I trust you, Mrs. Piper, and I can't explain my gratitude. I wouldn't even care if it's a whole lot short, and I hope I haven't inconvenienced you too much."

"Don't you worry about me," she assured. "I'll make it worth my while. You just think about getting your place all fixed up now."

Once Del left and the gate was closed, all went silent, while Jimmy peered through the porthole to watch as the empty wagons pulled away.

"Not yet," he prompted, waiting for the wagon to reach a safe distance. "They're not far enough away yet...not yet...not yet. Okay."

When he had given the word, Madeleine and Annabel removed their wigs and, together with everyone in sight, including Victor and Sherman, once they returned from the house, went to remove the shackles from all the slaves. They were all, of course, in shock to see all existing slaves work without instruction after removing their own shackles and with unrestrained smiles of excitement growing rapidly amongst them.

The new arrivals then watched in amazement as Misae approached Annabel and Madeleine to place her arms around both of them and share her joy, while they reciprocated with equal enthusiasm. To make the scene and the sudden turnaround all the more shocking, they had already resigned to the horror in believing they were bound for Del Hickory's farm.

Having stood in a similar position herself, Misae wasted no time in explaining circumstances to the people, to ask of injuries, and to show everyone where to get cleaned up, well-clothed, and well-fed.

In the midst of it all, it was realized that, in essence, Sanura had freed another 50 slaves by the simple act of reducing Del's barns to ashes.

***

After the early morning meeting, once Sanura and Talia had relinquished all the details they could possibly remember regarding their journey to Del Hickory's farm and of their escape to Blue Falls, they were completely overwhelmed by all they had experienced since arriving in the middle of the night. They understood the importance of the meeting, and the low light helped them to avoid getting too distracted by the many wonders they knew existed in every direction while walking from the Entrance, where they had slept, down The Books for the meeting.

Given the structure and thoroughness of the event, it was made stunningly clear to both of them that they hadn't stumbled upon a rabble of escapees hidden away in the mountains somewhere, but, instead, a highly organized and astute group of people; a comprehensive resistance.

Since from the moment they entered, right through the treatment process and up until the meeting, they were never imposed upon with noise, or questions, or demands of any kind; it was a daunting surprise to be interacting on such an intense level suddenly, where the lack of attention to detail could mean the difference between life or death for one or many.

The queen had said to them most graciously, "Usually, we would give you more time to settle in, but we feel acting quickly for the slaves you freed is vital."

They didn't need to be convinced, of course, and after all they had endured, answering questions for the people who ensured their safely was not in the least begrudged.

Once the meeting was over and a plan set in place, the queen stood and said, "We'll meet again soon. We're going to leave now and let the Guardians have a meeting alone before those going to Riverside have to leave."

She stood then with Isi, Jalen, and Ky Mani, but paused while the others left. Sanura and Talia stood to leave along with them, but Lesedi stopped them in their tracks and spoke their names while placing an amulet case into each of their hands. "Talia. Sanura. I said this is a meeting of the Guardians. It would be rude not to stay since you're already here. Elan has only just gone to sleep, I'm told, so you won't be seeing him. We will have a formal announcement and celebration when things have settled down again."

She didn't say any more, as the remaining Guardians had already been informed, but sent a knowing smile around the circle just as Annabel held out Misae's amulet and placed it in her hands. For a few moments, she regarded it with the deepest of thoughts, then looked to Annabel with a proud smile and placed it over her head as she left.

Both new arrivals looked from their amulet cases to each of the Guardians until realizing they were not the brunt of some cruel joke but had, in fact, walked into and sat at their table of destiny with all the proof around them in stunning glory.

Although she would never have guessed it, Sanura somehow believed it already, yet Talia needed convincing.

"Is it true?" she asked.

All the Guardians drew their amulets out and into full view.

After glancing over them all, Talia looked to Sanura adoringly, yet pensively, and said, "Sanura is most certainly a Guardian, she could have gone, but she came back for me. I just gave up."

"Not in the end," Sanura argued. "You found your strength."

"Any of us can be broken," Oni interjected.

Talia only shook her head then, confessing, "I was weak and I made things so much harder for Sanura."

Oni inhaled so deeply in that moment that all eyes turned to her, yet she was looking only at Talia when she finally voiced her thoughts: "It is a trait of the Guardian to know and see themselves so well."

Long after this conversation, Talia still struggled with disbelief, not only for the Guardian revelation, but for her sudden freedom and in a place which even her most insane imaginings would struggle to create.

When the other Guardians had left, they fell asleep at The Books for a short time just before dawn, after which Talia had woken with a start, sitting up abruptly, and it wasn't until she saw Sanura sleeping soundly next to her that she remembered where she was and resigned to being safe again. Yet, still hounded by feelings of inadequacy, and although she gave it her best shot, there would be no more sleeping after that, so she wandered quietly over to the edge of The Books to look out over the bottom half of Blue Falls for the first time in the daylight.

A moment later, she stood, cupping hands over her mouth, berating herself for the cry she let out when first struck by the vision and then quickly checked to ensure she hadn't woken Sanura. Quite a number of people were also sleeping in various places about The Books at that time, but no one seemed to have been disturbed, so she turned her gaze back to the wonder.

The storm hadn't quite subsided yet at that time, so great curtains of rain still fell from the ceiling, spraying a fine mist out over The Lake. Although she couldn't see The Falls themselves from where she stood, and even in the early light, the blue glow above the cascades could be seen clearly, growing brighter in every new moment. While lost in this vision, Talia was suddenly startled by an arm belonging to Sanura wrapping around her waist unexpectedly.

"Sorry," Sanura whispered when she jumped, "I didn't mean to scare you." She placed her head on Talia's shoulder then and, in her half-sleep, began taking in the view. Most abruptly, she raised her head again and gasped much the same as Talia had only moments before, and Talia almost laughed aloud.

"Am I still dreaming?" Sanura uttered.

Talia first thought the same. "No, it's real, if you can believe it."

"I think I need to wake up first."

Many silent minutes followed while they stood together, watching early-morning risers and all-nighters go about their business, children running to The Lake for a swim or to catch a prize for breakfast, and all manner of occupations which they could only imagine in such an enormous space.

"I want to see everything, all at once," Sanura admitted in that moment.

Talia had asked her to see the Hall of Dreams with her, so they first headed back to the Entrance again to walk through the tunnel and back and, although Sanura felt it pointless, she too wanted to see the Hall at least, and also felt the need to support her friend.

"I'm so very sorry," Annabel had told them, "But they're not here. If they were, you would be on the walls or in one of the Book of Dreams. I looked long ago and I look every time a new wagon arrives."

Annabel gave them no reason to hope that their parents were in Blue Falls, and Sanura was thankful for her direct assurance. False hope, she believed, became exhausting, and in the long run, it was much less painful to confront unwanted circumstances and to adjust the mindset accordingly.

Talia's approach proved more emotional; wanting to dream for as long as she could and to see the evidence for herself before accepting that she had come upon the place of myths and legends without them. Her heart had become as hollow as the tunnel itself by the time they came out again, and the experience itself hushed their journey down to The Ledge and The Falls, where they sadly drank-in the beauty for some time before making their way to The Hotpot.

They had eaten earlier in the day, but when they came down through The Nook on their way to The Falls, they were close enough to the Hotpot for an armada of delicious aromas to bombard them for the rest of the way there. After fasting for so long over the previous two days, their stomachs shrank considerably and filled all-too-quickly in their waking hours but, after a solid walk, energy levels revealed their true hunger, and it wasn't long before they found their way to the source of the smells which had slowly reeled them in all morning.

Talia was amazed at how little trouble her leg wound had given her so far during their walk. She noticed also that the swelling in her lips and cheeks together with Sanura's swollen lip had reduced considerably, and she commented to Sanura, "I can't believe how good my leg is already today."

"Same with my face, and my hand," Sanura agreed.

"They're amazing. Artetha and…Awinita." She struggled to remember. "So many names! Everyone I've met so far seems to be amazing in some way, and so kind."

Sanura could only agree.

"How about here?" Talia suggested, as they came out of a short path between two high boulders, somewhere inside the maze-like terrain of The Hotpot, to discover a hut built in to a niche in a stone wall. To allow for its uneven foundations on either side, the roof was made intentionally slanted, and the flat surface of existing stone below it became the counter at its front. On a sign mounted above the counter were the elegant, hand-painted words, Three Sisters And Fry.

Only a small number of people occupied the little hideaway at this time, and if they weren't eating, they were collecting from overhanging berry or grape vines, which seemed to fill the space like no other in Blue Falls, from what they had seen of it so far anyhow.

In this area of The Hotpot, the bowls of those eating were filled with offerings from either Three Sisters And Fry, or from another hut across the way dubbed The Catch-Cook. Since one of the golden rules of Blue Falls was that if you wanted to eat fish, you had to spear it for yourself, the latter hut offered a place where budding cooks who enjoyed experimenting with fish recipes could make meals of other people's catches for them. So the cooks who worked inside this hut were forever changing, yet the hut itself was never unmanned for there were so many people who loved to cook, to combine the rich herbs grown in Blue Falls with the many shared seasoning recipes to grace their freshly snagged perch, cod, or salmon.

When Sanura saw the name, Three Sisters And Fry, she halted them both and stared, as if she'd seen a frightening apparition of some kind.

"What's wrong?" Talia asked, wondering immediately if there were cause for concern, but then Sanura abruptly revealed her excitement.

"My mother used to make me Three Sisters all the time…and fry bread," she was struck with a sudden craving then. "Does that mean they have fry bread too?"

Talia smiled, somewhat with relief, and it warmed her heart that Sanura remembered something of her mother, thinking until this moment that she may have decided to block family from her thoughts entirely. "Let's ask," she said with equal excitement.

As they approached the counter, the woman standing over a large pot inside heard them and spun around. Her smile came about immediately. "Hello! Come for some of Ami's grub?" she asked, tightening the light-green bandana which she used to keep strands of thick grey hair out of her cooking.

"Hello," they both replied but didn't know what else to say because, both last night and this morning, food was simply brought to them without a request.

The woman's name was Amitola. She wasn't the only one to cook at the Three Sisters And Fry, but the most famous by far, for it was her creation, and she had lived in Blue Falls since its first year, so she could tell the newcomers in an instant; always sheepish and reluctant to ask questions.

"So, what have we got?" she asked, saving them from awkwardness. "Two bowls with some fry bread?"

Sanura suddenly felt like she might cry. "Yes…! Please."

Amitola chuckled heartily. She wasn't at all offended by Sanura's sudden brashness, in fact, the excitement brought her only joy. As she brought the bowls to the counter, Sanura's eyes were stuck to them all the way, and Talia appreciated the moment immensely. "Be careful," she warned Amitola. "She might bite your hand off."

This jab broke Sanura from her trance and she looked up to Amitola with nothing but love in her eyes. "Thank you!" She picked up the fry bread then. "It's still warm!"

"Just made it," Amitola revealed, still chuckling to herself.

Suddenly, Sanura was struck with an idea. "We don't have anything to give you," she said with disappointment, suggesting, of course, that they should pay somehow for what they both, Sanura especially, felt was a great gift.

"Child," Amitola replied, shaking her head as if she had also been blessed. "Your excitement for my cookin' is worth more than all the gold and jewels in The Cave put together. Besides, nobody pays for anything in Blue Falls. They should've told you that."

"They did," Talia admitted. "We're just not used to—"

"I know," she interrupted, already understanding. "You'll get used to it soon enough, don't worry, it's the same for everyone."

Sanura was already eating. The first thing she did was to dip one corner of the bread into the broth and bite into it impatiently, and it wasn't until quite a few spoonful later that she finally spoke. "You know," she muttered, still chewing with relish. "My momma could have made this."

"We've got an abundance of vegetables and herbs here," Amitola told them. "But I still keep the recipe simple because that's what the people remember. It's what they want, I've discovered, you know, the simple recipes we make in hard times when we don't have a whole lot to work with."

Sanura wanted to remark but her mouth was too full, so she just nodded eagerly and mumbled in agreement, "Mm hm."

Talia was a little less wolflike in her approach to the meal, but she enjoyed it immensely all the same, and she was so distracted watching Sanura that she ate at a snail's pace. In the end, Sanura had finished her second helping before Talia finished her first.

Because she wasn't conscientious in keeping up with every piece of news, and both Talia and Sanura had only pocketed their amulets for feeling it was too soon to feel comfortable wearing them for all to see, Amitola had no idea she was in the presence of two Guardians. They both sensed this from the beginning and were happy to maintain their incognito status just to have a humble and quiet experience.

When it was done, they sat for a good while longer to enjoy the peaceful niche they discovered, which would surely become a favorite HotPot meeting place, as it did for many who propagated the now-common phrase, Meet you at Ami's.

After thanking Amitola at least a hundred times, they stood with heavy bellies and left their short-term cocoon.

"Do you want to go and see Crystal Nest now?" Sanura suggested, as they walked out of the east end of The HotPot into an eye-opening view of the northern orchards, the Lake, and the tree line beyond it. "And we can see more of The Lake on the way. I had a dream last night after they told us about Crystal Nest."

"What dream?" Talia was curious, for she was reminded of her own. "I had a dream too."

"I dreamt I was in a maze made of crystal," she shared. "I was trying to find my way out."

Talia made an assumption, "Was it scary?"

"No, it was beautiful," she recalled. "And when I came out of the maze, it didn't matter how fast I ran, I just ran faster and faster, growing stronger and stronger, like a cheetah."

"I wonder what it could mean," Talia pondered aloud.

Sanura shrugged. "I don't know, but it was magical. What was your dream?"

"I dreamt Annabel threw me a sword and I chopped the heads off the two men who bought you and me," she remembered.

This surprised Sanura greatly, and she didn't know exactly how to feel about it or what to think of the casual way in which Talia shared her dream. "Whoa, what a dream," is all she could think to say.

"After Crystal Nest, can we go and meet Ky Mani?" Talia asked then, as if it were an extension of her dream.

While she didn't think Talia would be so keen, Sanura also wanted to begin with Ky Mani's teachings immediately but hadn't said anything yet for the fear of unnecessarily rushing Talia and for being disinclined to leave her alone while she practiced.

"It's up to you, but I want to start training right away," she added.

Sanura smiled inwardly for how her friend had already healed enough to find the inner strength to think about discovering her potential as a Warrior Guardian. "All right. I thought you'd never ask," she responded, all the while imagining that if she possessed Annabel and Madeleine's skills at Hickory's farm, she never would have run. Instead, she would have gone after them, one by one, until none of them were breathing, and then burnt it all down.

***

Although the storm had long since passed, raindrops still made their way down from the canopy to the forest floor, leaf by leaf, sliding through an endless maze of tiny green steps.

Mosi heard Layla sigh as she turned her face up into a ray of sunlight. She wasn't smiling exactly, but it was the first time he had seen her face without a frown and so, he fueled her positivity, recognizing that she had already done this for him somehow.

"Sunshine after the rain, there's nothing like it, huh?" he proposed.

"I haven't been in a place like this since… Oh, I can't even remember." She took one more deep breath then, before returning to the task at hand, that being the spearing of another fish. After hoping for salmon, she had caught two perch, but wasn't about to give up. With so many people to feed, it wouldn't go to waste.

Just before dawn, while still blessed by the cover of the storm, four of the less fatigued, one being Mosi, were sent in different directions on reconnaissance. When they returned with favorable news, all those but for the worst of the injured and the completely exhausted crept out to collect whatever provisions they could, throughout the morning, while the first team of volunteers kept watch from distant posts. Their plan was to stay all day then move further north under the cover of night and only move from their hideaway in the daylight if they knew hunters were on the way.

Mosi carved away at pine branches at the edge of the stream as he watched Layla, holding one of his freshly-cut spears in the air, waiting for prey to swim across the shallower places, admiring her tenacity to overcome the pain in her ankle and to fend for herself.

"You said I reminded you of your Montezuma," he remembered. "Well, you remind me of my Tamaya. Her leg could fall off and she'd keep going. But still, she's a gentle spirit."

149

His words found a greater smile in Layla, and in that moment, he became aware of his unexpected but apparent sense of duty to protect her, even though she was clearly self-reliant. Being completely devoted to the mother of his child, he knew his wasn't a romantic attraction, yet all the same, he couldn't deny his innate feeling of protectiveness.

"My daughter keeps me going," she said. "I just imagine she's here with me now, telling me why I'm failing to catch more fish, like she did when she was, oh, seven. Even at that age, she was running around, collecting food and medicines, trying to impress her father with all she knew about the forest and the rivers."

"I dream the same," he confessed, retaining a warm smile for Layla's story. "I was actually just imagining that I was teaching my boy how to survive in this place, how to shape a spear and catch a fish. It's like I'm creating false memories to fill that empty space with something."

Layla understood this mechanism, all too well, and sometimes, felt it necessary to take stock of her imagination to be sure she was never in denial about her circumstances or lost somewhere between fantasy and physical reality. Yet, as always, she found a smile whenever her daughter came to mind.

"You know, I was a warrior," he reminded Layla. "But we wanted Elan to have a different life, a more peaceful life, you know, once we were free, which is why we chose his name because it means friendly." A brief chuckle showed itself before he continued, thinking how ridiculous it was to believe one could suggest another's life path. "It was silly, but we thought he might perhaps be a healer or something with a name like Elan, but when you bring a child into a world like this, who knows what they will be."

"Believe it or not, my daughter's name means kitten," Layla said, enjoying distant memories.

Mosi chuckled. "Why did you choose this name? What is it?"

"She was born in a stable in the middle of a storm," Layla told him. "Maybe that's why I feel very close to her right now. After the storm we just went through, I was thinking of giving birth to her. Just before I went into serious labor that night, a tiny, drenched kitten crawled out from under the timber floorboards and curled up next to me to keep warm. All my screaming didn't even scare it away." She took a deep breath of yearning then but found an inner smile all the same. "So I called my girl Sanura, my little kitten."

***

With the atrocious condition of 50 new arrivals as evidence, it was clear that Del Hickory's idea of a slave in 'good health' was one who could still walk from one point to the next, or at least hobble there awkwardly. As the line of patients awaiting medical attention steadily grew longer, Tamaya became more and more resolute in her decision to honor the promise she made to the Princess and return with Elan to be a Healer at Riverside.

Almost all the damaged were too shy or fearful to immediately accept anything offered to them, and the only one, Misae noticed, who wasn't reluctant at all to utilize all surrounding resources, was somehow doing nothing for himself. He joined Shenandoah in helping others one after another to the showers or to the food baskets, encouraging them to eat and ensuring they were safe. Earlier on, she saw his eyes on her and on her trusted company, studying, analyzing, and evaluating the true circumstances for himself and for the other slaves. The energy in his great, muscled frame seemed inexhaustible, and it wasn't until the long line of patients neared its end that Misae found the chance to see to the deep lacerations in his back.

"I'm all right, my Princess," he answered, when she called him over. "There are others who—"

"These people here are the last to treat, and it wasn't a request," she interrupted, with a sternness which made him swallow and also ignited a look of surprise between Tamaya, Madeleine, and Annabel. "Sit," she demanded, pointing to the chairs before the Healers.

He sat, of course, without another word of objection.

Annabel smiled, shaking her head, and leaned across to whisper to Tamaya and Madeleine, "Don't mess with the Princess."

"What?" Misae queried with a grin.

They didn't answer, just chuckled to themselves reservedly and went back to work.

Elan was outside playing with Foxy and Bell, who had steadily become more excitable throughout the day for being out of a cage for so long, for the ocean of friendly attention and, most importantly, for the endless food scraps coming their way, all day and all night it seemed, thanks to the number of people. For them, it was sure they'd fallen into puppy heaven.

From an old sock, packed tightly with strips of hessian and knotted at the end, Elan had made a ball to play with and discovered that every time he kicked it, the dogs would compete to be the one to retrieve it first and bring it back to him. A couple of the younger men joined him in a game where they did their best to keep the ball away from the hounds by kicking it to one another and almost sent the dogs mad in the process, yet they laughed often and the game lent itself to heighten spirits.

Victor had stolen Shenandoah away once pressing matters were all but resolved, to go through the plans for Riverside.

Even after time spent with Annabel and Madeleine, unease soon became apparent in his reluctance to respond to Victor, or to respond openly and honestly. Victor had been in this situation countless times, recognized his symptoms immediately, and reached up to place a hand of friendship on the man's shoulder, to emphasize the encouraging words he was about to speak, but was even more saddened when this action caused Shenandoah to flinch suddenly. While completely understanding his reasons, the idea of being feared by a man twice his size and strength was ridiculous to Victor, and his gentle hand eventually found its mark.

"Nobody's going to turn on you here," he ensured. "You're with friends."

That's all he said in that moment, and it wasn't until he had led Shenandoah most of the way to the south-western wall in front of the river before he spoke again.

"The plan, Shenandoah," he began. "Is to build—"

Shenandoah interrupted with hesitance, "My friends call me Shenan or Shen, they say it's easier…if you want."

"All right, but only if you call me Victor and not sir," Victor proposed. His response was a welcome nod, so he continued, "What we want to do is build two tunnels coming from the barn closest to us. The opening to both tunnels will be the same, but the entrance to one of them will be hidden very well just inside, and this will be the actual tunnel which will pass us here and open up on the other side of the wall next to the river beneath the underbrush. The other tunnel is a decoy and it will turn away from the real tunnel and out into the center of the yard, where another door will open to a small room. As you can see, the trenches have already been dug, so we just need to go a bit further out, dig a hole for the room, secure the walls, cover them with the timber, and then cover the whole thing over to hide it all."

"Why?" Shenandoah asked, looking at the detailed plans in his hands, drawn out by Ky Mani and his team of war strategists.

"Two reasons, Shen," Victor answered. "The first is a meantime idea, in the case we're being watched too closely, or if war comes, we don't have to stop rescuing people. We can still save them without wagons on this side of the valley, which is where most of them will be coming from. When they come here or if we need to quickly hide them here, we can sneak them through the tunnel and up through secluded places to our other place. Everyone can also escape quickly in an emergency, but all that will have to end if we use it for its real purpose. The second reason is to create a decoy because we think they will soon increase the hunt for the ones who've been ruining their plans for a long time now, and even if war doesn't come, they won't stop until they get what they want, or until they've totally annihilated the people and the landscape to make sure the threat is gone. We've got a lot of people here now who want to help, so I don't think it will take a long time to finish it."

"But it's quite a plan," Shenandoah acknowledged after some moments of contemplation. "You must be sure you're going to be hunted. You must know your enemy well."

"Not well enough, but also too well," Victor confessed. "We also plan to place piles of crates and trailers everywhere, which will look like they're full of harvests or ready for the harvest, but, along with the fake tunnel and the underground room, they will all be booby-trapped."

'Booby-trapped?' Shenandoah was surprised by this idea, even though Annabel had already alluded to it.

Victor nodded and smiled, "Sherman acquired a shipment of black powder on the black market. A very large shipment meant for military, a hundred barrels or more. They're coming here, hidden inside deliveries of crates."

While Shenandoah considered all the information he had just accumulated, it became obvious that the people who had freed him were not only super-efficient but seemed to have endless resources at their fingertips. "It's a good plan," he said finally. "I take it that if the time came when you thought it was necessary, you would blow it all up and make it look like the secret underground nest they were looking for was destroyed."

"That's it," Victor confirmed. "They don't know who we are yet, but we've made a lot of enemies, and the ones high up will be looking. They're always looking for resistance."

"From what I hear about the events of last night and today, it sounds like you might have stirred that hornet's nest once again," he dared to suggest.

"Unfortunately, Shen, I don't think we just stirred it," Victor elaborated. "I think we beat it with a stick a few times."

A smile began to creep over Shenandoah when he thought of Del Hickory's barns. "And then, perhaps, set it on fire after that."

Victor chuckled, almost involuntarily. It was no laughing matter, but he clearly saw the relevance and the irony in Shenandoah's remark, so he simply agreed with, "Ah uh."

***

As if frozen in time, Del paused as he lifted a leg to board his carriage, then turned and walked quickly to the west side of the mansion to confirm an empty kennel.

"Where are the dogs?" he asked under his breath, before returning to the center of what used to be the open courtyard between all his buildings, and halted, looking around to all the men who were present the night before. "Where are the dogs?" he repeated, but no one answered. "Where are the dogs!?"

Mitchell and Tanner were put to work from the moment they finally got to their feet, and while they were too delirious to be productive at all, or even slightly effective, Del demanded they work until sundown before allowing them any food or water. Although many hours had passed, the amount of rubbish they moved into a trailer in the meantime was hardly noticeable, for even slight movements caused them additional agony. So when they heard Del ranting about the hounds, they were hardly moved at all, for their suffering was complete. It seemed, for them anyway, that there was no more pain to be had, and they hardly reacted to Del's question. All the other men shrugged.

"You don't even know," he realized, mystified, shaking his head endlessly while looking about the large, ashen piles of destruction, which were once integral pieces of the source of his healthy income.

Del might have stayed to abuse the men again, but he wanted to see two people before the end of the day, the first of which being Sheriff Downer, to discuss the death of his men.

Although he did learn that the two bodies found the previous day were indeed those he hired to teach Julian Winters a lesson in slander, the meeting otherwise proved unenlightening.

"I'm sorry, Del," the sheriff said. "I don't have anything more to go on. I'll see if I can question this Winters fella sometime, but I don't think any author is gonna have the experience to kill the way those two men were killed. It was too clean. The killer knew exactly what he was doing and there's no way Winters could've been responsible for the death of your six men last night. Plus, what do I say to him, oh, Del Hickory sent two men to shut you up for good, did you happen to kill them? He'll see that I know the truth about your plan for him and that I'm not going to do anything about it." After receiving no response from Del, but for his blank face alluding to agreement, he concluded his speech, "After that mother of a storm, there was no point searching the river banks all the way up to who-knows-where for clues, and since your men who survived only got as far up the river as just north of town, we don't even know where your men went before they were killed. If we knew which direction the 24 slaves went, we could organize a search party, but they could've gone to the southwestern hinterland or the northeast. My guess is the north because it's closer and there's more tree cover along the way, but still, it's a lot of land to cover."

As much as he didn't want to admit it, Del knew the sheriff was right in thinking he didn't have much to go on, even though he too believed that it was unlikely two slave girls slayed six men alone. So his next stop was the new army barracks, in the hope to enlist a formidable search party, yet this meeting proved more disappointing than the last.

Lieutenant Colonel Wright kept his secret delight for hearing of Del Hickory's recent losses well-hidden but not his certain dislike for the man.

"I wasn't stationed here to run errands for Del Hickory," he insisted, unconsciously running a hand through his clipped hair which needed no adjustment at all. He placed his hat carefully on the desk and sat as straight as a steel bar, meeting Del's eyes without the feeling of intimidation that most people endured in his place.

Air inside the newly built headquarters held a heavy scent of radiata pine, and the timber floors echoed every footstep of the lower ranks, as they busied themselves about a vacuous space, greatly in need of furnishings.

"I'm well aware of your history of service," he continued, noting Del's lack of argument with surprise. "Including your honorable discharge, but my orders were to award you the sole contract for slave-labor provisions and food supplies, etcetera, to this army, end of story. It doesn't matter now, as it seems clear that you're no longer in a position to keep up your end of the contract. So, we'll have to look for other food suppliers, unless, of course, you think you can rebuild before the end of this week."

"You're being stationed up here to secure the Midlands before the northern regions can get their heels dug in," Del enjoyed telling him, denoting his access to knowledge usually reserved for non-civilians. "I thought you might be interested to know if there was a hidden force somewhere capable of taking out a hundred soldiers and disappearing without a trace. It might be your men floatin' down the river next time."

"You said you lost six men last night," Wright argued. "Oh, and 20-something slaves."

"I did," he agreed. "But last year, a hundred soldiers—"

"Oh, yes-yes," Wright interrupted. "I was briefed on this. 100 men found in the river."

"Well, doesn't it interest you that the mayor and a highly-commended general were killed right before those men and now my men washed up the same?" Del posed, insinuating incompetence.

"My men tell me little girls destroyed your whole operation," Wright retaliated, with perfect timing to crumble Del's composure. "Not some mystical force living in the jungle somewhere."

Del looked about, noting many not-so-well-hidden smiles from all the ranks within earshot. All at once, he recognized exactly where he stood, and that was without any chance of cajoling Wright into doing anything he wanted. "Tell you what, Lieutenant, why—"

"That's Lieutenant Colonel," Wright corrected, as if grinding his heels into solid rock, and he spoke rapidly thereafter, giving Del no time to continue or to interject. "I think your men could have easily been overrun by that many slaves, so maybe you need to hire more suitable men for the job and not look to the army to mop up your mishaps. As far as the hundred dead soldiers are concerned, I'm sure I know more than you. The colonel's operation itself was questionable that night, since he received no orders whatsoever to be out with his men, and it seemed his operation was somehow connected to Chester Flinch, who also washed up at the same time with a bunch of his men. And since the colonel's sword was stuck in Flinch's body, it doesn't take a genius to figure out what might have happened between those two parties, but everyone wants to blame runaway slaves instead of acknowledging the cold hard facts about the people in question. Now I think I've made it clear to you where I stand, Mister Hickory."

Del sneered and his eyes narrowed. He stood then, understanding that Wright couldn't know the impossibility of Flinch and the colonel turning on one another, and spoke as he walked away. "Yes, you have, but I think you should save yourself a lot of time, Lieutenant Colonel, and just ready your men now for when your orders come through."

"What orders?" Wright spat with a large chunk of spite, disbelieving, but Del left without another word.

***

Since many of the new arrivals volunteered to help Misae with the Riverside project, when Tamaya finished treating her last patient, she went around again to collect all the new names in order to discover if they had loved ones in Blue Falls, before committing them to one place or the other. Having streamlined her methods with the first wave of newcomers, it wasn't long before she had recorded all 50 but for the last couple still receiving attention from the Healers.

"Got them all except these two," she informed them happily on approach, referring to the two men sitting before Misae and Tamaya.

After all, the man who Misae had to practically tie down in order to treat, inarguably sustained some of the worst of the wounds they had treated.

She shook her head like a worried mother. "Honestly, how did you think it would be all right just to leave these wounds to themselves. I've spent more time on you than I have on anyone."

156

"I'm sorry, my Princess," he replied earnestly. "I didn't mean to be a burden."

"No, I was saying, you should have been one of the first people to be treated," she elaborated, with more than a hint of disappointment.

Madeleine and Annabel shared a smile while cleaning up nearby, and when Tamaya found a break in conversation to ask the men for their names, Misae's patient answered first, and soon after, Annabel dropped the basin she was drying with a towel, as hers and all present Guardians' stunned eyes fell upon the man.

Tamaya didn't recognize the man's name, so she stood, looking back and forth between them all, trying to imagine the reason for their shock and sudden silence: silence but for the din of Annabel's steel basin hitting the floor like a struck gong and the seemingly endless reverberations which followed.

Annabel and Madeleine had heard his distinctive name for the first time this very morning, and because they thought to speak at the same time, it tended to balk everyone into speechlessness for a long while. Eventually, the man in the spotlight, Montezuma, waited on Misae for explanation, since she was sitting right in front of him and had just finished treating his innumerable wounds, but she could only shrug, even with knowing instinctively that another reunion was soon to take place. She pondered again over the tragedy and the magic which seemed to endlessly befall the Guardians.

"Do you have any children?" Annabel asked finally. "A family?"

The Guardians' reaction had bewildered him, but he managed to find his tongue eventually. "Yes. We have a daughter." He said no more then, until realizing they were waiting to hear names. "My daughter's name is Sanura a—"

Their immediate and obvious reaction to his daughter's name clammed him shut again, and he suddenly found his skin crawling all over. Misae sat back with a hand over her mouth, as Annabel snatched the booklet out of Tamaya's hands.

"Let me see that list," she said, while already going through it. "What markets did you say you came from, Montezuma?"

Misae answered in his place, "Southern markets at the River-Crossing," and when enough of her shock had abated, Misae asked him, "What's her mother's name?"

"Layla," he answered, swallowing very hard. "Do you know them?"

The name Layla was all the Guardians needed for confirmation, and Misae shared a quick smile with the others before turning to Montezuma.

"We know Sanura," she answered. "But her mother is not with her; I'm sorry."

Montezuma, like most, wasn't going to believe it easily, that his daughter was suddenly touchable, and the denial is his face was unmistakable.

Madeleine raised her open palms in question, stating: "Montezuma? Layla? Sanura? What are the chances?"

He barely nodded, as acceptance breached his barriers, yet wasn't sure what to ask first. "Sanura, is she safe and…"

"Yes," Misae confirmed. "She's only just come to us."

"Last night, in fact," Madeleine added.

While listening and reading at the same time, Annabel commented, as if the surprising information she was about to share was neither here nor there. "She's the reason you were all brought over here? She doesn't know it yet, but she accidentally rescued her own father."

In response to Montezuma's obvious confusion, Misae explained, "She's the one who escaped Hickory's farm and burnt the barns down last night."

"And freed more than 20 slaves when she escaped," Madeleine prompted. "So that makes 70-something if we count all of you, oh, and Talia, 70-something plus one."

"Quite a first day," Annabel remarked, still going through the list.

Madeleine laughed aloud and Misae half-giggled before saying with pride, "She also rescued another Guardian, Talia."

"What?" This was too much information for someone who had just rediscovered his daughter's whereabouts. "One of the Guardians?" he uttered.

Misae looked up to the others with the question, Should we tell him? in her eyes, and when unanimous shrugs answered, she told him the more startling news, "Sanura is a Guardian too, Montezuma, she's a Warrior Guardian."

Montezuma barely had time to process this information, when a revelation Annabel experienced at the same time became evident, as she wandered over to the window, suddenly wistful and light, looking through the open sashes to all the people outside.

"What is it, Annie?" Madeleine asked, finally.

Annabel turned to them, slowed by the wonder of her discovery, and lifted the booklet into the air. "A few of these people are up in the Hall of Dreams," she informed them. "And also, Talia's parents are here somewhere, both of them."

***

Chapter Six
The Darkness and the Light

Elan stood next to Jimmy, with his hands on his hips, in hysterics, as they watched Foxy and Bell play tug-a-war with the ball he had made. The once roundish object quickly turned to tatters and became elongated in the course of a long battle, which now lingered in stalemate with both hounds jaw-locked on the ball, each determined not to lose it. Their comical, muffled growls mixed with the occasional dance performance, where one lifted the other off the ground by spinning around rapidly, left Elan in rapture.

His mother called, and her voice surprised him yet again, filling his heart with an even greater joy. She stood by the carriage with Misae, Madeleine, Annabel, and those heading for Blue Falls, and when he approached, Montezuma, Kirra, and Tau, all unexpectedly knelt on one knee in front of him.

"Elan, my name is Montezuma," he began. "And this is Tau and Kirra. We're about to leave to see our daughters, Sanura and Talia, who we haven't seen since they were about your age, and we are told this is all because of your bravery."

While feeling somewhat intimidated, Elan managed a smile and to say, "It was all the Guardians, not just me. We work together. Sanura is nice, so is Talia. They can run really fast too, and they're very beautiful, except when they're covered in river mud."

His words earned Elan all-round laughter, however, Tamaya alone battled sorrow, for wishing Elan's father were there to see his son so modest in the face of valor and glory.

Elan studied Kirra's eyes and face with intent before remarking, "You look like Talia."

This comment broke Kirra into pieces, for no one had told Elan whose mother she was and it reconfirmed for her that she would see her Talia soon. All at once, she grabbed Elan, hugged him close and, although she didn't leave him much of a choice, he didn't really mind.

"Well, Elan, Warrior Guardian," Montezuma said, placing his hand on Elan's shoulder as they stood again to leave. "I owe you a great debt, and with your mother as witness, if you ever need anything, you only have to ask and I will be there for you. This is my promise."

Elan wasn't sure how to respond, so he simply nodded with, "Okeh."

This brought a greater smile to Montezuma. "I'll see you soon. We have a lot of work to do."

"Elan, Jimmy's staying tonight," Annabel informed him, mostly out of habit because before Tamaya arrived, she was always telling him of her comings and goings. "I don't know when we'll be back, it depends on the mission, but we'll be back soon."

"I'll look after Bell and Foxy," he said with joy.

When the carriage rolled away, Tamaya left Elan to play with the hounds some more and went with Misae back to where the tunnels were currently being constructed at the fence line. Misae looked over the plans again, while reminding herself of all Shenandoah mentioned regarding current constructions before he jumped into one of the tunnels himself and went to work.

After watching Misae bite her lips repeatedly, Tamaya became aware of the pressure she was under and said, "It's going well, don't worry. Look how much they've done already."

"I know," Misae agreed. "And there's nothing more important than this mission at the moment and for people to be reunited with their families. It's just that there's been so many interruptions to this project already, right from the very beginning, before I even came here, which is part of the reason I chose to do it. I feel something very powerful has been working against us."

She looked into Tamaya's eyes then as if searching for an answer there, and, in sensing her mystification, Tamaya could only ask, "What is it?"

It took a lot longer for Misae to answer than Tamaya expected, and this led her to believe that Misae might have been battling with her current thoughts for a great deal longer than just a month or two.

"Now that I'm here, I can feel it," Misae answered. "I feel the shadows and the darkness. I feel them attacking my soul, trying to distract me, trying to make me sick, trying to put fear into my heart."

This idea was not at all foreign to Tamaya. "Then you should be confident, my Princess," she said with surety. "Because if the darkness believes you can succeed enough to put extra effort into causing you trouble, it only means there's every chance you will succeed."

Misae's head tilted as this idea began to turn her thoughts around. "I didn't think of it like that."

160

"All you have to do is follow your instincts," Tamaya added. "What are they telling you now?"

This time, she didn't have to think for very long. "They're telling me that we're behind, that we should be finished and prepared already, ready to use Riverside as a decoy at any time."

This was a dilemma Tamaya knew she had no chance of helping with, not in any physical sense. "It's a shame there's so much going on, but maybe you could try to talk to the others as soon as you can, about how to speed things up, if you really feel we should."

Misae nodded with newfound contrition. "I do, and I will, as soon as I see them."

***

After an awe-inspiring exploration of Crystal Nest and of the torrents at the opening next to Dead Man's Fall, the two wandering Guardians strolled through the fruit trees and vines of the northern orchards. With a mini fruit and berry banquet in hand, they stopped by The Lake to sit on a large rock for a little respite and to devour their delicious collection.

They were all but finished, sitting silently, gazing across the water when Talia nudged Sanura. "Look!" She pointed, as a boat appeared from behind a large rock with its spinner dolphin figurehead leading the way. Rich red lines in the grain of its cedar body highlighted themselves as it drifted through a curtain of sun rays. The sight could be deemed magical, and it brought yet another smile to both their faces.

Nuru spotted them at the edge and guided the boat over with precision at the oars. He slid up alongside them and gently halted as the hull found the shallower sandy bank. "Are you waiting for a ride?" he asked, with a beaming smile, but they only looked to each other curiously. "This is where people usually wait for me, if they want to go out on the boat," he explained, struggling to avert his eyes from Talia.

Talia, however, seemed more captivated by the intricate designs in the timber vessel. "It's a beautiful boat. Did you make it?"

"No," Nuru said with unseen disappointment. "I wish I did. Victor's grandfather made it, but I did all the carving, and I also named it. It's the Dreaming Dolphin."

"Can you take us to The Falls?" Sanura asked. "I want to see it from the front."

161

"Yes!" he answered, all too excitedly. "Usually, it's very expensive, but for two beautiful young ladies such as yourselves, I'll forget the fee today." His eyes still hadn't wandered much from Talia.

"Really?" Sanura replied, detecting his game. She decided to have some fun and took on a fake but serious tone. "Since they told us we pay for nothing here, that makes you a criminal, and do you know you're admitting your guilt to a Guardian, and flirting with a Guardian also. She might just have you expelled from Blue Falls for your insolence. Talia?"

"Guardians?" Nuru uttered, as his face dropped. He heard that three new Guardians had come to light but wasn't expecting to see any of them under such circumstances, and he certainly wasn't expecting one of them to have his heart on a plate before he'd even heard her speak. "Talia," he repeated aloud, unwittingly.

Talia did well to hide her amusement. She took her amulet case out, let it swing in the air for Nuru to see, and Sanura did the same before they pocketed them again. Nuru's smile had vanished completely and shame washed over him. It wasn't until Talia's grin crept out that he realized they were playing.

With a newfound yet hesitant smile, he stood and bowed to them. "Forgive me, my Guardians."

"We'll let you off this time without a beheading," Talia proposed. "But only if you take us to The Falls as Sanura requested, and then down to the other end to see the forest from the Lake."

"And," Sanura added. "You have to take us out anytime we want, day or night."

Talia giggled. It was too much to ask, even for the most prima-donna of princesses.

Yet, Nuru didn't seem to mind. "This is not a punishment," he answered with a cheeky grin, reaching out a hand to help them aboard. "It's more like a gift."

He won Sanura over with that comment. They boarded easily with the tip of the hull resting on the sandy bank and, after cleverly using an oar against the rock to push them away from the shore and to spin the vessel around at the same time, Nuru had them safely negotiating through scattered swimmers and in front of The Falls in no time.

After some minutes to take in the sight, he turned them around again and started heading toward the other end of The Lake, when someone caught their eye, jumping up and down and waving wildly at the water's edge from where they had departed.

It was Annabel and they could only just hear her calling out. It sounded as if she spoke their names, but all the children splashing and yelling around them muffled out her voice, while it was obvious she pointed emphatically to three people standing between herself and Madeleine.

"Sorry, Nuru," Talia said. "Can you take us over? She's calling us."

With her sight fixed on the shore, Sanura slowly reached across to Talia's arm and proceeded to squeeze it tighter and tighter while her eyes latched on to one of the men there, standing tall, his head held high; much how she remembered her father.

Talia looked to Sanura's grip on her arm and was about to question it but, after seeing the shock in her eyes, she looked back to the shore herself again to discover a great shock of her own. She too recognized someone standing there, two people in fact. Without thinking, she stood abruptly and Sanura followed suit before they realized what a great mistake that was, considering they were not positioned in the exact center of the boat.

"No!" Nuru tried to warn them, but it was all too late.

The boat dipped savagely to Talia's side and when she reached out automatically to grab Sanura's arm, she pulled them both overboard. It was your classic double-rookie fiasco.

When they both surfaced, they might have been battling with laughter, but, instead, they started swimming immediately for the shore, stopping every few strokes, hoping to confirm from a new position that their minds weren't playing tricks on them. They could make out Madeleine and Annabel easily, both keeled-over, laughing hysterically, but neither of them had seen their parents in over ten years and wouldn't be sure it was them until coming face-to-face.

Nuru let the boat drift, sitting with his head in his hands and a longing in his eyes as he watched Talia swim away. "I could've taken you over," he muttered to himself.

Montezuma and Tau waited with arms outstretched at the edge, and Kirra stood between them with a hand over her mouth, shaking with desperation to know for certain if it was Talia swimming toward them.

The impromptu swimmers both halted just a few lengths from the edge and treaded water there, staring at their parents with minds floundering between the juxtaposition of sureness and incredulity.

"Well, are you gonna come out?" Annabel asked, still giggling along with Madeleine.

It was only then that they moved closer to the edge and accepted the hands which came to lift them onto land again. Sanura first looked about quickly for her mother, but the sorrow in Montezuma's eyes, for his awareness of her unspoken question, was all the heartbreaking confirmation she needed. She began to weep then, as she walked into her father's arms, as he did, for it just didn't feel right to have the gift of seeing his daughter again without sharing it with her mother.

After long embraces, during which Talia shook her head most of the time, she looked back and forth in wonder between her parents and Madeleine and Annabel. "How? How did you do it?"

"It was Sanura, not us," Madeleine stated. "They wouldn't be here if not for her."

Annabel nodded and shared a knowing glance with Madeleine that it was time to leave them alone. "We'll tell you how later," she insured, as they wandered off to meet the other Guardians at The Armory.

They had walked quite a distance before hearing Sanura call their names as she sprinted to catch up. "I just remembered the mission tonight," she panted. "I wanted to wish you good luck. And if you see a one-eyed man, can you…" She went silent then, since she hadn't thought it through.

"Take his other eye out?" Annabel guessed with a grin.

"And take his friend's eyes for Talia," Sanura smiled. "I wish I was coming with you."

"We know," Annabel replied.

"If we see one-eyed man and his friend, we'll make sure no one touches them," Madeleine stated, confusing Sanura somewhat.

"So we save them for you," Annabel enunciated.

Upon those words, Sanura's humorous demeanor turned when she realized her fellow Guardians weren't actually joking. Their eyes held only sureness, and she seemed to draw on their inner strength somehow, while feeling far behind, like she was the only one who didn't know she was in the presence of true sisters.

"I want to search for my mother," she said, as a wave of great pain surged through her heart. They nodded in unison and their purposeful gaze hadn't changed. "Can we?"

"I thought I told you already, you don't ask permission for anything," Annabel reminded her gently. "You just have to make it clear what you want and we all make it happen somehow. There's no in-between."

"Talk to your father about where we should start," Madeleine suggested. "We can start this week, one day a week maybe until things settle, then we can go more often."

Annabel nodded in agreement. "You can come with us as our slave, and your father too, because we've never seen your mother. If we just take a carriage, we can go to more places and if we see anyone posted in the Hall Of Dreams, then we'll just have to take them and find a way to get them home if it's too much for the carriage. We were planning to do more runs to the markets in the future anyhow with wagons, since the drop will be closed for good."

For a while, Sanura lost herself in a depth of gratitude that left her speechless. "How do I thank you?" she asked eventually. "I don't know."

"Right now, there are more than 70 people who don't know how to thank you, Sanura," Madeleine offered as a reason for her to feel worthy of blessings.

Sanura was thrown again. "70? I don't understand."

"Del Hickory brought 50 slaves to his house before he knew about his sheds burning down," Madeleine explained. "Long story, but I bought them all. Your father and Talia's parents were amongst them, and also seven other people who have family here in Blue Falls."

"If you didn't burn those sheds down, your father wouldn't be here right now," Annabel added. "They'd all be Hickory's slaves."

"Which is pretty much a death sentence," Madeleine proposed. "There're only three heroes in this story. You, Elan, and Misae, she's the reason those horses you mentioned never showed up."

This idea mystified Sanura, thinking of how convoluted the events of the last two days had been, and all ending with her father's sudden presence. She stood in silence for a moment, trying to believe in it, then looked back to her father for confirmation to see him waiting impatiently by the Lake.

"I'll be with you in spirit tonight," she said, with hope and adoration shining from her eyes, then she hugged them both quickly and ran back to her father.

***

For many months after fleeing, when thinking of his home, Nathaniel's mind darted to that last horrific night and quickly filled with visions of his associates' startled faces, as death gulped them up and licked its lips. Swords pierced hearts and opened throats, splashing his body over with warm, red insidiousness, and, now, he wondered if their last sounds, their vague but urgent utterances mixed with agonizing grunts and groans, might echo in his ears forever.

After the train pulled in, he had walked across East Bridge and couldn't help but to look upstream toward the boat sheds on the water's edge, one of which staged that ghastly event, and when his stomach dropped, he felt, for one moment, that he might vomit, but it passed once the sheds were out of view. The next thing, his sickness turned to sorrow, the deepest of sorrows, being the result of yearning for lost dreams unwittingly discarded through the art of mindless endeavors.

Somehow, his legs kept moving toward his old home, to Helen, but he knew not why. There wasn't much chance of reconciling, he knew that, for this also meant he would have to confess to all his misadventures, if she didn't learn of them already, and would only result in the same predicament; being alone in the world again.

It wasn't long, of course, before he came walking back down the hill, berating himself for ignoring his instincts, and knocking on the door. He wasn't there for five minutes, for after refusing to answer Helen's poignant questions, she turned him away, warning him that the new sheriff had been around, asking for his whereabouts after following up on an unsolved case.

"Why did you ask what Madeleine told me?" Helen queried suspiciously, with a distance and coldness in her eyes most perplexing after so many years of marriage. "Madeleine hasn't said anything. Does she know something about it?"

There was no way to answer, of course, without breaking his wife's heart again, so he just looked into her eyes for a few moments longer, sighed and said, "I'm sorry, Helen," then turned and walked away.

While Helen sat on a swinging bench in her garden with Susanna, trying to regain peace of mind yet again with a flood of tears blocking the way, Nathaniel stood, lifeless, looking over a message board in the post office, hoping to find work of some kind.

A handwritten message, Carpenters And Laborers Wanted, caught his eye. He was no carpenter, but anyone healthy enough could perform laborer's tasks, and since presenting itself to be the only hope of work on the whole message board, which also offered accommodation and food, he noted the address and immediately made his way there.

Shortly after arriving, he realized why the name, Del Hickory, felt so familiar. Until that moment, he thought the man must have been a local businessman and perhaps a customer at the bank where he used to work, but, no, Hickory's reputation in the southern regions never failed to reach gossipers in the Midlands and so, Nathaniel had heard plenty of unwanted stories in the distant past.

"Welcome aboard," Hickory said, after Nathaniel had said only that he was looking for work. "I'm sure you'll do better than those two idiots."

He referred to Tanner and Mitchell, who were still working to clear rubble but now at a completely useless rate. Their bodies were stiffened, and lethargy reigned supreme.

"What happened to them?" Nathaniel asked, albeit hesitantly, being unsure as to whether he actually wanted to know the answer.

Del sniffed, regarding the men with disgust, "They're responsible for this whole place going up in smoke. But since you need work so bad, you should thank them because now, we need all the hands we can get. Your first job is to help us on a hunt tonight to find the slaves these morons lost. We start rebuilding tomorrow."

Nathaniel didn't know how to respond at first.

What have I walked into?

"The notice said you needed laborers," he dared to mention.

"When you work for me, you do as I ask," Del insisted. "Unless you've got a problem huntin' slaves now?"

There was no chance of Nathaniel daring to dispute Del's devious motivations, and some of his men looked like they'd skin him alive just for smiling at them.

"N-no," Nathaniel lied.

"Well, good," Del uttered. "We'll get you a musket. We're heading out soon."

***

"There's one thing I'm confused about," Madeleine declared, as they walked along the highest northern ledge toward the Armory. They merely strolled, knowing others wouldn't arrive for some time, and for the chance to speak of Sampa in private. The ledge also offered the best view from the northwestern end of Blue Falls, whereas from the ground, the view was limited to the pathways leading to the west side of The Books, down to The Hotpot and beyond to the northeastern orchards. A vantage point from the high ledge gave way to a unique sight of Blue Falls from where they could see all that visible from below, plus The Lake and the trees leading up to the Dark Forest. "I've been thinking about it," she added. "Oh, and also, you lied to me."

Without hesitation, Annabel objected, "I did not."

"You don't even know what I'm going to say," Madeleine laughed.

Yet, Annabel's resolve stayed. "It doesn't matter, I know I've never lied to you."

"Well, you said when you killed the men the day we found the princesses and Elan, it was the first time you killed," Madeleine proposed.

"First of all, I didn't tell you that," Annabel stated, laying out her case. "Someone else told you. Second, it is true, it was the first time I killed, in Earth. And third…I didn't lie to you…see? Sorry, I thought I had a third thing, but…"

"All right, I'll let you get away with that," Madeleine chuckled. "Now, the idea which confuses me is how you could spend so much time in Sampa and not be missed in Blue Falls."

Annabel grinned. "Gosh, it took you long enough to think of this."

"Be quiet," she snapped but with amusement. "I thought of it yesterday, but I've had a lot to think about, so I forgot."

"Actually, I would've told you yesterday, but I didn't want to overload you with information, and it's a difficult one to believe and get your head around," she confessed. "My mother explained it to me on the first day, but it still took me a few visits before I understood and I only believed it because I tested it many times to be sure, but, simply put, while a Guardian's inside Sampa, no time passes in Earth, and vice versa."

"What?" As Annabel insinuated, this idea was immediately unbelievable. "You mean, you can stay there for any length of time and come back to the same day?"

"The same moment," Annabel specified. "Up until the last time anyway, I wasn't able to stay for a very long time because I got too anxious thinking about everyone here, but it's stupid because when I come back, it's always the same time as it was when I left. It's too strange, so I didn't last longer than a few months for a long time."

"A few months!" Madeleine exclaimed.

"It'll take you a while to accept it," Annabel offered with understanding. "I stayed much longer last time. Now, I don't see how it could be any other way. Like this, it guarantees the Guardians will be truly effective in both worlds, and one won't be neglected when you're focused on the other. And do you see how the worlds are connected? Whatever happens in one, has an effect on the other."

Madeleine thought on it for a while and felt she was beginning to understand. "So you come back the same age?"

"Ah uh, the same moment, remember?" she reinstated. "Everything is the same."

"Hmmm." Madeleine pondered on all the possibilities. "So what happens if I injure myself in Sampa then come back through?"

"The injury would be gone because you didn't have it when you entered," Annabel explained. "That's if you actually managed to injure yourself."

They continued in silence for a while, as Madeleine digested all the new facts, before she remembered another question. "Oh, that's what I wanted to ask. Does Sampa have a ruling government or something, like Earth, or are you the...ruler of Sampa?"

Annabel chuckled. "No. Like in Blue Falls, I'm just a Guardian. The Sampa people are waiting for their queen to enter the realm along with the Guardians. They recently decided the next rightful queen should be Lesedi, so long as she enters in time, and so, they wait, and their council waits for her to take her place to lead the people with the Guardians at her side. They know she can't be the queen of Earth and that she's already in league with the Guardians here, and so it would be insulting to ask her to step down for an existing ruler in Sampa when she enters. There's no throne, but if there were, I would be the Keeper of that throne, to be sure no false leaders come to power before the chosen, and unless the people are being enslaved, they live exactly how the people in Blue Falls live until then. This is what they want, which is why, for now, I only spend minimal time in Sampa, so there's more chance of Lesedi taking her place for the longest time possible."

The obvious entered Madeleine's mind. "But what about Earth? What about the millions who won't be lucky enough to find Blue Falls and Sampa?"

"The queen can't lead a country which is already completely controlled by those with great power," Annabel proposed. "You know they will just continue to desecrate her people and their ways, and when most of the Earth's population supports the agendas of their leaders, she is truly powerless to make change. In Sampa, all its people and the people we bring, will respect and follow Lesedi's leadership, and there's every chance to create a world where everyone is free and safe and living in good health again. That's if we Guardians fulfill our quests, of course."

"Freya wasn't exaggerating," Madeleine realized once more, with confirmation found in Annabel's learned beliefs, together with the evidence of her own research. "The Earth will be taken over."

"It's already happened," Annabel sighed. "We're so very far behind."

Madeleine shook her head, knowing, but still struggling with denial all the same. "And what? We just escape to Sampa and leave Earth to waste away?"

Annabel shook her head. "No, not the Guardians. We can still move between both realms and even though we can't go to war against the enslavers on Earth, we can still try to awaken as many people as we can, but once the people of Blue Falls enter the gateway into Sampa, they can't return to Earth, so they need to make a choice."

"Oh my goodness," Madeleine uttered. "I'm glad I don't have to face that choice. What about the queen, can she return?"

"No," Annabel answered, with a portentous tone. "The queen can't come back."

"So where's the gateway?" finally, Madeleine asked, having meant to ask since their first conversation.

"In The Auditorium," Annabel shared with a smile, knowing how well it remained hidden in plain sight.

Madeleine had spent a great many hours there, during celebrations and talks, yet saw no signs of a gateway, but it made sense to her, being situated on the same side of Blue Falls as the Guardians' doorway. "Really? How do you know?"

"I found it by accident a long time ago," Annabel confessed. "Long before you came. I was in The Auditorium, practicing with Ky Mani, Jojo, Akachi, and Oni."

"Practicing silence?" Madeleine asked, thinking of the lessons Guardians undertook in The Auditorium, whereby they were challenged to make their way around the perimeter of the cavern as quickly as possible with a weapon, without being heard by those sitting quietly in the center. Given one could be heard simply whispering in any part of the huge space, silence was surely a difficult skill to master.

"Yes, silence," Annabel confirmed. "One day, I went close to the wall in the center at the highest point on the northern side, and blue lines started to appear, like they do in the Guardians' doorway, but this was a gateway, much larger. Three diamonds started to appear right in front of me like the other door, but I think they were following me when I moved along the wall. Anyhow, when I saw it, I backed away quickly before the gateway had the chance to fully come out and brighten, you know, like the Guardians' doorway."

Madeleine was amazed. "Oh my. Well, I guess no one saw, so that was lucky."

They were nearing the entrance to the Armory, so Annabel lowered her voice and, after shaking her head with some regret, confessed, "Actually, Oni saw it, but she was the only one."

"What?" Madeleine only just managed to keep her voice hushed. "How do you know? Did she say something?"

"No," Annabel answered, without doubt. "Everyone else was looking the other way when it happened, but Oni went to the wall after I moved away from it and when it didn't reveal itself again to her, she looked back to me as if she was going to say something. She must have seen the fear in my face and I was trying to shake my head without anyone else seeing, but anyway, she just smiled and never said a word about it."

"Nothing?" Madeleine asked, greatly surprised. "Ever? She's never said a thing about it?"

After shaking her head with equal wonder, Annabel added, "This is Oni. Oni at her most high. Her intuition is greater than any I have known, even greater than Isi, I think. She understood somehow and also trusted me, without me saying a single word."

Ironically, it was Oni who first appeared to them, and from inside the Armory. They were unaware that she had been in there for some time already, selecting all her guards and pieces of uniform, and came outside to sit on one of the stone benches, to look out over Blue Falls while she donned her blackened gear. She smiled eagerly upon seeing her fellow Guardians, saying, "Tonight, we rescue 20-something people."

Both her joy and smile had a contagious effect on Madeleine and Annabel.

"Someone seems sure we're going to find them," Madeleine insinuated.

"The queen's right," Oni stated. "There's only two places they could be hiding, the lower northern forests or the upper northern forests. And since they won't be silly enough to travel in the daytime, they haven't had enough time yet to make it that far north."

Both Annabel and Madeleine agreed. They couldn't fault Ky Mani and the queen's logic, nor their highly-detailed plan.

Without knowing exactly what might oppose them on the mission, it was decided that Ky Mani, Jalen, and the chosen Shadow Warriors would each take a sword similar to Annabel and Madeleine's, lightweight and sheathed in black, and a sling-bow to ensure they weren't hindered or snagged when running at full speed, which was an important factor to consider in the denser parts of the forests. Different types of blades including throwing knives were optional, as were any other light weapon; so long as it reflected no light and wouldn't hinder the unit as a whole.

The chosen Guardians to accompany Jalen and 31 Night Panthers for the mission were Madeleine, Annabel, Akachi, Oni, and Kachina, and they too chose minimal weaponry for the same reasons. Akachi chose her sword and throwing knives, which she threw with great accuracy, as did Oni, who also selected knives in addition to her shorter staff which, although few people knew it, snapped apart in the center into two sticks with short blades at each end. Annabel and Madeleine chose their swords and sling bows, and while they all wore wrist, arm, and ankle guards, all garments were lightweight, tight-fitting, and black.

After everyone's input had been voiced, a plan evolved which saw a team of 38 divided into two equal groups of Protectors and Seekers.

The idea was to go silently without detection and to avoid confrontations of any kind. Kachina, Oni, and Akachi were to join half the Shadow Warriors in the Seekers unit, while Madeleine, Annabel, and Jalen joined the other half to form the Protectors who would provide a buffer between any posing threat and the Seekers unit, whose main objective was to find the runaways.

Ky Mani's role was to act as a go-between and to coordinate the movements of both units based on his reconnaissance to ensure they would be aware of any presence long before any possible danger came close to the Seekers or the escapees.

It was just on dusk when all the warriors were fitted-out, and those of Blue Falls fortunate enough to witness them leave on their nocturnal mission saw what looked like a string of lethal shadows make their way silently to the Entrance, amazing all by how well-prepared they were already in mind as well as body.

Lesedi waited for them at the Entrance with Naira, Sayen, and Isi, and not too far from them, all the parents waited also to give their blessings for the mission. When it came time to depart, Lesedi looked over the Guardians and Jalen, noting that if she didn't know each one of them intimately, they would be very frightening indeed. After shaking her head in awe, for the fierce and mighty force before her, she shared some final words of encouragement: "Remember, my friends, I'll be posting additional Warriors between here and the ridge behind the falls in case you're followed and need assistance, and we'll have a large team of Healers ready to go all night and all day until you return. Let's hope it's tonight. All our hearts are with you, Warriors. May you be blessed with quick success and return home safely to us."

***

Chapter Seven
Twisted Fates

Livid was Wright, and rightfully so, upon receiving his mission orders, and so surprised that he froze, stark-faced before the private who had delivered the message for at least half a minute before dismissing him. Adding salt to the wound, his orders included allowing Del Hickory and his men to accompany them on the mission, so that Del could potentially identify his 24 lost slaves. Given that it wasn't the first time a questionable individual with equally questionable connections had undermined his position, it might have been all-too-easy to swallow, but Del's permanent, smug grin added another hefty layer of challenge. Sadly for Wright, all he possessed in his ego's armory were sneaky verbal attacks which he let fly every so often.

"So, I guess your reputation for never losing a slave is well-and-truly out the window 'ey?" he jeered, enjoying his own words immensely.

Only he, Del, Doyle, and Will were mounted and kept to the rear so as to keep their approach as discreet as possible. They all moved along steadily together but for the few soldiers chosen for reconnaissance, who went ahead in a number of directions with orders to report back periodically.

"It's not over yet," Del implied. "You can bet, when I find them, I'll make such a good example out of 'em, there won't be any attempts after that. By the way, I know this is your army and all, but I would've brought more than 50 men. I mean, considering you have, what, a thousand or—"

"This army," Wright interrupted sharply. "My orders and my decisions are not yours to judge. They'll hear us coming miles away if we walk in with hundreds of men. I think I've made it very clear how I feel about your presence on this mission, Hickory, so I suggest you keep your opinions to yourself or I'll have my men escort you back home for making too much noise." He veered his steed away then, giving Del no time to respond.

As always, Del just smirked anyhow. He didn't care too much for competing with younger hotheads, and he would have done it alone but didn't have anywhere near enough men left to handle such a task. Either way, an uneasy feeling in his stomach continued to worsen, and he was happy to be riding far behind the unit.

Up ahead, in the middle ground, Nathaniel waited for his moment to escape; it wouldn't be too long now. All the while, sweat steadily built on his brow and trickled down his temples. Along the way, he learned about the demise of Hickory's men, and this new information did nothing to ease his troubled mind.

Sounds all too familiar, Nathaniel thought, with panic striking his heart. He knew a thing or two about the highly tuned skills their supposed prey was most likely to have, which turned the hunters into the hunted and, although the crescent moon was another seventh brighter this night than when he arrived in Black Sand Valley, the ones they hunted might as well be invisible.

We could already be surrounded.

After much contemplation, he decided the best place to make his getaway would be after the clearing but before the edge of the northern forests, so then he could double back to the outskirts of town along the other side of the river via Dead Man's Fall.

I should have stayed on the docks.

It was the Lieutenant Colonel's plan to follow the river until they reached the last place Del's men were seen and then veer northeast into the northern forests. From there, he would split the men into search teams like a comb spreading out, looking for any signs left by the runaways or by a supposed hidden force. Although their orders were not to harm the escapees, except in the case of a life-threatening situation, the men were armed with swords and musket rifles, and while ordered to go silently, their boot-laden footsteps alone could be heard a long way off, let alone the rattling of water flasks, the clinking of swords, and the squeaking of leather equipment belts and satchels. Consequently, a sentinel for the runaways heard their approach and returned to set Mosi's emergency plan in motion long before they came close to their target.

The food was taken up, the fire extinguished, and in seconds, they were making their way out of the gorge with the intention of turning west onto a narrow goat track which would eventually lead them northwest and into the northern hinterland beyond Crystal Lake. This wasn't the shortest route at all, but Mosi and Layla hoped that any posse hunting them would assume they fled due north, as most would surely do, rather than to move closer to the enemy first and risk being seen. This way, due to the cliffs along that part of the stream, after the men discovered their hideaway and searched that area, they would have to come back the same way they entered the gorge in order to follow them. So, as hoped, by the time Wright's reconnaissance had crossed over the goat track and into the gorge, Mosi had already led his people west.

Nathaniel saw his opportunity to make an escape. Before the gorge, a small nest of trees on the west side of the clearing, where the terrain sloped downward, looked ripe for providing enough cover to conceal him as he ran, so long as he timed it right. To his great fortune, while procrastinating with fear, one soldier made his way quickly to Wright to inform him they had found a recently used fireplace and Wright immediately hastened his unit north.

It was the perfect distraction, for the men's eyes were all forward and their ears filled with their own increased noise production, so he veered further and further to the left of the group until he was alone in that space and when he moved behind the clump of trees, he just never came out again. Once the horses had passed, he dropped the musket rifle and ran westward as fast as his jelly legs could travel.

***

"Yes, my Queen," Isi replied. "One of the tests we spoke of will be tonight."

Queen Lesedi dropped her shoulders and exhaled abruptly. With her instincts confirmed, she imagined Misae in harm's way again, and this, in turn, led her to remember the dream she experienced in the few hours of sleep she stole in the early hours of the morning. It seemed a most important dream, and one of Misae, so once the mission was underway, she asked Isi to sit with her on The Ledge by The Falls to speak with her alone.

"And Misae?" she asked, as three children ran past them and leapt into one of the ponds. Their sudden screams of delight washed over her restless mind like waves of urgency. "Will she be in danger again?"

"No." Isi was certain. "Misae will not become a part of the mission tonight. She has her own task. Now that all the Guardians have been found, the last of their potential weaknesses will be tested, and it's the darkness that will somehow bring about this test."

"Haven't they been tested enough?" Lesedi conjectured.

"So long as there's a chance of breaking the bond between the Guardians, they will be tested," Isi relayed. "And since a chance will present itself tonight, the darkness has been preparing for a long time to surprise them. It will be the cruelest of tests, one most tempting for the Guardian to fail."

All of a sudden, Lesedi felt the way she did at the time Isi told her Misae would be in danger; that feeling of helplessness and despair. "The darkness is aware that the last of the Guardians are coming together and now, stand to fulfill the prophecy."

"Yes. Ever since the Riverside project began, there have been many delays and all from dark forces on the outside affecting the project and the Guardians," Isi concluded. "Not because of any mistakes we've made. We feel this is no coincidence, that it's the darkness surrounding us now causing these setbacks. If you think about it, Riverside is almost finished and would have easily been finished a long time ago."

"That's true," Lesedi could only agree, after having endured so many unforeseen setbacks herself during the development phase of the project.

"Misae's powers are growing quickly, as a warrior and also as a seer," Isi said then, surprising his queen with a subject deviation: yet she would soon see the relevance. "Your daughter only had to discover what she was, and now, the true Misae will shine through as a great force on her own. We sense now she struggles with her own instincts but will be the one to devise a plan which will somehow guarantee the event you were leaving to chance, hoping it would happen on its own."

"Are you saying it will guarantee that our decoy plan happens?" she asked.

"Yes," Isi asserted, and again without doubt.

Lesedi shook her head. "But they're not ready now."

"No, they're not," Isi agreed.

Urgency gripped her again for a moment. "How sure are you of this?"

"Of the final outcome, not at all," Isi was careful to remind her. "You know, with the Guardians, we can't see this, but for me, there's no doubt Misae will want to initiate this plan, but she can only do that if they are prepared, if Riverside is finished."

"What does she need?" It was a queen's and a mother's question, and Isi was reluctant to answer, so she added, "Isi, just tell me honestly what you think."

"It's not what I think, it's what Misae will see. As with all the Guardians, she too has been hounded by the darkness, and now, she may not be able to bring her ideas to life as quickly as she would like."

"Why does that matter?" she asked. "Will it be too late then?"

"Maybe." Although instinctive, it was still a guess, and Isi wasn't afraid to admit his unsureness. "I'm telling you this because you asked to talk to me, but as you can see, my Queen, I haven't given you much proof of anything because it's difficult to know what might be relevant to you."

"I had a dream last night," she felt impelled to tell him, suddenly. "I was standing on a mountain top looking over Riverside and I saw Misae down below, trying to protect the people. She was building a wall of men, between them and the enemy, and she only needed three more men to close the gap in the wall, but she didn't have anyone left to fill it."

Isi didn't respond immediately. He left Lesedi to ponder on the dream again for a long while before asking, "And what did you do?"

She shook her head. "I had an army of warriors behind me, and I wanted to order them into the battle but we were too far away," Lesedi answered. "It was way too late to do anything."

While beginning to see the connection between her dream and Isi's intuitions, Lesedi suddenly realized that Isi had been up to his usual illusive tricks again. Her eyes narrowed and the slightest smile appearing in the corners of his mouth confirmed her suspicions.

"Isi, how do you know my dreams?" she asked suspiciously, hoping to see his thoughts by looking deeper into his eyes, but it didn't work. "You knew I was going to ask you about this tonight."

"I don't think the Guardians are the only ones being tested at this time," Isi answered, albeit ambiguously.

"Are you saying that I am also being tested?" she asked, with mounting apprehension. "And my dream was trying to show me something?"

"If you were close enough to the battle, what would you have done?" he posed.

Lesedi didn't need to think about it. "I would've sent my army in, of course."

"But you said she only needed three people," Isi contested, with curious eyes denoting the significance of this inconsistency, and after a long pause, added, "I believe the gap in the wall represents your connection to Misae."

"But it's a gap," Lesedi argued. "It's a disconnection."

Isi agreed with a nod. "But for you and Misae, your dreams hold all the missing links you need."

Lesedi looked away then to cast her eyes over the plateau and the lake, watching mothers play with babies in the shallower pools and children diving from the rocks within the blue hue of the Falls. In the low light of evening, the vision painted a stark contrast for her troubled mind, for looking over the trouble-free multitudes around her while her thoughts rested on the Guardians' dangerous yet intrepid mission.

Somehow, for Misae's sake, she needed to be a queen, a protective but non-controlling mother, and a supportive ally.

Supportive ally.

So many times recently, she had denied her urge to offer Misae additional assistance of all kinds, for fear of interfering and undermining her daughter's need to fulfill her chosen quest alone. After talking to Isi, she started to wonder if these fears prevented her from acting on her instincts as she normally would if it were someone other than Misae overseeing the Riverside project. The dream passed through her thoughts again. The gap in the wall.

"Oh, Isi," she said finally. "You talk to me so casually of things that I could easily ruin with a poor choice and somehow trust that I will use the information wisely, whatever that means. I understand you don't know the outcome, but what do your instincts tell you about my choices and the decisions I'll make at this time?"

Isi found just the hint of a smile again as he answered, "I believe in my queen."

***

All of a sudden, Mosi called for everyone to freeze and to be silent. They had been running for many minutes, so those injured, or still weakened by yesterday's trials, didn't mind at all to pause for a moment, while Mosi, who had also been carrying Layla, showed no signs of tiring.

After listening with intent for a few moments, he quickly ushered everyone off the path and gently returned Layla to her feet to position himself at the edge of the trees where he could still see a good portion of the path in both directions. The footsteps he heard came closer and he could see that it was just one man of light frame, running fast and weaponless it seemed, yet Mosi's knife was at the ready nonetheless.

As the man came alongside, Mosi snatched him up and held the knife at his throat. "Make a sound and I kill you," he threatened, while contemplating what he should do with his catch.

"Wait!" Layla said, when she saw the man and after moving closer, she uttered with great surprise. "Terry?"

"Yes!" Nathaniel blurted out. "It's me."

"I know this man, Mosi," Layla said. "He's the one who set us free."

Mosi's suspicion remained. "Then why is he with these men?"

"I'm not," Nathaniel shook his head and swallowed. "I'm not with them, I'm trying to get away from them. You saw me running. I swear to you, I'm not."

"Let him go, Mosi," Layla said. "He doesn't have a weapon."

After Mosi complied, Nathaniel turned and raised his hands in a servile manner. "I'm going back to town. I'm not following you and I'm not with them."

178

There was no time to discuss it further. Mosi picked Layla up and had just given the signal for everyone to move again when the sudden but silent appearance of many shadowed figures stopped them all dead in their tracks.

Mosi's automatic reaction was to place Layla down again and raise his knife, ready for an attack, but he was quickly surprised when, instead of soldiers, Ky Mani, Oni, Kachina, and Akachi drew closer to reveal their faces in a stream of moonlight. More warriors appeared behind them then, just as Ky Mani ran off alone.

Kachina stepped forward.

"I'm Princess Kachina," she said. "We are the Guardians. We're here to take you to—"

Just then, Kachina spotted Nathaniel a little farther back and due to his new appearance, she only recognized him personally when she drew closer and before anyone even saw her move, she had unsheathed her sword, flashed past them, taken a handful of Nathaniel's hair in her grip, and stood, holding her sword at his throat.

Nathaniel could feel the sting of the blade on his neck repeatedly, like tiny little hints of the horror yet to come and, while doing his best to remain completely motionless, his heaving lungs had other ideas, not to mention the uncontrollable shuddering which his great fear dumped into the mix. He needed to speak but also knew that anything coming from his mouth might only provoke her into sliding that blade along his neck, especially if it were merely to beg for his life. In any case, in this moment, it was more important for him to appease his utter astonishment.

"H...how did you m...move so fast?" he stuttered.

Kachina didn't answer, but Nathaniel felt her grip tighten, he also caught a fleeting glimpse of her face and recognized his past victim, now holding his life in her hands.

"Wait!" Layla implored once again. Kachina's deadly gaze didn't change at all, yet it somehow personified her want to stab the man repeatedly.

Although Layla didn't know it, Nathaniel's only saving grace, the only reason he wasn't already choking on his own blood, was the fact that his own daughter's name reverberated inside Kachina's head.

"What is this man doing with you?" Kachina asked then, her voice turning to ice as she battled a mixed-up conscience while her bladed hand yearned to strike.

"His name is Terry," Layla blurted, frightfully. "He helped us escape."

Kachina's eyes narrowed and her grip tightened again. "He's lying to you. His name is not Terry!"

Layla wasn't immediately sure how to respond to the claim, and since her Terry didn't argue, she could only assume the accusation to be true. "All right, maybe his name's not Terry, but he did help us escape."

Kachina released Nathaniel suddenly and pushed him away. She was so rough that he almost stumbled over.

"Thank you," Layla said.

"I didn't spare him because he helped you," Kachina said, still riddled with fury and spite; a part of her still unsure. The handle of her sword creaked under the weight of her intense grip and they realized she might not have truly decided yet. "It makes up for nothing. I spared him for his daughter's sake." She looked deep into Nathaniel's eyes then and said with absolute scorn, "She's wise and talented and courageous. Is there a worse punishment for a father than to repel her from his life?"

Mosi insisted, "We have to keep moving."

Kachina turned quickly then and moved closer to the others, farther from temptation. "No. We wait for Ky Mani's instruction," she informed them, without compromise; not that anyone would dare to question her now. "There's another team of our people between us and the unit of soldiers. When we get the word the way is clear to the west, we move out, and if that man takes a single step in our direction, I will cut him into pieces."

Layla looked to Nathaniel with great confusion, yet quickly found her own resolution when he responded with a face full of shame and without the ability to maintain eye contact. Her Terry had done nothing to defend himself against the princess's claims, and she also seemed too knowledgeable on the subject, too sure, and altogether too frightening to even think about defying.

Ky Mani returned then, followed closely by the other team. "They're too close," he said. "The Protectors must stay. Take them now, Seekers, go now while the west is clear."

Just then, Madeleine spotted her father, but didn't recognize him until she flashed over with a speed equaling Kachina's and rested the tip of her sword over his Adam's apple. Then, her eyes widened as she recognized the cowering man. "Father?" Utter shock fell upon her, as she lowered the sword. She turned to Kachina with questioning eyes, knowing she and the others would have certainly seen him standing there, then turned back to note the line of fresh blood across his neck. Assuming what might have taken place, she could only look to Kachina again, startled, as she could think of nothing to say in that moment.

Kachina only repeated Ky Mani's suggestion, "We have to go, Maddy."

"Madeleine, how did you move so fast?" Nathaniel asked, enduring a new wave of shock.

"Is that all you have to say?" Madeleine asked, mystified. "What are you doing here!? Are you with these men?" She turned to Kachina, Oni, and Akachi again. "Go. I'll take care of this."

Kachina nodded and the Seekers team left quickly with the escapees without another word, while Ky Mani, Madeleine, Annabel, and Jalen stayed with the unit of Protectors.

Madeleine turned to her father again with rushed instructions. "Wait five minutes, then go west and south again back to town. If you keep going west, one of them will kill you. Do you understand?"

Nathaniel nodded. "But I want to talk to you, Madeleine," he implored with sincerity ringing clear in his voice.

Madeleine had no time to think at all, so she relented. "Meet me at East Bridge after dark tomorrow."

They were all gone in the next instant, and Nathaniel could hear nothing of their footsteps, as if they had simply vanished. Suddenly, he was alone again, but for the lithe, dancing shadows of the trees.

Wait five minutes, she said. He started running at 11 seconds.

***

Surprised for having dozed off, Misae sat up abruptly when Shenandoah and Jimmy entered the sitting room of the mansion. While battling the sleeplessness in her busy mind, she paced around the empty bottom floor for hours and couldn't remember sitting in a lounge chair, let alone reclining into it and closing her eyes.

"Sorry to wake you, Misae," Shenandoah said quietly. "But Sherman's here. There's nothing to worry about, but you better come out and see."

In her half-sleep, this information dazed Misae even further. She looked over to the window, squinting, to note its blackness. "Is it almost dawn or…?"

"No, not even close," Jimmy sniggered. "I'm sorry, you look so tired, but we thought you might want to know right away. We'll meet you outside."

Before she could ask another question, they left her alone again, so she sat up straight, rubbed her eyes, and tried to wipe the sleep out of her face. Both legs were reluctant to move at all, and she noted, in that moment, how nothing brought on lethargy like torturing oneself with a short nap after being sleep-deprived for so long. Nonetheless, curiosity countered her pain, and after wandering out into the courtyard, she was very pleased to have been woken.

How did I sleep through this?

Sherman stood next to his horses at the head of a long wagon just inside the gate, and beside him, gathering up and organizing an array of working tools, were 50 of the largest and strongest Shadow Warriors. With her mouth ajar, she looked at her hands to ensure she wasn't dreaming, then proceeded to close and open her eyes wide a number of times, hoping to refocus again on reality. Eventually, she believed the sight, though with utter astonishment, as all the Warriors smiled and waved.

Sherman walked over then and handed her a folded piece of paper. "The queen asked me to give you this and wait for anyone who wants to come back with me."

"Thank you, Sherman," Misae replied, grateful yet pensive, and most distracted by the letter. She walked back to the steps of the house to open the paper under a lamplight and read:

Misae, I'm sending you these men to be sure you have all you need for whatever you decide is best for Riverside. If there's anything else you want right now, tell Sherman tonight and we'll send it over tomorrow. I love you. You are my light.

Misae swallowed her tears. She hadn't seen him yet, because he was still unpacking the wagon when she first came out, but Montezuma was also there when she returned, sorting through a mass of equipment.

"Montezuma?" she said with great surprise. "Why are you back so soon? What happened?"

"We missed you, my Princess," he grinned, continuing with his work.

Misae feigned amusement. "But what—"

Sanura appeared at the wagon door then, with an armful of supplies, and answered the question poised on Misae's tongue. After discarding her bundle, she went straight to Misae to surprise her yet again, but with a hug this time, then stood back with a smile of great warmth. "Thank you, Misae, Princess Misae."

Still dopey from an inkling of slumber, Misae struggled to formulate complete sentences in her mind, and all she managed, at first, was to speak her name, "Sanura."

"Yes," Sanura giggled.

"Why are you thanking me?" she asked.

"Those men, the ones who came here looking for us, they might've found us, if not for you," she explained.

Misae smiled with acknowledgement, yet she never felt comfortable with praise and so, she was thankful when Elan appeared rubbing one eye lazily with a fist. After sneaking past his sleeping mother, he came out to see why the hounds had howled.

"And this one," Sanura said, as she picked Elan up into her arms and spun him around on the spot. "This one is my hero."

Elan was suddenly awake and glowing with joy. When she put him down again, he looked to Misae and said, "This is Sanura."

Misae snickered and ruffled his hair, then turned to Montezuma. "How many warriors?"

"50," Montezuma answered with delight.

"And the mission?" she asked, looking between Sanura and Montezuma.

"They weren't back yet before we left," Sanura answered. "So we don't know yet; I'm sorry."

Although the Warriors went about unpacking quietly, the commotion soon woke almost everyone, including Tamaya, and so Misae found herself quickly surrounded by multitudes. She took this unexpected opportunity to inform them all that, although they vowed to stay and help with the project, no one but for those who could handle long hours of heavy work needed to remain. Yet, she did suggest that anyone was welcome to stay, if that's what they wanted, but also welcome to go to "Our other place," as she put it, tonight, to begin a new life in a safe and beautiful new home.

Many were initially reluctant to abandon their post but, after further consideration of the team of massive warriors, the numbers of the willing increased enough to fill Sherman's wagon. This pleased Misae greatly, for the sake of those who would only be working out of obligation and for the fact that most of those who remained were the fittest and strongest. Together with the warriors sent by her mother, she now had an overkill of assistance; exactly what she wanted, what she had been dreaming about all day.

Once Sherman and his wagonload were set to leave, he asked of Misae: "So, any requests for the queen?"

"Yes," Misae answered. Fully awake again, she pulled a folded piece of paper out of her coat pocket. "Give this to the Armory and my mother please, and can you ask my mother to send enough wagons in three days to take home everyone but the 50 warriors. Also, with the wagons, please bring everything the armory had time to make, and also bring all the favorite weapons of these 50 warriors."

Misae's portentous words lifted every warrior's head and paused them all mid-stride, as if they were of one mind, resonating with Misae's insinuation. A smile slowly crept over all their faces, then found its way to Sherman.

"Also, thank you, Sherman," Misae said finally. "And can you please thank the queen for hearing my call?"

***

When another sentinel returned with confirmation of having found the escaped slaves' hideout, Wright ordered his men to reform and to move forward at double speed, yet they had just reached the end of the clearing when one of his men called, "Over there!"

"Hold your fire!" Wright ordered immediately, knowing how quickly hair-triggers spawned. He saw them too. "I want half you men to break away, head east, and try to cut them off. The rest stay behind so we can surround them. Move!"

"Wait!" Del called, as his horse started prancing for all the sudden excitement. "Why would they go east? That doesn't make sense."

"You saw them as well as I did, Hickory!" he shouted. "They're going east, now do you want to catch them or not?"

"It's an ambush; I'm telling you!" Del blurted. His horse was spinning on the spot now and he too was set to fly, in the opposite direction. "Don't you see? They want everyone to empty their muskets at nothing so they can move in. Will, Doyle, get ready to go."

One of the soldiers in the lead cried out in pain. Soon after, many others did the same and their shrieks ended abruptly, like death interrupted their call for help, then a long series of musket blasts rang out before Wright could even think to shout another order. Soldiers could be seen returning then, running flat-out, attempting to retreat, only to be cut down two, three, ten at a time by something unseen.

Wright's 50-man unit had been reduced to just a few retreaters in only seconds, but he himself had seen nothing but mere shadows of the enemy.

"Fall back!" he shouted. "Fall back!" Yet, his efforts went mostly unheard behind the remaining few blasts and screams.

A shocking realization came to Del then and his eyes filled with horror when he turned to his men. "They're gonna flank us," he stated, blank-faced, and only an instant before he turned his horse to bolt away.

Doyle and Will needed no encouragement to follow, and Wright himself only needed to witness another couple of his men falling down to acknowledge their sudden and awful predicament before sending his thoroughbred into a galloping retreat.

Del and his men had just reached the middle of the clearing when a fleeting shadow named Jalen leapt up out of the grass, rising as high as the men on horseback, and spun swiftly in the air.

All they heard was a "swish" before Will's head rolled off his body.

Wright had caught up to the others by then and the remaining three leaned over further in the saddle, hoping to keep their heads. In horror, they continued on, as Will's tenacious body galloped on with them for a good long while before slipping silently to the ground.

Soon after, adding to their bewilderment, a woman's voice shouted out from behind, "Don't hit the horses!"

Just as these words registered in his mind, Del realized that he had fallen well behind the other two men on taller horses. "Ya!" he screamed, but his worst fears came to life in the same instant. An arrow found its mark at the top of his left shoulder and remained there, sticking out just under the collar bone. He screeched like a wild monkey while his legs almost lost their grip around his only means of escape, when he sat up abruptly to take a glance at the dark steel of the arrowhead shining with his blood in the half-light of the moon.

The others didn't look back to see if Del was still with them. They were married to the gallop in all ways, waiting for that shot of pain to find them too, but it never came.

***

Chapter Eight
Licking Wounds

"Don't hit the horses!" Del hollered. Ropable, he sat at his kitchen table with all that was left of his men standing around, not knowing what to do to help him with his wound. "They lopped Will's head off and said don't hit the horses! Ha!" After laughing hysterically for a few moments, he started coughing for not having swallowed a swig of whiskey well enough.

Wright agreed to send one of his doctors over after returning to headquarters, but Del still awaited the fulfillment of that promise, furious and impatient beyond sanity. They did their best to stop the bleeding and while barely half an hour had passed, every moment seemed endless, as the pain increased in his shoulder and pounded his head in sympathy.

"How did it end up sticking out the top like that anyway, boss?" one of his men, Pete, asked with innocent curiosity. "Were they lying on the ground when they shot you?"

"No, you idiot!" Del spat, without restraint. "I was leaning over and they shot me from behind. Now, why can't anyone take it out!? Because I swear, if anyone touches it again without taking it out of my shoulder at the same time, I'll kill you. Do you hear me? I'll kill you!"

"Were you walking or galloping, boss?" Pete asked, but only received an awkward sneer from Del, so he elaborated, "'Cos if you were galloping, that's a pretty good shot." He saw Del's anger rising quickly again, so he attempted to backtrack but succeeded only in digging a deeper hole for himself with over-explanation. "I mean, for a nighttime shot, and with a short bow, or sling bow, whatever it was, 'cos that's not a regular longbow arrow, no sir, and still getting you without hitting the horse, well, now you have to admit that's accurate…that's…I'm just saying they must be a great marksman."

Del went calm; more from perplexity than anything else, that Pete would be stupid enough to provoke him under these circumstances. "Great marksman?" he repeated. It looked like he might laugh hysterically again but refrained somehow. "Accurate? I swear, Pete, if you say another word to me tonight, I'll use my good arm and show you how accurate my shotgun can be when I aim it at your head! Now get out of my sight you pathetic idiot!"

Mitchell and Tanner were listening from the adjacent living room, sharing grins of enjoyment every time Del went off. While the others were out, searching, they both cleaned themselves up and ate a giant meal, so they were sure to become the subject of abuse if they entered the room. There was nothing they could do to help anyhow, even if they wanted to, which they surely did not. It was certain, if not for them, there would have been no need for Del to go hunting in the first place, so their wounded hides enjoyed their measure of inadvertent revenge very much.

Doyle was a part of the excursion, so he couldn't stand aside so easily and, although he was happy to be alive and without an injury like Del's, he would never say anything to that effect; not out loud anyway. "We can't take it out," he admitted. "It's got prongs running in both directions along the shaft. We have to find the middle point and try to cut it there. Then we can pull it out from both ends."

"But that part could be somewhere in the middle of my shoulder!" Del realized, adding more despair to his plight.

Doyle nodded. "That's what we're saying. The middle part is somewhere inside your shoulder. We can't get to it. We can't even see it."

"Ah!" Del screamed and swiped the whiskey bottle off the table with his good arm, which only increased pain levels for having jerked his body around suddenly, and he yelled again in retaliation. The bottle smashed, leaving a thin, honey-colored pool over white marble tiles. "Get me another bottle!" he demanded.

Once a new bottle arrived, and he had taken another couple of hefty chugs, he looked around to the four men in the room. "Where're all the men? And where are those idiots, Tanner and Mitchell? I should've taken them with us, ha!" He enjoyed that idea for one moment, of them being chopped up with the soldiers, then wondered in the next if the two had absconded. "If they've run off, I'll hunt them d—"

"They're here, boss," Pete interrupted. "But this is it. You took Will and the rest with you, and the new one."

"I thought I told you not to speak," Del threatened, before remembering Terry and realizing he had apparently led the timid man to his death, yet his expression didn't waver from an equal balance of grimace and sneer. Not that he would have felt it either way, but his pain was too great to take on any feelings of remorse, and he also began to feel very ill indeed.

Whilst his head swayed gently back and forth, his glazed eyes looked between the pathetic remains of what used to be a useful and willing league of men, while his mind revisited the utter destruction surrounding his mansion. He wanted very much to voice an entanglement of retributive thoughts, but agony now demanded all his energy, and he was also lost to know who to be angry with, or who to be angry with the most.

***

"You know, I've never been great with numbers," Akachi admitted. "But there seems to be a lot more than 20-something people here, so maybe Sanura needs to work on her arithmetic or something."

Kachina laughed. "Let's see when Oni gets back."

It was a relief for them to be so close to home and walking and talking in full volume without having to keep watch in any direction. The queen had left enough Shadow Warriors between Dead Man's Fall and home to battle a whole battalion, so they walked at an easy pace.

"39," Oni informed them, as she bounced back to their position. She had just run down the line and back to count all the people they'd found.

"See, arithmetic lessons," Akachi reinstated. "That's almost 40!"

Oni screwed up her face. "What?"

Her confusion only fueled Kachina's giggling.

"Just don't ask her to count the enemy before an attack," Akachi added. "Oh yeah, there's about five or ten, she'd say, suddenly we're facing 250."

"Akachi!" Kachina objected, though she laughed some more. "She even said she didn't know for sure how many there were."

Oni caught on, "Oh, I get it. No, one of them told me they're not all from Hickory's place."

"Ha! Akachi," Kachina jeered. "Now you owe Sanura an apology."

"What? She's not even here," Akachi objected.

Kachina's humor slipped away then, thinking of the battle which surely took place. "That was a lot of muskets going off."

"This was the plan, remember?" Oni said to reassure her, and also herself a little. "To draw their fire to the wrong place while under the cover of trees."

Akachi contradicted her own nod of agreement with, "All the same, I won't be happy until I see them."

When they entered Blue Falls, it seemed like all those present when they left hadn't moved at all while they were away, but one of the queen's sentries ran back to inform her they had seen the Guardians coming back across the plateau at Dead Man's Fall with the runaways, and it wasn't long before a massive greeting party awaited their imminent arrival.

Lesedi was, of course, hoping to see both units walk in together and so, while seeing the first team and the escapees brought her great joy, she couldn't help but to nurse concern, so her first question to the ones who had arrived was, of course, "Are the others far away?"

"We're not sure how far," Kachina answered. "We ran into some trouble and stuck to the plan."

"The Protectors stayed back to act as a decoy," Oni elaborated.

"How big was the trouble?" Lesedi asked then.

"50 to 60 soldiers with Hickory. They came searching like we thought they might," Kachina told her. "But we were all still inside the tree line."

This was reassuring information for Lesedi, being the ideal terrain for her warriors to confront an enemy armed with muskets and the like. The plan, if the Protectors needed to stay back and create a diversion, was for the Seekers unit to completely disconnect with them and focus solely on returning with the runaways as quickly as possible to Blue Falls. There was no point in them trying to rejoin the other team after that because they could never know where they might have gone. Secondly, there was no way of knowing what they might have had to do, or how far they had to go, in order to draw the enemy away, and thirdly, they might ruin the Protector's unknown plan by suddenly appearing in the very place they were trying to lead the soldiers away from. So they would wait two hours before sending two search units out; one via the roads, in case the unit was captured and escorted back through town, and another back the way they came, to search the hinterland.

This plan was agreed to by all and vowed to be followed by all and, given the scenario within which they found themselves, they knew it might be a long time before seeing the Protectors again, and so everyone focused immediately on treating and welcoming the new arrivals.

Although Layla had many helpers along the way, it was Mosi who took the last shift and carried her into the healing bay. When he put her down on the bed, he stood, stretched his back, took a giant breath, and exhaled heavily with great relief. After turning on the spot a couple of times in amazement, he turned back to Layla to share a smile of elation.

As usual, Artetha and Awinita stood at the helm of the healing bay, surrounded by an inundation of willing helpers. Once all the injured were in place, they walked from bed to bed, offering advice to other healers where needed, and while no serious injuries exposed themselves, they came upon a multitude of cuts, grazes, bruises, and sprains, such as Layla's swollen ankle.

The Shadow Warriors were prepared to go back out again if the Protectors didn't return before their deadline, and so they went to the HotPot in the meantime to replenish energy levels. Oni, Kachina, and Akachi, however, stayed for the return of the remaining warriors, and briefed the queen further on the mission, with Naira, Sayen, and Victor listening on with intent.

Before too long, the healing bay and the Entrance slowly filled with the roar of hundreds. It was most unsettling for the newcomers until they realized the outcry was one of universal joy for the return of the second unit of warriors. The remaining Shadow Warriors entered first and after sharing nods and smiles of confidence with the queen and party, they headed straight for the Armory. Jalen's smile was one of pure delight, and the queen shook her head with apprehension as his huge frame wandered by, glistening with red streaks.

When the queen saw how well they had all soaked themselves in the enemy's blood, she held her breath until she counted the three Guardians and Ky Mani, who entered soon after, covered with an equal amount of the enemy's coagulated losses. Yet, not a single Shadow Warrior or Guardian went to the healing bay. Lesedi's smile was great, but it could only be seen in her eyes, as she covered her mouth in awe, that the mission seemed a complete success.

The cheering and singing from their great audience went on for a long while, denying the healing bay its customary silence, but no one seemed to mind.

Ky Mani approached first. "Mission accomplished, my Queen," he said simply, but with much pride, then followed the Shadow Warriors to the Armory.

The appearance of their fellow Guardians brought relief and excitement for Kachina, Oni, and Akachi.

"What took you so long?" Akachi asked. "Not that we were worried but, you know."

Madeleine proceeded to tell them that, before they made their way back, the Protectors split up and left an obvious trail in many directions. To further ensure a clean getaway, they took the time to confuse the surrounds of the battleground, hoping to lead hunters into believing they might have escaped to any number of places, none of which being in the direction of Blue Falls, of course.

"And Jalen also wanted to make a statement," Annabel added.

All present but for Madeleine raised their eyebrows with curiosity.

"That's a story for another time," Madeleine decided, then turned to Kachina to share an embrace with her, during which she whispered, "I'm so sorry. Thank you, my sister."

While the queen had no idea what had transpired between Kachina and Madeleine, it was clear to her that it must have been something most significant, as they embraced for a long while and shared some tears in the process. She turned to Isi, ready to share a knowing smile, only to find his dimples were way ahead of her.

***

"We only saw them because they wanted us to," Wright concluded, in hindsight.

When he returned, he immediately brought a number of his officers together to brief them on the incident and to inform them of his new plan of action.

"It's a good thing you had a horse, Lieutenant Colonel sir," one of them suggested, with a not-so-well-hidden insinuation which might have seen him at least get an ear lashing for insubordination if not for Wright's own feeling of guilt.

"Yes, well," Wright floundered. "We won't be surprised next time."

We? Next time? These became sardonic questions on all their minds. Every one of their 50 comrades were lying dead somewhere, while their senior officer returned alone, without a scratch, arrogantly expecting the men to follow him again without question and with loyalty and confidence.

"I'll meet with the Major General sometime over the next couple of days, and we'll formulate a strategy," he informed them, hoping to restore their faith in his leadership.

Yet, to them, this only fueled their idea of his incompetence for essentially attempting to pass the responsibility and the problem up the ladder.

"What happened to Hickory and his men?" another of his officers asked.

"Oh, that reminds me," he was prompted. "Can someone send one of the doctors down to his place? Hickory and one of his men got away, but Hickory was wounded. Tell the good doctor to take his time, it's nothing too serious."

"Yes, sir!" came the eager response from a nearby private.

***

"Look at them," Mosi urged. "Look at the blood. I think the men who were hunting us are very unhappy at this time."

"They're frightening," Layla thought aloud, watching the Guardians in wonder. "Look at the way they hold their swords, like they were born with one in their hands."

Artetha chuckled. Upon noting the severity of Layla's injury, she had taken ownership of the treatment herself and first wrapped the ankle with a poultice

191

of comfrey before using with a mix of her healing balms made in part with tamanu, coconut, or tea tree oil, to treat lacerations on her legs and arms.

Mosi enjoyed very much simply sitting quietly and breathing gently, having nothing urgent to think about.

"Well, I was here when three of them were born anyway," Artetha informed them with a grin. "And I know, for sure, they didn't come out with swords in their hands."

"Really?" Layla asked. "Three of them?"

Artetha nodded proudly. "They look terrifying," she admitted. "And if you're the enemy, you should be very, very afraid because if they've got you in their sights, you're already dead. But any one of them would risk their life for any one of us. They're all in black and bloody now, but you'll see; they are truly beautiful souls and when they're not on duty, you forget how lethal they are because they're so kind in spirit."

Layla and Mosi watched the Guardians for some time, reflecting on Artetha's words, trying to imagine any one of them being gentle. They found this to be a challenge, especially after seeing them in the field and witnessing two of them in action, somehow moving faster than a panther at full flight, snatching up their prey before the prey even saw them coming.

In the next moment, Layla's heart skipped a beat as Kachina raised her sword and pointed it in their direction, yet, she was only sure when the others looked over and directly into her eyes that they were talking about her. Annabel and Madeleine approached the healing bay then, with eyes hardly swaying from Layla's hesitant glances, and the subsequent uneasy feeling left her breathless; that was, until she heard their gentle voices.

They didn't speak at first, as they knew Artetha liked to have the first and final words whenever they returned from their latest dangerous adventure, so they paused, carrying only hints of smiles until the expected came.

"Mm hmmm," Artetha muttered, shaking her head. Typically, she took on a disapproving tone with them, while in their absence, to anyone else, sang nothing but their praises. "I'm just gonna assume that none of that blood is your own coz I don't even want to look at you. Just tell me you didn't take any kiddies out with you this time."

"No," Annabel sniggered. "Not this time."

"I'm sorry to bother you with it now," Madeleine said to Layla and Mosi. "But I wanted to talk to you before tomorrow, if you don't mind. Kachina told me the man who was with you helped you escape; can you tell me what happened?"

Layla nodded. "He told me his name was Terry. We were on a ship bound for Port Harroway. He brought us a key in the middle of the night when we were just offshore, told us how to escape, and gave us the signal when it was clear to go."

"Why?" Madeleine asked, with regretful suspicion. "Why did he help you?"

"I don't know," she admitted. "He was sick during the journey and I helped him, maybe that's why."

Madeleine looked to Mosi, hoping for more information.

Mosi only shrugged. "I wasn't on the ship with Layla. I escaped from Hickory's farm."

"Your name is Layla?" Annabel snapped out, before Madeleine had time to ask the same.

Layla nodded and Artetha stopped working in that moment to stand up straight and observe Annabel's face, knowing instinctively that she and Madeleine just had an epiphany of some kind.

"Do you have any children, Layla?" Madeleine asked, just ahead of Annabel this time.

Layla nodded again. "I was just talking to Mosi about how to go about searching for them here. How would we do that?"

"Your name is Mosi?" Annabel won the race again this time, yet, in Madeleine's defense, Annabel had heard his name spoken many times by Tamaya in recent days. "Wait, you two are together and you have children together?" she proposed, wanting to be very clear on their circumstances.

"No," Mosi answered. "I mean, yes, my name is Mosi, but we're not together. I have a son, and Layla has a daughter."

There was a long pause then, before they realized the Guardians waited to hear their children's names, while they were both still distracted, wondering why their own names seemed familiar. That uneasy feeling Layla felt earlier quickly returned.

"My daughter's name is Sanura, and Mosi's son…" she failed to finish her sentence for the obvious affect her daughter's name had on Madeleine and Annabel.

"And my son's name is Elan," Mosi concluded.

"Montezuma and Tamaya," Annabel dared to offer, yet both she and Madeleine now clearly saw Sanura in her mother's eyes and Elan in his father's. Either way, suspicions were quickly confirmed by the startled reactions to the suggestion of their partners' names.

"Hold on," Annabel said, as both she and Madeleine spun around looking about the Entrance, while failing to see Sanura and Talia anywhere. "I'll be back in a second."

She was about to run off to ask the queen or Victor of Sanura's whereabouts when Artetha stopped her. "Wait, Annie. They're not here. Sherman took them to Riverside."

Both Mosi and Layla sat with mouths open, looking back and forth between the Guardians and Artetha, speechless, while their heartbeats steadily accelerated.

"What?" Annabel exclaimed. "What are they doing at Riverside?" She looked to Madeleine to note the same disappointment in her face. "No, not again."

Madeleine sighed. "Well, Elan and Tamaya are there anyhow."

"All right, you two," Annabel said suddenly, turning both their heads rapidly. "We'll go and get cleaned up, and when Artetha's finished and you've cleaned up too, we'll take you to Riverside where they all are, apparently."

"Now?" Layla blurted out.

The Guardians nodded in unison, and since Layla and Mosi had already witnessed the acute and unwavering conviction of the Guardians, it was certain they were not being tricked or being offered false promises, even though the claims might only be believed upon seeing their families.

"How do you know them so well?" Mosi asked, yet unsure, and feeling as if it were far too easy to have found his family this way.

"I don't think there's a single person in Blue Falls who doesn't know Elan," Artetha chuckled.

"We'll be back soon," Annabel said. "Mosi, you can ask Artetha all about your son. She was his momma until Tamaya arrived, and she also healed Sanura's wounds, Layla."

As Madeleine and Annabel left for the Armory, both Mosi and Layla turned to Artetha. Neither knew what to say or ask first.

"You can close your mouths now," Artetha said with great happiness, acknowledging their persistent doubt. She went back to her work. "It's true, they're all with us. Actually, I think Elan saw Annie more as his momma, but, anyway, I do have the pleasure of his company a lot." Her smile faded then as she raised her eyebrows with a touch of apprehension and sighed deeply. "Better hold onto your hats," she warned. "Both of you have another big surprise coming up."

***

"I want to be there," Talia had said, with a racing heart fueled by excitement, "Can I...I mean, can we please come with you?"

194

Yet again, Annabel found herself saying to a Guardian, Talia this time, that she never had to ask permission for anything, if she wanted to go to Riverside, whether it was to witness Sanura reunite with her mother or for any other reason, then someone would take her to Riverside, without question. No one decided the movements of the Guardians but for the Guardians themselves. This was an absolute, and well known to all. When they're left to work without impediment, left to follow their instincts when seeking lost ones or defending innocents, magic was sure to happen, and no one would ever dare to obstruct their proven and exalted powers in any way, shape, or form. To the people, it would be like defying the very blessings they themselves had incurred and, while the Guardians' loyalty remained with Queen Lesedi, and they were unlikely to deny her requests, this remained their choice alone.

Talia still struggled with this kind of autonomy and although she grew stronger, emotionally, with each new moment, a feeling of immense gratitude fed the reluctance she maintained to ask for anything, however minor. After only one night and one day with her newfound parents, her joy hadn't come down from its peak yet, and, in fact, had only escalated further with the appearance of Sanura's mother and Elan's father. She sat across from her parents so she could cast her eyes upon them the whole way to Riverside, hoping to rid that urgent feeling deep inside of disbelief mixed with the fear of losing them again. She also wanted to make eye contact with Layla and Mosi sitting beside her, so she sat in the corner while telling them the story of her escape.

Layla and Mosi rode most restlessly, writhing hands and wiping tears of anticipation away. At one time, halfway through Talia's story, their pain and joy became too much for all five passengers. With emotions easily swayed, having each experienced their own recent emotional upheaval, they all wept together from the top of Ridge Road down to West Bridge before the great flood ended.

"This is going to kill me," Talia confessed. "I've never cried so much for being so happy."

Unwittingly, Talia had left them hanging on her story at the point where Sanura came back to rescue her, hence the reason for their unanimous breakdown. Speaking of the moment Sanura reappeared, Talia revisited her emotions on the night, setting forth a contagion of tears, and the interruption created by all was so long that Layla had to prompt Talia to finish telling her story.

When she was done, Mosi voiced his realization, "Layla, your daughter is the one who set me free, and Tau, Kirra, and Montezuma wouldn't be with us if she didn't burn those barns down."

"And Mosi," Talia said, drawing his attention. "Sanura and I might not have made it at all without Elan's help."

Layla and Mosi smiled to one another, but these stories didn't help their heartbreak so much; to know that, in their absence, they had missed their children growing so talented and well-loved. Their urgency to see Sanura and Elan escalated with each new piece of information, and if either one of them were in control of the carriage, they might have rivaled Annabel's recent bolt through the forests on Primrose.

Up top, in the driver's seat with reins in hand, Annabel said to Madeleine, "Who needs sleep anyway?"

Madeleine chuckled yet shook her head at the same time in sympathy for her body's aches and pains. Their tiredness exacerbated the chill in the air, yet the bouncing carriage provided somewhat of a distraction from the hurt while the moonlight and the layer of mist hovering all around lulled them into a dreamlike state within which discomfort could be ignored.

"How is Sanura going to find the doorway while she's at Riverside?" with a hint of woe, Madeleine posed.

"You'll have to let that one go," Annabel advised. "How long did I watch you come and go, doing this, that, and the other? A year or something? And just when I thought your time might be coming, Kachina discovered your father in her book."

"You probably thought it would never happen," Madeleine supposed. "How did you do it?"

Annabel shrugged. "Like you now, I didn't have a choice. But at least we can share the pain from now on. You know I was only guessing at Sanura anyway."

"I know," Madeleine acknowledged. "But what you said about her makes sense and look at how her actions have affected so many different outcomes. Yet, again, when I think of what Kachina did last night—"

"You mean, what she didn't do," Annabel corrected.

"Yes. Exactly," she sighed. "I wonder, like you first did, if it won't be her."

"The darkness can be cruel sometimes," Annabel surmised. "Breaking somebody into pieces and then putting revenge on a silver platter right in front of them, knowing how much they want it, knowing the damage it would cause to take it. She could've done it, you know, and hidden it from us if she wanted to. I've thought about it, and the timing of it all. They would have said she killed one of Hickory's men, someone Layla knew as Terry, and none of us would have cared too much to ask anything about it."

Madeleine had thought of this herself; a slightly different scenario, yet the same idea. "I wonder when we'll get the chance to go to Sampa. It's strange, thinking how no time will pass here while we're in there anyway, but we haven't even had the opportunity to walk to Crystal Nest together."

"I wanted to talk to you about that and see what you think," Annabel replied. "I've been thinking of this for a very long time, and my instincts tell me if I walk in with you, the Timuillain will see that we're one giant step closer to fulfilling the Sampa Prophecy and opening the door for all 11 Guardians. They'll attack with everything they've got, knowing it's their last chance to take full control and so, many innocent people would die in the process."

"You're suggesting we wait until the third Guardian finds the doorway before even making my presence known to them," Madeleine intuited.

"Yes," Annabel confirmed. "It will also be much less difficult for you if we do it that way."

Madeleine thought aloud, "I keep forgetting that for you, or us, no time has passed in Sampa since you were there, so it doesn't matter how long we take."

Annabel nodded. "I think this would be the strongest tactical move, even though I'm already missing people there very much. At the moment, there's just a few smaller battles going on and I know this is only because the Timuillain, for now anyway, are almost totally focused on manufacturing weapons and recruiting armies."

"What do you think they'll do when 11 Guardians walk in together?" Madeleine posed.

"Attack anyway. Well, the thing I told you, the people want from us, is for us to close the Wall of Amity. There's a wide abyss stretching right across Sampa from south to north, separating the east from the rest of the realm, and there is only one bridge across it. The east holds the Timui Mountains, where mostly all of the Timuillain live, the Timu, as we call them. The abyss is actually the base of the Wall of Amity, when it's down, of course. It's where the wall rises from."

Madeleine didn't understand. "What do you mean?"

"The wall is the same as the wall surrounding Attunga, the Guardians' realm. It looks like the blue opening in our doorway into Sampa, like the blue mist we walk through, but no one except the Guardians can pass through any of these blue walls. So, when the Wall of Amity is raised, the Timu can't pass through into the rest of Sampa, and the people of Sampa can't pass through into the east, which is why it was called, The Bridge of No Return."

"That means we have to get everyone out of the east before we close it," Madeleine proposed. "But how could we do that if, like you said, the mountains are full of catacombs, and if Sampa is so vast?"

"No," Annabel answered. "The prophecy, which has been kept by the Elders of Amity for thousands of years, says that the people of Sampa can still return to their side of the realm through the Wall of Amity if they cross at the Bridge of No Return, but they just can't go back through again. Same for the Timu, once they cross into the east, they can't go back to Sampa. When they reigned, one of the many lies the Timu miseducated the people with was to tell them it was given its name because if you crossed the bridge, you would be tortured and killed by the Timu. It was just another way of confusing and hiding the prophecy, and spreading more fear of the Timu among the people of Sampa. It also scared people out of exploring in the east."

Madeleine released a great sigh. "Sounds like we've got some work to do. Well, since I don't know anything about Sampa and I trust you, I think we should wait like you said and go in with all the Guardians."

"All right," Annabel replied, pleased for Madeleine's trust and support. "If the third Guardian takes too long to find the doorway, maybe we could go for a quick visit and we'll disguise you or something. I hope we can work out how we're supposed to raise the Wall of Amity before then."

"You're joking?" Madeleine asked, then saw in her blank face that she wasn't. "You don't know how to raise it?"

"A long time ago, the Timu somehow hid the location of whatever the Guardians use to raise the wall," Annabel elaborated. "Only the Guardians of old knew where this was, and the Elders say it was easy to find but the Timu went to great lengths in hiding it. I've been looking for years myself but I can't find it. It's not in Attunga and I have a special team of seekers searching Sampa for it. They've been searching for as long as I have."

As the horses crossed East Bridge, their steps on the hardwood slats added an ominous drum to the Guardians' post-battle silence as Madeleine pondered on the idea of joining Annabel and all the Guardians to fight a great war in Sampa. It was too much to think of at that time, so she rested her head on Annabel's shoulder instead, and let her mind drift off to wherever it wanted to go.

"So I'm supposed to drive and hold you up," Annabel complained, yet in jest. "Maybe I could juggle for you too or something?"

"Can you juggle?" Madeleine's wandering mind asked.

"I can actually," she admitted.

"That figures," Madeleine scoffed. "That shot you took at Hickory was amazing. They'll be telling stories about that one for generations."

"Don't hit the horses," Annabel remembered aloud. "Did you think I'd take a shot if there was any chance of hitting a horse?"

"Sorry, it was just automatic, you know?" she answered in defense.

"Anyhow," Annabel concluded, with some disappointment. "I think I was a little high. I was aiming for his heart, but I guess we'll find out tomorrow."

Once Misae and Shenandoah had shown the Shadow Warriors where to find everything they needed and where to sleep, one of them stepped forward and declined on behalf of all.

"Respectfully, my Princess," Cayman said. "It is our intention to work day and night. We'll work in shifts and take catnaps when we need them, so the work will never stop. We plan to work like fury until it's finished. You don't need to stay with us the whole time, of course, you just need to give us enough work to last us through the night."

"Whose idea was this?" Misae asked.

"It is the collective wish of all of us," he answered. "We want to help our Princess achieve her goal, to see her home and safe again."

Misae found Tamaya smiling, as were Montezuma and Sanura, who were already informed of the Warriors' plan on the way over.

"Well, you were worried about time, my Princess, so here's your answer," Shenandoah suggested.

After Cayman announced that they were well-rested and more than capable of achieving their objective, he added convincingly, "And as you can see, we're not exactly weak and feeble."

Upon looking through the men's collective volume of great muscle again, Misae silently agreed with Cayman, and since their presence and motivation was, after all, her own dream manifested, she found no reason to deny their wishes. In fact, they were in complete harmony with her own.

She went with Shenandoah, Montezuma, and Sanura to set the warriors to work immediately, and although they had warned her, after setting-up lanterns and torchlight in every place, they immediately began working at a rate which both startled and inspired. Within just an hour or so, she could already see major advancements in every aspect of their plan.

At one point, after her third circumnavigation of the area, she turned to Shenandoah to express delight, but tiredness rendered her speechless. It didn't matter though; Shenandoah understood her elation and also noted her fading energy levels.

"Misae, why don't you get some sleep now?" he implored. "As insane as these men are, they have enough work now to keep them busy until morning."

Misae was all set to accept the idea when a distant voice rose over the surrounding clamor. They all looked over to see Talia running toward them, calling Sanura's name. Given their recent experiences and the fact that everyone knew of the Guardians' mission on this night, it wasn't too difficult for all present to think the worst of Talia's presence and her high-speed approach only added to the suspense.

Sanura also didn't believe it was Talia until she came closer and one of the torchlights exposed the white teeth in her beaming smile, contradicting the swell of tears sitting dormant on her eyelids.

"Talia, what's wrong?" Sanura blurted, stark-faced.

"Nothing," Talia replied, a little breathless. "But you have to come with me. Where's Elan and Tamaya?"

Talia's question only brought more confusion for all, as they tried to make a connection between Sanura, Elan, and Tamaya, but failed to guess what the matter could be.

"They're sleeping," Misae answered, for Sanura was struck silent. "What's going on?"

"We have to wake them up," she said. "I have to show you something. C'mon!"

She impelled them to follow and, while hesitantly, Sanura obeyed. Misae trailed behind, with curiosity leading her through a haze of lethargy.

They hadn't moved too far at all before Talia halted abruptly and looked back to Montezuma, who hadn't moved at all. "Montezuma!"

He pointed to himself. "Me?"

"Yes!" she answered with a giggle. "You too, c'mon."

When they passed the barn, Talia went inside and returned with the mystified souls of Elan and Tamaya, and led them all to the entrance where they found Madeleine and Annabel standing near a carriage with Kirra and Tau, while two sweat-lined horses grazed placidly nearby.

Misae looked to Annabel and Madeleine with narrowing eyes. "What are you two up to?" she asked suspiciously. "I don't trust those grins of yours."

They both shrugged, giving nothing away, while Talia went to the carriage and opened the doors.

"They're here now," she told the occupants.

Mosi was quick to step out first, having no injuries, and Talia helped Layla as she stepped down ever so carefully. Every time she sat for a long while, her ankle would become stiff again and the first few steps thereafter were always challenging, so she wobbled a good deal after her feet touched the ground just to stand balanced.

No introductions were needed, of course, except for Elan perhaps, but he worked things out for himself when his mother screamed briefly before running into Mosi's open arms. Sanura and Montezuma's reactions were not so impulsive at first, as they froze for a few moments, looking between themselves and Layla. Layla wanted to run to them, but her ankle predetermined that impossibility. In any case, despite her obvious injury, it wasn't long before Sanura nearly knocked her off her feet with a flying embrace, and Montezuma was soon there with his arms around both of them.

Misae looked to all others then and nodded toward the construction site, suggesting they should leave the reunion alone.

On the way back over, Misae and Shenandoah heard the story of the mission from Annabel and Madeleine, and Misae's first question to Annabel surprised them all.

With more than just mild curiosity, she asked, "Do you think you killed Hickory?"

"He didn't come off his horse," Annabel answered, noting her purposeful tone. "But who knows what happened later. Why?"

"Because if he's dead, it ruins a plan I wanted to ask you about. Not that it matters, and I guess it's good if he's dead," she added, not to make Annabel feel guilty. "But all the same, I'd have to forget it and start over. It's just an add-on to the plan we already had, and if you only injured him, that's okay, it actually works better for the plan."

They were most curious, of course, and when she finished telling them her idea, she was pleased to hear Annabel exclaim, "Misae, it's brilliant. It guarantees we get what we want. We just have to do it right and be ready at Riverside when the time comes."

While Madeleine went over and over the plan in her mind, searching for any possible contingencies, she couldn't find one either, aside from the obvious dangers of course, so she also nodded in agreement. "It's really good. How did you come up with it?"

"I was thinking about Hickory's connections with the army and, I don't know why, it just came to me," she admitted modestly. "I'm glad you like it."

After a quick stroll and little more than a glance over the site, Annabel finally noticed the radical advancements and remarked, "Whoa! Someone's been busy."

"Where did these ones come from?" Madeleine asked, referring to the newly arrived Shadow Warriors, hammering through the work like the possessed.

Misae smiled. "Momma bear."

Just then, Cayman appeared out of nowhere, his face and body glistening with sweat under the torchlights. He pulled a folded piece of paper from a small pouch slung over his shoulder, unfolded it, and handed it to Misae.

"Mission accomplished, my Princess," he said, and the deep base in his voice somehow added promise to his words. He pointed to one of the rectangles within a map he had drawn on the paper. "Ex is ammunitions. They keep everything in there, except for swords and a few muskets with the guards on patrol. I'll sit down with you and list everything tomorrow."

Misae nodded. "Thank you, Cayman. Did you run into any trouble?"

"I wish," he replied, laughing briefly and shaking his head, then wandered off, leaving Misae to look over the map. So curious about Cayman's findings, she temporarily forgot about Madeleine and Annabel in her presence.

They looked to one another, with faces captured by awe and fascination, then to Shenandoah, who only smiled knowingly.

"Misae, since when did you become a warlord?" Annabel asked in half-jest, extracting a giggle out of Madeleine.

Misae looked up from the page with equal amusement. "That's Princess of War," she corrected. "Wow, I'm really awake now. Are you both too tired for some sword practice?"

***

Chapter Nine
Don't Lose Your Head

Wright did well to hide his great disappointment when the doctor returned to inform him that Del Hickory was going to be all right. He blamed Del directly for the death of all his men, since, if not for his slaves escaping and his connections with Wright's superiors, they would never have ventured into the hinterland in the first place.

It took all morning for him to organize a legion to traipse into the hinterland again, simply to retrieve his lost men, as he wasn't planning to have a repeat performance, of the massacre kind. This time, wagons were loaded with cannons and Gatling guns, and all the things he was thinking of last night while bolting, flatstick with his tail between his legs, out of the forest and all the way back to the barracks.

200 men led the way this time, in the strictest of formations, all armed to the hilt and walking on thin ice as if waiting for the ground to open up and swallow them whole. Under the guidance of four senior officers, most of the men surrounded the area while others went to work, collecting bodies, and smaller units were sent out to the east, north, and west on reconnaissance in search of clues as to where a hidden force might choose to dwell.

While overcompensating for his epic failure, Wright shouted orders with exuberant confidence, yet, most ironically, his exhibition was all for not. They could have walked in completely weaponless and with just enough men to fill a wagon or two with the dead, for there wasn't another living soul in the entire region.

When the men were all in position, Wright moved his horse forward to inspect the scene. Trails of dead air wafted past his nostrils periodically as he meandered through fly-ridden corpses, and when he came to where Del's man, Will, had gone down, he pulled his steed up and stared in horror at what they'd found. Will's head had been stuck at the end of a stake and throughout the morning, birds had taken his eyes out and feasted well on the rest of his face.

While staring horrified at Will's head, another stinky trail came Wright's way, and a moment later, he vomited, barely managing to direct the flow away from his horse's withers, and subsequently backed away, lurching over the saddle.

One of his concerned soldiers called out, "You all right, Lieutenant Colonel?"

Wright spat a few times before responding. "Of course I'm all right. Just got surprised is all. Now let's get this cleaned up! I want us out of here by 1400!"

"Yes, sir!" came many replies. One particularly green, enthusiastic soldier shouted, "Yes, sir! Lieutenant Colonel, sir! Right away, sir!"

Wright believed, for a moment, that he was being mocked, until he spun around, ready to scold someone, only to watch the young man in question hop to it with vigilance.

"Yes, good then," he muttered to himself, realizing he had merely projected his own imaginings, that his men saw him as an incompetent and cowardly leader.

The scouts returned to inform him they had found many tracks leading north, northeast, and due east, and although he wondered if the attackers had fled to the east coast, knowing the hinterland would probably be searched thoroughly, he still pondered on the idea of the ground beneath his feet being the ceiling of a secret hideaway. Part of his initial orders were to establish a base, prepare for war, and investigate the alleged existence of an underground group of rebel slaves, but he was to search throughout Black Sand Valley, not in the north or the east.

His men also found piles of the dead soldiers' weapons on the bank of a stream to the northeast and, although skeptical, Wright held no proof to deny one of his officer's suggestions that they had ditched the weapons for their cumbersome nature before crossing the stream, as they also discovered that same trail continued on the other side of the water, again to the northeast.

After a conference with his officers, he decided that it was both pointless and dangerous to split the men up to search farther afield at this time, and once the wagons were loaded, he gave the order to move out and return home.

One of his officers asked, with some disgust, "Is that all we're going to do?"

"For now," Wright replied. "My orders are not to waste any more resources on this, for the time being anyhow. The men will get their war, Major, you can count on that, and the one that's coming will clean out this infestation, don't you worry. Let's just hope these soldiers are willing to fight against the white armies of the north who have taken it upon themselves to fight for the likes of those who slaughtered our men."

***

Come dawn, sleep had successfully denied Del all but a few brief moments of its serenity. By the time the doctor arrived, he had lost consciousness many times, much to the doctor's delight, for Del's delirium helped him immensely to go about cutting the arrow out without the unending screams he would have otherwise endured if operating soon after the event.

It was a messy and long operation, whereby he ended up cutting the arrow into five pieces before having to pry the last two lengths out using a combination of clamps and other makeshift instruments which he created on the fly. In the end, he bound the wound tightly and interweaved bandages around Del's neck and chest to be sure his dressing would continually apply pressure to the wound.

At first, they carried Del to his bed, only for him to find that lying prone or slightly elevated increased pain to unbearable levels and, since he couldn't lie any other way for the same reason, they brought him back out and into the living room where they lowered him into a large, well-cushioned chair.

While his men had been working tirelessly to assist him for hours, he moaned and groaned nothing but unintelligible frustrations the whole time, and again now, due to all the movement. They were more than happy not to have understood a single word he uttered in his misery and happier still that the doctor had come and gone to release them from the burden of responsibility. Finally, they could ignore him and rest themselves for the remainder of the night.

Mitchell and Tanner hardly helped at all throughout the entire time. They hadn't slept much themselves since their dreaded, farcical night, and even now, they suffered with constant aches and pains. They'd never before enjoyed watching someone suffer as much as watching Del spit and vomit for hours, while slowly becoming more and more frightened and desperate. None of the many revenge fantasies they dreamt up even came close to equaling the spectacle they witnessed, and they would have gone off to sleep but for the enjoyment factor in staying to watch.

The all-encompassing agony from Del's lashings had finally begun to wane, yet almost to Tanner's disappointed, for once again, the deep ache in his eye socket became his most prominent affliction. It never failed to remind him of his escaped prize nor to fuel denial; that he was unlikely to ever find her. If she were with the ones who attacked Wright's army and wounded Del, then the chance of ever coming face-to-face with her again was less than zero. Even so, he satisfied his violent needs with unending delusions of how he might exact his revenge. Mitchell too, concocted all kinds of torturous ideas on how to go about teaching their escapees a lesson, for having brought a lashing upon his otherwise immune world and shaken his ego into nothingness. Both victims merely waited for better health, dreaming of an opportunity to wreak havoc on two young women, and in the meantime, they begged their deity to bring them the justice they deserved.

Mid-morning, Del was heard yelling orders and complaining that no one had come to see him in hours. Although it was true, there was nothing more they could do for him other than to surround him with food, water, and blankets, and to help him get to the bathroom when needed.

This was not good enough for Del. Pain came in unrelenting waves and while he harbored myriad sadistic thoughts, in his current condition, he could act out none of them. Instead, he had to somehow find patience, to somehow endure absolute frustration, to resign to healing, and to forget about putting his own hands into anything for a while.

"Where's Doyle?" he demanded, before being reminded that he had given Doyle a mission for this day. "Oh yeah. Where's Tanner and Mitchell?" he asked then. "They better be working!"

"They're working, boss," Pete answered.

Del yelped then, as if hit with another arrow, before asking, "What did the doctor say?"

Pete replied again, for being the only one around, "He's gonna come back tonight and change the dressing."

There was nothing else important enough for Del to say or ask, so he went silent again. Talking, together with bursts of anger, made him feel like passing out and also increased his discomfort three-fold, he finally realized. Resting his head back, he closed his eyes, contemplating, You want your freedom? Well, guess what? You're getting war instead, and it's gonna flush you out.

***

She was right, that young woman, whose name Nathaniel may never live to learn. He could think of no worse punishment for himself than to have repelled Madeleine away and out of his world.

How did you move so fast and when did you become so deadly?

Seeing his daughter in action, fighting for a cause his own behavior once worked against, dragged the disappointment of past apathy into his safety-zone

206

of personal identity, and forced him, yet again, to reveal unto himself another layer of misconception.

Will she come?

Even though she said to meet him after dark, Nathaniel arrived at East Bridge long before the sun wandered out of sight, waiting nervously on the riverbank until then with a view of the road in both directions. Never before in his life had he spent so much time alone than over the last few seasons, and yet, even now, he was no closer to being comfortable with it than he was in the beginning. In his current state-of-mind, silence became suffocating, a crisp and haunting breeze whispered something of his conundrums, and the stars seemed to mock the lack of love in his life with their not-so-distant sparkle.

A carriage rolled in slowly from the east, with two visible silhouettes in the driver's seat. The soft thudding of hooves found his ears first, then the squeak of dry wheel bearings and metal springs. He sighed with relief as it turned off the road to pull up nearby, and when Madeleine jumped down, he thought his chest might implode under the weight of desperation.

"Thank you for coming," he said, as she approached, yet she stayed a few paces away, and her undeniable coldness struck his greatest fears like a lashing.

"To be perfectly honest, I only came because I knew you'd keep looking if I didn't," she replied.

"Maddy—" he began, realizing he hadn't called her Maddy since she was a child. She stepped forward in that moment, placed a cotton drawstring bag in his hands, and subsequently deleted the speech waiting on his tongue. "What's this?"

"Money," she answered. "A lot of money. Remember the last conversation we had about you never returning to Black Sand Valley?"

His eyes flashed back to hers then. "Yes, but, M—"

"It's either that," she interrupted. "Or you could go and talk to the new crooked sheriff and tell him about all your crooked dealings with all your crooked friends. Maybe he'll recruit you, knowing what we've discovered about him."

Unfortunately, for Nathaniel, history denied any chance of rebuttal and left him juggling fruitless words around in his mouth. Eventually, he managed to say, "I've changed."

"Good," she stated, turning to leave. "Let's hope it continues, and if you're thinking of seeing Mother before you leave, I strongly recommend that you don—"

"I already tried," he confessed.

Madeleine halted and turned, furious. "Why? Why would you do that? She only just started to find some happiness again."

He shook his head and despair found every crease in his face. "I had to do something. I can't just…"

Suddenly, realization struck him silent and he was unable to voice the words, I can't just walk away from you and Helen, because he was certain now, this was already his path and not only that, but he had paved the way long ago when he decided to do things which may one day be forgiven, but certainly never forgotten; things his daughter would surely be reminded of by his presence alone, promising an eternity of disgust.

"Start a new life for yourself somewhere," she said, arrogating his only course of action, while walking away again. "Somewhere far away. There's nothing for you here. Let's go, Jimmy."

After climbing into the seat again, she turned one last time to look Nathaniel's way. It lifted his heart for a moment, thinking she might say something hopeful before leaving, but she merely left him with an expression of great disappointment; the final vision of his failed attempt to recuperate something out of all that was lost.

Long after the carriage had gone, he stood petrified, staring into the obscurity which slowly swallowed them up, as the darkness closed-in all around.

Madeleine, I never got to say I love you.

How she might have responded if he were to have voiced his affection, he couldn't know, but he did wonder if he had saved himself from yet another stab in the heart and a most expected frosty reaction by keeping this love to himself.

It didn't matter about the darkness, the cold, or his empty stomach, and direction failed him, for there was nowhere he wanted to go without his daughter, without his wife, without any hope of his dreams keeping alive.

Yet, his legs moved themselves toward the station. While he had no prior plan at all, but for getting some money together and attempting to meet with Helen and Madeleine, and since he couldn't stay in town for fear of being recognized, there was nowhere else he could think to go. His parents were gone, as with his older brother, so there was no one waiting for him anywhere in Earth, and he felt the brunt of this solitude all at once after watching Madeleine roll away, sitting next to a man he'd never even met.

Nathaniel dared to acknowledge that no one would be thinking of him now, but for those who despised him or those who surely did what they could not to think of him at all. This very idea stopped him in his tracks, yet he didn't realize he wasn't walking for a long while, as he stared at a black feather on the ground which had broadcast its appearance in his path with a flashing of blue moonlight over its vane.

After picking it up, he wiped the dust of its barbs and quill, then stood gazing at it for minutes while attempting to gather his thoughts into some kind of coherent plan. He was reminded of the bay windows in Madeleine's bedroom where she had hung many of the feathers she found over the years and how they would drift about in the breeze beside strings of seashells all tinkling together. The sound they made almost came to his ears again in that moment, as he imagined standing at Madeleine's doorway when she was a little girl, watching her sleep and listening to the shells, some of which they had collected together at a fun-filled trip to the beach.

Though he tried to understand, it was yet unclear how life had brought him to a standstill on a path by the river near East Bridge, under the moonlight, holding a crow feather in his hands as if it were a lost dream he'd just found. When he finally started moving again, it was in awe for having discovered a new level of hollowness, for even his modest of wishes had been denied.

At the first lamplight on the path leading to the ticket office, Nathaniel pulled out the little money he had left and counted it before opening the bag Madeleine had given him to add enough for a train ticket. It wasn't the place to count it, but Nathaniel only needed to rummage through the stacks of notes quickly to see that she had given him a small fortune, enough to buy a house or two, maybe even three, and yet, his sorrow killed any excitement which this gift might have delivered under different circumstances.

As he removed a bill and shoved the bag deep inside his coat, the Ticketmaster called out from afar.

"Are you hoping to catch this northern train, sir?" he asked, indicating the one warming up on the tracks, sending clouds of steam out into the darkness. "It's about to leave and it's the last train out tonight."

Julian went to the window. "Where's it headed?"

"North," he answered. "All stops to Mount Illusion and there's plenty of sleepers if you're going that far."

"Mount Illusion," Nathaniel repeated, thinking of the place known for its undying anti-slavery mentality, which was also the subject of rumors that its base was a place where escaped slaves could find sanctuary. Good, he thought. No slaves. It was also a two-day journey. Sleep. Forget.

"Yes, thank you, I'll take a one-way sleeper to Mt. Illusion."

The whistle of the train sounded.

"We've got two minutes," the Ticketmaster said, rushing to write up Nathaniel's ticket. "Will that be economy or first-class?"

Oddly, Nathaniel's mind washed over his money bag and over the memories of Helen, Madeleine, and Layla's disappointed eyes all at the same time. Without realizing it, he paused, holding his breath for a long while, waiting for a wave of sadness to pass.

"Sorry, sir, but we must make haste," the polite man prompted, snapping Nathaniel back to the task at hand.

"I'm sorry, good sir," Nathaniel replied. "Economy will be fine, thank you."

***

While she tried ever so hard, Madeleine couldn't hide her amusement when Julian stumbled down the stairs and into the foyer of the hotel with his beret and pipe, barely avoiding a fall, then stood straight again, adjusting his ensemble like nothing had happened.

"You okay, Mister Mitten?" Barnaby asked, most concerned, remembering the time he himself tripped down the narrow staircase and ruined his hip for a good six months.

"Julian!" Madeleine said upon seeing him. "I was just asking if you were in."

"Julian?" Barnaby repeated, taking up his register to check the mistake.

Julian shook his head secretly. "'It's Walter actually. Perhaps you forgot?"

Madeleine finally caught on. "Oh, yes, sorry…Walter. I'm terrible with names. I'm sorry, no wonder you couldn't find him in your register, Mister Dixon."

Julian laughed awkwardly and led Madeleine away to speak in private.

"So very super sleuth," Madeleine jeered, still enjoying the sight too much for Julian's ego to withstand. "I almost didn't recognize you."

"You're not supposed to recognize me at all!" Julian exclaimed, with a voice hushed between his teeth.

Madeleine noted his genuine concern and took on a more serious tone, "You look very nervous. Are you all right?"

"To be honest, not really," he confessed. "I'm afraid someone's going to recognize me and it'll get back to you-know-who. If I try to go home, what if they follow me again?"

"Why don't you stay with my mother for a while?" she suggested. "The place is huge, so you won't be a burden on anyone, and she won't mind, in fact, she'd probably welcome the distraction at the moment. If you need anything, you can go to the store on the north side and just lay low for a while."

Julian's tension lessened to some extent. "That sounds like a good idea, thank you."

"Go pay for your stay," she said. "Jimmy's waiting with the carriage outside. We've got a few passengers, so you'll have to ride up top, but we'll drop you there before we head back."

With much appreciation, Julian nodded, retrieved his bag, gave a most suspicious Barnaby some money, and then left with Madeleine. He was very pleased to find the street virtually deserted, but for one or two distant wanderers, and smiled to Jimmy standing at the door of the carriage, chatting to the passengers hidden inside.

Jimmy smiled in return, though it was difficult for him not to feel heartache whenever he saw Madeleine with Julian. He held no confidence that she would ever feel the same, and although he had resigned to this disappointing reality long ago, acceptance never lent itself to numbing feelings at all.

"I'll ride inside," Madeleine said to him. "If you don't mind, we're going to drop Julian off at my mother's place."

"Okay," Jimmy agreed, with both hidden joy and guilt for knowing Julian would soon be gone again. While listening to Madeleine, he noticed a man step out of the shadows behind her, a little further up the street, and didn't think anything of it until he came closer to reveal his murderous eyes which were locked onto Julian.

It was Doyle, unbuttoning his trench coat. When Jimmy saw him pull out a crossbow and raise it in the air, he hastened to push Maddy sideways and behind him out of the way.

"Maddy, watch out!" he yelled, as Doyle let the arrow fly.

Julian, also with his back to Doyle, didn't have time to notice what was happening or to take any emergency action, and as a consequence, luck came his way. The arrow which was meant for him instead, found a place high in Jimmy's shoulder, and the impact sent him reeling backward into Madeleine arms.

Doyle was long gone before Madeleine looked up again, and although she also saw his face before he turned, her concern for Jimmy was too great to think of chasing him.

"Jimmy!" she exclaimed. His body, limp and heavy, brought her to her knees as he cried out in agony. When Annabel jumped out, she looked up to her, wide-eyed and furious, and said only, "Artetha!"

Annabel nodded frightfully. "I'll drive, you look after him. Help us, Julian!"

Raised voices shocked Julian into action, after having been frozen until that moment, and he helped them to lift Jimmy into the carriage. With many grunts and groans, voiced through gritted teeth, Jimmy objected but he was inside and on the floor with Madeleine, and Annabel was up top with reins in hand, just a few moments later.

Julian stood at the door after that, not knowing what to do, until Madeleine looked up from Jimmy for an instant to see that he was still standing outside.

"Julian! Get in!" she demanded.

After he rushed in, Annabel let out a "Ya!" and the wagon launched into action.

Kirra and Tau sat fearfully, but Talia spoke up, "What can I do?"

"Find me some material or something I can use to stop the bleeding," she asked, trying to brace Jimmy through the greater jolts of a frantic ride. "We have to apply pressure around the wound. Jimmy? Jimmy!" Finally, his head lolled over her way and swayed a little in rhythm with the smaller bumps. "Jimmy, don't fall asleep," she begged. "Look at me."

After finding nothing of use, Talia stole her father's shirt and handed it to Madeleine, who then wound it around the base of the arrow and applied pressure to it.

"Stay awake, Jimmy," she repeated, then looked up to all present in despair. "There's nothing else we can do until we get home."

Jimmy clutched Madeleine's arms then. She could see he was trying to say something, but his voice was too quiet, so she leaned closer and he whispered in her ear, "Maddy... I love you."

***

Artetha was never so frightened, as she was upon seeing Annabel's face when she came pelting into the Healing Bay, screaming her name at the top of her voice.

Given the Guardians' perilous exploits, the last thing she expected was to see Jimmy being rushed into the bay, sporting an arrow. She didn't even ask what happened, only bellowed orders to a number of her most experienced healers while she and Awinita went about preparing Jimmy for what they needed to do.

"Out!" she demanded of the crowd which had quickly formed. "Everyone! Leave us."

Madeleine stayed in defiance. "I'm not leaving," she stated, with a voice breaking into pieces, yet stepped back a few paces to avoid being in the way.

Artetha ignored her, focusing on the task at hand.

Madeleine turned to Annabel, who had also refused to leave and barely managed to speak the words. "It's all my fault, Annie. I should've been watching—"

"If you're going to do that, you can get out, like I asked," Artetha interrupted.

Though she fought somewhat, Annabel managed to lead her away a few paces.

Madeleine couldn't silence her thoughts, but she lowered her voice. "I should've seen it coming. Why wasn't I watching?"

Annabel was too distraught to think hard on the question, but in seeing Madeleine's horrified state, she tried to say something worthwhile, yet it was merely her own regret which floated to the surface. "I could've kept watch. I should've kept watch."

"It's not fair, Jimmy's never hurt anyone." Madeleine thought of his last whispered words and only just prevented herself from breaking down for Annabel's sake.

Placing a supportive arm around Madeleine, Annabel watched her uncle, while his subdued body swayed gently back and forth as Artetha went about her desperate work.

They'd forgotten about Julian, who had attracted many a curious onlooker, as he wandered stunned-faced over to the wall to look out and beyond into Blue Falls.

Blue Falls, he mouthed, but no sound came out of his mouth. When he looked back to the healing bay to see his friends huddled together, guilt riddled his mind and denied any excitement for his discovery.

It's my fault. I should be the one lying there.

***

Chapter Ten
Just Breathe

"It's all they had planned, all they hoped for, that we should be fighting one-another and, so long as we are, they are winning, they are laughing."
~ (Excerpt; The Guardians of The Falls – Julian Bartholomew Winters.)

***

"The Panthers are your warriors, my Queen, not mine," Jalen said, in all sincerity. "If you choose to send them on any mission without my knowledge, this is your right. We are all in your charge."

With legs hanging over the edge, they sat on a granite ledge overlooking Crimson Lake. Finally, Lesedi had found an opportunity to sit in this place after wishing for the chance since the first day she walked through Crimson Cove. Lamplight seemed to draw a red hue out of the long seam of ruby on the adjacent wall, and for Lesedi, its bloodlike nature seemed to predicate the immediate future.

She sighed. "I'm sorry to admit, Jalen, for a long time, I misunderstood your cause, and now, it seems your work is proving invaluable."

"This was the purpose, my Queen," he explained. "To do what I can to redeem my worthiness among the people."

"No one blames you or Kachina for what happened, Jalen," she assured. "I don't know how many times I've said that now. Not even me, and I lost three daughters that day. I know you blame yourself, but they would have come for us eventually, you know this."

Jalen let himself believe that at times, yet this resolution quickly evaporated in the loss of his parents and the memory of his love being dragged away into the darkness together with their subsequent permanent detachment. Nevertheless, he didn't dwell on it anywhere near as much as he did in the beginning.

"So what is your request, my Queen?" he asked.

"I want you to lead the Shadow Warriors to Riverside in the middle of the night, three nights from now," she answered. "It's imperative that no one sees you, no one at all. The same when you return from the mission, of course."

Jalen's head tilted with curiosity. "What is the mission?"

"I don't know yet," she admitted. "It's my daughter's plan and I can't talk to Annabel or Madeleine more at the moment, they're too upset, of course, but in any case, I can only guess that the Panthers are finally going to get the war they wanted."

Jalen thought of the man, their friend, who had driven the wagon which brought him to Blue Falls and to freedom. "How is Jimmy?"

Lesedi shook her head sadly and shrugged. "Artetha removed the arrow, but he's barely breathing now, and his heart was very faint, last I heard. We just have to wait."

"It was a long ride back home," Jalen insinuated with disappointment. After some moments in silence, watching red streams of light meander all over the walls, Jalen thought to ask, "And the Guardians?"

"They will get to Riverside another way, but you will be working with them," she said, then added reservedly, "Kachina also. You were in different teams last time, but that wasn't intentional, it was just the best formation for that mission. This time, I hear you will be working together, and if you think this will jeopardize the mission, then I need to know now so we can do what's necessary to avoid any problems."

Jalen never spoke of Kachina with anyone, and while his mind had accepted his great loss, his heart refused for all time to do the same. Reassuring the queen also meant thinking and talking about his feelings honestly, and it wasn't easy at all, but he swallowed his pain for the sake of her confidence.

"My feelings have never changed, my Queen," he confessed. "And I haven't told anyone, so I trust you to keep it to yourself, but I will wait forever for Kachina. She doesn't want me now, but there is no one else for me. I've tried, I can't bring back what she used to feel, but during a mission, when I'm fighting for my people, this will be the last thing on my mind."

Jalen's honesty proved undeniable. Lesedi smiled pensively for his broken dreams and nodded in belief. "Very well. I trust you, Jalen, and I pray you will find your peace with it in time."

"I have found enough peace for now, my Queen," he claimed, but with sincerity. "I realized, some time ago, my personal losses are like grains of sand in the desert of our ruined world. Who am I to expect so much?"

Lesedi turned away from him then to look out across a sea of lamplights, being reminded of the night sky and the widespread devastation of her people witnessed over the years. Although she didn't expect those words to come from

Jalen, she couldn't have agreed more. She too had impossible expectations, such as the return of her late husband or a life for her daughters which didn't involve hiding or willingly placing themselves in harm's way. Jalen was right, loss became omnipresent at some point in their history, and in the end, one realized, albeit in the company of melancholy, that their own dreams were no more important than those lost to anyone else.

"They tell me my daughter wants to stage a battle without our warriors sustaining any casualties," she said flatly. "I'm not sure yet how she plans to perform this miracle, but if there's any chance of that and also stopping the never-ending search for Blue Falls, then I want to give her all the support she needs."

Jalen's curiosity mounted. "No casualties," he repeated, enjoying the words immensely. "So how many Shadow Warriors am I taking with me?"

Noting Jalen's mischievous eyes, Lesedi replied, "She wants another hundred. Just Shadow Warriors, the very best of the best. Just you and the ones I trust will not fail my daughter."

As Lesedi stood to leave, Jalen stood with her, lifting his head with confidence and ensured, "We will not fail you or Misae, my Queen."

Her smile was thin but filled with hope, and after walking a few paces, she turned to add, "You know, Jalen, bears will hibernate, but, eventually, they all have to come out and live their dreams."

***

"I've missed you, Neema," Madeleine confessed, with a sadness unlike anything her lifelong surrogate mother had ever seen before.

They sat together with Annabel on the edge of a bed, watching Jimmy. It was almost dawn, yet he remained unconscious, and neither Madeleine nor Annabel had moved from the healing bay for more than a few minutes. Victor and Sherman dozed off in nearby chairs not so long ago, and Artetha, although she tried to get some sleep also, kept herself awake, listening to Madeleine and Neema's gentle whispers. Annabel hadn't spoken for a long while. Most of the time, her eyes were fixed on Jimmy's chest, watching it move ever so slightly up and down, while being compelled occasionally to rush over and listen to his breathing to be sure he was still with them.

"Whenever I think of the hardest times in my life," Madeleine continued. "I remember, you were there for me every time, sitting on my bed and talking to me until I felt better again."

"I wish I could think of something helpful to say now, Maddy," Neema responded with regret. "But I'm lost. I miss you more than you could know, my girl, but I know you've been busy, so I don't insist. I don't want you to think I haven't been thinking about you."

"I wouldn't think that, I just feel guilty for never seeing you," she admitted.

Neema shook her head and sighed, "That's silly. Things are what they are. I understand, and I've got Jamero now, thanks to you."

This idea always made Madeleine smile, yet, for now, her lips barely moved.

"I don't know Jimmy like both of you, but I'll never forget the first time I saw him," Neema remembered. "Annie, you weren't there, but it was the day Maddy brought me here. When I walked out to the carriage, he said, 'Good morning, Neema!' with his great big smile. He was the first white man ever to talk to me like an equal, you know, to use my name and look me in the eye."

Neema's story found some joy in Madeleine, yet equal sadness for it only exemplified the integrity of a man lying frightfully still just a step away, and she failed to speak for a time, remembering all the occasions Jimmy had picked her up from here and there. Every time he greeted her with the same constant smile and a, "Good morning, Maddy!" or, "That's a beautiful flower in your hair, Maddy." He would inquire as to the kind of flower, say how she wore it so well, and compliment her choice of dresses and coats, just to make conversation or, unbeknownst to Madeleine, just to see her smile again.

"I miss your pancakes," Madeleine said out of the blue. "When Jimmy's better, can we make him some of your pancakes?"

She only received an enthusiastic nod in reply. Yet, again, she had brought Neema to tears, but Neema fought them well in her wish to be strong for Madeleine.

"The ones with lemon and maple sugar," Madeleine added. "I don't care if they're not good for you."

"If you don't invite me, I'll never talk to you again," Annabel said, leaning her head on Madeleine's shoulder. "Wake up, Jimmy," she whispered then.

***

Not in so many words, but Madeleine asked Julian to go away. She gently impelled him to go exploring until Jimmy's circumstances were better understood. Although Julian told them he wouldn't go far, curiosity led him on and on, and it wasn't long before he found himself staring at The Falls, trying to cope with juxtaposed feelings of elation and depression, while watching playful children leap into the ponds all around.

Aside from the fact that an innocent man was now hovering with death due to his actions, his own need to publicly share his opinions, he had also brought the worst of devastations into the world of someone he hoped never to disappoint. If he had chosen, instead, not to use names, he never would have attracted the attention of the likes of Del Hickory.

Madeleine, you should be standing here with me, he believed at least, and she, in turn, should be speaking with excitement about all the places he was like to explore in this vast labyrinth of wonder. Together, they would take a long journey through every place, and in his journal, he would enter many catalysts for future enthralling literary endeavors.

I'm so selfish, he decided then. How are you fairing, Madeleine?

Just then, Julian became aware of a nearby presence which hadn't moved for a long while and turned to see a young man watching him from the other side of The Ledge.

While competing with the voice of rushing water, he called, "Hello."

"Hello," Isi replied, approaching with a reserved smile.

Although Julian expected him to say something more, Isi only stood there regarding him, as if waiting for Julian to speak.

"My name's Julian," he said finally. "I'm a friend of Madeleine, in case you're wondering why I'm here."

"No," Isi replied. "I know why you're here and it's not to sit and stare at The Falls all depressed."

Greatly taken aback, Julian's eyes opened a little wider and he found himself standing straighter all of a sudden. "What do you mean?" he asked, pretending.

"Do I really need to explain, Mister Julian Winters?" Isi asked bluntly.

Never before had Julian been spoken to in such a manner by someone so young and somehow, Isi's presence alone felt ominous in a way, that their meeting was destined, more than random. He saw a certain knowing in Isi's eyes, one which unsteadied the solid rock beneath his feet and broke him free of his dismal trance. "How do you know me?" he asked with suspicion.

"If you're going to ask obvious questions, we're not going to get very far," Isi stated. "If I were to tell you that no white person, except for you and a Guardian, has stepped inside Blue Falls in almost 20 years," he proposed. "What would you say?"

"I'd say that's remarkable," Julian said without doubt. "Is it true?"

"Yes," Isi answered. "A white man fell in one time, but that doesn't count because he wasn't invited, and he's also dead now."

Julian swallowed. "Did you kill him?"

Isi placed a hand over his chest. "Me?"

Julian back-peddled. "No, not you specifically."

"The man committed suicide," he answered, eventually. "Accidentally." Julian only frowned with confusion, so Isi posed, "Like the character, D'Arcy, in your book, Silencing the Truth, but instead of a cliff, he fell from the ceiling of Blue Falls."

Julian looked up to see the opening aglow. It must be dawn.

"You've read my book?" Being obvious, it was more of a shocked statement.

"Most people in Blue Falls have read your books," he verified. "All the Blue Ones for certain."

"Blue Ones," Julian repeated. "I've read about them. What are they? Are you one of them?"

Isi nodded. "We were all born here, as children of the new world, unaffected by the conditioning of the outside world. We never stop asking questions, never stop learning, and we're highly intuitive. For instance, from what I've learned of you so far, I can tell that your father neglected or abandoned you, and when he was around, he was cold and harsh. You feel guilty for your mother for some reason."

Julian's mouth waxed agape. This boy had just dissected his life in no time, leaving him speechless and he wondered, What else do you know?

"I can also elicit information," he went on, as if hearing Julian's thought. "Like when you say, or I say, Madeleine..." After a pause then, to reflect on Julian's reaction, he continued, "I can see by your energy that your feelings for Madeleine run much deeper than friendship, and by your following body movements that you don't feel worthy of fulfilling that dream." It was obvious to Isi that he had struck the chord he was aiming for and so he added for comfort's sake, "Some people are afraid of us, but in essence, we only speak the truth, the truth in what we see and feel."

After time, Julian resigned to the pellucidity of his emotional shield and asked what he believed to be his first honest and relevant question: "You said you know why I'm here. Why?"

Isi smiled ever so slightly. "Are you working on another book?"

"Yes," Julian answered, though skeptically. "It's a book about the prophecy. I think I'm going to call it The Guardians of The Falls."

"I like it already," Isi said, then asked. "And how is it going?"

Julian hesitated, wondering if he should repeat his usual glazing over of the truth, but decided, instead, to speak of his undeniable disappointment. "Terribly, in fact," he admitted. "I'm confused about the whole idea now; I haven't written anything worthwhile in months."

Isi turned on the spot and waved his hands over the expanse of Blue Falls. "Despite the work of people like you and Madeleine, the outside world knows little to nothing about a hidden war these people and many others out there have been fighting, and for how long now? Everyone seems sure that another open war is coming to this whole continent, and at the same time, people will be drowning in propaganda. At this war's end, the shadows will hope everyone is a perfect slave and automatically believe everything they say. Truth will be hard to find, but you're already published and you have access to papers and journals. Right now, you're inside Blue Falls, surrounded by the truth from elders to children to Blue Ones. You have the queen and all four princesses, when Misae gets back, to hear the entire truth and learn everything you can about their stories, their history, all the legends, the prophecy, the Guardians and the Earth. Also, it seems you're the only person given this chance."

These ideas washed around in Julian's head like a whirlpool of creativity, and he couldn't deny the pertinence in any single notion.

"The darkness came for you, Julian, not Jimmy, not Madeleine," Isi reinstated. "This can only lead one to believe that you might have the power to achieve something valuable."

Surprising Julian greatly, Isi began to walk away then.

"Wait," he objected. "Where are you going?"

Isi turned only to ask, "Does it suddenly feel like you're very far behind?"

Julian nodded, with a sense of urgency rising quickly from deep within.

"Well, now, you stand with us. We are all far behind," he concluded. "Because only the darkness could be capable of first imagining the horrors they continue to bring and we, first, have to believe anyone could actually commit such atrocities before we can even begin to think about how to react to each one. The problem is, we just can't believe it, but this is just lack of acceptance and the refusal to challenge what we think we know, or to challenge what we want to believe. Such as it is for you to believe the idea that you too have a purpose for being here greater than to satisfy your own curiosity."

His last words silenced Julian, as he began to envisage the magnitude of the prophecy and its relevance to his own circumstances.

You're right Isi, we are so far behind.

***

Firelight caught the resolution in Kachina's face and revealed it to all the Guardians around her. By the lake, six of them had built a small fire to encircle and enjoy while discussing all they knew of the coming mission. None but for Oni and Akachi were sure why Kachina had brought her Book of The Doomed down with her, only to begin picking all the gemstones out of the cover with a pocketknife. Yet, when she proceeded to tear pages out, scrunch them up, and offer them to the most vengeful flames, Naira and Sayen, and even Talia, also understood completely.

The first to become ash was the page containing Madeleine's father. Quite a few more followed before she stopped feeding individual pages and left the remainder of the book in the hands of the temporary but unforgiving blaze she'd just created. Looking up then, she first met with Oni's eyes to share a smile, before offering the same to the others.

Not a single one of them could think of sleeping since hearing the news of Jimmy's condition, and there wasn't much more to say about the little they knew of Misae's plan, thus a long, tired silence prevailed until Akachi snapped everyone out of their trancelike state, after all had been subdued by the warmth of the flames for so long.

"Whoever did this is about as dead as someone can be, without actually being dead," she concluded.

"Can you imagine what Annabel will do to them?" Kachina pondered aloud.

"Or Madeleine," Akachi contested. "She's so upset, but you can tell she'd like to kill a few barbarians."

Jojo turned to her sister to complain. "Akachi, where do get these things from?"

"I make them up, of course," she retorted. "What do you think?"

"Of course you do," Jojo agreed, then turned to Kachina to ask, "Kachina, did you see Annabel take that shot at Hickory?"

Kachina shook her head. "No, but I wish I did. Only Maddy, Jalen, and a few Panthers saw it."

"I heard she was a hundred paces out," Jojo added in question.

"That's what Maddy said," Kachina answered. "Jalen and I didn't really talk on the mission. We said hello, but…"

"That's a good start," Oni implied. "Better than nothing."

Kachina nodded. "It's all right. I thought I was going to feel really strange, but it wasn't so bad. We were focused on the mission anyhow and in different teams. He didn't try to push anything too, which was good."

As if he had manifested from their conversation, Jalen appeared then and did well to hide the better part of his nervousness, though he stayed a pace or two away to speak. His presence surprised them all of course, none more than Kachina, as she was just remembering the sadness in his eyes when, after the mission, she could sense that he was too afraid to say anything more to her than goodnight.

Given the shock of Jalen's efforts and for the fact that he wore a light-brown cotton shirt and long, dark pants for the occasion, nobody responded immediately. When most had only ever seen him bare-chested and usually wielding some weapon or other, the transformation was astonishing.

"I'm sorry to interrupt," he began, graciously. "I just had a meeting with the queen about the new mission and I wanted to talk to you all about it, but I don't want to interrupt if you're having a Guardians' meeting."

Jojo decided to break the awkwardness following his words with some play. "Yes, that's right, suddenly I'm a Guardian now, surprise!" she stated, jumping to her feet, proceeding to dance around Jalen as if trying to provoke him into a battle. "And since you interrupted, I'm going to have to give you a good beating. Let's see what you got, warrior!"

Jalen smiled, turning on the spot to watch her silly and harmless strikes at the air around him.

"Watch out, Jalen," Akachi warned. "She might stand on your foot. We look the same, but we definitely don't have the same skills."

Jojo dropped what she was doing and ran to attack Akachi for her comical but slight remark, but Akachi was prepared for this already and was up and running before Jojo even came close. As the chase went on a good distance, they received a few laughs from the circle, but the humor quickly faded in the wake of Jimmy's predicament. Even so, the partial relief was most welcome by all and served as an impromptu icebreaker for Jalen's unexpected presence.

"Come and sit with us, Jalen," Kachina incited, again surprising everyone present. She thought to be the first to ask, believing he might not feel comfortable doing so unless the invitation came directly from her.

His heart faltered then, like she'd thrown a beehive into it, but he just took a deep breath and looked for a place to sit, anywhere but right next to Kachina. Jojo and Akachi returned then, with lethargy, like they'd run really hard when they didn't feel like running at all and flopped back into the circle.

"It's too early for this," Akachi insisted. "Or late, however you look at it."

While it was only for a moment or two, Jalen and Kachina looked directly into each other's eyes for the first time in a very long while to share a slight and clumsy smile.

To avoid another awkward silence, Oni piped up, "So, Jalen, tell us about Annabel's sling-bow shot."

***

However careful Artetha was to draw her smile thin and hesitant, it spread like wildfire throughout Jimmy's small audience when he woke enough to take a sip or two of water. As she rested his head gently back down again, it pleased them all greatly to hear him moan ever so quietly, and although his eyes barely opened at all, it seemed he tried to do so.

Madeleine jumped up, paced silently back and forth for a short time before returning abruptly to sit back down again next to a stunned Annabel. They were so quiet in their reaction that neither Victor nor Sherman were woken by the turn of events.

"It's a good sign, isn't it?" Madeleine whispered.

Artetha was reluctant to answer with surety. "We're not out of the woods yet," she whispered in reply, with deep lines of concern across her brow. "But, yes, it's a good sign." In actual fact, she felt his chances were better than good now, but she never liked to encourage false hope.

Just then, Julian entered the healing bay like a lost puppy and asked quietly, "How's he doing?"

"He kind of woke up and had some water," Madeleine answered, though she didn't really feel like talking, especially not to have a long conversation about Blue Falls with Julian at this time.

Julian sighed some of his dread away, "Oh, that's good. That's positive."

Madeleine nodded and felt obliged to ask, "Did you have a look around?"

"Yes, a little," he replied reservedly. Under the circumstances, he didn't want to show any excitement. Plus, he harbored a thousand questions for Madeleine and knew it wasn't the time to ask any of them, but they filled his mind nonetheless, leaving him speechless.

Static silence followed and, sensing Madeleine's reluctance to talk, Annabel hopped off the bed and turned to Julian. "Come with me," she said. "I have an idea."

After receiving a naive shrug from Madeleine, he could only follow, as Annabel led him down to the beginning of the rail tracks.

"Drop your bag," she said, reaching high above her head to a pocket in a nearby ledge to retrieve a key. "You won't need it."

"What are we doing?" he asked. "What are these rails?"

"You'll get to see all of Blue Falls. It's the best view. The two tracks go different ways. The one down there is the Swing Rail," she answered, turning to a nearby chest to remove its padlock. "You sit in a kind of swing which glides you slowly all the way down to The Lake, and you can use the brake to slow down or stop when you want to look for longer at the places you like."

"That's brilliant," he said with delight. "To see it all so effortlessly. The view must be amazing."

Annabel removed a harness from the unlocked chest, inserted the wheels into the bottom of the rails, and slid it up to chest height. "Walk back into this."

Julian did so, and without fuss, due to all the talk about gliding and braking. He looked to another nearby open chest containing a great many swing harnesses then regarded his own more closely. "This one seems different."

"It's an even better view from this rail," she told him, clipping the pieces of harness together in the quick release mechanism at the center of his chest. "Use the pedals to push yourself up," she directed then, while assisting in lifting him by the harness into a horizontal position.

This surprised Julian. "What? You're lying down the whole way like this?" he asked curiously, nervously.

"Yep," she answered calmly. "Now, you see this big button on your chest? That's the release, the harness flips right off when you punch that. At the end of the track, where the rail rises up over The Lake, punch it then and the harness will fly off. Believe me, you don't want to hit it before then unless you want to die broken into pieces. Are you ready?"

"What? No," he contested.

"You remember my name, right?" she asked then.

"Of course," he replied, muddled now. "It's Annabel. Why?"

"Because you will surely want to curse it at some point on the way down," she said frankly. "At a few points actually."

Julian's stomach dropped. "Why? You said it'll show me all of Blue Falls."

"Oh it will, I didn't lie," she confirmed. "You'll see it all in about 20 seconds. This harness doesn't have a brake either, by the way."

"What? Wait. I don't think I want to—"

"My uncle's fighting for his life," she interrupted. "And I know it's not your fault. He made his own choice, so nobody can blame you but, still, he took an arrow in your place, so you don't get to mope around feeling all sad and sorry for yourself. Think about that on the way down, if you have time. Make sure you hit that button all right. Above the water, not before. Oh, and don't forget to dive perfectly or fold your legs up. A belly-flop might kill you."

"Wait!" he tried, one last time, but it was too late.

"Remember," she reinstated, ignoring him completely. "Make sure you hit the button when you're over The Lake, otherwise it's a horrible death for you. All right, time to go."

Annabel let go of the harness and gave the bottom of his heals a lazy kick as he slipped away, then she called after him just as his speed began to accelerate rapidly. "By the way, this rail's called the Plummet!"

She walked back up to the healing bay then and sat next to Madeleine again as if nothing had happened, but asked, "Did he wake up again?"

"He moved his head a few times while you were gone," Madeleine answered. "Not much, but it's something. Where's Julian?"

"Julian?" Annabel feigned. "Oh, I showed him where the rail was so he could see some more of Blue Falls."

Madeleine might have accepted that for the whole truth, but she saw the guilty smile Annabel struggled to conceal. "Which rail, Annie?"

"Well, you know, Julian didn't specify which one he wanted to try, so I chose one for him," she answered, hiding even less of her sly grin.

"You didn't," Madeleine said, with both amusement and horror rising. After Annabel did nothing to deny her suspicions, she gasped and struggled to whisper, "Oh! You did! I'm surprised we didn't hear him scream from here."

"No chance," Annabel argued. "He'll be way too frightened to scream."

***

As the track lifted him high above The Lake and his highspeed run rapidly decelerated to zero again, Julian couldn't believe he was still alive. He punched the release button then, as commanded, and let out, "Yahooahhh!"

Since he curled his legs up and wrapped his arms around them as the harness slid away, his entry into the water possessed none of the grace of Annabel's elegant dive, but he was thankful to have avoided a belly-flop. The water rushing back in at his neck as he entered the water with a bomb-dive felt like it could have taken his head off before he went under completely.

Despite his poor form, the long drop sent him deep down where he spread his body out and opened his eyes to the flashes of blue sapphire all around. Even in the early morning light, the sight was mesmerizing and glorious, especially witnessing it for the first time, and while suspended there, he wished his body didn't demand more oxygen.

When he resurfaced, something felt different. He didn't gasp or splutter, only took a deep enough breath to keep him down there again for even longer in the crystal-clear waters, where shadows made by schools of fish drifted through morphing, ribbon-like streams in countless shades of blue.

Once he'd had his fill of the Lake, Julian walked back toward the Entrance, following the rail with his eye until he came upon the harness sitting idle in a dip in the track above the entrance to Crimson Cove.

Nanook was there taking it down and looked around to see Julian watching him with hair slicked back and clothes still drenched from his swim. Smiling curiously, he questioned, "This was you? I heard it go past The Nook and expected to see Annabel."

Julian nodded and answered with the words he had repeated countless times already, whenever a new person looked at him strangely, "I'm a friend of Madeleine."

"Is that so?" Nanook replied. "So you must be Julian Winters. So what possessed you to try the Plummet?"

"Annabel," he was embarrassed to admit. "She didn't tell me it was...quite so fast. In fact, she didn't tell me anything, not even what happens if you don't disconnect over The Lake."

Nanook chuckled. "You glide back down here with the harness, of course."

"That's it?" Julian asked, blank-faced now.

This amused Nanook even further. "Yes. What did she tell you?"

"She said I'd die if I didn't hit the release and go into the lake," he admitted, with shame for being so easily misled.

Nanook couldn't help but belly-laugh at that point. "Oh, boy, what did you do, man, to annoy Annabel so much?"

"I got her uncle shot," Julian answered, remembering suddenly with a twist in his stomach.

"Ah." Nanook's smile left him quickly and his face filled with empathy. "We are all thinking of Jimmy. Everything has a purpose, my friend."

Julian sighed. "I'd like to believe that."

"Such as your presence here and now," Nanook elaborated. "Dear Maddy tells me you're writing a book about the Guardians and the prophecy. I am Nanook, the one who discovered all 11 names of the Guardians. I created their amulets and I'm also the keeper of The Cave."

"What's The Cave?" Julian asked in wonder, as it seemed most significant to Nanook.

Nanook grinned. "Follow me. If you don't know what The Cave is yet, then you are in for a very big shock, my friend."

"I just had one of those," Julian uttered. "I'm not sure if I'm ready for another quite so soon."

Julian followed Nanook, who, at one point, chuckled again, saying, "Oh, Annabel, Annabel. She really is the most unpredictable Guardian of them all."

Halting in his tracks, Julian questioned, "Annabel's one of the white Guardians?"

Nanook turned with a frown of bewilderment. "My goodness, man, yes, of course, it's Madeleine and Annabel. How can you not know this?"

With slowly widening eyes, Julian barely voiced the words, "Madeleine's a Guardian?"

Nanook shook his head, feeling a little guilty for enjoying Julian's additional shock so much. "Come, it seems you have a lot of work to do, Mister Julian Winters."

***

While watching Jimmy sleep, Madeleine wished her journal were close by so she could have written something to appease her busy mind, like: Imagine discovering upon someone's death that their heart was with you all along, yet it was never known to you and neither acknowledged nor shared. What kind of love is that? Why would it come for them, while the one who possessed their heart remained far out of reach? And was it enough for them, to have known and felt that love all alone?

"I haven't seen Julian at all. Do you think he died?" Annabel asked in jest.

"What?" Jimmy mumbled, suddenly waking. He turned his head slowly and blinked away sleep until his eyes focused on them.

"No, Jimmy, not really," Madeleine struggled. "Just...don't worry. No, Annie, I think we would have heard about that already."

"Jimmy, we're leaving for Riverside now," Annabel informed him.

"And it wouldn't feel right without hearing you say good luck," Madeleine added.

It had only been a couple of days since the arrow was removed. Although Jimmy's condition had improved immensely, he was still slow to respond, and any significant or sudden movements brought about dizziness very quickly.

"Good luck," he said, smiling as best he could. The last thing he remembered was standing at the carriage, talking to the passengers, the next thing he was being fed from a water bottle by hands he couldn't see with blurred vision in his semi-conscious state. The unknown space of time in between continued to pester him. "I still don't remember what happened."

"Maybe you won't," Annabel suggested. "It's like that sometimes, and maybe it's better."

"It doesn't matter, Jimmy," Madeleine reassured him. "It only matters that you get better. You might remember in time, but just rest now. We'll see you soon."

***

The wagons had been loaded with all but for the Shadow Warriors, the Guardians, and, to Tamaya's dear fright, Elan and Mosi.

Even Shenandoah agreed to leave after Misae said to him, "We couldn't have finished this plan so well without you, Shen, but now it's up to the Guardians and Warriors. I would never forgive myself if something happened to you."

They embraced then, before he stepped up into the wagon, during which he said for her ears only, "And what will I do if something happens to you?"

Elan refused to leave. He walked away from his mother when she headed for the wagon to stand with arms folded next to his fellow Guardians, stating, "I'm not leaving them," with eyes holding the same fire as the ones at his side who now possessed his undeniable loyalty.

All the Warrior Guardians, including Princess Misae, said nothing of consequence during the standoff, knowing it was not their place to interfere with a mother and her child, nor to affect the natural course of a Guardian's path.

"And what will you do, Elan?" Tamaya asked, imploring him to revisit his decision. Her predicament felt hopeless. Having never had the chance to build an air of authority over her son nor to learn how to relate to his motivations, she didn't feel confident at all in demanding anything of him. Still, she repeated, "What will you do, Elan?" then looked between Mosi and the Guardians. "What would he do?"

"Elan," Misae drew his attention and repeated his mother's question. "Warrior Guardian, you've heard the whole plan. What will you do?"

Elan knew that his mother wanted him to decide there was nothing he could do and to leave with her. However, he knew that Misae, although she worded the question exactly the same, expected an actual answer, a worthwhile answer, a strategic reason for his presence.

"I can let the horses out," he answered with confidence. "There's not much cover over there at the gates, but I'm smaller and I won't scare them. I can even hide behind one of the fence posts or the water troughs. The Shadow Warriors can't do that."

"Maybe not, but they are more practiced in the art of invisibility and silence than you, Elan, and they can hide in many ways," Misae argued. "The moon is almost full. How will you get the horses to move away?"

"Maddy told me thistle is their favorite," he told them. "It's true; I've been giving it to our horses, so if I take some with me, they'll follow. Or I can take some barley from here. You see, Momma? I won't be fighting soldiers."

"If they don't follow you quietly, Elan, you have to be prepared to scare them into running away somehow and then get away yourself without anyone seeing you at all," Misae reinstated, having already covered this with all those aboard the mission.

Mosi hadn't said anything in a while. Like Tamaya, he struggled to employ his motivation to be a protective parent, especially in light of discovering his son to be a Warrior Guardian and, having heard the story of Elan helping two Guardians escape, he couldn't doubt that his boy was worthy enough of the task for which he volunteered. Finally, he looked to Elan with a smile of pride.

"I will stay and help my son. I'll be his backup, in case anything goes wrong, and I'll wait on the fence line for him to return."

This idea felt a little better for Tamaya, yet now, she would have to think of them both in danger's way. She fell silent and looked to her long-lost Mosi, knowing he also felt unsure how to be a parent for a Guardian child. In the end, her heart could only rest on her trust for Mosi and her belief that nothing could break them all apart again. She shared with him a concerned but supportive smile.

Misae's plan contained no one but Shadow Warriors and Guardians, Sherman and Ky Mani to coordinate the final escape, and every person knew how emphatic she had been about this prerequisite for the mission. Although she herself was not at the same skill level as the other Warrior Guardians, aside from Sherman, Sanura, and Talia, every other person was a highly-trained and lethal warrior who could take-on multiple enemies at one time with ease. Sanura, Talia, and Sherman were involved in Misae's plan, but they were never to confront soldiers in combat at any time, so she held no concern for their safety, and she had been waiting to see what Elan might elect to do. Under the circumstances, and although she didn't want to alter her plan even in the slightest, she could hardly deny Mosi's wish to be there for his son, so, instead, she weakened a piece of her own rigidity.

"All right," she decided all at once. "Let's send two Shadow Warriors to go with Mosi and wait in support of Elan, and by this time, Annabel and Oni, our two finest archers, will be in their second positions in the field with their bows, so they can provide cover from there. Cayman will be in between both of you until he completes his mission and joins with Annabel and Oni again so he can also move in if Elan's in trouble. If something happens to put Elan at risk, then everyone is to abandon this part of the plan and move in to protect Elan until he is safe, then continue only if there's still time. If I think for a second that we're not going to fulfill this mission with zero casualties, then I'm shutting it down and getting everyone into the tunnels and away immediately. I know I've said it many times, but is everybody clear on that? I will do it. We all know if that ammunition shed doesn't go up, we have to evacuate immediately. So if I call to abandon the plan, the Guardians will defend the barn until everyone's in the tunnel and then go themselves. The soldiers will still trigger the trap whether we take out the shed or not, so move quickly."

Everyone knew the adjustments Misae was forced to make regarding Elan, however minor, could potentially ruin the entire plan. Tamaya abruptly realized this and that if she had not contested Elan's will at all, he may have been content to stay away from the greater danger, just to be a part of it, and the plan would have been left as it was, being one highly-trained warrior going alone to free the army horses before the next phase of the plan was to be executed.

Even so, Elan was most delighted to be on a mission with his father there to witness it all, while Tamaya silenced herself, for fear of inciting another unwanted redevelopment, and stepped her troubled soul into the wagon without another word. Mosi sighed, feeling her great concern and went to the wagon, followed closely by Annabel.

Taking Tamaya's hand, he looked into her eyes with confidence and said, "We will see you soon. This, I promise you."

"You can't promise that," she contested, trying to keep from breaking down. "I already lost you both once. You don't need to risk your lives tonight."

"Elan fights for the future freedom of our people," Mosi proposed. "I want to stand by my son. He's something greater than we could have imagined, and I don't think it's for us to hold him back."

After a few deep breaths, Tamaya nodded ever so hesitantly and sat back against the wall of the wagon next to Bell and Foxy. Mosi offered an awkward smile, then went back to Elan, but before Annabel joined them, she also looked into Tamaya's eyes, yet pointed to her own, which were filled with a promise: "You see these? They won't leave him the whole time."

Tamaya tried to show some hope but nothing eventuated. Annabel's words helped somewhat, given her awareness of the Guardians' abilities, yet she folded her arms and let out a huff of self-loathing. "I'm sorry, Annie, it's my fault," she admitted, with great remorse. "If I didn't say anything—"

"It was meant to be," Annabel interrupted, then smiled. "At least he's not running off alone this time, right? Trust us, Tamaya, we love Elan more than you could know."

That much was surely true. "I know," she nodded, concealing the better part of her inner turmoil, and waved lazily as the wagon rolled away through the closing gates.

***

Chapter Eleven
Stirring Hives

"Complacency beckons for a downfall."

~ Oni, Warrior Guardian.

***

Del woke, sat up abruptly, and the sudden movement sent a surge of agony back and forth between his shoulder and his neck. Through gritted teeth, he cursed his own stupidity before falling silent again to listen for what might have stirred him from slumber.

Nothing; not a sound all about, but for the branch of a tree brushing at the window for the gentle breeze outside.

Parched he was, so after grumbling to himself about the challenges of doing almost anything in his current condition, he clumsily donned a gown and went to find some water. After lighting a lamp above the stove in the kitchen, almost unnecessarily for the grace of the moonlight, he turned and froze there, water jug in hand, upon discovering Pete's head sitting in the middle of the long hardwood table in a pool of blood, with dead eyes alluding to his sudden, frightful demise.

The bamboo water jug dropped from his hand and cracked open on the tiles as Del spun on the spot, searching all around, waiting for something to jump out of the shadows. After half a minute, still nothing had come for him, only more silence, so he stepped out and into the living room to where a cabinet held all his favorite weapons – whips, muskets, and swords – only to find the doors ajar.

Dreaded expectations were confirmed after looking inside to find only whips hanging uselessly from their hooks. After moving quietly from window to window, one of the panes finally revealed the source of all the anomalies. With much reluctance, he walked to the front door and out into the courtyard where Mitchell, Tanner, and Doyle all sat, roped off around his whipping pole.

Jalen and Cayman stood just outside the doorway, with giant curved swords in hand, and both nodded toward others, insisting he joined them. Realizing he was trapped long ago, Del yielded and walked to meet face-to-face with Misae, Sanura, Talia, Madeline dressed as Vivian Piper, and Annabel dressed, of course, as her daughter, Penelope.

"You?" Del asked of Vivian. "You're helping them?"

"Well, you know, they have a lot of gold and jewels," Madeleine said, heavy in accent. "And their home is right under my land here, so share and share alike, as they say."

With scorn, Del looked to Sanura and Talia, who had worn gold bracelets and also sapphires and rubies in their hair for the occasion. Misae wore warrior's shielding like Jalen and Cayman, yet clearly none of them were desolate escapees but part of a well-kept and well-organized resistance.

"It's her!" Tanner blurted suddenly, upon further inspection of Sanura's face. "Mitchell, it's them!"

Mitchell's heart sank even further from its place of no hope. They were indeed the ones who got away and who brought the most stringent of punishments upon them, vicariously through their boss, yet he remained almost completely unmoved and reluctant to speak after witnessing Pete's head fly off his body right in front of his eyes. He could still feel Pete's sticky blood on his neck and face.

Sanura found a deadly grin and Talia's proved even less warming. She looked at Mitchell, as Sanura looked at Tanner, with all kinds of murderous ideas swimming around in her mind.

"Boss, these two are the ones who burnt your barns down!" Mitchell informed him, just as Jalen forced Del into sitting next to his men.

"You idiots," Del said, without the usual strength of anger behind his words. "If they don't kill you, I swear I'll do it myself."

"You'll be too busy dying, Del," Madeleine said. "Besides, we're definitely going to kill you all. You don't think we could let you go after this, do you?"

Del was tied off like the others, as Madeleine announced: "Time to take out the competition, Del."

"You never sold my slaves, did you?" Del asked, while knowing the answer.

"Nope," Madeleine replied. "They just went underground like these two young ladies, while your moronic helpers stumbled all over the countryside and got themselves all sliced up for dinner."

"You wanna know why all the searching over the years has failed?" Annabel cut-in. "Not just you, but every other piece of scum before you." After receiving nothing but a hateful glare from Del, she continued, "Because while you're all searching north and west, they've been right here under your noses the whole time, and they've been digging for 20 years. Two of your men came to our house that night, and after Princess Misae slit both their throats, she sent her warriors to rescue these two and chop up the rest of your friends."

Although it pained him to move, Del squirmed inside his ropes, wishing he could get to Vivian and Annabel to fulfill his desire to strangle both of them. "Princess?" he scoffed. It was all he could think to say at the time.

"That's right," Misae answered. "And I'm the princess who's going to destroy that army next door tonight."

"Hope you don't mind," Annabel added like a stab, in her best Penelope voice. "But they need to go through your land. It's the best strategy."

Doyle remained quiet, knowing as well as his boss that no words would help them out of their current predicament anyway. He received particularly threatening looks from both Vivian and Penelope but didn't know they were reserved purely for him, as Vivian, of course, didn't look at all like the woman who was with the man he failed to murder just days ago.

"You're going to attack the barracks?" Del asked, believing and disbelieving all at once.

"Our warriors will rise up out of Vivian's land and strike while they're sleeping," Misae said with pretended lust. "They won't even know what's happening until they're all dead."

"You see, Del, these people needed protection," Madeleine began, then paused to enjoy her own greed. "And me? Well, I need to be rich, Del. It's plain and simple, and now, I'm swimmin' in it. Like you, this army posed a threat to both our interests, and since I can't possibly dispose of a whole army on my own, we decided to work together for the common good. We gave Chester Flinch's greedy little solicitor a great big pot of gold to draw up a backdated contract, which Chester was happy to sign for us, of course," she chuckled. "Before we put the Colonel's sword through his heart."

"Chester was most congenial," Annabel said, smiling eerily.

"It was you," Del realized, astonished. "All of it."

"Silly, silly boys," Annabel mocked. "Too busy talking big to realize you're just little puppets." She tapped each one of them on the top of the head then with the end of her sheathed sword, saying, "Puppet, puppet, puppet and...puppet."

They each flinched and scowled, only encouraging greater amusement in all but themselves.

"You little rats keep getting in the way," Annabel added, hoping to fuel their hatred. "So we play games with you for a little while, just like a cat, then we sink the teeth in."

Sanura spoke for the first time, "I didn't think I wanted to do it, but I'm sure I do now. Give me a sword someone."

Before anyone had a chance to move, Sanura, instead, reached inside her coat, pulled Tanner's own knife out from a sheath around her waist, which she had momentarily forgotten, and an instant later, poised, kneeling at Tanner's side with the blade across his neck. Tanner lifted his head up and back as far away as he could, but already felt the sting of the steel, his own craftwork, yet again.

"Recognize this?" she asked, knowing he most certainly would. "How's the eye?"

Tanner only sneered at her threat, but to his surprise, his own knife kept cutting, sliding back and forth across his neck, and the pressure increased with every new slice, until one last heavy slash opened a wide gorge in his throat. He jerked around, slopping his blood all over Mitchell, who sat stunned, watching his friend with one shocked eye, trying to reach around and clasp at his shirt in a pointless effort to seek assistance.

"Give me that," Talia said, taking the knife from Sanura, surprising the other Warriors again.

Mitchell jumped when he saw Talia's eyes lock onto his, as she came to stand over him. Tanner still jerked around, making gurgling sounds next to him, making his sure demise even more disturbing.

"No," he pleaded. "Don't do it…I—"

"Shut up," Talia said. "Your death has arrived. Face it like the demon you've become, not a mouse." She stepped either side of his outstretched legs, sat on his knees, grabbed a handful of his hair to pull his head back, and then placed the knife at his throat. "But first," she said, bringing her face so close to his that he could feel her warm breath on his face. "I want you to think about all the things you were going to do to me."

Mitchell shuddered uncontrollably and felt a sting periodically about his neck. He'd never seen more stunning eyes, like the oasis of love he had never found, and denial helped him to believe that such beauty couldn't possibly want to end his life.

"Are you thinking of it?" Talia taunted. "Is it everything you dreamed of?"

Everyone without exception believed Talia was going to cut his throat as Sanura had done to Tanner, and so, great surprise came upon all when she, instead, rested the tip of the blade against his chest and slowly pushed it into him. First, she used one hand, then both, with increasingly more pressure and more body weight, until one last shove sent the blade in to its hilt.

She sat back then, looking into his terrified eyes, as his body convulsed under the weight of his failing heart, before standing again to say, "You can keep the knife."

"Two down, two to go," Madeleine claimed then, before Mitchell had even expired, drawing rapid attention from both Del and Doyle. "Jalen. Cayman. Your turn."

Both warriors stepped forward and stood over the seated, cowering men.

"Wait!" Del shouted, truly acknowledging only then that his moment had actually arrived, but was duly lost for anything else to say thereafter. His memory kept bringing up additional proof of his odiousness rather than ideas to support a righteous plea for reprieve, and while his tongue froze, two monstrous swords were lifted high into the air.

Both men closed their eyes in that instant, only to hear a musket shot seconds later instead of the sound of a blade shearing their heads off.

Jalen reeled back, grunting loudly and gripping his chest as he spun around.

Cayman reached out to prevent him from falling down. "Jalen!" he called.

"Everyone back!" Misae yelled, and they all fled as quickly as they could while assisting Jalen along the way.

Moments later, Sherman approached, musket in hand. "I think I got one, boss!" he shouted excitedly, then ran off after them.

"Wait!" Del called, but the man was gone. He couldn't believe his luck; that the new laborer he hired was smart enough and already loyal enough to think for himself and to ambush his boss's attackers.

"Get the knife, hurry!" he shouted, urgently.

Doyle struggled, but after time, managed to pull the knife out of Mitchell and cut his own ropes loose.

As he jumped up to cut Del's ropes, they heard Sherman's gurgling screams cry out from somewhere in the outer darkness.

"They got him! Hurry!" Del panicked. "Quick, we've gotta get to the barracks."

They'll be back.

His shoulder injury was long forgotten and the pain from every long stride ignored while he bounded with Doyle to the barracks as fast as possible, expecting all the while for a shadow to leap out and lop their heads off.

***

"I'm going to miss being Vivian," Madeleine confessed. "Sometimes, it's annoying, but other times, it's kind of fun."

Annabel understood well. "I know what you mean, and Penelope was really starting to come out of her shell I thought."

Sherman sniggered, "Don't say things like that, Annie, I worry that you're slipping."

"That happened long ago," Annabel replied in jest. "Anyhow, it's time they both died."

After hearing the gunshot, Misae rushed in to meet with them at Hickory's place as planned, followed closely by Kachina and Akachi carrying weapons and shielding for Annabel and Madeleine. Far behind them, another 100 warriors waited at the boundary for their princess's command with bows and loaded quivers.

"Phase one accomplished, my Princess," Jalen said to Misae, yet he couldn't help looking at Kachina when he said it. The fierceness in her poise left him breathless.

"Okay, no time to waste," Misae replied. "Let's go with phase two. Second places, everybody!" Her signal echoed into the distance, by way of her warriors, and all the way back to Riverside, where all remaining warriors readied themselves also for the second phase of Misae's plan.

***

"C'mon, Elan," Annabel thought aloud. "Cayman's coming back now."

"It's okay," Oni assured. "Hickory hasn't been there for long."

Their longbows were nocked with arrows of Misae's design, having a row of thin splits in their flint tips to create greater sparks upon impact, and they had positioned themselves at the edge of a thick bush in the middle of the clearing between Del's property and the barracks. From there, they watched Elan make his way to the top of the paddock, where all the horses had congregated, to encourage them to follow the others he had already led out through the open gates just moment earlier. He taunted them with clumps of thistle until they moved.

With two Shadow Warriors at his side, Mosi waited, crouched at the lower boundary fence, and even from the Guardians' distance, they could see that he constantly resisted the urge to get up and run to assist his son. At one point, he stood quickly and then dropped again suddenly.

"There," Annabel said, prompting Oni to look toward the barracks.

"I see him." Oni dropped her flint arrow along with Annabel and they both reloaded with regular steel-tipped arrows.

Cayman returned in that moment and found a place beside them. "It's done," he said. "What's happening?"

Neither archer responded nor looked his way. Their bows were up with strings drawn, ready to fire, though not in the direction of the barrel of black powder that Cayman had just planted, as he expected. Moving behind them, he looked along their arrows to see a soldier walking down to the fence seemingly to empty his bladder, not five paces from where Elan sat, crouched behind a fence post. The man hadn't seen Elan yet, but the horses moving together out through the gate quickly found his curiosity.

"Stay where you are, Mosi," Annabel whispered, trying to reach him telepathically.

"The soldier will see the gate," Oni supposed. "Even if he doesn't see Elan."

In that moment, they both saw Elan slip his knife out of its sheath and ready himself to move.

"No. That's not happening, Elan," Annabel said, as they watched Mosi and the warriors slowly rising to their feet, ready to run.

"Shoot?" Oni asked, with eyes locked onto the man, who now seemed to be looking in Elan's direction. "Let's wait 'til he turns."

Their fingers burned as the strings cut in.

"Yes, when he turns," Annabel affirmed. "On three, okay?"

The man was doing up his pants now, but his gaze hadn't swayed from Elan. Instead, he was trying to peer around the fence post.

"One..." Annabel began, as the man slowly turned. "Two... Three!"

They let fly, gripping fists and cringing for the surge of fingertip pain, yet their eyes didn't leave the fletching of their arrows for an instant.

Cayman watched on in awe. To him, the distance seemed impossible and he wouldn't even attempt it himself. Instead, he would run and try to take a closer shot or else distract the man somehow. Before this moment, he was concerned that the Guardians were positioned too far from the black powder barrel he'd just planted to successfully make that shot, yet the soldier stood one-and-a-half times that distance away.

Flying in parallel, both arrows found their mark not so far from one another in the man's chest and sent him slamming into the ground. There came hardly a sound, at least not from the Guardians' distance, and a moment later, Elan was up, ushering horses out again.

Mosi and his two-warrior chaperone all stood up straight, motionless and in shock. Although they looked in every place, they failed to see the archers' position in the meadow, and it wasn't long before Elan returned to him. Being so stunned, Elan had to physically push his father to get him to move off again.

The Guardians were pleased, as there existed an unspoken yet friendly rival between the two of them, where archery was concerned, and neither wanted to be the one who just missed. However, their flint arrows were again in place a second later, and although they hadn't drawn them yet, they were too focused on the next shot to think too much about the last.

***

"What is it, Private? This better be important," Wright threatened. He sat up in bed and fumbled around with the oil lamp at his bedside. "What's all the shouting outside?"

"Del Hickory's here," the private said, as the light hit Wright's annoyed, sleep-lined face. "He's demanding to see you."

"Hickory?" Wright repeated, adopting a most grumpy tone. "What's he doing here?"

"He thinks we're about to be attacked, sir," he answered sheepishly, neither believing nor disbelieving himself. "Something happened at his place."

"Again? Oh, what now?" he asked, though rhetorically and with a mix of boredom and annoyance. "All right, I'll be out in a minute."

Still doing up his belt, Wright found his way outside to meet with an anxious and furious Del Hickory standing outside in the courtyard between the officers' buildings, dressed in a gown somewhat bloodied at the front by his wound which had begun to weep through the doctor's dressing.

"What is it, Hickory?" he demanded. "Haven't you done enough?"

Beside himself, Del hollered, "What took you so long!? They're coming!"

"Who's coming?" he asked impatiently, unmoved and rolling his eyes. "What are you talking about?"

With a good amount of spitting and cursing, Del shared an enraged and rapid story of what had happened at his property, what he'd learned of hidden places and about the coming attack. By the end of his venting, it was clear to Wright that Del wasn't drunk or delusional, yet he believed both the idea of an attack and the numbers he claimed were exaggerations born of some obviously traumatizing experience.

Del finished his speech with, "Don't you see? We've been searching in all the wrong places. They've been right under our feet the whole time!"

"Calm down, Hickory," he said, most patronizingly and looked in every direction around the lines of barracks. He couldn't see the horse paddock for the buildings from his position, yet the surrounding land appeared still and silent. Nothing presented itself to be a threat, except for Del himself, threatening to spread fear amongst his men unnecessarily. "Get a hold of yourself, man. You're going to spook my men."

***

They could just make out Del's raised voice but couldn't see him or the officers for the ammunitions shed.

"When Elan gets back, you call it, Cayman," Annabel said. "Tell us when you think Del's had enough time to share his story and when they're about to move."

Mosi and Elan could now be seen running low along the boundary fence with the two Shadow Warriors and, given that Elan's explicit and well-repeated orders were to retreat immediately to Annabel and Oni once the horses were out, it wasn't long before they all fell in behind only to remain silent, as the Guardians held their bows at the ready again.

"You see it? Between the second and third stumps, dead-center," Cayman confirmed, yet he had already made it very clear and since it was also the plan all along, nothing needed to be said at all. It was only the excitement for what was to come which had him repeating things.

He ran quickly then to the southwest a good distance, in order to see down past the ammunitions shed to where many men began to group around Wright and Hickory, and as the Guardians raised their bows again, he raised his arm in the air, ready to give the fire signal.

***

"Get a hold of myself!?" Del blurted. "I'm telling you—"

"Take a look around, Del," he interrupted. "I don't think a bunch of your slaves are stupid enough to—"

Before he could finish, everyone ducked at once, as an explosion rang out from behind the ammunitions shed and there wasn't time to stand straight again before a series of massive blasts sent them all diving to the ground, covering their own heads. Shrapnel, aflame, flew in every direction, spraying all around and over the rooftops of the closer buildings, as smaller blasts continued unendingly. Cannonballs pierced barrack walls and came down from above with thuds and crashes.

All at once, fires sprang up and started building all around. Men screamed death pains and when the larger explosions ended, Wright stood up and spun around to view the damage, staring wide-eyed in disbelief.

Del got to his feet and shouted, "Do you believe me now!? Do you think you're under attack now!? Maybe you need some more time to think about it!"

239

Wright wasn't listening, being too busy minding the fact that he just lost all his ammunitions – rifles, cannons, Gatling guns and all his black powder – and they possessed but swords and fists with which to defend themselves. In his daze, he was yet to direct his men.

"Your orders, Lieutenant Colonel!" his major demanded, bellowing in his face after being ignored three times already.

Receiving only continued bewilderment from Wright, the major decided to direct the men himself, "Men! Get your swords! I want a blockade on the north side immediately! Go! Go! Go!"

When at least 200 men had formed, he stood on a crate to see past them and further into the distance toward Del's property. Nothing of merit presented itself, but then, without warning, 100 arrows came spraying into the compound and each seemed to find a body in the newly formed blockade. While agonizing screams filled the air, Wright, Del, and Doyle all ran into the officer's barracks as the few soldiers who had found a musket fired pointlessly into the darkness, spending the last of their ammunition.

"Hold your fire!" the major called, all too late. He was so distracted by the new attack that he didn't see Wright run away and just as he pondered over the most effective order to give the men, in the absence of any senior officer, another wave of arrows came, then another, and another. They kept coming, reaching farther back into the compound each time where hundreds collected, readying themselves for battle.

Being in such a confined space, and so well-defined for targeting by lanterns and torchlights as the major quickly determined, at least 50 men were dropping with each new delivery of arrows. As the bodies quickly piled up around him, and since no other officers were in sight, the major decided there was only one thing left to do.

"Charge!" he hollered. "Charge!"

All the remaining men cried out at once and starting running north, with their swords in the air, before the major picked up a sword himself and ran after them.

***

"Here they come!" Misae shouted. "There's still too many. Before the first unit of archers retreat, I want you all to fire two more arrows, now!"

Just moments later, the arrows were released before half the archers retreated with all the bows, leaving the other half to join the yet unused third of the Shadow Warriors. Together, this 100 warriors and the Guardians retreated only as far as the Riverside entrance, where they stood, waiting for the soldiers.

Everyone was clear on Misae's plan for this phase. Her force of Warriors could drive off and annihilate a few hundred soldiers under these circumstances, but the idea was to make them think the warriors were retreating into the barn and into the tunnel in order to draw them all into the compound before the trap was triggered. Forcing them to attack also lured them into a bottleneck at the Riverside entrance, making it a simpler task for so many lethal combatants to draw them in without suffering losses.

"Remember!" Misae called. "They don't all need to be inside before we retreat. Don't try to be a hero. We don't need heroes tonight, just stick to the plan and move into the tunnel immediately. I want everyone out alive! Got it!?"

The unanimous cry which followed filled Misae's heart with pride and gave her more courage, more confidence in her plan coming to fruition.

"All right, spears ready!" she ordered then. "Let's slow them down at the entrance."

100 spears were held in the air, awaiting flight an instant later.

Misae defied her fears somehow, perhaps because she stood at the front line with Annabel, Madeleine, Ky Mani, Oni, Akachi, and Kachina. Unbeknownst to her, they were all ready to cut down anyone who seemed even slightly capable of injuring her in any way. Even without this knowledge, she trusted them with every ounce of her being, and, in that moment, believed she wouldn't mind dying at their side.

"Now!" she ordered, and the spears flew.

Jalen found his way next to Kachina at the frontline, as the soldiers entered the gate. He turned to her, wanting to speak his heart's desire but, instead, he said with a mischievous smile, "I'm going to take down more than you before we leave, my Princess."

Kachina's eyes narrowed, yet she failed to hide her enjoyment in his challenge. "We'll see."

The soldiers came then, all screaming away their energy, after barely scraping past the entrance without collecting a spear on the way through. Contrarily, the Guardians and the Shadow Warriors stood still, calculating, ensuring that their very next movement would result in the death of a soldier, which is exactly what happened. The simultaneous strike from the line of warriors not only wiped out the front line of soldiers but sent a shockwave back through them. As they collided into one another somewhere just beyond the frontline, the new line of soldiers at the very front were bounced back into the line of Guardians and Shadow Warriors again, who subsequently cut them down effortlessly as they stumbled unbalanced into an unyielding force.

"Now!" Misae shouted above the clamor. She worried they were doing too well and risked encouraging the soldiers to retreat already. Although there was no time at all to think about it, the combined and unexpected power which came from the warriors shocked her to the core. Not only that, but she had already defeated two advancing soldiers herself and, again to her surprise, it wasn't the spectacularly fearful challenge she had imagined. In fact, the soldiers seemed completely incapable of defending themselves against her. Even though she knew her skills were nowhere near as advanced as the other Guardians by her side, they still seemed more than adequate to defend herself easily against her current enemy and she was almost disappointed that it was time to retreat.

Jalen sliced off a soldier's arm with his giant sword, who had raised it against Kachina, then opened the man's chest and abdomen with a second strike.

"Stop protecting me!" Kachina demanded.

"I'm not!" Jalen replied. He sent a grin her way but wasn't too sure if she saw it. "It's just one more for me! I've got seven so far, how about you?"

"Stop stealing my kills!" she shouted then, and Jalen laughed at his first opportunity.

Most of the Shadow Warriors had retreated into the barn by then and into the tunnel. The Guardians were the last to reverse inside, while holding off a flailing, steely line of ferocity, and the doors were slammed in the soldiers' faces as the last of them entered.

Without pause, they all entered the tunnel then and closed the first door behind them. Just inside the entrance, the secret door, which looked just like another part of the tunnel wall, opened into the actual tunnel for their escape. As planned, this one was closed and bolted before they followed the others out and under the fence into thick brush on the other side from where they could make their way easily to hidden tracks leading northwest and to Blue Falls.

The longer tunnel, being that which the soldiers were intended to explore, eventually led to the sealed room full of black powder and steel pellets. A volatile trap was set so in the act of opening the door to the room, two large pieces of flint would be forced together over piles of black powder surrounding the barrels.

The soldiers would have to spend time breaking through this door. Misae supposed this would give them all the time they needed to escape, for the soldiers to collect themselves inside the Riverside walls and to fill the tunnel before breaking through the door.

While the soldiers could never have known, the tunnel was also lined with hidden barrels and pockets of black powder, along with almost every crate, box, and trailer within the Riverside fences. Like the barrels inside the room, most of these were covered in sacks of musket pellets and metal offcuts from the Armory. This arrangement was carefully designed to create a domino effect, sending a series of explosions back down through the tunnel and out into the shed, which would then set off all surrounding hidden deposits of black-powder barrels including those inside and around the mansion itself.

Having gathered on the other side of the fence, Misae announced that phase four of her plan was now underway. Immediately, everyone but the Guardians, 30 Shadow Warriors, and Jalen started heading northwest toward home. Those remaining only moved far enough away to be at a safe distance before any blasts occurred, and they were ready to move in again if, for some reason, the trap failed to detonate.

In this case, Misae's contingency plan was for the Guardians, Oni and Annabel, with their bows and flint arrows, to go alone and in stealth to approach the Riverside entrance at a good distance from the west. From there, the archers were to be protected by their fellow Guardians, while they targeted any one of the loaded barrels somewhere close to the gates, which would, in turn, set off the chain of explosions in reverse order, resulting in the same destruction. This was purely an emergency plan, as the core of the mission was for the soldiers to believe all their enemy went underground before any blasts, so the archers would have to hit their mark first time or risk exposing their presence to soldiers who may also decide to come after them. It was of no consequence to Misae's plan if some of the soldiers survived the night, but none of her people could be seen themselves from the moment they went into the tunnel.

So, for now, they slid down into a hollow, waiting for the soldiers to breach that inner trapdoor and, having faith in Misae's strategy, they readied themselves to follow the others home just as soon as that first boom rang out.

***

By the time the major found his way to the frontline, none of the men were fighting at all, and he couldn't see a single enemy warrior, alive or dead. He'd passed through copious quantities of lifeless soldiers, ripped open, bloodless, dismembered, and decapitated, but hadn't seen even one of the enemy.

Shadows.

"We've got them cornered, Major!" one proud soldier exclaimed.

"What's going on?" the major demanded.

"They retreated into a tunnel under the barn, sir," he replied. "We broke through the first door and now the men are trying to break through another door far down inside the tunnel." The corporal was very pleased to be the one debriefing the major and stood awaiting praise, but the major wasn't at all pleased with any part of the battle so far, since he also estimated that little more than one-tenth of the soldiers were all that remained.

It's too quiet.

"Did anyone see them go into the tunnel?" he asked. "And did you search the house?"

The corporal nodded eagerly. "Yes, sir, there's no one in the house and we saw them go into the tunnel before they closed the barn door. I saw the savages with my own eyes."

Turning on the spot, the major surveyed the inner grounds with his stomach turning knots.

If this were a legitimate farm, then where were all the current harvests? The livestock?

Watching the remaining soldiers take up strategic positions behind trailers and piles of crates, the major saw a strange pattern which led him to wonder why so many piles of unknown goods were scattered all over the grounds instead of being collected in one place or in the barn. He went to one of the trailers then, pulled the canvas cover back and quickly found the reason for his dreaded suspicions.

"Fall back, men! Retreat! Retreat!" he yelled at the top of his voice, just as a massive, haunting thud sounded and a shockwave rumbled throughout the grounds.

***

All barracks except for the headquarters and one other continued to blaze, since there wasn't enough manpower left to fight the flames, and would most likely be reduced to ash completely unhindered. Only a handful of injured soldiers, Wright, Del, and Doyle remained.

Not that Wright was doing anything at all to rectify a complete disaster area which was once his chariot, intended to lead him to fame and reverence. His war wasn't meant to be like this. This is what happened to the other side, after he had unleashed cannons and thousands of muskets, and at the end of his fantasy, he was the one standing beside the flag, smug with victory.

They had just finished watching Vivian Piper's entire estate explode into the air, as if a giant with a red-hot pitchfork turned up immense volumes of the earth and, even from their distance, they could see the silhouettes of soldiers in the sky against a red and orange backdrop, spinning and turning in pieces. Wright stood outside headquarters thereafter, turning himself, but around and around on the spot, in shock and utter disbelief while his buildings crackled and spluttered away.

"Well, you're just a born leader, aren't you?" Del remarked. He would have said much more, but Wright shot him a look of utter despair and even he couldn't cut the man down any further.

After many long minutes, void of anything eventful, the three of them ventured cautiously through Del's land, over to Vivian's property and although they all expected to come upon a terrible scene, they were still completely unprepared for the horror they found.

It was as if that same giant had prepared a tossed salad made of diced, stir-fried soldiers, red mud and shredded timber, but hadn't eaten yet. The barrage of internal and external explosions turned the mansion into Swiss cheese, and all its remains were either burning or smoking. They couldn't see a living soul in sight. Everything, even the men, had been shredded or shattered into fragments, and countless smaller fires still burned away quietly to themselves.

Try as he might, Wright couldn't imagine how he was going to survive debriefing without rapid demotion or how he might explain surviving again, and again without injury, while a thousand men all but perished. Expecting more ridicule from Del, he avoided making eye contact for a long time and was finally surprised to find that he seemed somewhat sympathetic, in expression anyhow, if not in mind.

"Guess that's the end of that," Del stated.

***

With wistful hearts, Lesedi, Sayen, and Naira had waited with Isi at the opening next to Dead Man's Fall for what seemed like an eternity to witness the end of the fourth-phase to Misae's plan. Although only those at the very front could see anything worthwhile, both Crystal Nest and the opening were filled to bursting with people who didn't care to join the Panthers outside along the ridge to catch a glimpse of what promised to be a spectacular display under the night sky. This event in no way ensured the success of the mission nor the safety of her people, and so, like her daughters, Lesedi watched on, thinking only, *Misae, are you safe? Are our people safe?*

Explosions seemed endless and making the scene more ominous was the fact that the sound took so long to reach them. Countless fireballs were seen first but the blasts and rumbles didn't come for many moments later. The vision wasn't so frightening without the relevance of sound, yet the sounds when they came alone seemed to reveal, with more potency, the true power and weight behind the detonations.

Once it was over, Lesedi looked to her daughters to see that their expressions mirrored her well-hidden fear. "This was the plan, remember?" she said for reassurance, as much for herself as for them. "This means they sprung the trap. We have to trust Misae. C'mon, let's get to the Entrance."

Lesedi wasted no time, remembering how difficult it was to find their way around the masses of individual crowds formed in waiting for the return of the warriors.

Most of the population had collected around The Books, The Hotpot, and in the northwest of Blue Falls, for above them, on the ledge outside The Armory, a huge gong had been mounted for the hopeful sounding of the Warriors' return and the success of the mission.

Awareness of the greater prophecy had become a virus among the people once it was revealed to them that another three Guardians were in their company and that the so-called ancient myth of Sampa was not such an untouchable dream after all.

Every new crowd she came upon was a celebration, waiting to happen and some, the greater believers and the obsessed, were already celebrating. When the queen halted at these every so often, in wonder, and to share hesitant approval, they would say, "We believe in the Guardians, my Queen. They will not fail us."

"We'll hear the gong soon," a child's excited voice called out from somewhere within the masses, but disappointingly, Lesedi couldn't find them.

"We love you, my Queen!" she heard from many others as she walked away.

While most distracted by thoughts of the mission, the people's new wave of unity warmed Lesedi's heart again and gave her much hope on her journey up to where the truth, however welcome or dreaded, would surely find itself, and soon.

The Entrance became so packed full of excitable spectators, Lesedi wondered if she would have to usher people out of the healing bay when she arrived, but found, to her delight, they had respected this space as always, and only Artetha, Awinita, and their army of healers were waiting in their usual places.

Inside the circle, Tamaya waited with Shenandoah, Layla, and Montezuma in one place, and Tau, Kirra, Julian, and Victor waited in another, soon to be joined by Jojo, Tatsuya, and Kachina's parents, Imari and Zalika, looking just as jittery. All present attempted to share hopeful, encouraging faces with one another, yet mostly succeeded in sharing their fears.

While only a small percentage of the population saw the explosions with their own eyes, a deep rumbling could be heard from any place within Blue Falls, even in the deepest caverns, and startled the calmest of spirits. An eternity came and went, and then another, while anticipation built and restlessness flourished, then finally, they heard a cheer slowly moving through the crowds as some of the warriors began to arrive.

First, many Shadow Warriors came through, all smiling proudly as they made their way to the Armory, and only five of them stopped into the Healing Bay for minor treatment. These were mostly the workers sent days earlier and looked nothing like they had seen the frontline of a battle, yet the fact that Misae had decided not to keep them behind gave Lesedi great hope. Ahead of the next group of Shadow Warriors came Sherman, Talia, Sanura, Mosi, and Elan, who all inspired a great uproar, mostly for the three new Guardians appearing together for the first time.

Although Sanura and Talia's parents knew they would not be a part of the battle itself, it was still a great relief to see their faces again, while noting with intrigue how their demeanors had changed noticeably since they were last seen, Talia's especially, and could only assume their presence on the mission spawned confidence of a kind.

Tamaya, this time, didn't crumble into pieces but, instead, met Mosi's eyes with pride in her heart and with the warmest of smiles Mosi had ever seen in her much-loved face. Elan ran ahead to jump into her arms. "We did it, Momma!" he shouted joyfully.

While the arrival of these three Guardians inspired all, none of them could answer anyone's questions regarding the final battle which took place, for they were long gone, running for home as per the plan, while swords went clashing far behind.

So, they all waited again for a long while, each moment ten times as long as the previous, before a new wave of Shadow Warriors started coming through, blood-soaked unlike the last. The first of which assisted 10 injured men into the healing bay. These had various open wounds to the abdomen, chest, legs, and arms, but they were all conscious and didn't need to be carried.

Lesedi watched the healers go to work right away and her hope stumbled for seeing the wounded as she turned her eyes again to a new group of Shadow Warriors coming through.

Only a few of these went to the healing bay, and walked in without assistance, while the rest continued on to the Armory. Many more minutes passed then, without a single new arrival, neither warrior nor Guardian, and in this time, Isi approached Lesedi.

"That's every Shadow Warrior, my Queen, except for Jalen," he stated with confidence. "Three of us counted them, as you asked."

"Thank you, Isi," she replied, without averting her eyes from the entry and the next outcry sought to stop her heart completely. She reached for her chest as the screaming and shouting bellowed throughout the Entrance and rose from the depths of Blue Falls in retaliation.

The crowds were leaping into the air all around her, and it wasn't until the new arrivals came close that she could make out each and every one of them; Misae and the last of the Guardians, the last of all who had stayed for the mission, approached with Jalen and stood before her. None were injured, yet they all looked as if they had been swimming in a river of blood.

On the way back, as they knew how she disliked it so, they all conspired to bow to Lesedi on one knee when they returned, and as they did, Jalen looked up to say, "Mission accomplished, my Queen."

She shook her head with disapproval, yet with an unstoppable smile, and replied, "Up! All of you." Then, she turned to Isi, "Do you have it?"

An arrow was passed forward to the queen, a regular arrow but for a small, tightly wrapped ball of sand at its end instead of the usual pointed tip. "Oni? Annabel?" she queried. "Who's going to take the shot?"

They looked to one another only to share a knowing smile.

Annabel passed her bow to Misae and said, "You can make this shot. I've seen you do better."

At first, Misae thought to decline and let modesty pass the honor onto one of the gifted archers, but the greater part of her wanted to be the one to share with all the signal to confirm the success of her mission and the future protection of Blue Falls.

"Okay," she accepted, with ambition biting at her bottom lip.

As the arrow found its nocking point, Misae thought of the day she volunteered for the Riverside project and could only vaguely remember her fearful heart at the time. Since then, she had killed and transformed, before building a battleground and killing some more, and now that fragile heart she once possessed was nothing but a foggy travesty. She turned then to find Shenandoah not too far away with a smile made just for her, and with a full heart, she drew back the string to look down the shaft to the center of the gong far away.

I'm not missing this shot.

"There's only one arrow," Oni said abruptly, with a cheeky grin, just as Misae was about to let fly. "I thought you should know."

Misae lowered the bow again for a moment. "Thank you, Oni," she sniggered.

While watching her daughter's eyes lock again onto her faraway target, a copper disk glinting with hope for the future, Lesedi stood in awe. She almost gasped aloud with the sudden realization that, in that moment anyway, she wasn't looking at her daughter at all but an adored leader of the people who braved to fight right beside her Warriors. In that moment, she saw an icon, a Warrior Guardian, a legend, and a veteran Princess of War.

Before the gong had delivered its undeniable and drawn-out proof, there remained no doubt in Lesedi's mind at all that Misae's arrow would deliver its long-awaited message.

***

"Are you sure you don't want some help, Neema?" Annabel asked.

"No, for the tenth time, Annabel, I've got it all under control," came her blunt reply.

Annabel sent Madeleine and Jimmy a cheeky smile. "It's taking forever, that's all."

"Where are your manners, child?" Neema berated.

"I lost them the moment I smelled your delicious pancakes, Neema," Annabel confessed. "I want. Gimme now."

Neema smiled and shook her head. "I'm cooking one at a time, are y'all gonna fight over them like wild dogs?"

"I might, Neema," Madeleine admitted. "It's been too long."

"Well, the first one's for Jimmy," she stated. "And if either of you are pathetic enough to steal a pancake from a wounded man, then I might whoop you one with my spatula here."

"Why don't we divide the first one into three?" Jimmy proposed, gracefully. "Or four, sorry, Neema."

"How 'bout you just enjoy it, Jimmy, and let those two wolves drool all over themselves in the meantime," Neema insisted. "They ain't gonna die to wait a few minutes."

Annabel sighed. "I'm just playing, Neema, but they do smell delectable."

"Delectable, huh?" Neema repeated. "Fancy words, even if they are complimentary, ain't gonna get you the first pancake, girl."

"Forget it, Annie," Madeleine insisted. "Neema's like a lie and manipulation detector after learning all of my sneaky tricks over the years. Not much gets by that one."

"There...one down," Neema said with glee, dropping a steaming, hot pancake onto Jimmy's plate.

Forgetting his injury momentarily, Jimmy leaned over abruptly to smell his breakfast and in his hasty movement, caused a wave of unexpected pain to pass through his chest and up through his neck. He sat back again to grimace for a moment or two.

"You okay?" both Annabel and Madeleine asked in unison.

Jimmy nodded and replied with positivity, "I just keep forgetting. It's a good sign I guess."

"A few weeks and you'll be as good as new, Jimmy," Annabel assured.

With a genuine smile, Jimmy agreed, feeling good about the success in his recovery so far. He picked up a small wooden pot and splashed lemon juice over his pancake, then added a sprinkle of maple sugar. "Like that?"

"Exactly," Madeleine confirmed. "You wait."

Jimmy rolled it up like Madeleine told him, chopped off the end with a fork and dropped it onto his tongue. After only a moment of chewing, he sighed aloud whilst hastily preparing another piece on his fork, ready for immediate gorging.

"I told you," Madeleine chuckled.

With eyes practically rolling back in her head, Annabel watched on with envy and anticipation.

"Annie can have the next one, Neema," Madeleine offered. "She might pass out otherwise, or drown in her own saliva."

Soon, they were all eating anyhow, Neema included, and in the end, Annabel had eaten so many, she sat back, wallowing in self-disgust. "Oh boy," she said, exhaling all at once.

"I told you they'd catch up on you," Madeleine reminded her.

"You weren't wrong, but it's worth it," Annabel decided. "Thank you, Neema, with all my heart. I want them every day please."

"I'm glad you liked them," Neema chuckled. "I've enjoyed this very much. You girls make me laugh so hard; it hurts."

"Well, at least we're good for something," Annabel supposed. "Because I can't make pancakes like that for you. They're the best."

"She's right," Jimmy agreed. "Thank you, Neema."

"Y'all welcome," she said, then kissed them all on the top of the head. "I'm gonna meet Jamero now. Keep safe and well, Jimmy."

Soon after she left, Annabel stood and groaned while patting her belly. "I was going for a swim but there's no way now. I'll sink to the bottom forever."

Watching Annabel's overly relaxed demeanor, Madeleine found herself sighing deeply with relief. "It's really nice, isn't it? Not to have anything urgent to do or think about. Just to relax without a busy mind. I can't remember the last time."

"Me neither," Annabel agreed. "Let's enjoy it while it lasts. We'll be doing the market runs again soon, if war doesn't come first."

"Oh yeah, The Drop's closed now," Jimmy realized. His mind had been too preoccupied with healing of late to think too much about the developments of Blue Falls and the like. "We'll have to go to the markets now if we want to bring more people here, but I don't mind, I kinda missed us all heading out with the wagons before sunrise. So what will happen with the place next door?"

Madeleine shrugged. "I'm guessing, after they've finished clearing and searching it, the government will seize Vivian Piper's whole estate and sell next door off to a farmer."

"And who knows about Riverside," Annabel pondered.

"They'll probably keep searching Riverside until they realize they could dig for months and months and still not even come close to digging in the right place," Madeleine supposed. "The property is too big for that. If they think there's gold and jewels underground, they might persist, but they'd have to open up the whole place like a mine and they're not going to do that; I don't think. I wouldn't put it past them, but if the residents have anything to say about it, that's not going to happen."

"Either way, the Riverside plan worked perfectly," Jimmy acknowledged. "And Misae's planning, well, I still can't believe the Guardians and 150 warriors defeated a thousand without losing one of our own."

"I don't think that will ever happen again," Annabel suggested, sadly. "But it would be nice if every battle were like that."

"Let's just hope there's no more battles and the war never comes," Jimmy said with great expectation.

Annabel and Madeleine flashed a knowing glance to one another and failed to hide it from Jimmy.

After pausing to ponder on their potential secrets, he asked, "So what do you two think about the prophecy? They're saying Sampa is real and it's here somewhere."

"Between us, Jimmy," Annabel replied, after sharing looks of agreement with Madeleine. "And it has to stay between us. It's true. I've known for a long time, but I haven't been able to share it with anyone for many reasons. It's a long explanation, but what it comes down to is that the Guardians have to find a way to open it for the people."

"We're hoping it's going to happen soon," Madeleine added.

Jimmy looked to her. "So you know too?"

"Yes," she nodded. "I've only just learned about it, but I can guarantee it's true."

"Well, that's all I need to know," Jimmy smiled. "I trust you both know what you're doing."

They sniggered at the same time and Annabel shook her head. "I don't know about that, Jimmy. So what are you up to now? I'm going to get some more sleep. And in case you think I'm lazy having a fat nap after pancakes, I didn't sleep much last night. The celebration never ends."

"I don't think you're lazy," Madeleine said in support. "I'm going to do the same later, but first, I promised this one I'd take him outside to feed the horses."

"You're not lifting anything," Annabel demanded.

"No, I won't, I promise," Jimmy ensured.

Annabel didn't completely believe him. "Good. I'll meet up with you both tonight. Make sure he doesn't do any work please, Maddy."

"I will," she confirmed. "We'll just take it slow."

After she left, Jimmy sighed inwardly for being alone with Madeleine.

"Thanks," he said. "It means a lot. I've been missing the little things, you know, like being with the horses, giving Aaron his favorite oats, carrots for Jessie, and, don't be mad, just a handful of barley here and there for Primrose. She loves it, but I never give her enough to make her crazy."

"It's all right," Madeleine giggled. "I do the same, and besides, she's crazy anyway. She loves thistle too."

"There's a bunch of it growing by the tool shed," he said excitedly. "Have you seen it?"

Madeleine shook her head, smiling and enjoying Jimmy's elation for one of her favorite pastimes. "C'mon, you can show me on the way to the horses."

***

Unwittingly, Nuru had become somewhat of a loner, drifting by himself across the water most days in the Dreaming Dolphin, taking couples and groups for rides, who mainly wanted to talk amongst themselves, or helping those with an ambition to spear a fish from the boat in the middle of the lake.

He didn't mind so much, the long hours of solitude, for many years as a slave, they would lock him up alone at night, and his imagination never failed to keep him company. On this day, as with most days recently, he imagined that Sanura and Talia had come for another sail, and he was given the chance not to make a bumbling fool of himself before Talia.

Warrior Guardian, your beauty could break my heart on its own. Who am I to think of you?

252

Although his only wish, the last thing Nuru expected was to see Talia sitting on the rocks at the edge of the lake.

"Someone told me this was the place to sit if you wanted to go for a boat ride," Talia reminded him. "Can you take us around? The last trip was cut short, if you remember, and I didn't get to see all of it."

"Cut short," Nuru repeated with a chuckle, remembering the Guardians' accidental dip into the lake. "It would be my pleasure to finish the tour." After letting the boat slide up onto the sand, he sat, ready.

"Well? What are we waiting for?" Talia asked.

"Ah…Sanura?" he answered with confusion. "You said us, I thought maybe Sanura was coming."

"No, silly," Talia replied, with a warm smile that he hadn't seen before. "Us, being you and me."

***

Finally, the greater pain in Del's shoulder had all but subsided, and only milder aches and pains remained. Work on the new sheds was well underway, and his new team of employees seemed to work well under his and Doyle's direction. It wouldn't be long before he could store harvests and house slaves again, so his evenings were spent with newfound positivity for his future income and the ability to fulfill the task appointed to him in manipulating those in power around him, from magistrates to army officers, to bankers and lawyers, and to exact his superiors' hidden agendas.

Unfortunately, for Del's future aspirations, the Guardians and all those involved decided that two weeks was long enough for him to have met with any illusory employers to share all the misleading information derived from his own misadventures. Thus, phase five of Misae's plan had been initiated, which subsequently and conveniently sought to avenge Jimmy's undeserved infliction; a plan involving only Annabel, Madeleine, and Jimmy, after a clandestine delivery executed this day while Del occupied himself in town.

"Boss," Doyle said, handing him a tumbler of whiskey.

"Cheers," Del replied, accepting with relish. He took a chug and exclaimed an elongated, "Ah."

Doyle took a seat next to him on the eastern veranda of the mansion and, likewise, rested his feet on a stool, whiskey in hand. Looking out into the twilight, he claimed, "Things aren't going too bad now, boss."

"Hmmm, we'll see," Del replied, and after looking about the verandah, asked, "What are these barrels doing here?"

"That's the beer and wine for your party, boss," Doyle answered. "The delivery came while you were out. 11 barrels, right? They said you told them to put some up here, some in the cellar, and some in the dining hall. Good idea, so we don't have to move 'em around too much after your guests arrive. I told the men not to touch any one of them or I'd…" Doyle's voice faded out then as he watched Del's face go white and stark, as if he'd just seen a ghost. "What is it, boss?"

Del's eyes turned slowly to the barrels again. "Guests? I ain't havin' no party, Doyle, wh—"

Shocked, Del jumped sideways in his seat as two arrows came whizzing in, impacting Doyle. One entered his chest, the other, his face. They both wedged themselves solidly into the timber backing of his chair and pinned him there, while his arms and legs flailed around pointlessly.

Horrified, and disgusted by Doyle's freakish, urgent groans, Del dropped his glass, as he watched the man's body jerk all around spasmodically. After jumping to his feet, he looked quickly over all the paddocks but saw nothing of consequence immediately, so he leapt inside the doorway to peer out ever so slightly, unable to take his eyes off Doyle, shuddering and gurgling in his struggle with death.

From so far away, Del couldn't possibly hear Madeleine whisper to Annabel and Jimmy, "I was a little high," or for Jimmy to whisper in reply, "Nup, Annie's through the heart, yours through the brain, perfect."

Looking closer at one of the arrows, Del's heart skipped a beat, for written on the fletching was the word, bang, and, like a great and stunning slap, it occurred to him all too late, that running inside was exactly what they wanted him to do. Slowed by fearful realization, he looked between all visible barrels to note with a swallow that he was surrounded by them, but, before he could take a single step, two flint-tipped arrows came pelting in from afar, finding one barrel each on the verandah. Together, they triggered a series of explosions which sent him bouncing off fireballs and flipping into the air all aflame.

While barely conscious, and in his last moments, Del thought to have seen his stock whip snaking alongside, as he drifted back down into the jaws of an inferno, his glorious mansion.

The End

Epilogue

A fistful of weeks had passed and yet, Sanura's intensity for warrior training had dwindled not at all. Day and night, she practiced, with hardly a pause but for sleep and nourishment, and her fellow Guardians believed she rivaled even Kachina's drive when she first came to Blue Falls with fire brewing in her heart. When Ky Mani and the Guardians proved unavailable, she went to Crimson Cove to practice with Jalen or with any willing Shadow Warrior until exhaustion forced her to sleep again.

During the mission at Riverside, when it was her turn to enter the tunnel, Sanura had stayed for as long as she could to watch the Guardians in action as the soldiers entered the gates. Talia was pulling at her, but she resisted just long enough to see that first impact along the front line which sent the soldiers reeling and set the precedent for the remainder of the battle. In that moment, seeing them move as one, steadfast and sure, she wanted to run to their side to fight with them and felt it not enough to have killed a bound man before running from the battle into a tunnel and far away. Yet, to follow her whims would have been to jeopardize the mission, she knew that well, and so, she left with Talia, but with a resolute mind, thinking, I'm so far behind, but next time, I will fight.

While she spent more and more time with Nuru, Talia also trained with ferocity, feeling far behind herself, but even then, she only spent two-thirds of Sanura's time practicing. On this particular day, however, something had changed and Sanura's usual focus began to blur toward the end of practice.

Aside from Julian watching-on while writing notes from the sideline, and, of course, Foxy and Bell, who had ditched Elan again, having discovered the scents of their original kidnappers' somewhere near The Nook and followed them all the way up to the Dojo, only Madeleine, Annabel, and Sanura remained in the Panther's Den at this time, having stayed back to demonstrate for Sanura something she queried at the end of Ky Mani's lesson.

Although given plenty of warning before the Guardians' training session, Julian arrived late, after being distracted along the way, talking to Taneli and

Jabari as they worked away on three additional columns in the Hall of Dreams, creating statues of the three newly exposed Guardians; Elan, Sanura, and Talia.

It was easy for anyone to be delayed while walking through the tunnel. Lanterns drew out every line of the sculptors' immaculate work and cast long, broken shadows of each figure across the uneven rocky surfaces of the walls and ceiling. More and more, the hollow space took on an air of sanctity, silently demanding hush and respect, while containing an abundance of heartbreaking dreams yet to manifest themselves. Julian limited his questions for the dust-covered men, keeping himself quiet illustrating the pages of his journal with new sketches of father and son chiseling away, searching for Talia somewhere in the stone, and subsequently lost track of the time he had spent absorbing inspirational energy found in such a well-loved place.

Having discovered the truth about Blue Falls, the Guardians, and more of the prophecy, Julian had met with the queen and all the Guardians individually to learn about their lives and how they came to find Blue Falls.

Yet, or so it seemed at first, the end to his research might never be found. The more he learned, the more there was to discover about the hidden and unique talents of each extraordinary member of the Guardian circle, the queen and princesses. This never-ending dig left him wondering if he would ever feel as if he had compiled enough information to complete his book with confidence in having done enough to portray a true and complete picture of Blue Falls and the prophecy. Somewhere along the way, he had also come to realize that something was still being hidden from him, and, since he believed it was not just the Guardians but also the queen and all the Blue Ones keeping this secret, he decided not to question it any further, for now. Instead, he focused on all the information uncovered thus far, which was more than enough to correlate all at once anyhow, while beginning to trust more in the natural process and believing all would be revealed to him in good time.

"How's the book going, Julian?" Annabel asked, drawing his face away from the page. She stood nearby, but her eyes hadn't left Sanura and Madeleine as she watched their movements very closely.

Julian surprised himself for his positive reaction to her question, when, many weeks ago, his stomach would have dropped at the very mention of his stagnating manuscript. "Good, actually. Yesterday, I wrote about some of my own experiences, like my first time on the Plummet."

Annabel chuckled and looked his way for a moment. "Hope you didn't curse too much. Young people might be reading that book."

"No," Julian smiled. He had forgiven Annabel that very day, and, in fact, to her great surprise, hugged and thanked her for the unexpected chance to experience something he never would have tried if fully aware of what the adventure offered. "I'd like to try going down with someone else. That would be fun."

"Goodness, Julian," Madeleine exclaimed, eavesdropping to some extent. "Did I just hear what I thought I heard? Gosh, soon you'll be picking up a sword."

Julian only smiled; this idea had already crossed his mind more than once.

"Well, there're three harnesses," Annabel suggested with a mischievous grin, looking also to Madeleine.

"Don't distract me," Madeleine said, blocking another solid attack, yet Sanura seemed to lose concentration quickly thereafter, taking on an unexpected vagueness.

"You know, Julian, thinking back, I probably should have asked if you could swim," Annabel shared with a snigger.

Julian chuckled along with her. "I didn't think of that, but maybe you would have done it anyway."

"Are you all right, Sanura?" Madeleine asked suddenly, most concerned. "I think we should quit for today. You look exhausted, and for the first time I can remember."

"You push yourself very hard, Sanura," Annabel concurred.

"I'm sorry," she replied lazily. "I asked you to show me these tactics and I'm not myself. I think I should go and meditate and clear my head."

"We can show you next time," Annabel suggested.

Sanura nodded reluctantly, as she wanted to practice but knew it would also be wasting their time to continue. "I've been having strange dreams," she confessed. "The same thing over and over, about Crystal Nest, and they're distracting me today, I don't know why. I'm sorry."

In that moment, Annabel and Madeleine had the same hopeful thought and did well to share it with one another secretly, silently.

"Oh yeah?" Annabel responded with nonchalance, as if it were neither here nor there.

Sanura looked to them all, misty-eyed, as if entranced. "Yes. I think I'll go there now and meditate for a while."

It wasn't long before she left and Julian got wind of the silent communication and reserved excitement shared between Annabel and Madeleine.

"I get the feeling I missed something," he intuited, suggesting more secrecy.

"Actually, Julian, some might say you're blessed," Annabel argued. "Because if our instincts are correct, then, apart from two Guardians, you were the only one here to witness the very moment in the prophecy that the people have been waiting for, and for hundreds of years."

Julian frowned. "Okay then, I definitely missed something."

***

"I'm sorry to bother you so late, sir," Lorena apologized. "But I've been sent to inform you right away, there's been another problem in the Midlands."

"What now, specifically?" the man replied with annoyance, while rolling eyes for only his dinner guest to see.

"I'm sorry, sir," she answered, without a hint of remorse in her voice, and if he had bothered to look into her dark blue eyes, he might have seen scorn. "Specifically, Del Hickory. He and what was left of his men have perished. His mansion was also burnt to the ground this time."

After a deep breath, a sigh and a pause to absorb the mild angst this news brought about, he asked, "Is that all?"

"Yes, sir. They told me to await your instruction," she informed him.

"Tell them to do nothing."

"Nothing at all, sir?"

"That's right."

"Very well, sir," she ensured, re-adjusting a couple of unruly blonde locks which failed to comply to the bun she created only moments ago. "Enjoy your meal."

"You don't seem too worried," Dorjan noted, once he believed they were alone again.

Yet, neither diner was aware that Lorena hadn't left at all but, instead, slipped behind a partition at their backs to listen in on their conversation.

"Dorjan," he answered flatly. "I don't care. Any hidden slaves will be taken care of when we fill Riverside and all the Midlands with armies from the south anyway, and when we set the northern regions against those armies, there'll be no way of going anywhere without either army seeing them, but that doesn't matter either. Slavery with chains is slow and ineffective. It will go on hidden, but it works better when people think they're doing something for themselves. Make them rely on comfort and convenience, make it difficult to obtain, then they'll do whatever you ask to keep it. It's time for our next chapter now, but I am starting to believe your fantasies about the Guardians rising again, which is why you're here."

"I told you they're not fantasies," Dorjan reinstated, with his dark eyes doing little to hide long-term frustration. He pulled his long black hair behind both ears and sniffed away the travesty of ineptitude which had been cast over him by all those who believed the Guardian Prophecy to be merely a myth. "The Guardians exist and even if they don't know who you are, they've been working against you. If they took part in that battle, I don't believe, for a second, they went down with all the rest. How many times have you tried to control all the Midlands now and failed?"

No reminder was needed. "Well, since you're supposed to be the best hunter and our deadliest mercenary, I think it's time we put that to the test, along with your fantasies, don't you? If the prophecy is true then two of them are white, so they won't be hiding underground all the time. Bring me some heads and I'll give you whatever you want. Maybe you'll even find yourself some gold and jewels along the way."

"You already know what I want, a place of my own on your side of the ice," Dorjan prompted.

His dinner partner's eyes narrowed somewhat. "All right," he lied. "Even though I don't think they offer any real threat, they'll be a nuisance in the future, so if you eradicate our Guardian problem, I'm sure I can justify your request to the members. Done."

Dorjan grinned with anticipation and confidence. "Something in the more tropical regions."

"We'll see," came his reluctant reply.

A suited messenger approached their table then. "I'm sorry to interrupt your dinner, sir," he said. "But they sent me to inform you of a recent incident in the Midlands regarding Mister Hickory."

"What?" Dorjan asked, most suspiciously, while looking about the restaurant. "They just sent someone about this?"

"Impossible," the messenger stated. "There's only one messenger at a time, and I'm it until Friday."

Lorena spun around in her hidden place, covering her racing heart with both hands, then moved quickly away, nursing virtual confirmation of the *Guardians' existence, which was somehow known to her all along.*

Where do I look for you, Guardians? she pondered with seemingly impossible expectations, *How can I warn you?*

***

CPSIA information can be obtained
at www.ICGtesting.com
Printed in the USA
LVHW080739141220
673102LV00028B/158

9 781645 361701